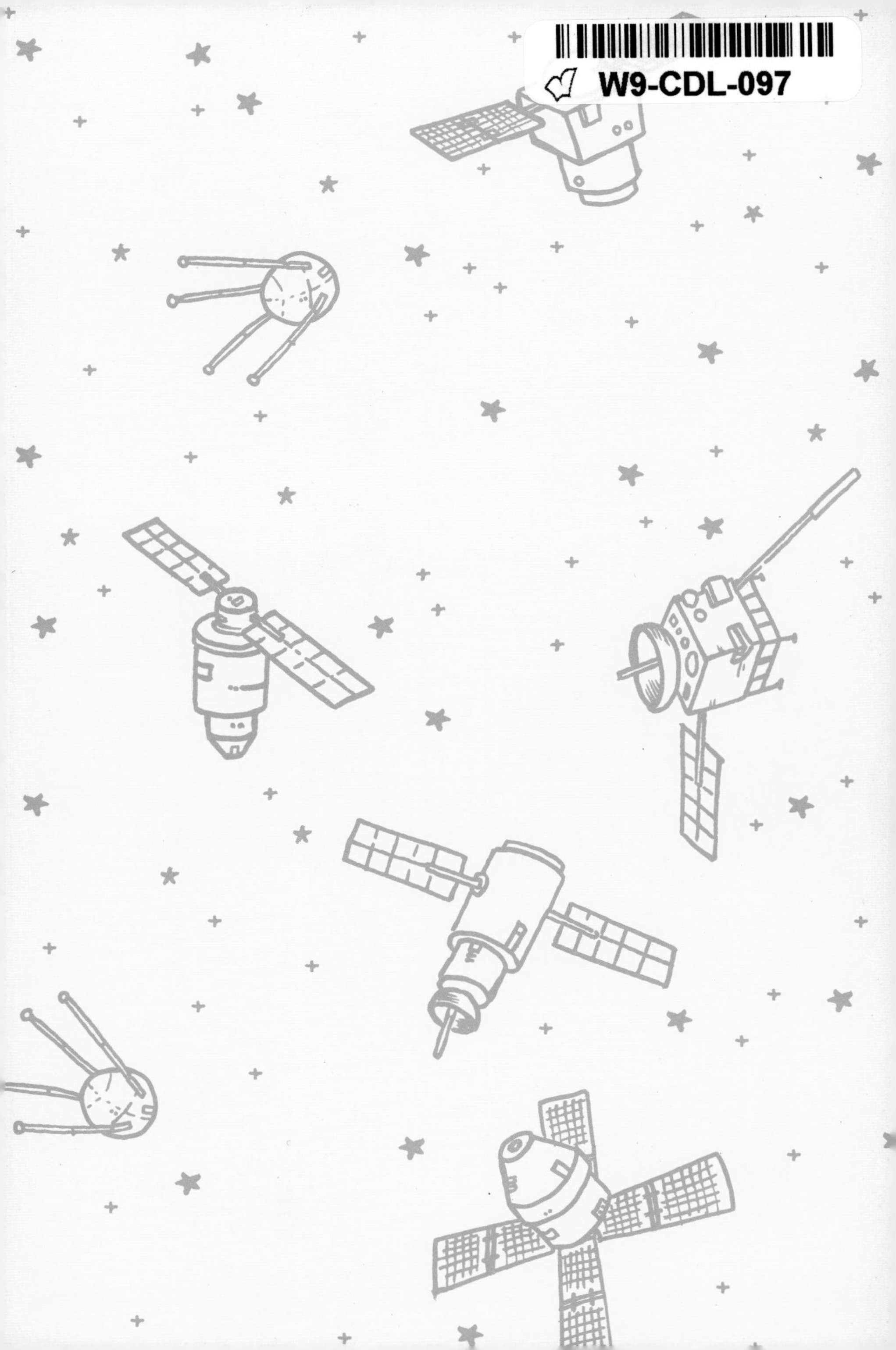

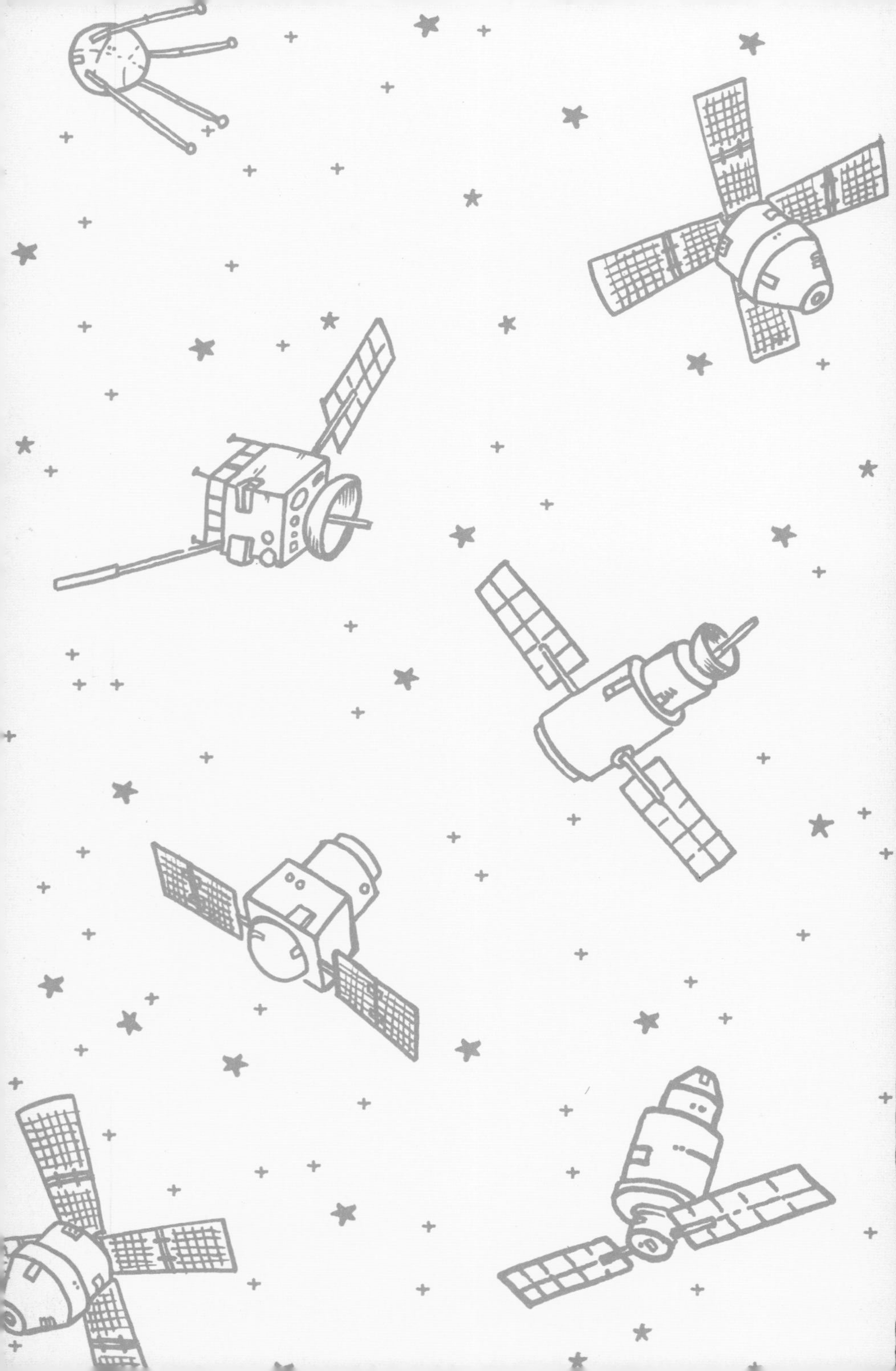

CatStronauts

ROBOT RESCUE

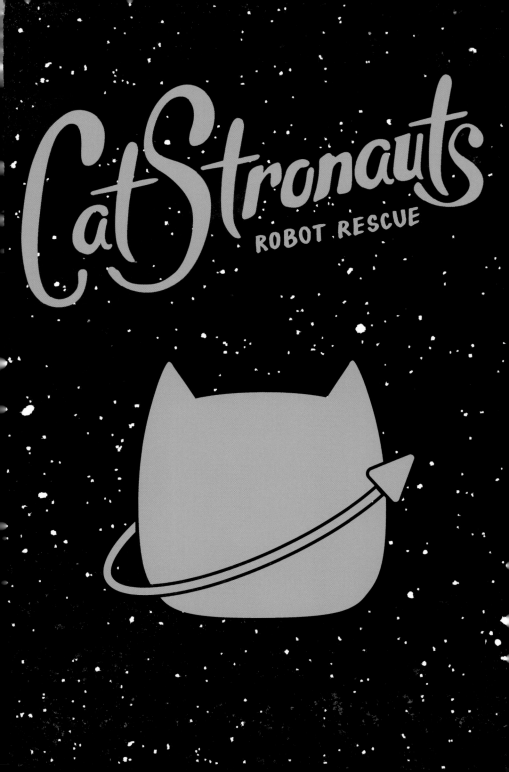

CatStronauts

ROBOT RESCUE

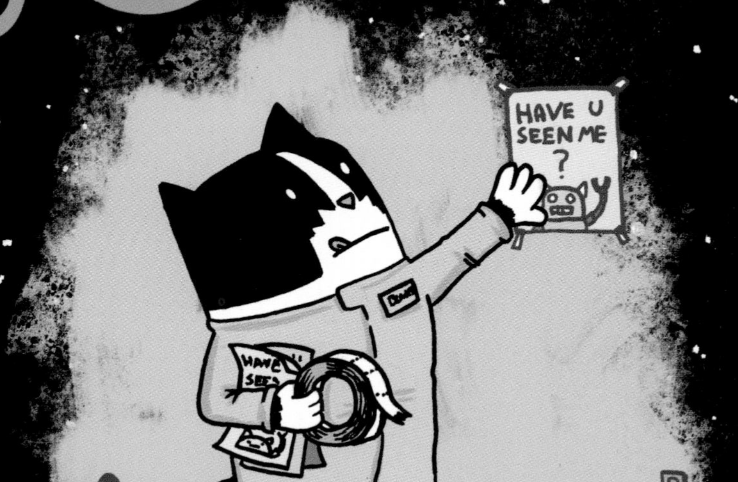
HAVE U SEEN ME ?

BY DREW BROCKINGTON

Little, Brown and Company
New York Boston

Copyright © 2018 by Drew Brockington
Catstrofont software copyright © 2016 by Drew Brockington
CatStro_Thin software copyright © 2017 by Drew Brockington

Cover art copyright © 2018 by Drew Brockington. Cover design by Angela Taldone.
Cover copyright © 2018 by Hachette Book Group, Inc.

Little, Brown and Company
Hachette Book Group
1290 Avenue of the Americas, New York, NY 10104
Visit us at LBYR.com

First Edition: April 2018

Little, Brown and Company is a division of Hachette Book Group, Inc. The Little, Brown name and logo are trademarks of Hachette Book Group, Inc.

The publisher is not responsible for websites (or their content) that are not owned by the publisher.

ISBNs: 978-0-316-30759-8 (hardcover), 978-0-316-30756-7 (pbk.), 978-0-316-41219-3 (ebook), 978-0-316-41217-9 (ebook), 978-0-316-30755-0 (ebook)

Printed in China

1010

10 9 8 7 6 5 4 3 2 1

For my mom

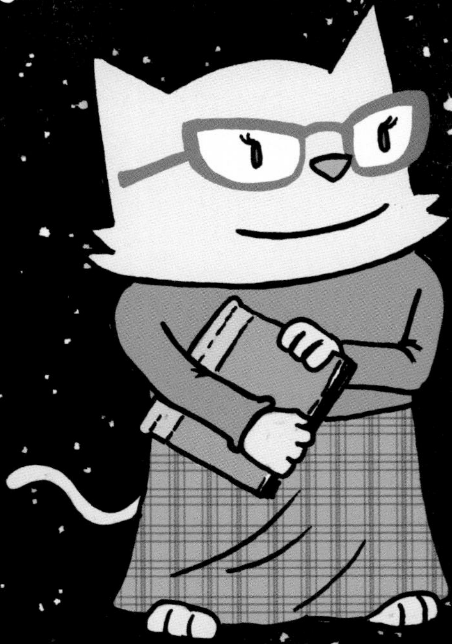

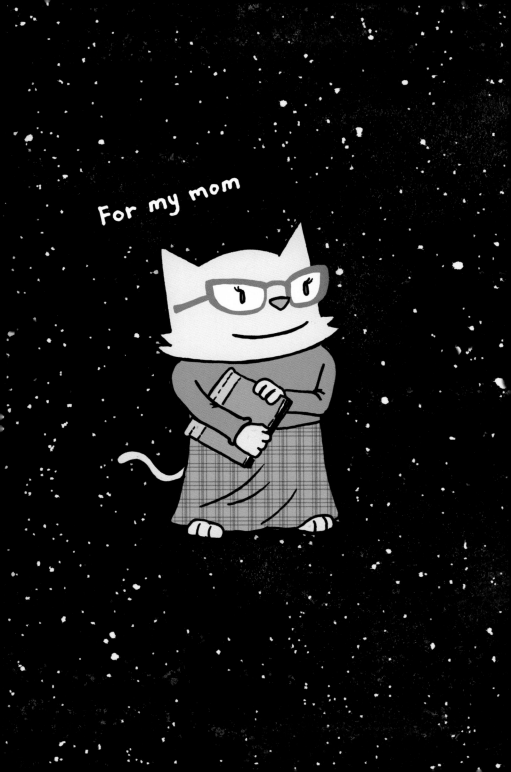

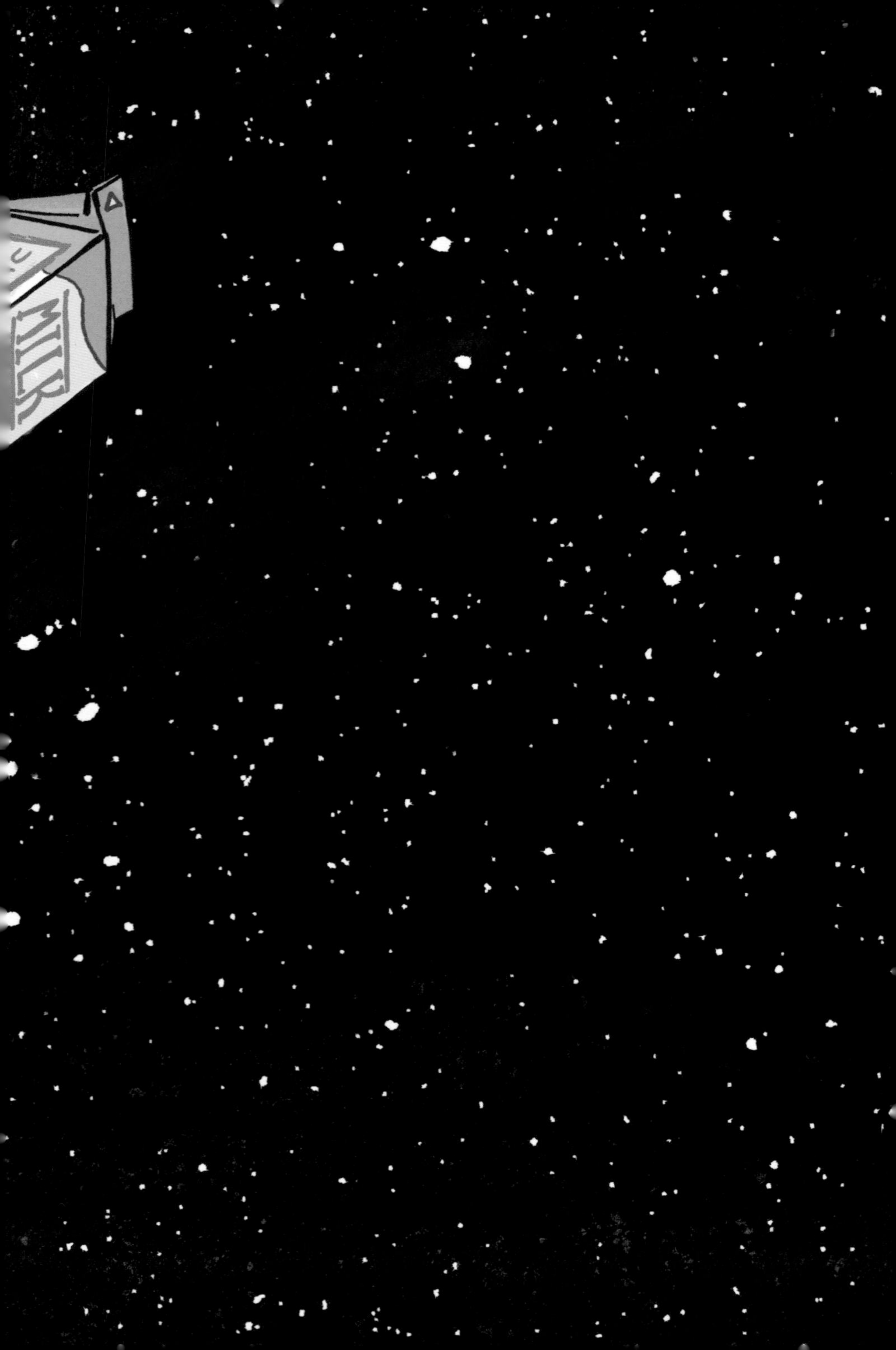
MILK

CHAPTER 1

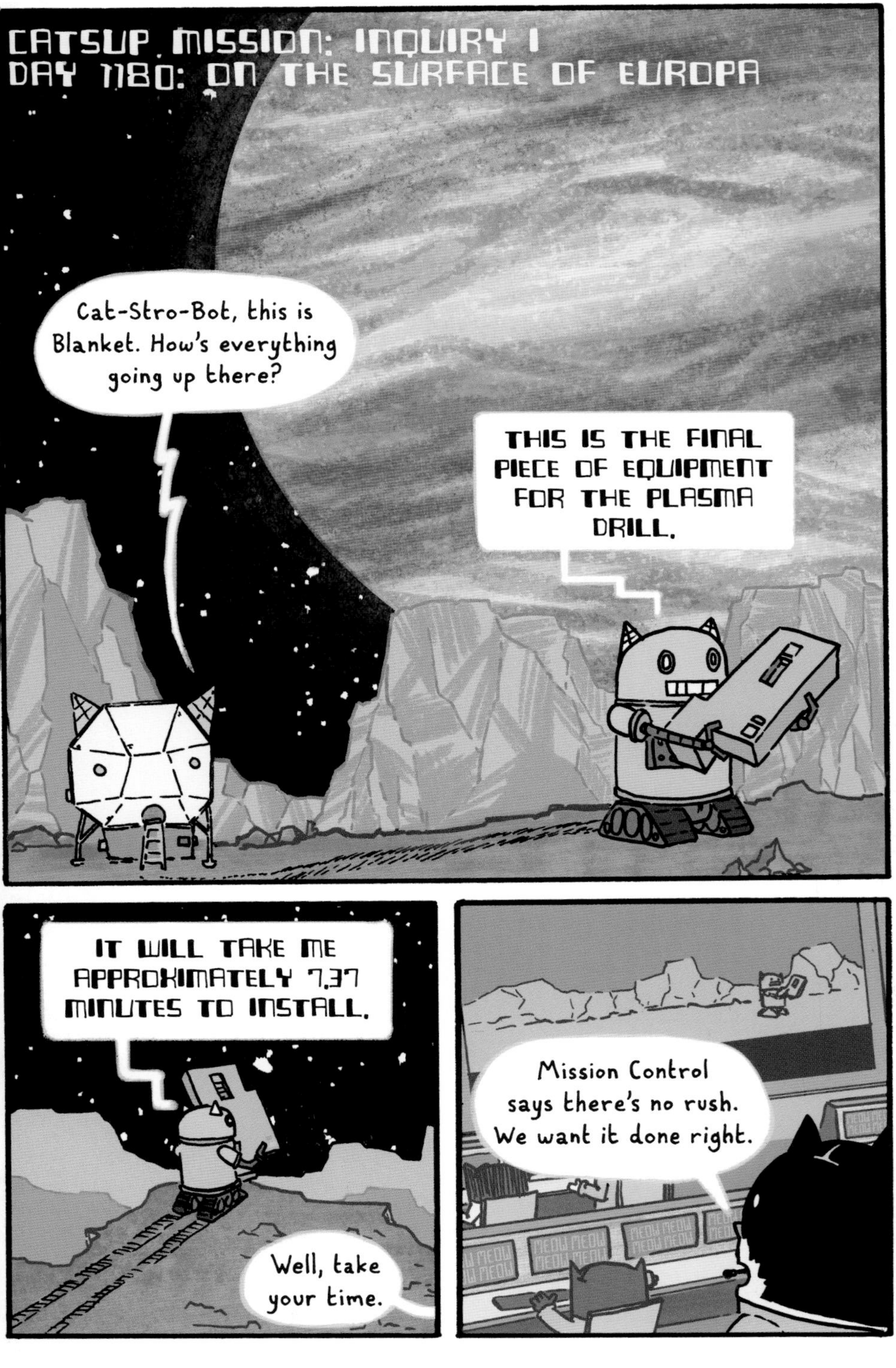
CATSUP MISSION: INQUIRY I
DAY 1180: ON THE SURFACE OF EUROPA
Cat-Stro-Bot, this is Blanket. How's everything going up there?
THIS IS THE FINAL PIECE OF EQUIPMENT FOR THE PLASMA DRILL.
IT WILL TAKE ME APPROXIMATELY 7.37 MINUTES TO INSTALL.
Well, take your time.
Mission Control says there's no rush. We want it done right.
MEOW MEOW MEOW MEOW

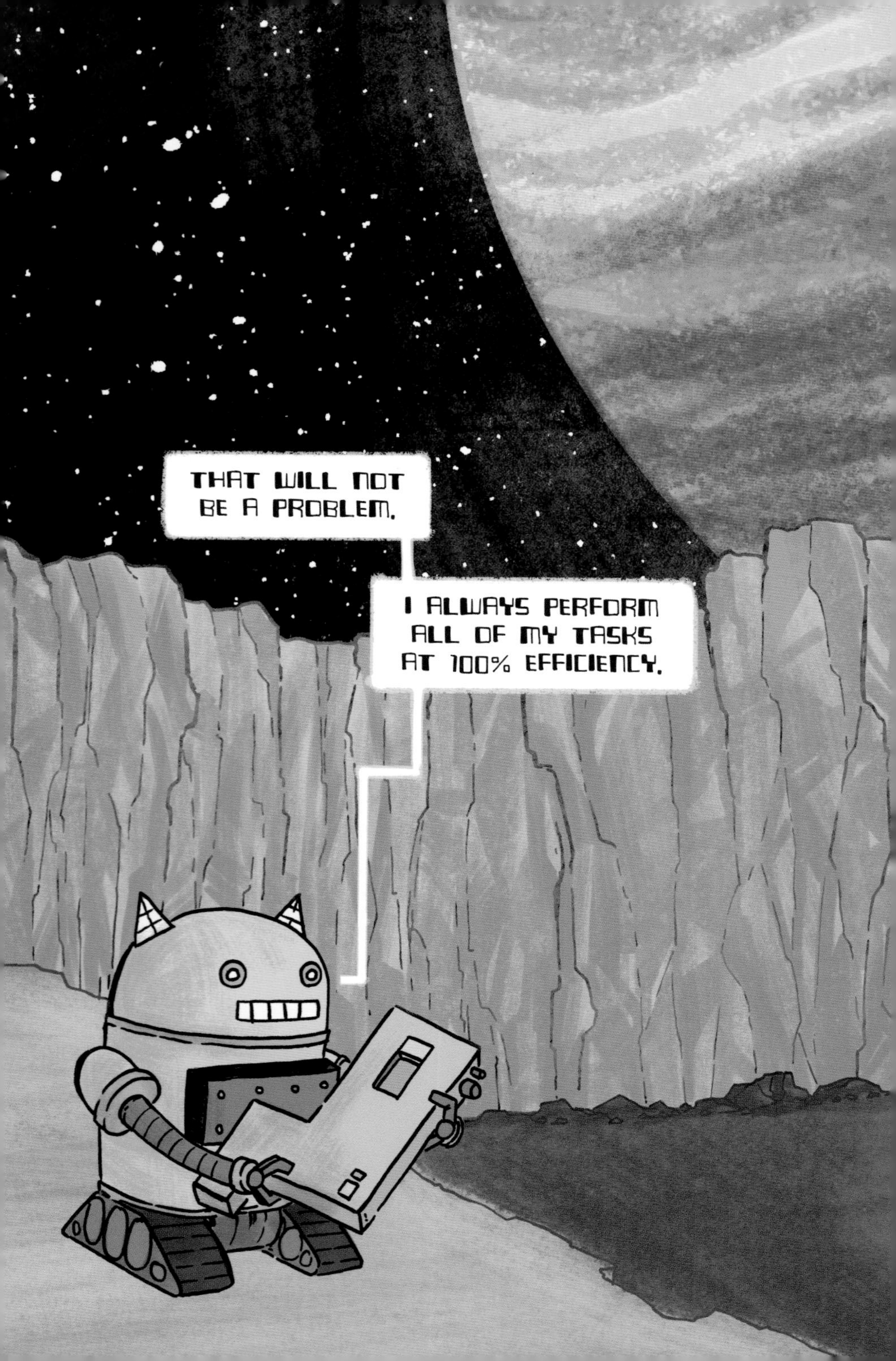
THAT WILL NOT BE A PROBLEM.
I ALWAYS PERFORM ALL OF MY TASKS AT 100% EFFICIENCY.

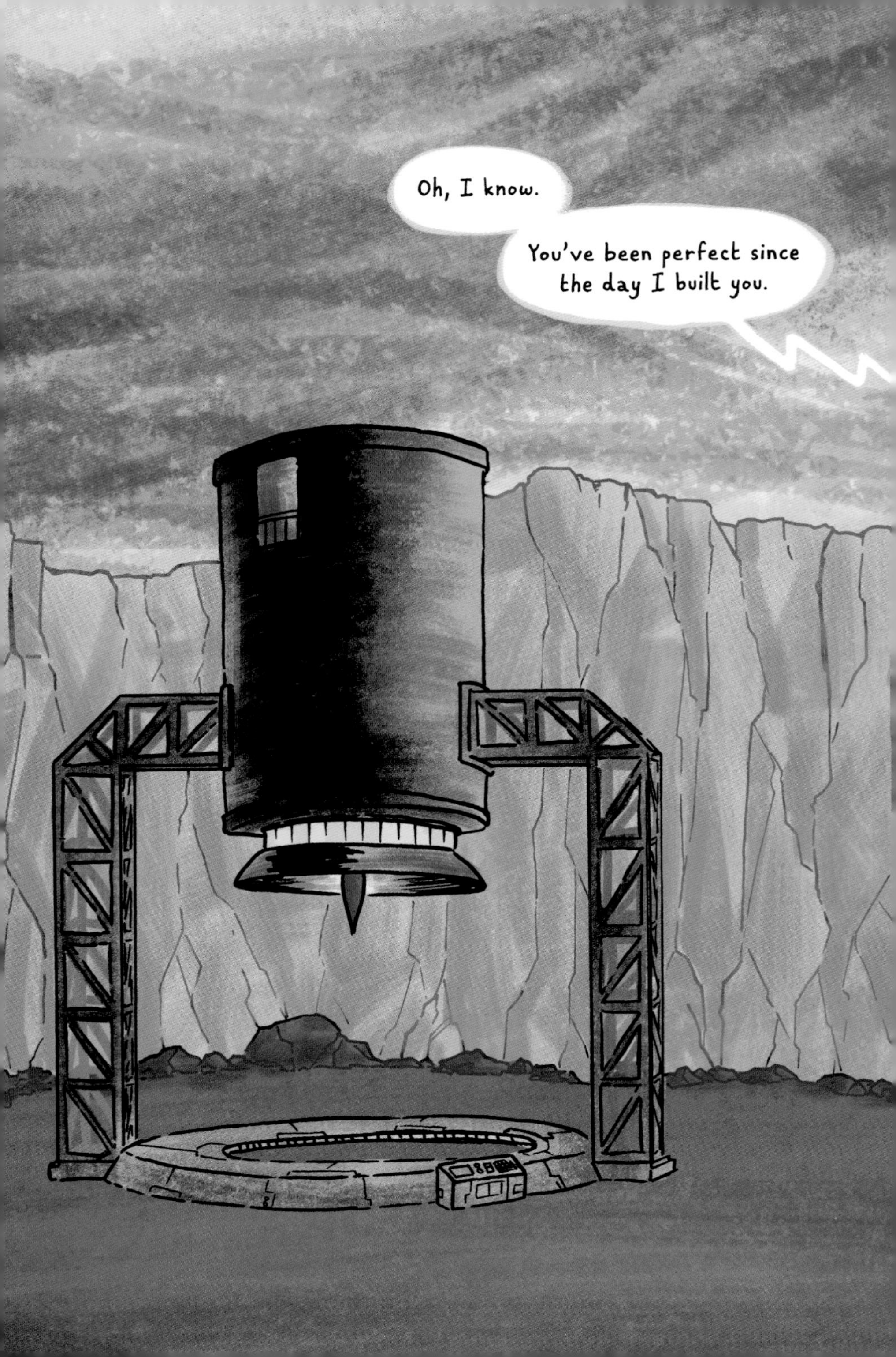
Oh, I know.
You've been perfect since the day I built you.

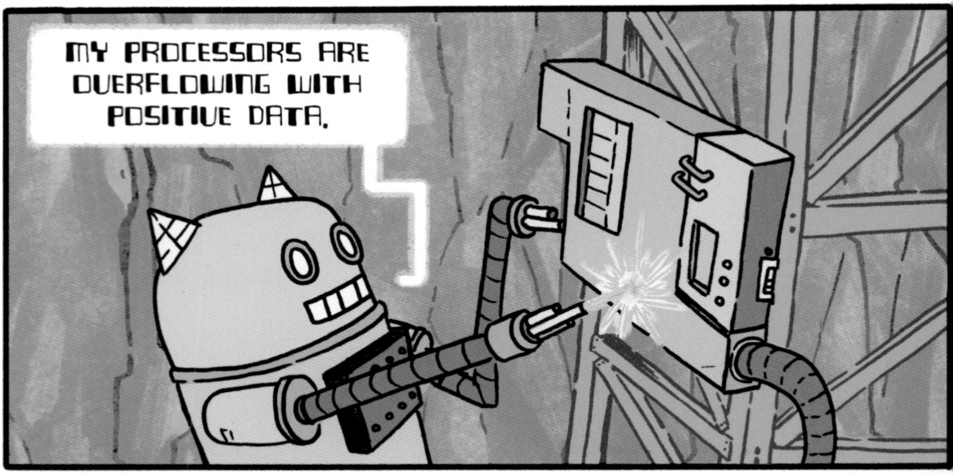
MY PROCESSORS ARE OVERFLOWING WITH POSITIVE DATA.

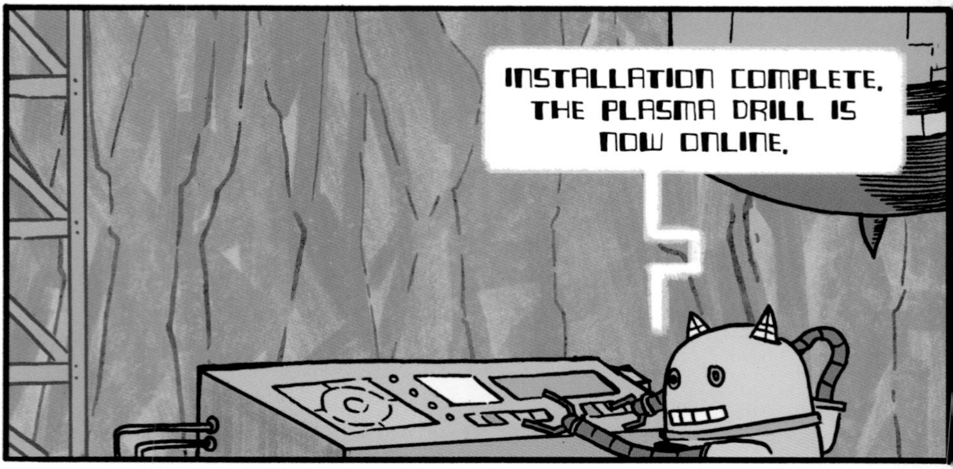
INSTALLATION COMPLETE. THE PLASMA DRILL IS NOW ONLINE.

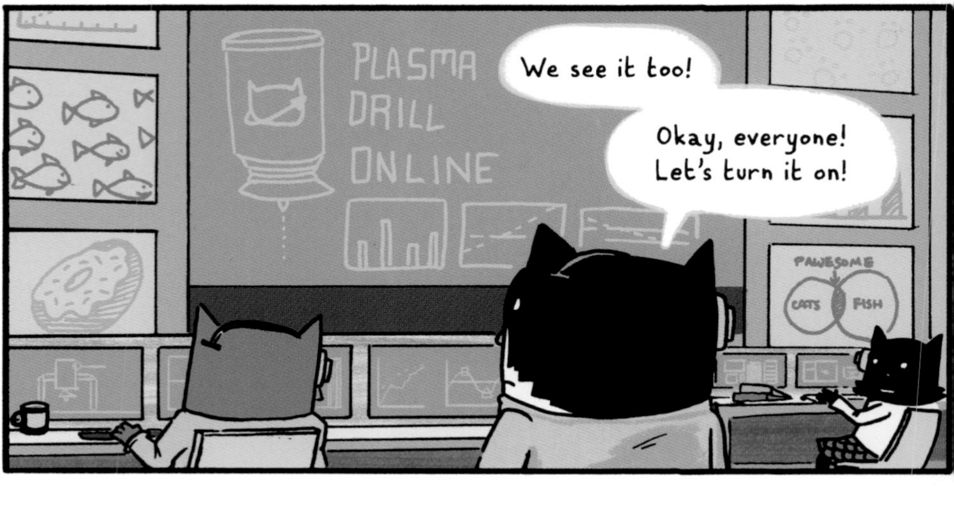
PLASMA
DRILL
ONLINE
We see it too!
Okay, everyone! Let's turn it on!
PAWESOME
CATS
FISH

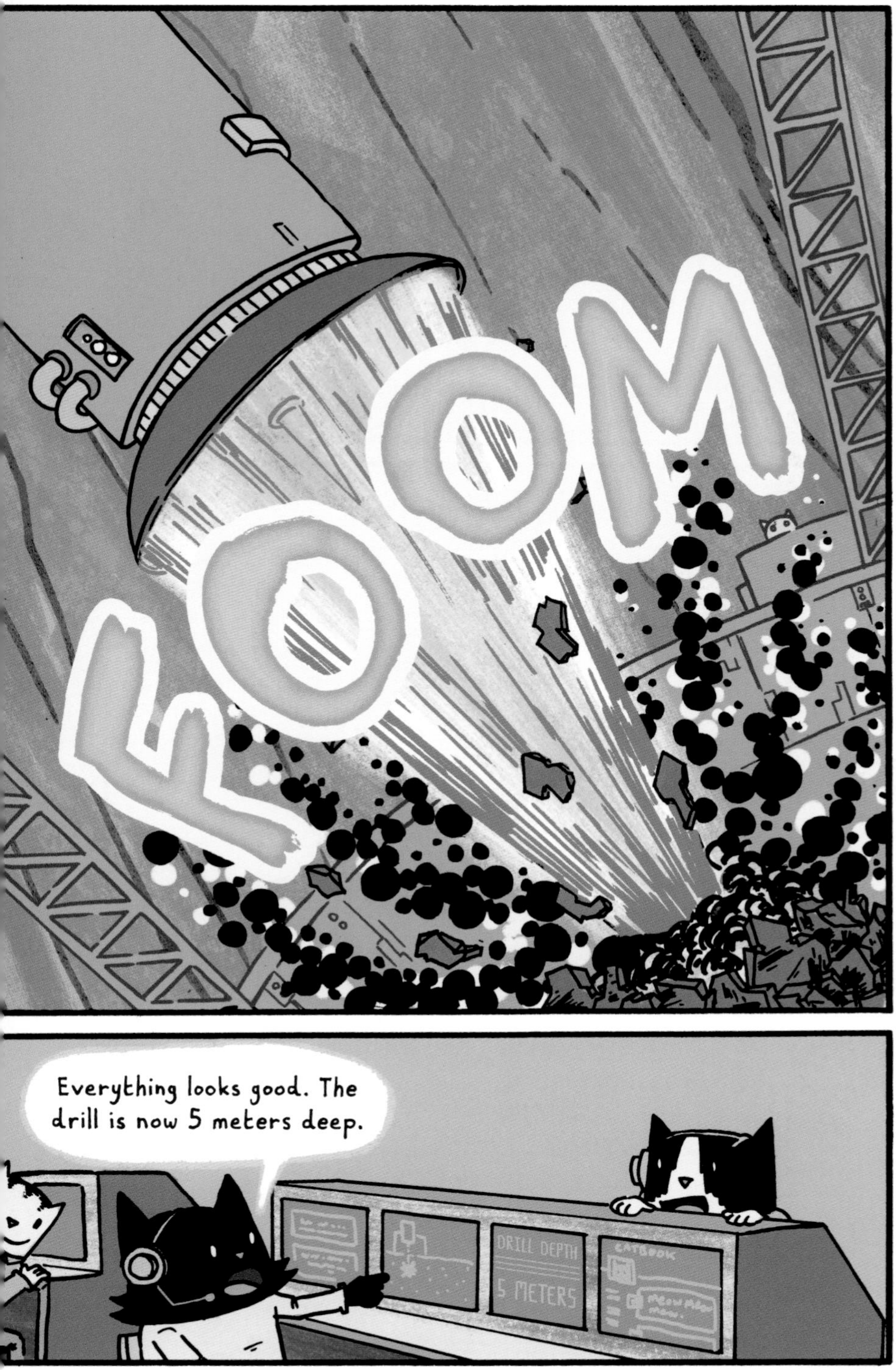
FOOM
Everything looks good. The drill is now 5 meters deep.
DRILL DEPTH
5 METERS
CATBOOK

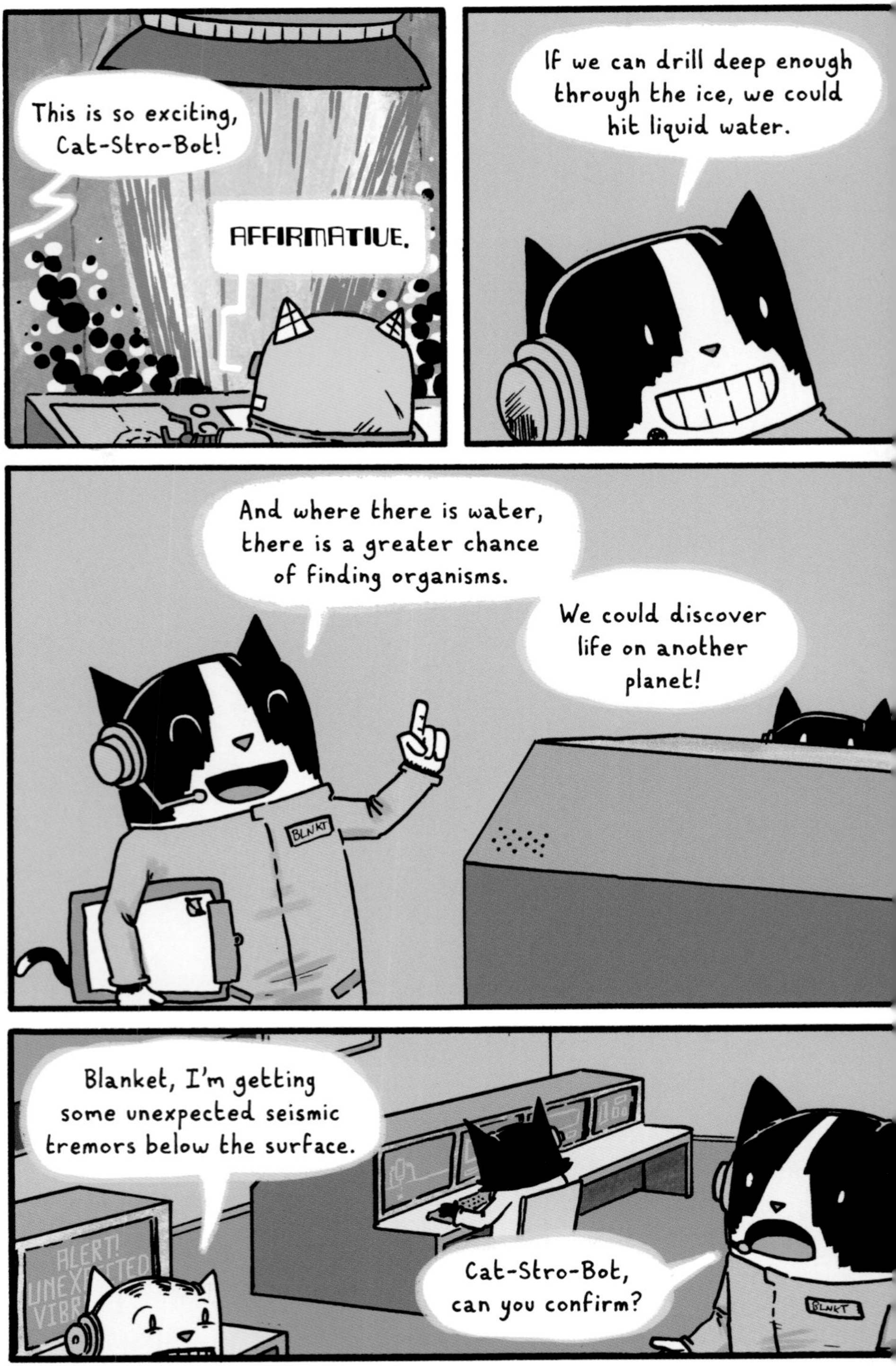
This is so exciting, Cat-Stro-Bot!
AFFIRMATIVE.
If we can drill deep enough through the ice, we could hit liquid water.
And where there is water, there is a greater chance of finding organisms.
We could discover life on another planet!
BLNKT
Blanket, I'm getting some unexpected seismic tremors below the surface.
ALERT! UNEXPECTED VIBR
Cat-Stro-Bot, can you confirm?
BLNKT

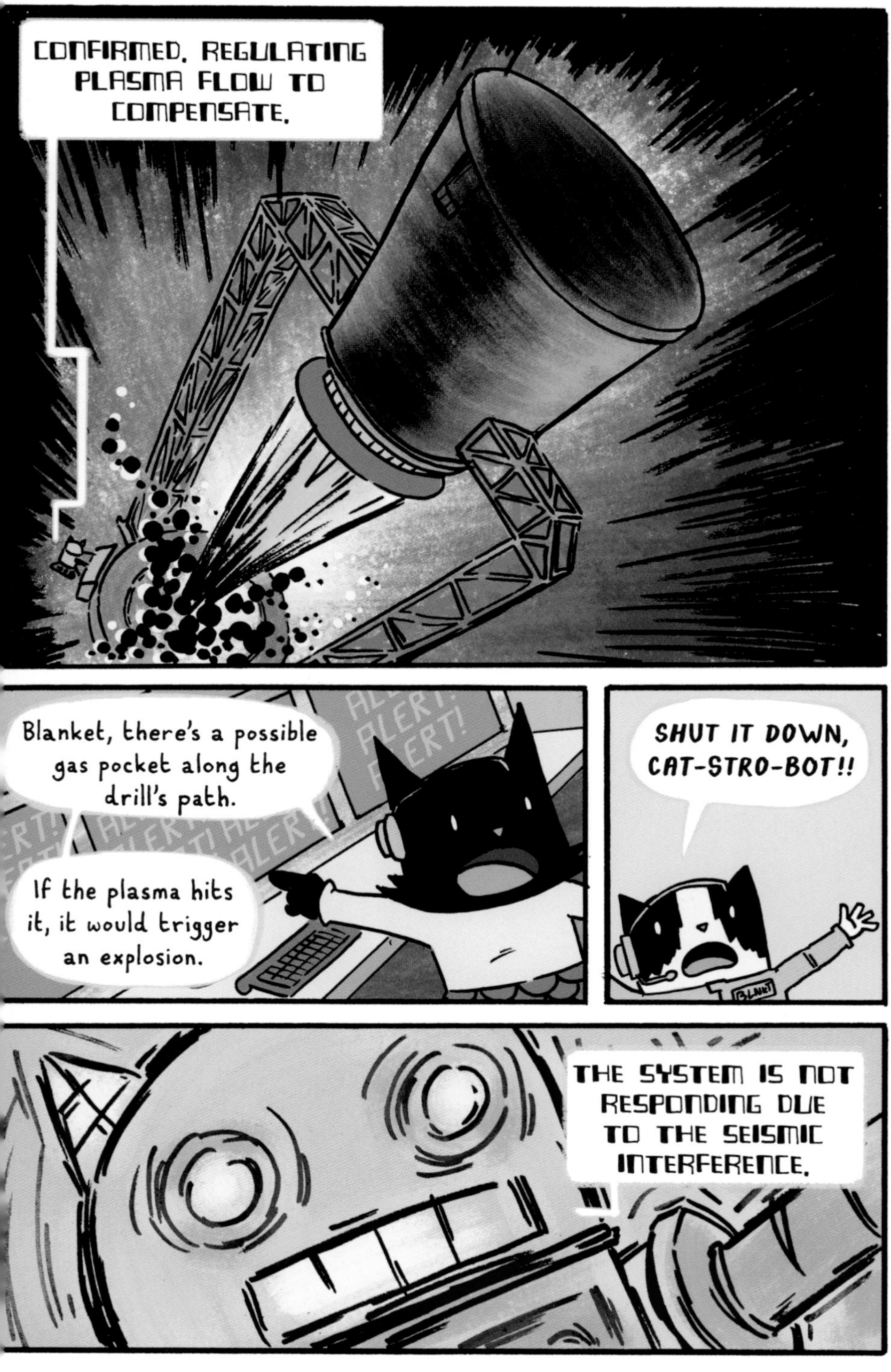
CONFIRMED. REGULATING PLASMA FLOW TO COMPENSATE.
ALERT! ALERT! ALERT!
Blanket, there's a possible gas pocket along the drill's path.
If the plasma hits it, it would trigger an explosion.
SHUT IT DOWN, CAT-STRO-BOT!!
BLNKT
THE SYSTEM IS NOT RESPONDING DUE TO THE SEISMIC INTERFERENCE.

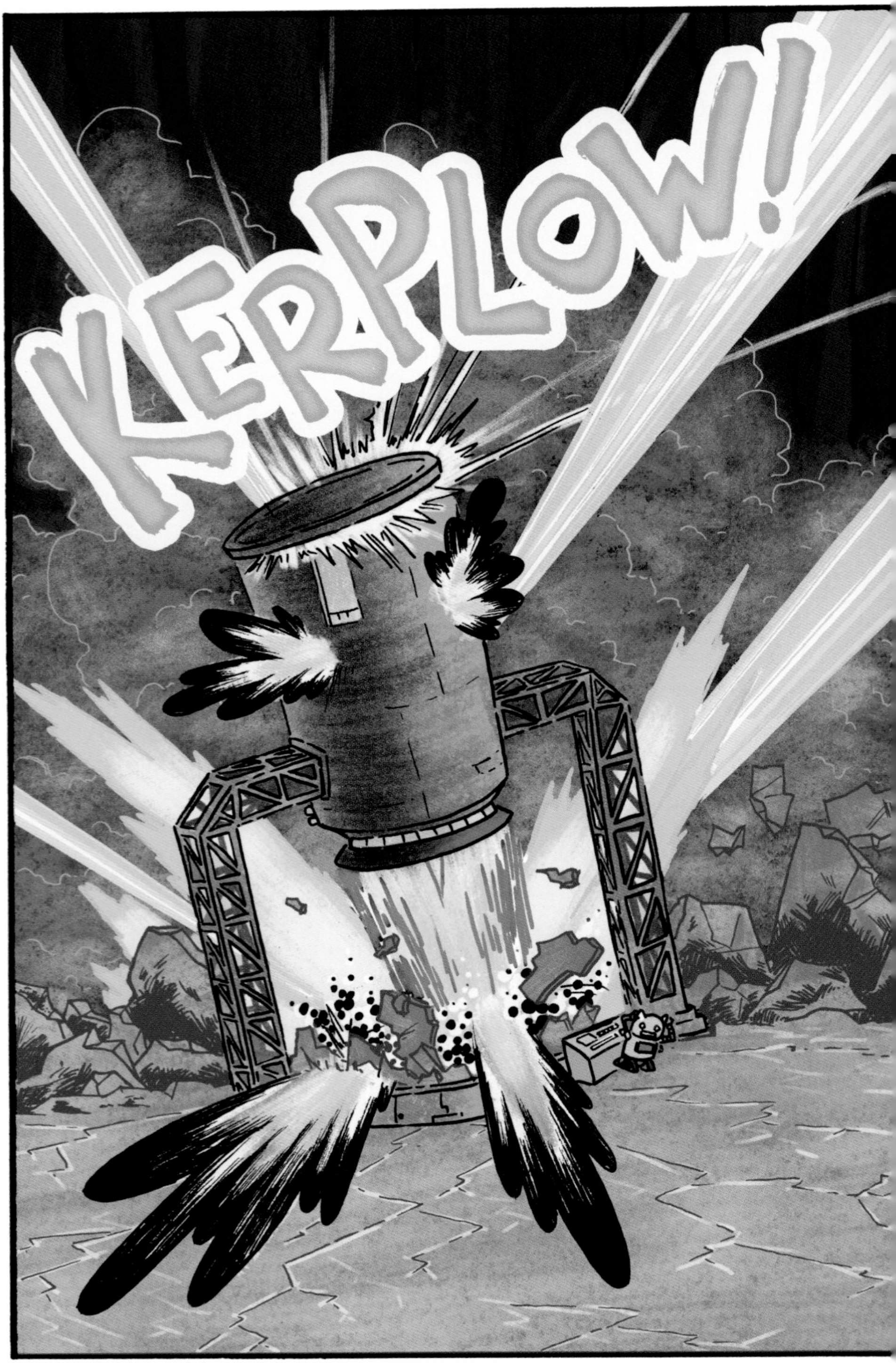
KERPLOW!

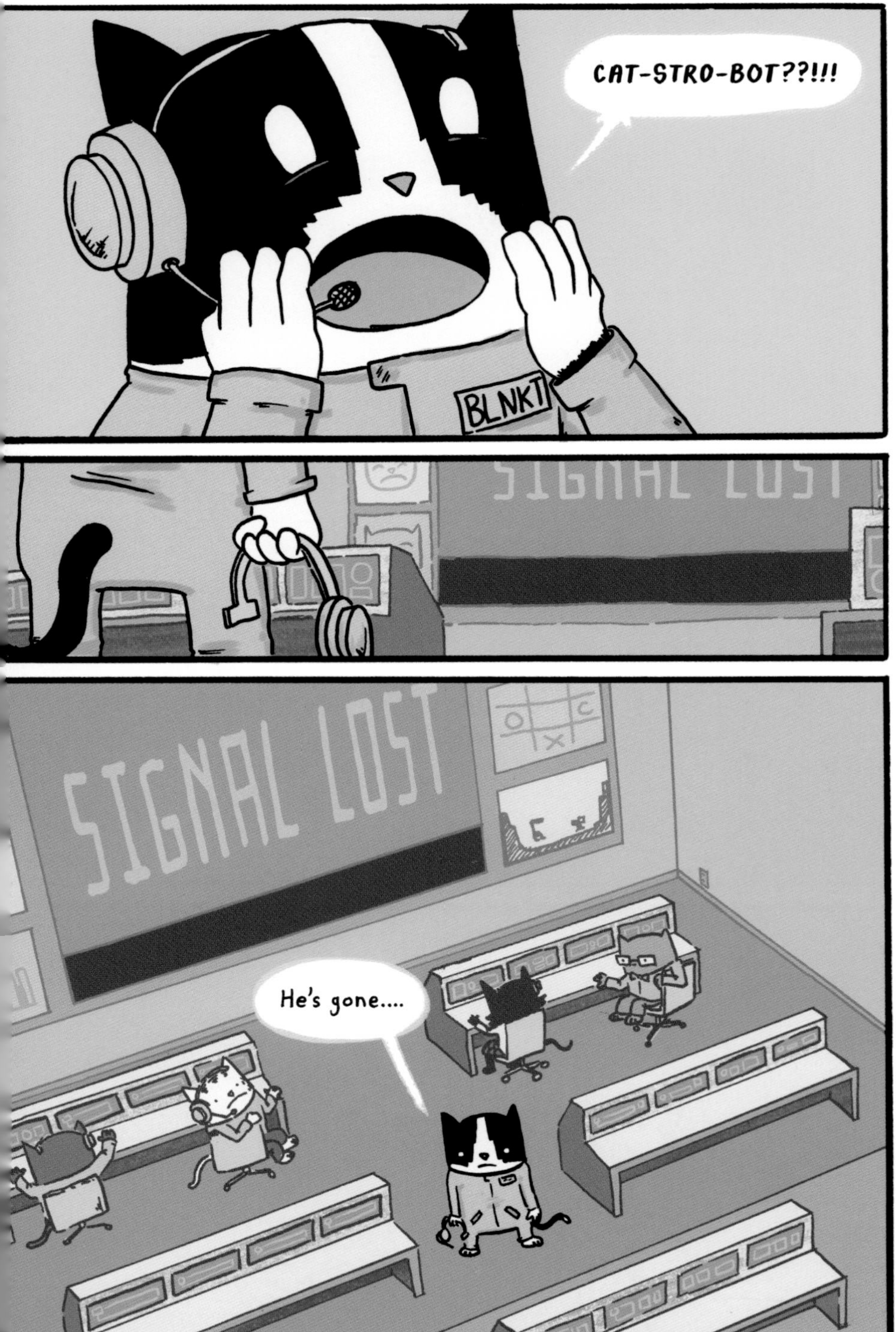
CAT-STRO-BOT??!!!
BLNKT
SIGNAL LOST
SIGNAL LOST
He's gone....

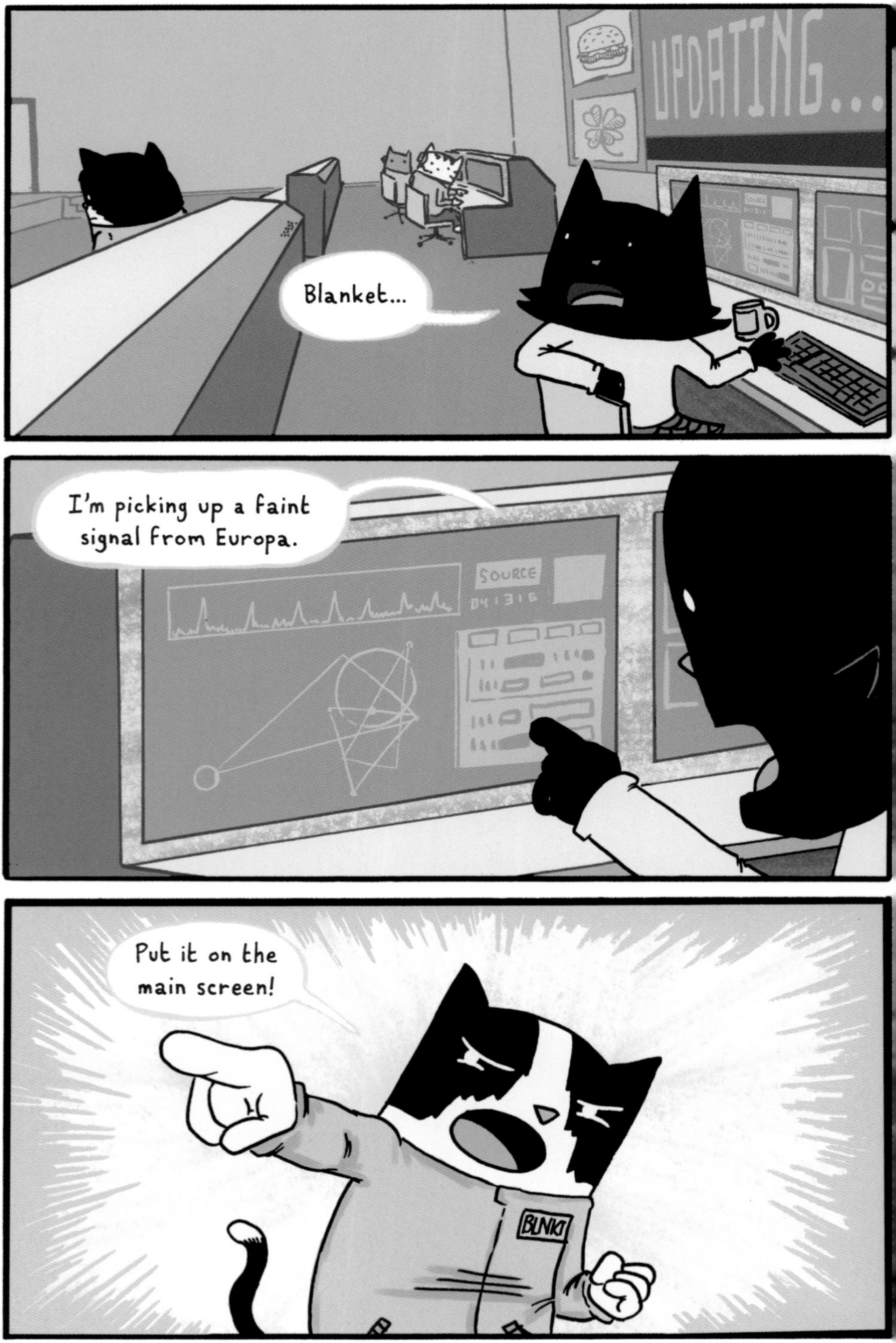
UPDATING...
Blanket...
I'm picking up a faint signal from Europa.
SOURCE
Put it on the main screen!
BLNKT

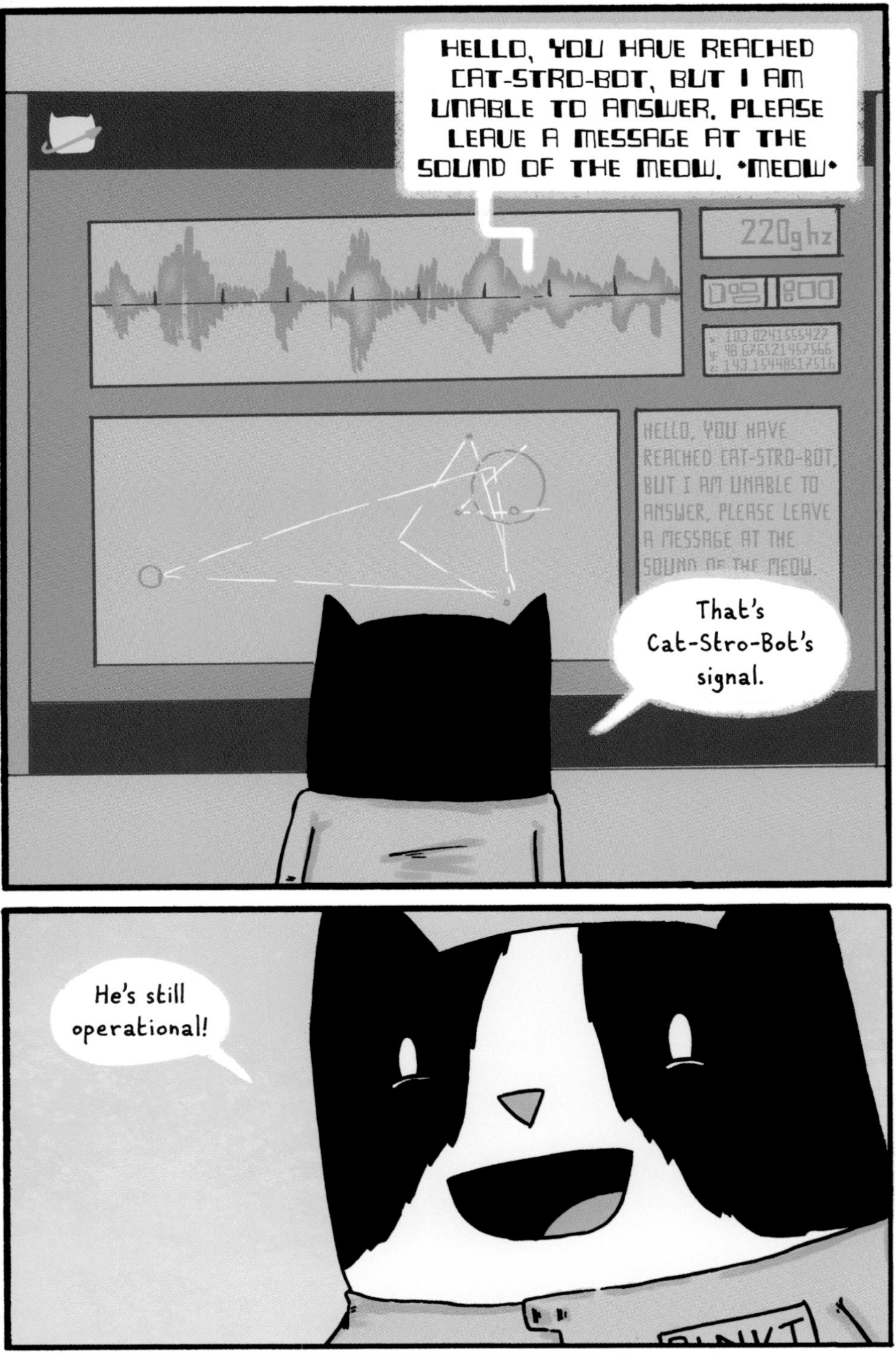
HELLO, YOU HAVE REACHED CAT-STRO-BOT, BUT I AM UNABLE TO ANSWER. PLEASE LEAVE A MESSAGE AT THE SOUND OF THE MEOW. *MEOW*
220ghz
That's Cat-Stro-Bot's signal.
He's still operational!

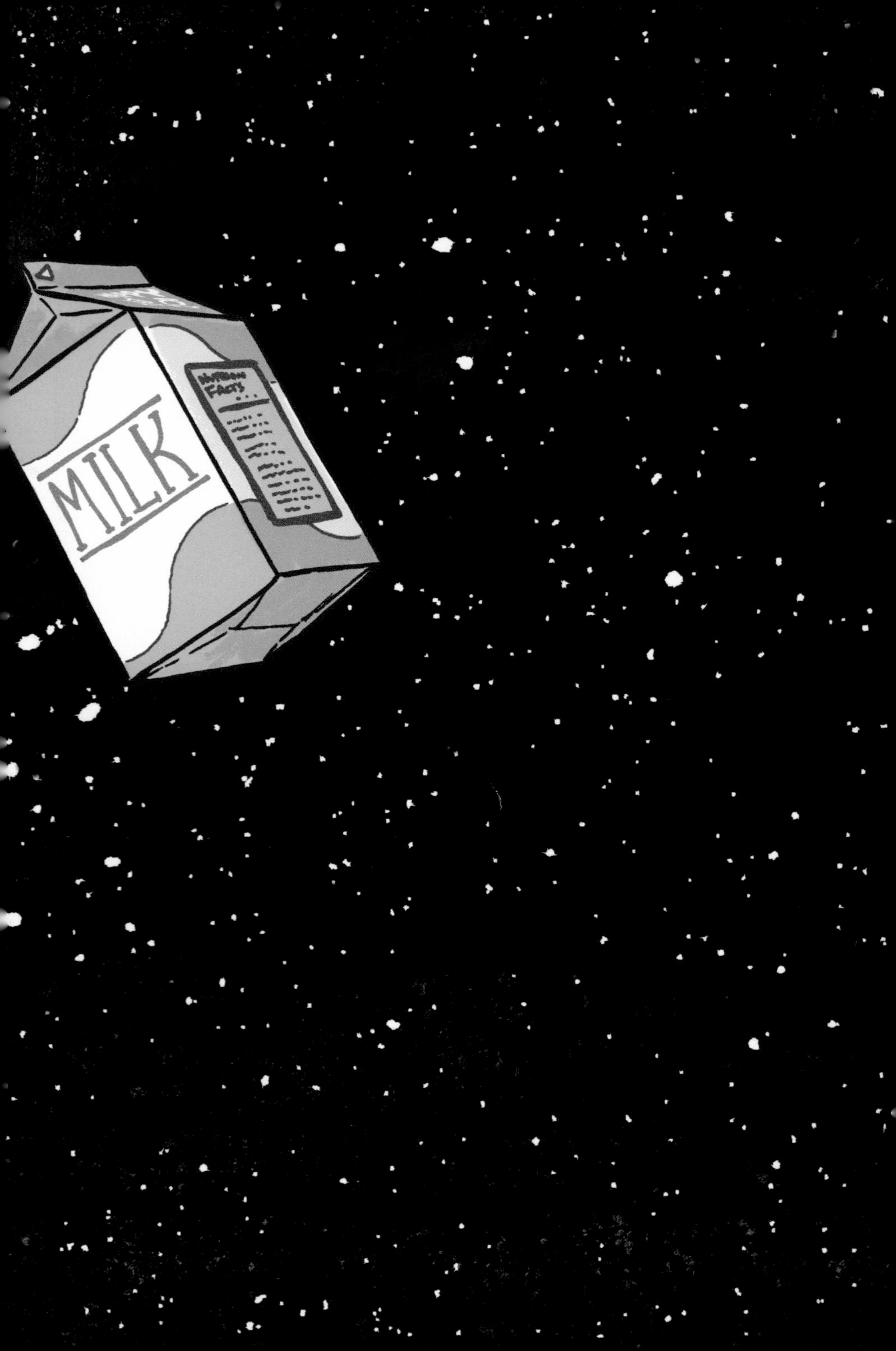
MILK

CHAPTER 2

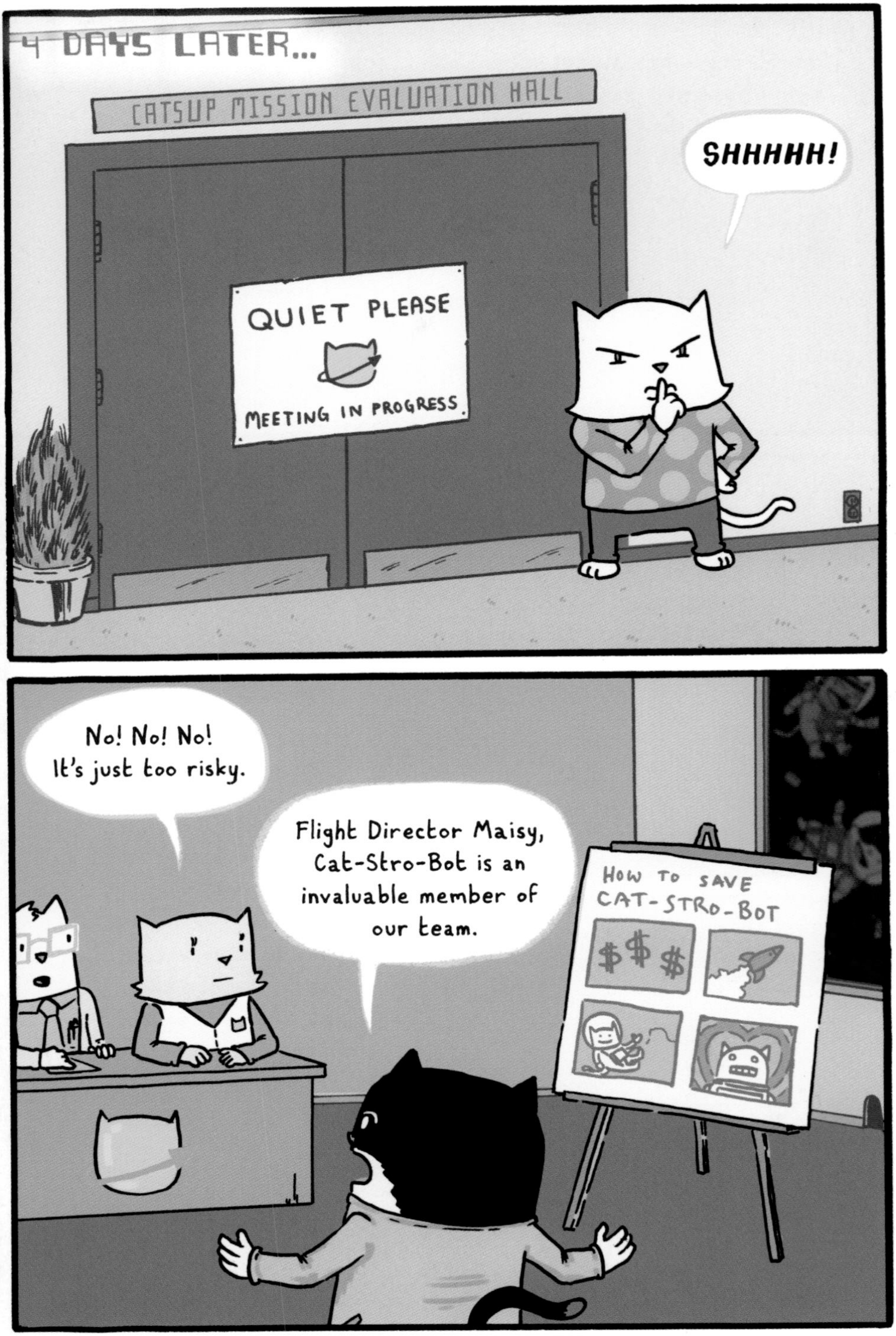
4 DAYS LATER...
CATSUP MISSION EVALUATION HALL
SHHHHH!
QUIET PLEASE
MEETING IN PROGRESS
No! No! No! It's just too risky.
Flight Director Maisy, Cat-Stro-Bot is an invaluable member of our team.
HOW TO SAVE CAT-STRO-BOT
$ $ $

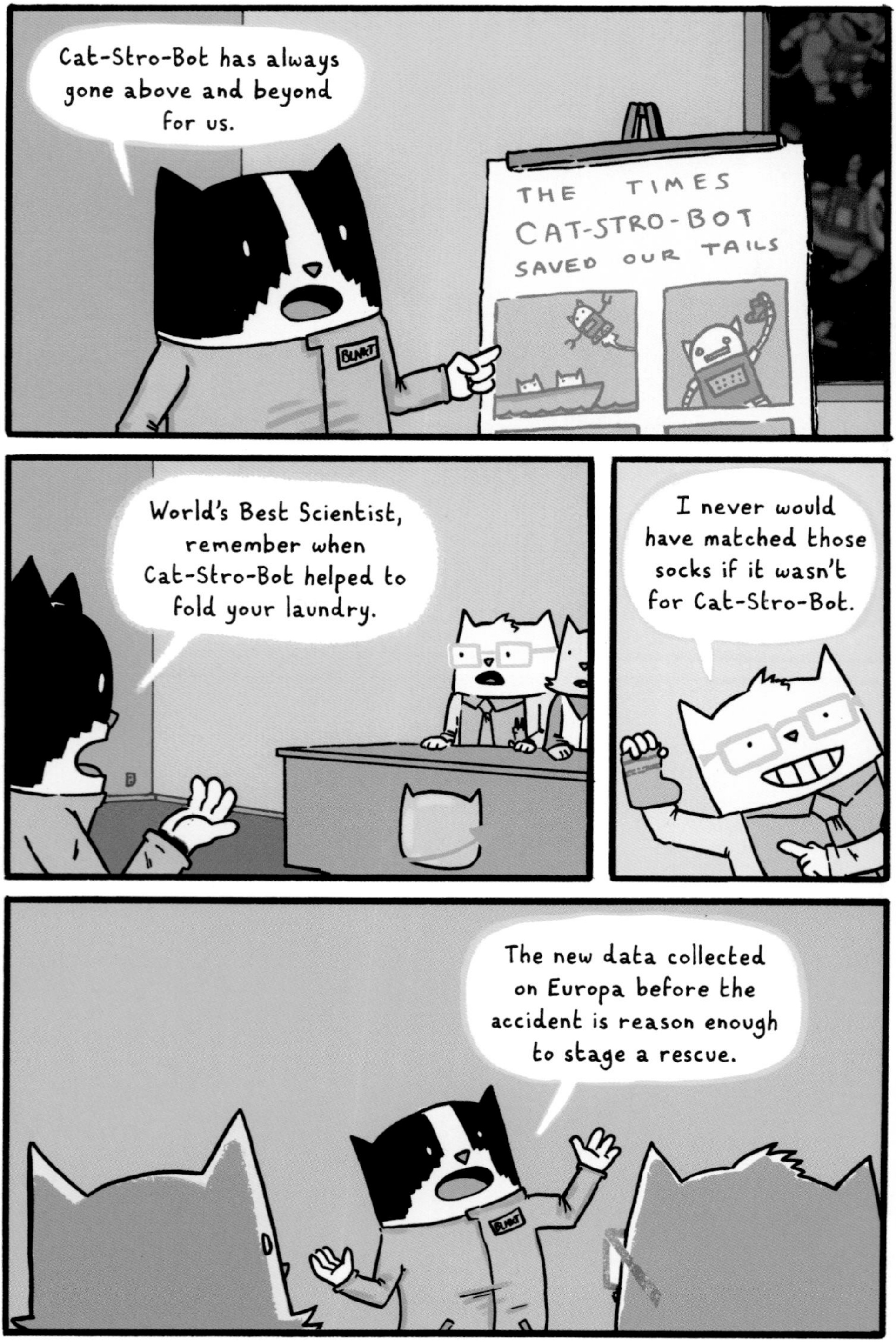
Cat-Stro-Bot has always gone above and beyond for us.
THE TIMES
CAT-STRO-BOT SAVED OUR TAILS
BLNKT
World's Best Scientist, remember when Cat-Stro-Bot helped to fold your laundry.
I never would have matched those socks if it wasn't for Cat-Stro-Bot.
The new data collected on Europa before the accident is reason enough to stage a rescue.
BLNKT

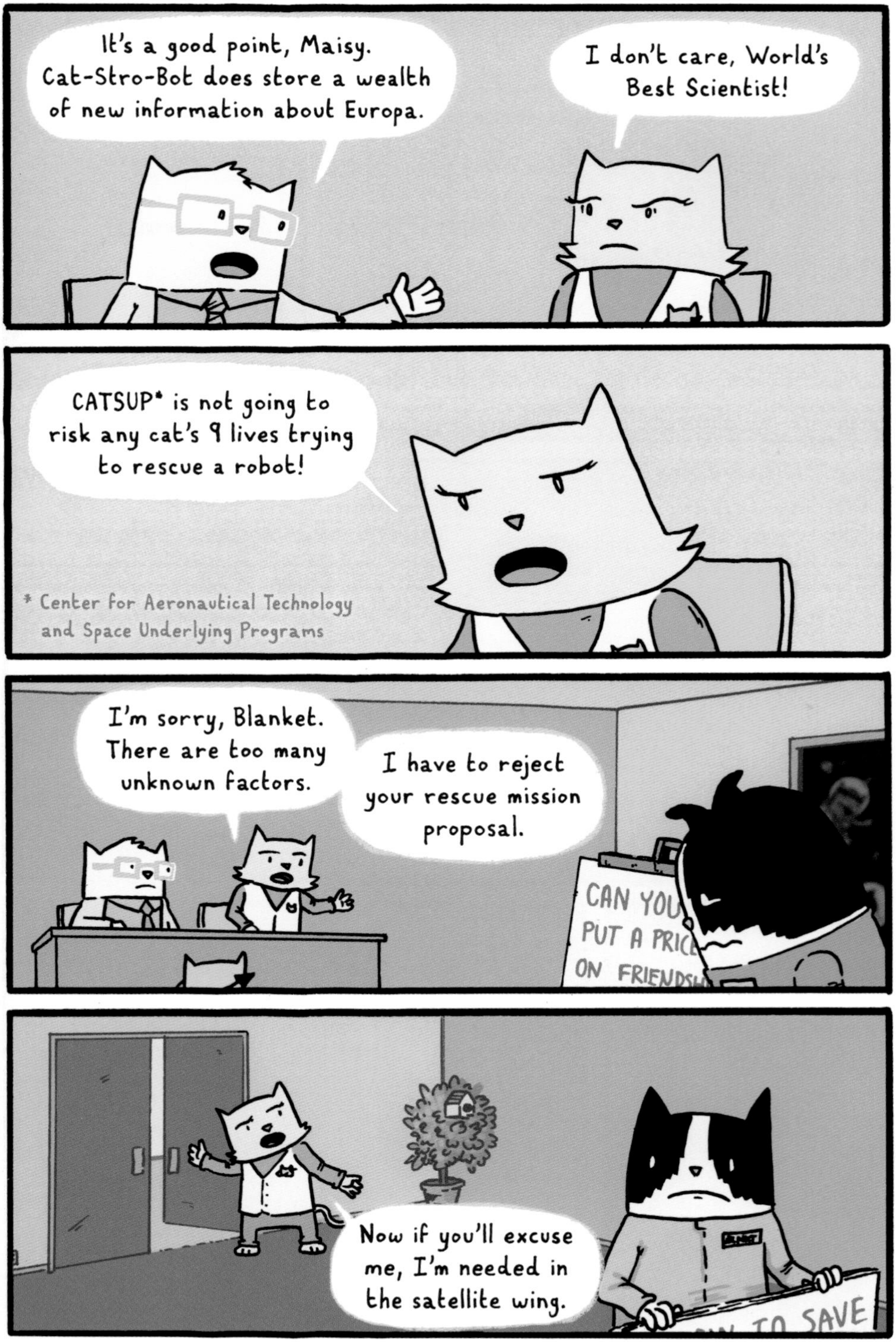
It's a good point, Maisy. Cat-Stro-Bot does store a wealth of new information about Europa.
I don't care, World's Best Scientist!
CATSUP* is not going to risk any cat's 9 lives trying to rescue a robot!
* Center for Aeronautical Technology and Space Underlying Programs
I'm sorry, Blanket. There are too many unknown factors.
I have to reject your rescue mission proposal.
Now if you'll excuse me, I'm needed in the satellite wing.
TO SAVE

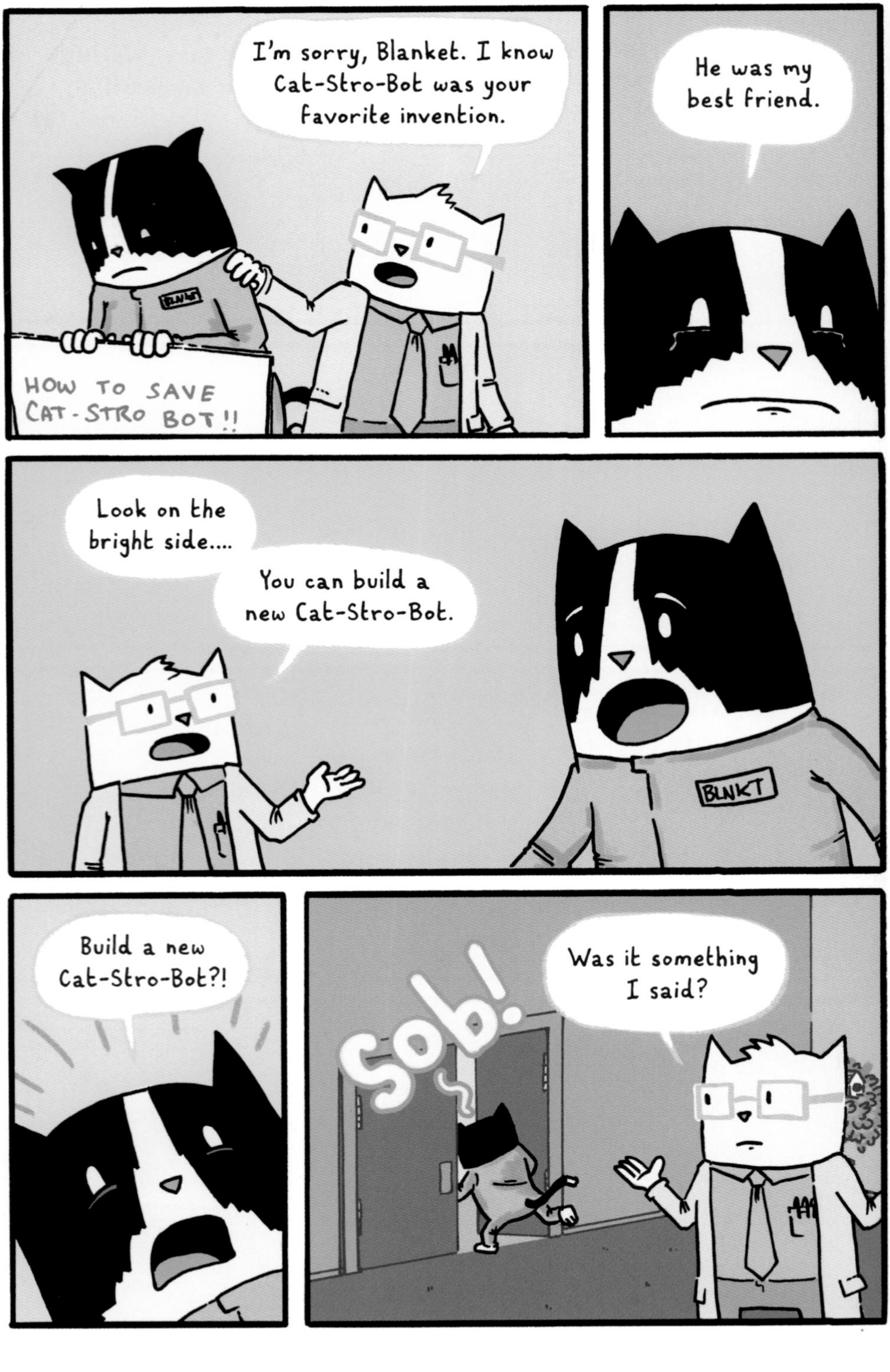
I'm sorry, Blanket. I know Cat-Stro-Bot was your favorite invention.
BLNKT
HOW TO SAVE CAT-STRO BOT!!
He was my best friend.
Look on the bright side....
You can build a new Cat-Stro-Bot.
BLNKT
Build a new Cat-Stro-Bot?!
SOB!
Was it something I said?

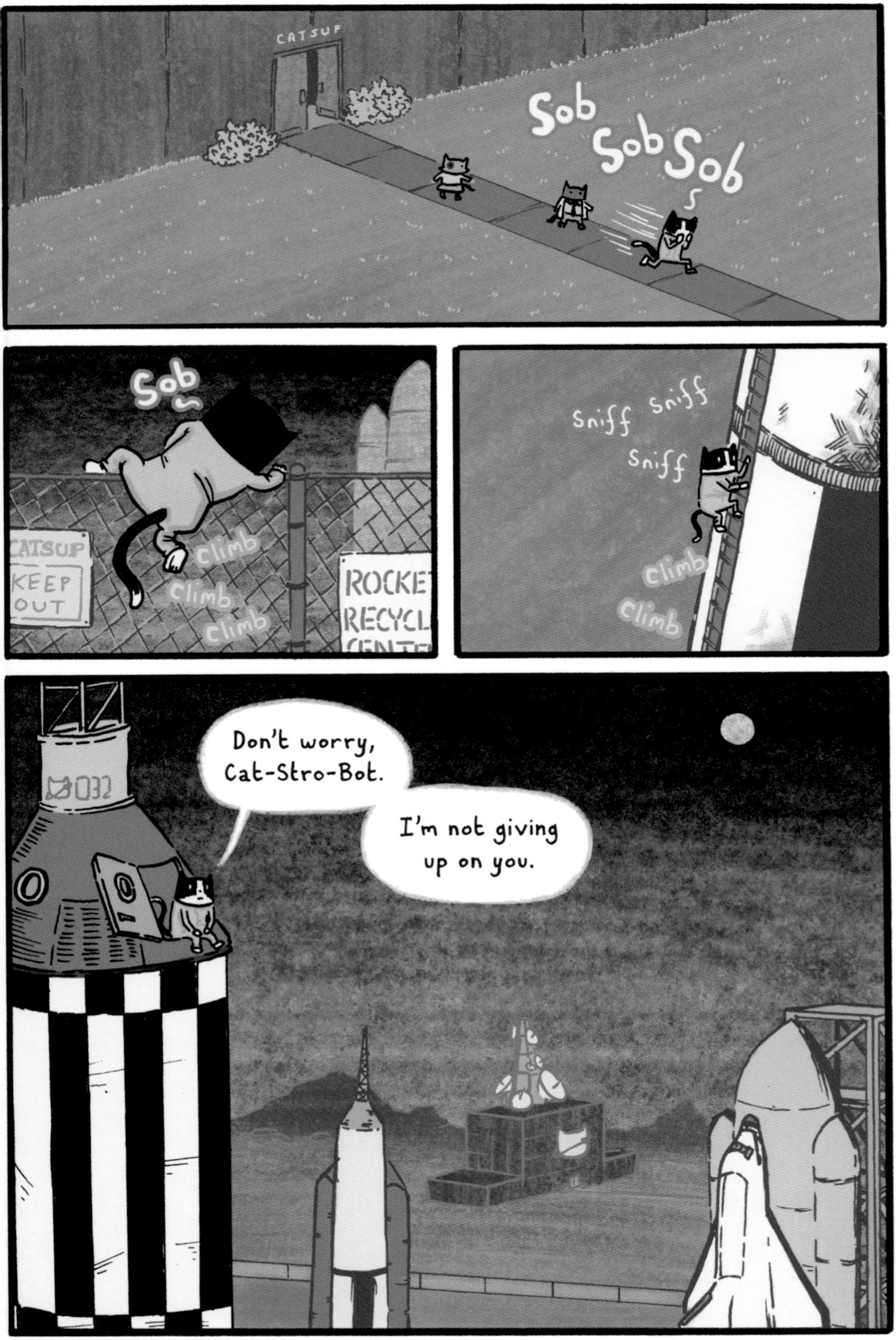
CATSUP
Sob
Sob
Sob
Sob
CATSUP
KEEP
OUT
climb
climb
climb
ROCKET
RECYCL
sniff sniff
sniff
climb
climb
Don't worry, Cat-Stro-Bot.
I'm not giving up on you.

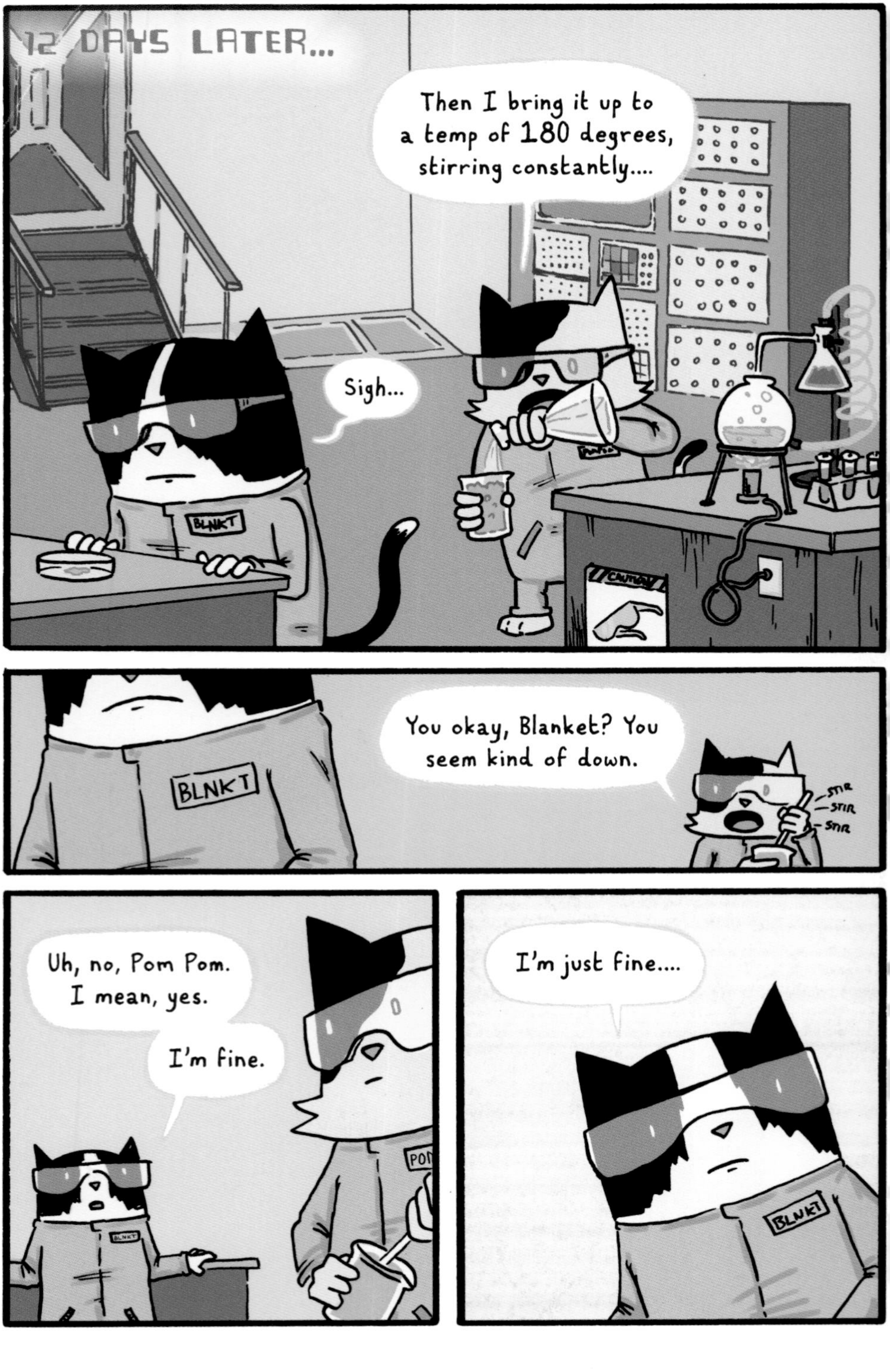
12 DAYS LATER...
Then I bring it up to a temp of 180 degrees, stirring constantly....
Sigh...
BLNKT
CAUTION
You okay, Blanket? You seem kind of down.
BLNKT
STIR
STIR
STIR
Uh, no, Pom Pom. I mean, yes.
I'm fine.
I'm just fine....
BLNKT

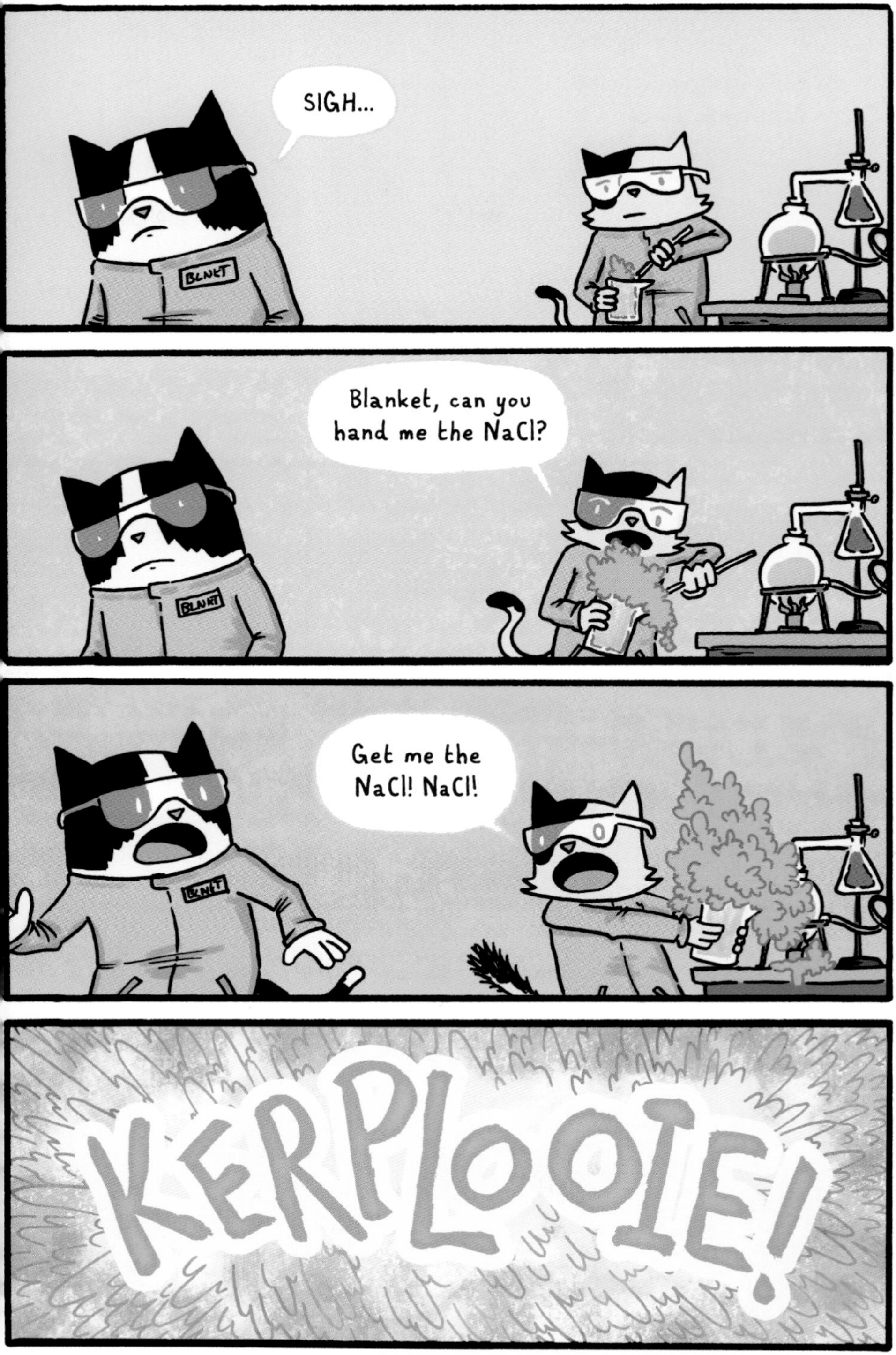
SIGH...
BLNKT
Blanket, can you hand me the NaCl?
BLNKT
Get me the NaCl! NaCl!
BLNKT
KERPLOOIE!

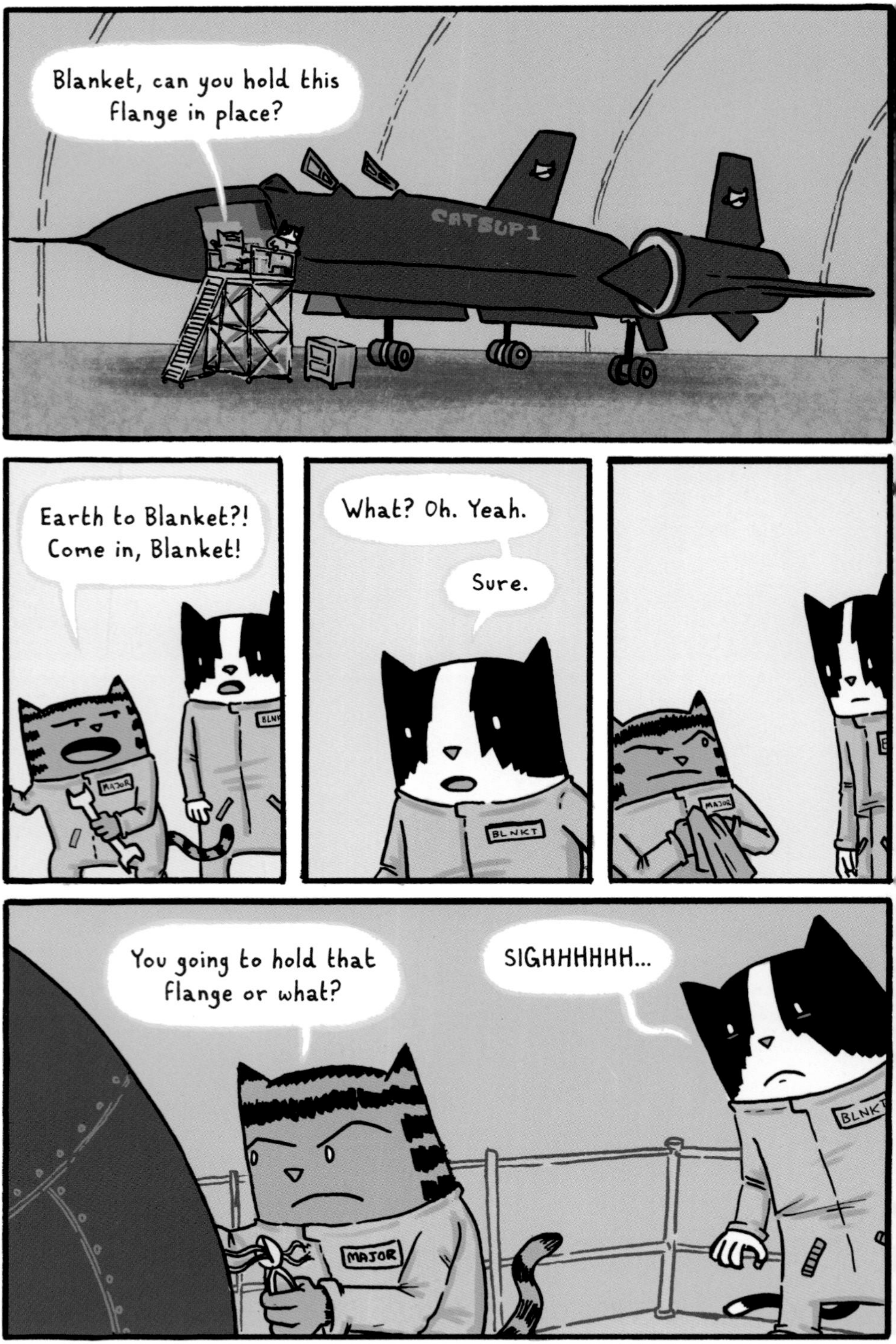
Blanket, can you hold this flange in place?
CATSUP 1
Earth to Blanket?! Come in, Blanket!
BLNK
MAJOR
What? Oh. Yeah.
Sure.
BLNKT
MAJOR
You going to hold that flange or what?
SIGHHHHHH...
MAJOR
BLNKT

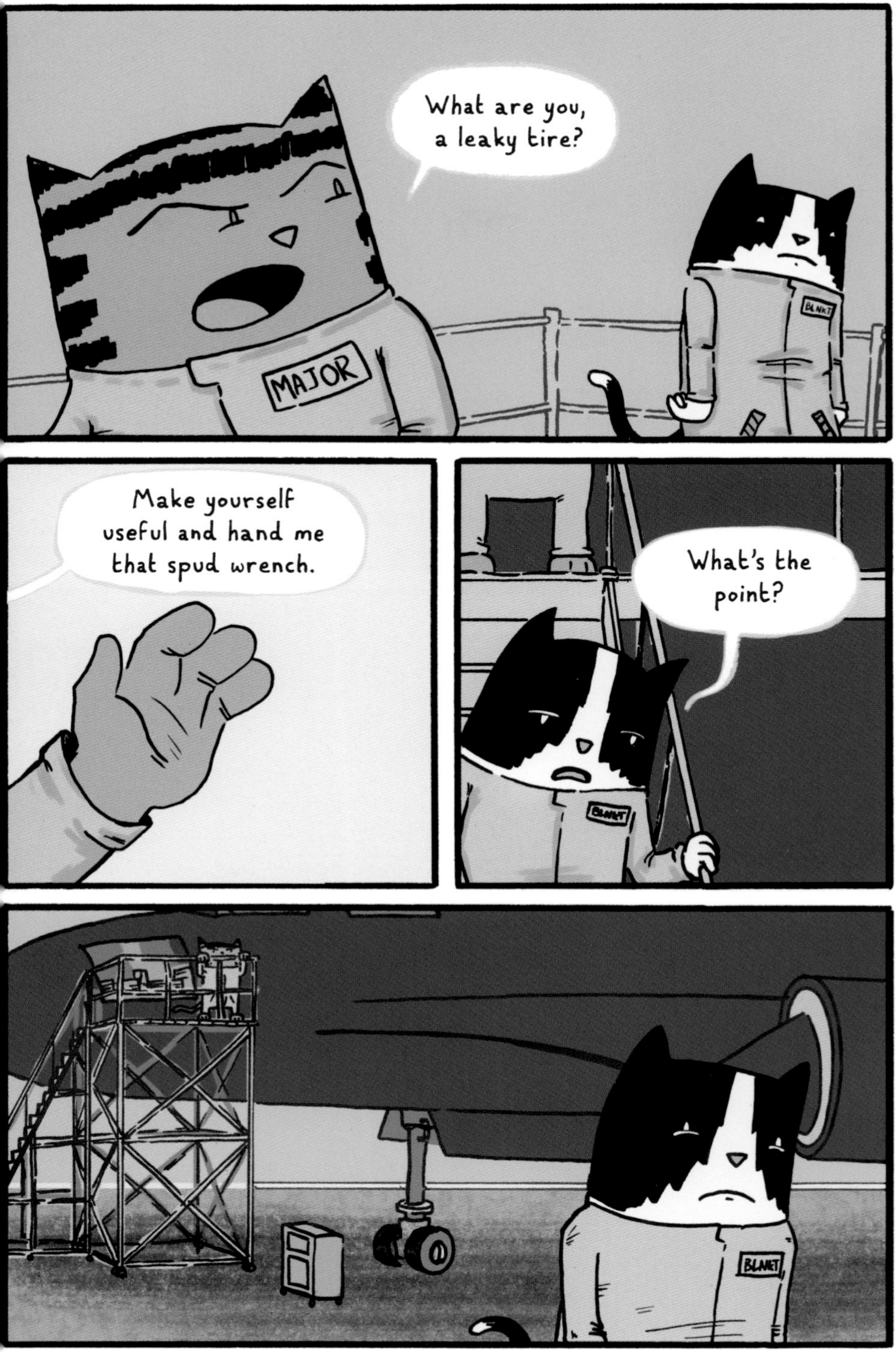
What are you, a leaky tire?
MAJOR
BLNKT
Make yourself useful and hand me that spud wrench.
What's the point?
BLNKT
BLNKT

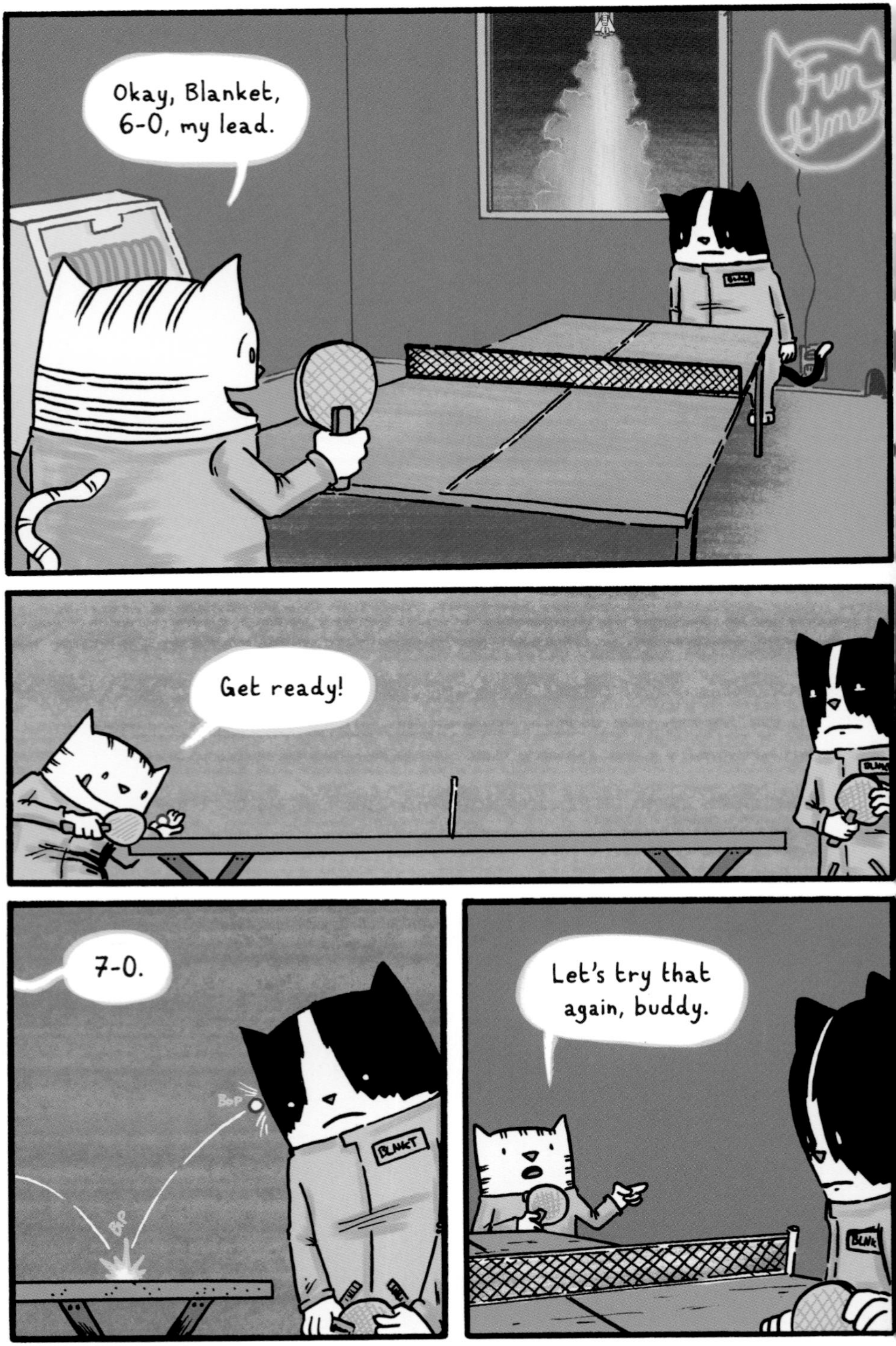
Okay, Blanket, 6-0, my lead.
Get ready!
7-0.
Let's try that again, buddy.

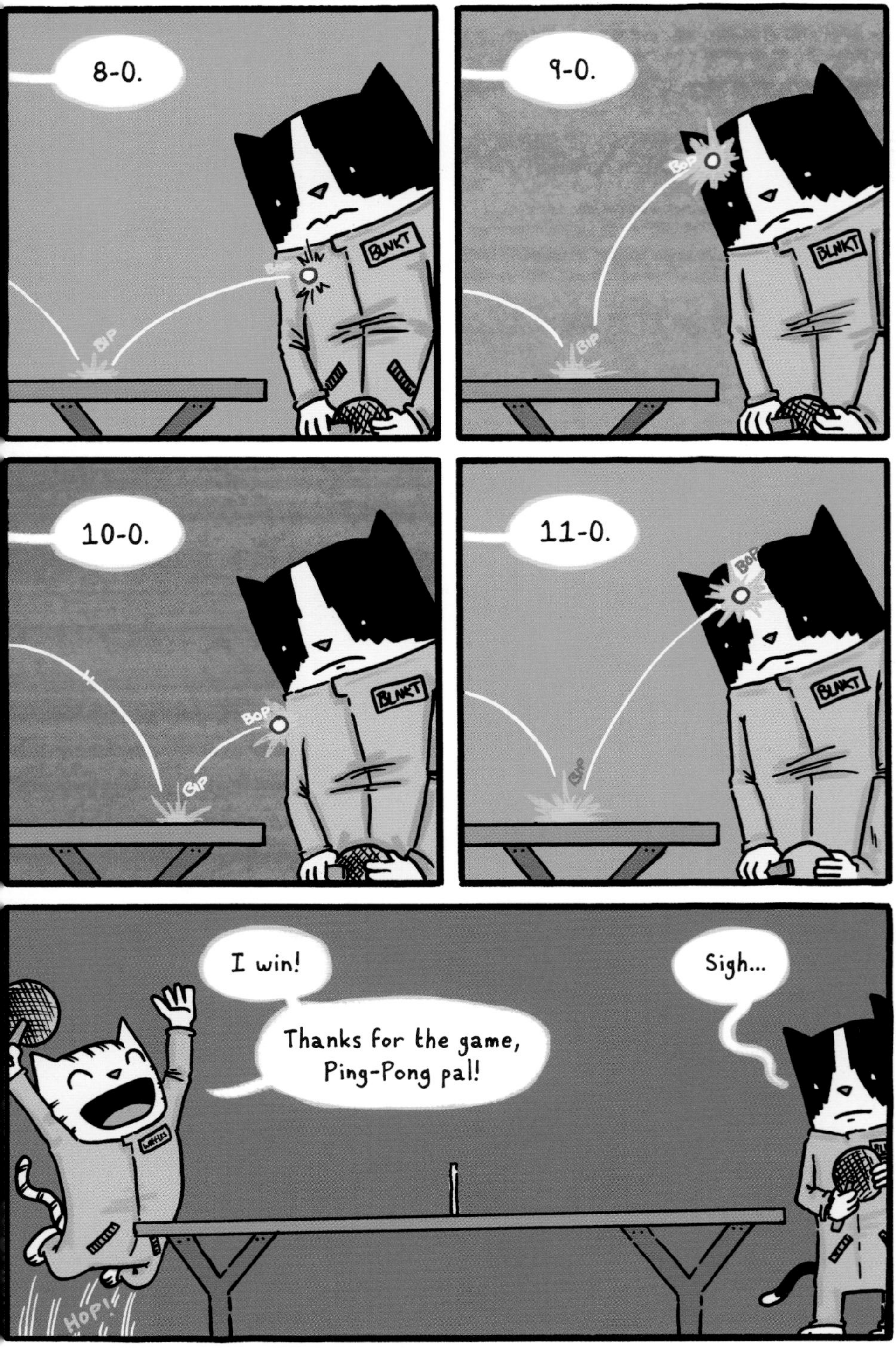
8-0.
BLNKT
BOP
BIP
9-0.
BOP
BLNKT
BIP
10-0.
BLNKT
BOP
BIP
11-0.
BOP
BLNKT
BIP
I win!
Thanks for the game, Ping-Pong pal!
Sigh...
HOP!

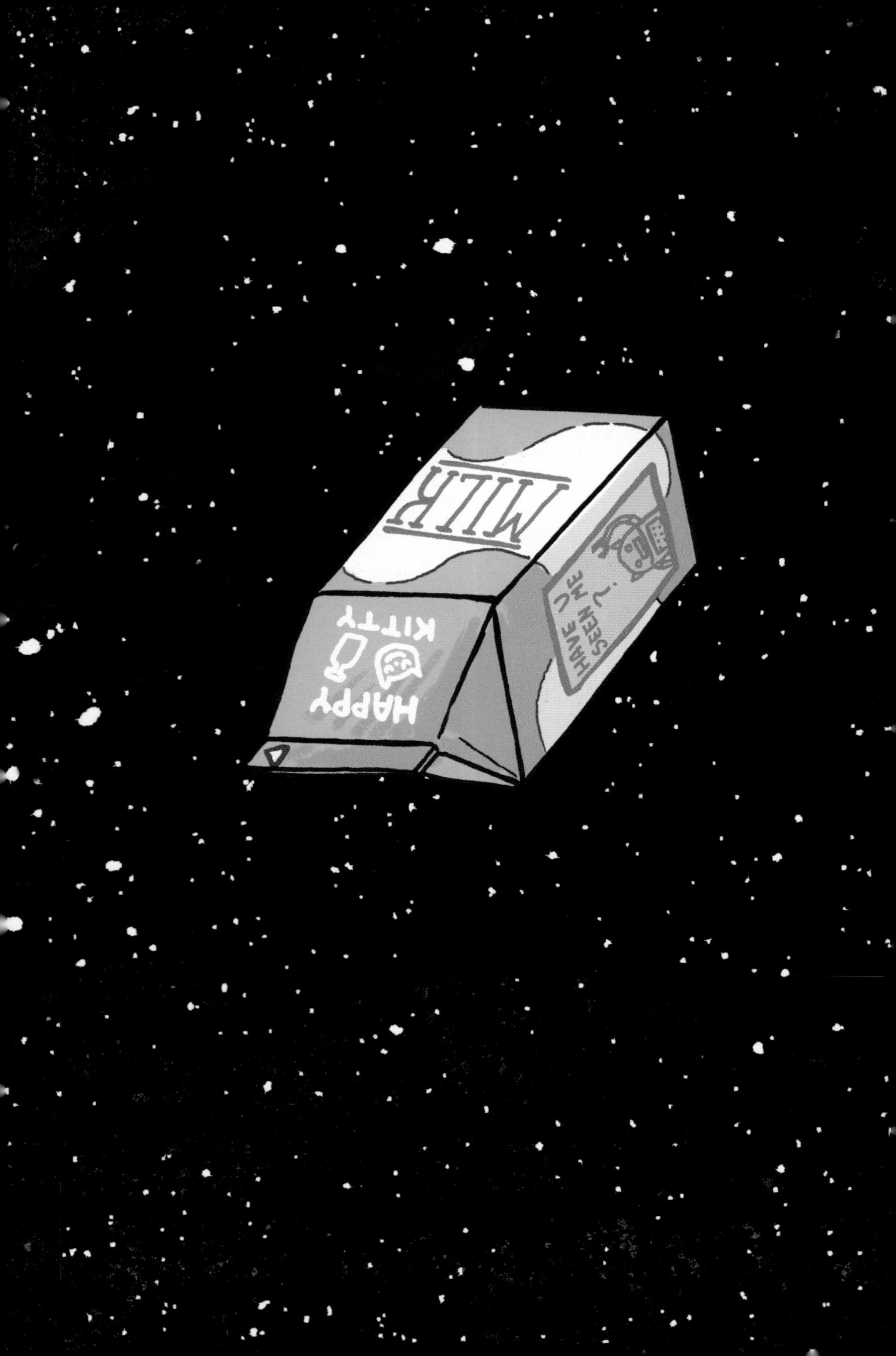
MILK
HAPPY KITTY
HAVE U SEEN ME ?

CHAPTER 3

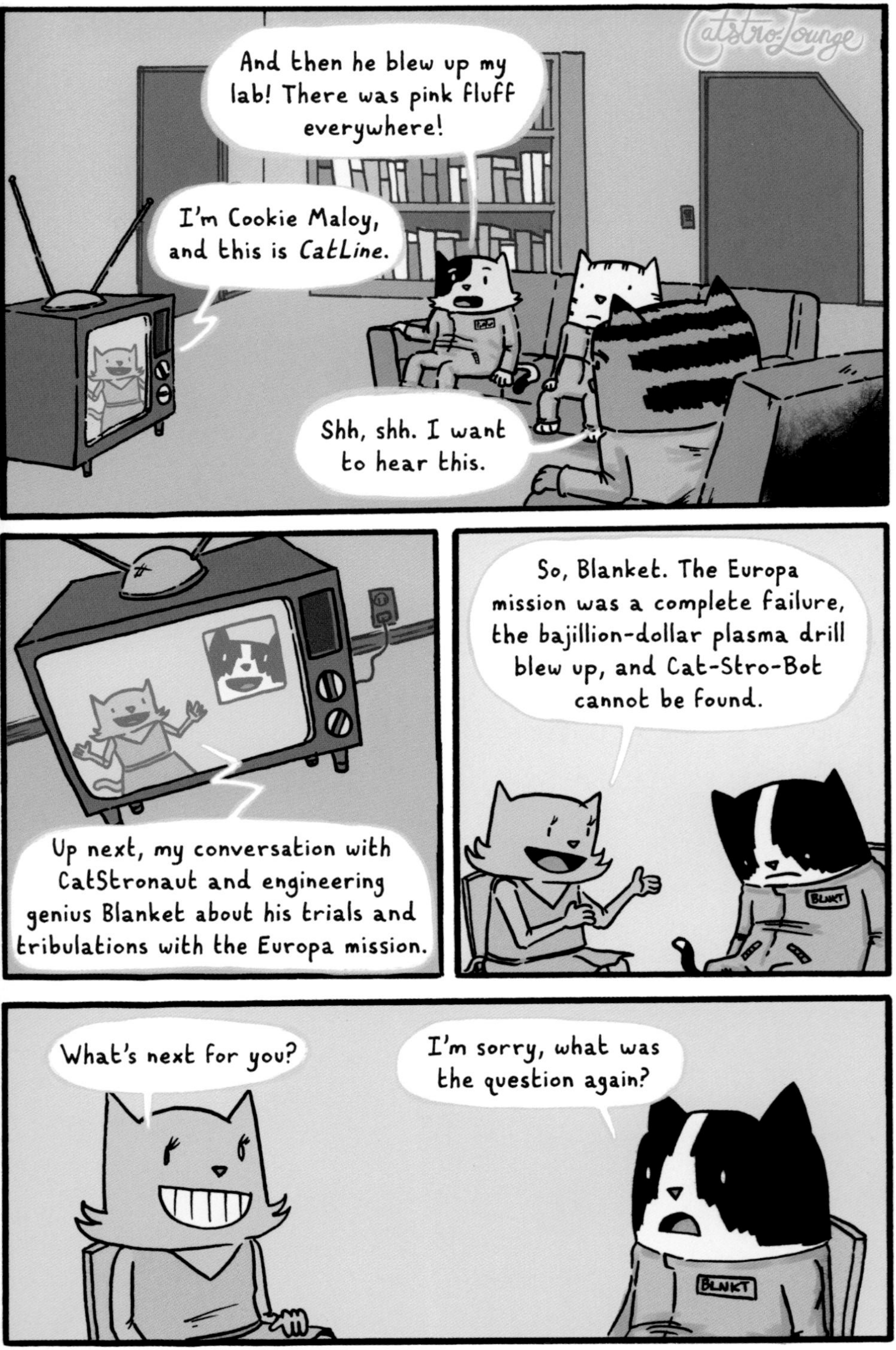

Catstro-Lounge
And then he blew up my lab! There was pink fluff everywhere!
I'm Cookie Maloy, and this is *CatLine*.
Shh, shh. I want to hear this.
Up next, my conversation with CatStronaut and engineering genius Blanket about his trials and tribulations with the Europa mission.
So, Blanket. The Europa mission was a complete failure, the bajillion-dollar plasma drill blew up, and Cat-Stro-Bot cannot be found.
BLNKT
What's next for you?
I'm sorry, what was the question again?
BLNKT

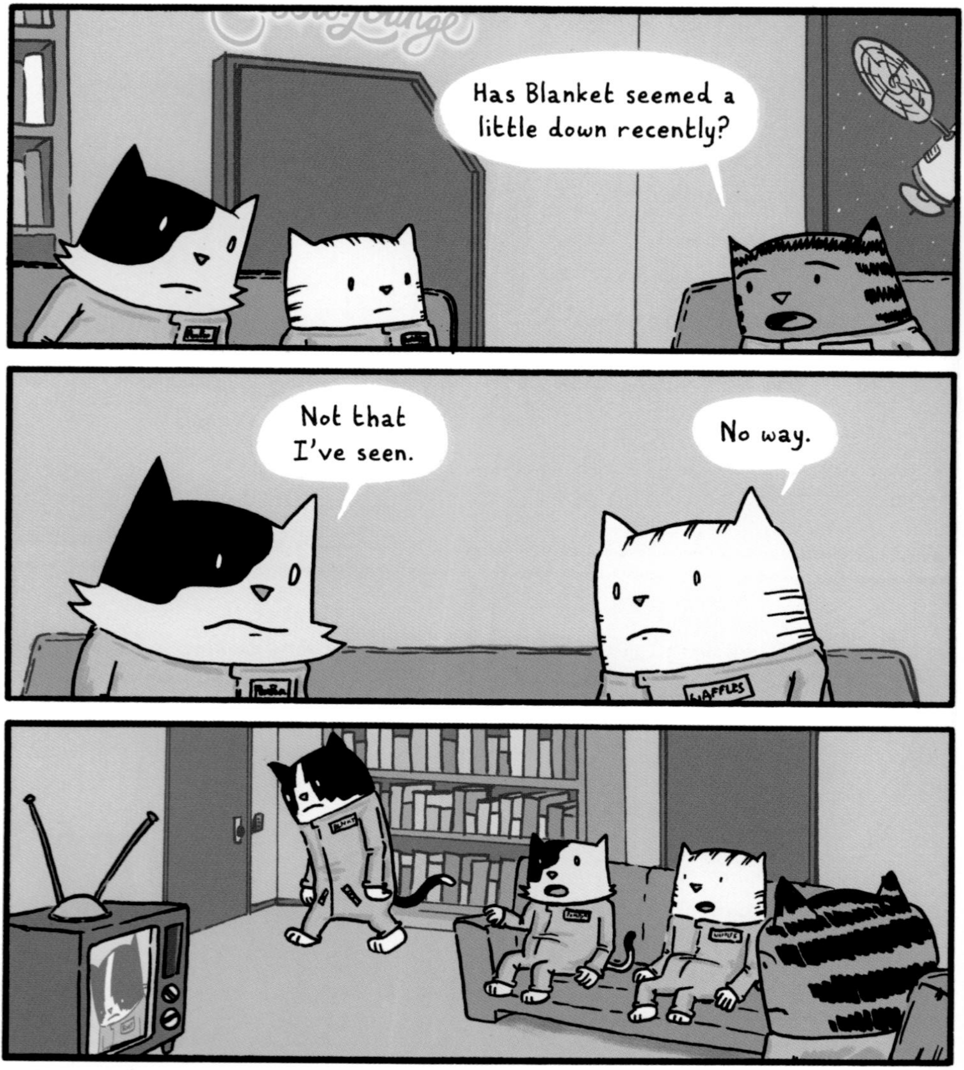
Has Blanket seemed a little down recently?
Not that I've seen.
No way.
Now that you mention it...
Ever since the Europa incident...

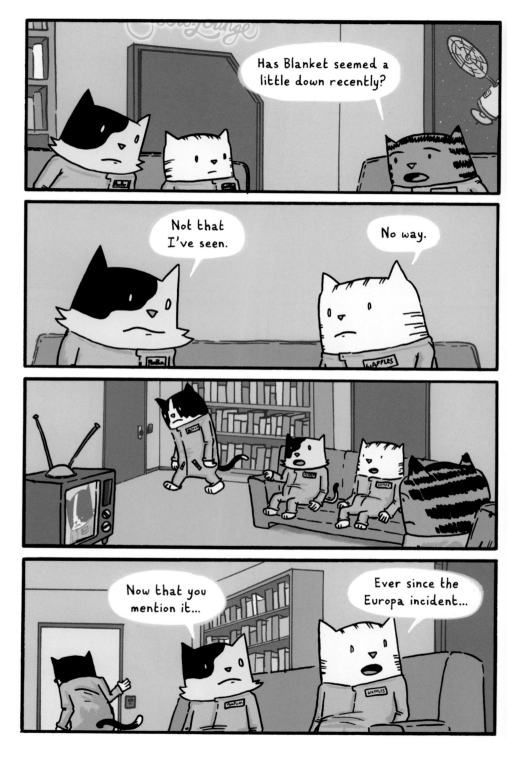

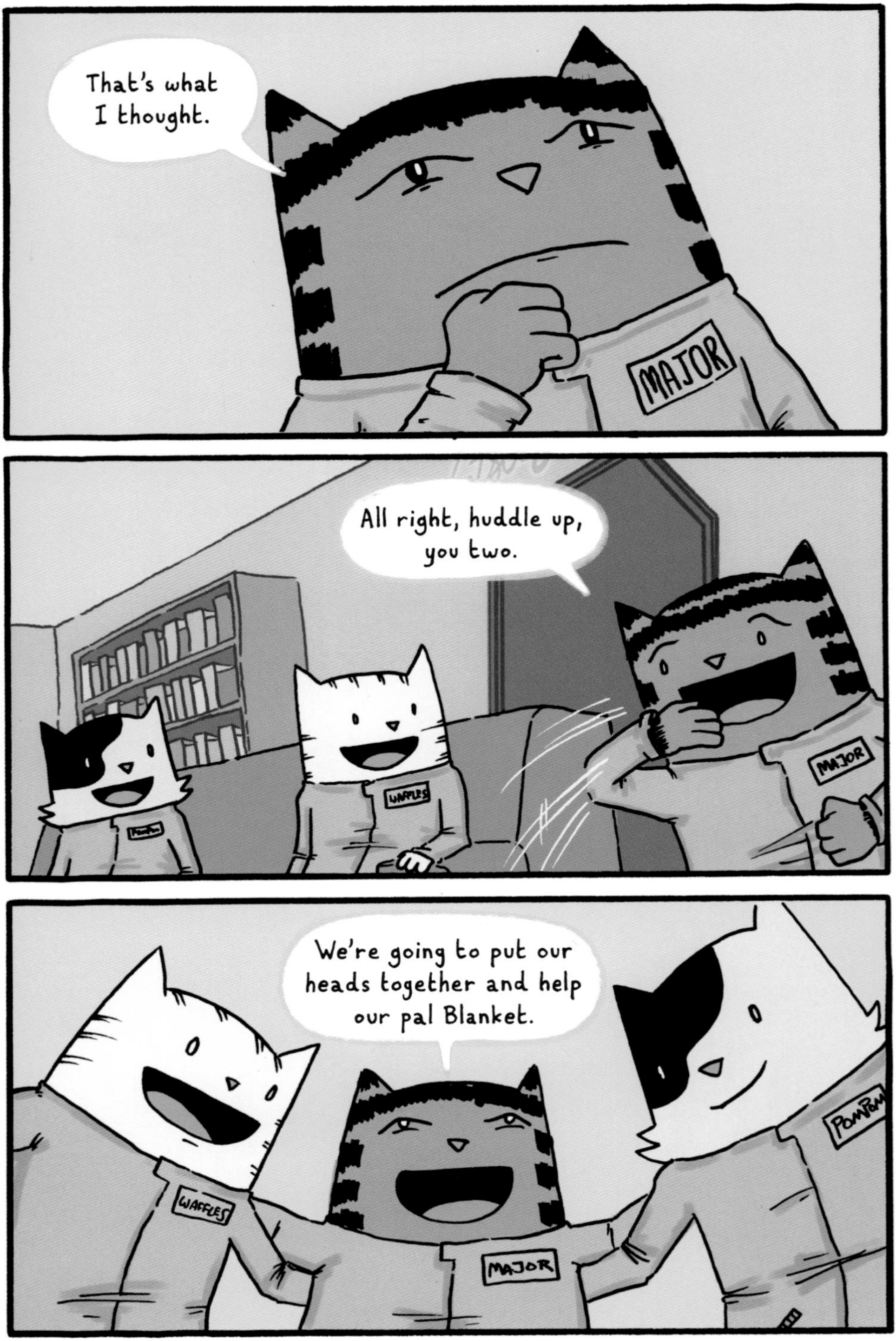
That's what I thought.
MAJOR
All right, huddle up, you two.
WAFFLES
MAJOR
We're going to put our heads together and help our pal Blanket.
WAFFLES
MAJOR
POMPOM

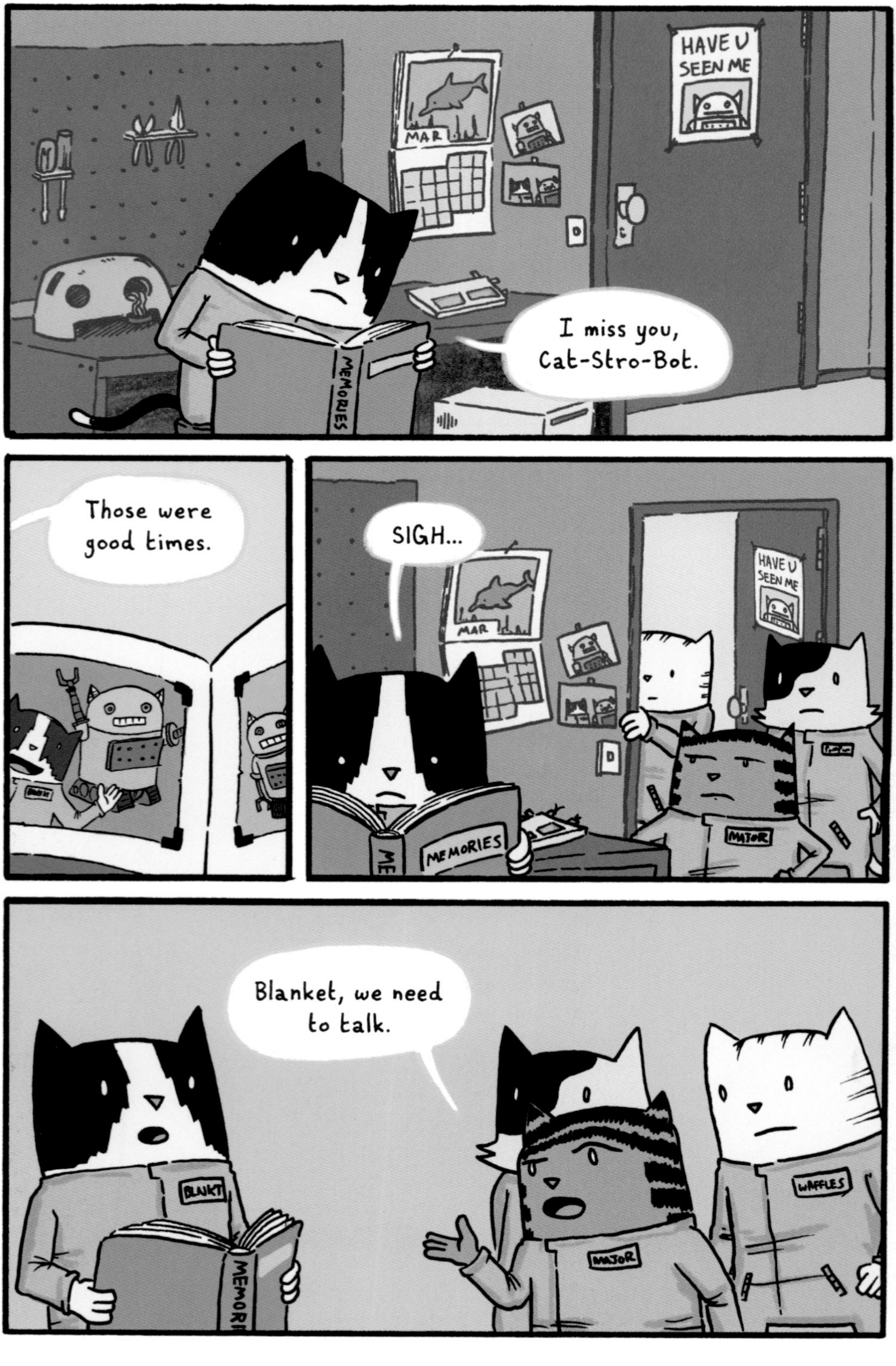
HAVE U SEEN ME
MAR
MEMORIES
I miss you, Cat-Stro-Bot.
Those were good times.
SIGH...
HAVE U SEEN ME
MAR
MEMORIES
MAJOR
Blanket, we need to talk.
BLNKT
MEMORI
MAJOR
WAFFLES

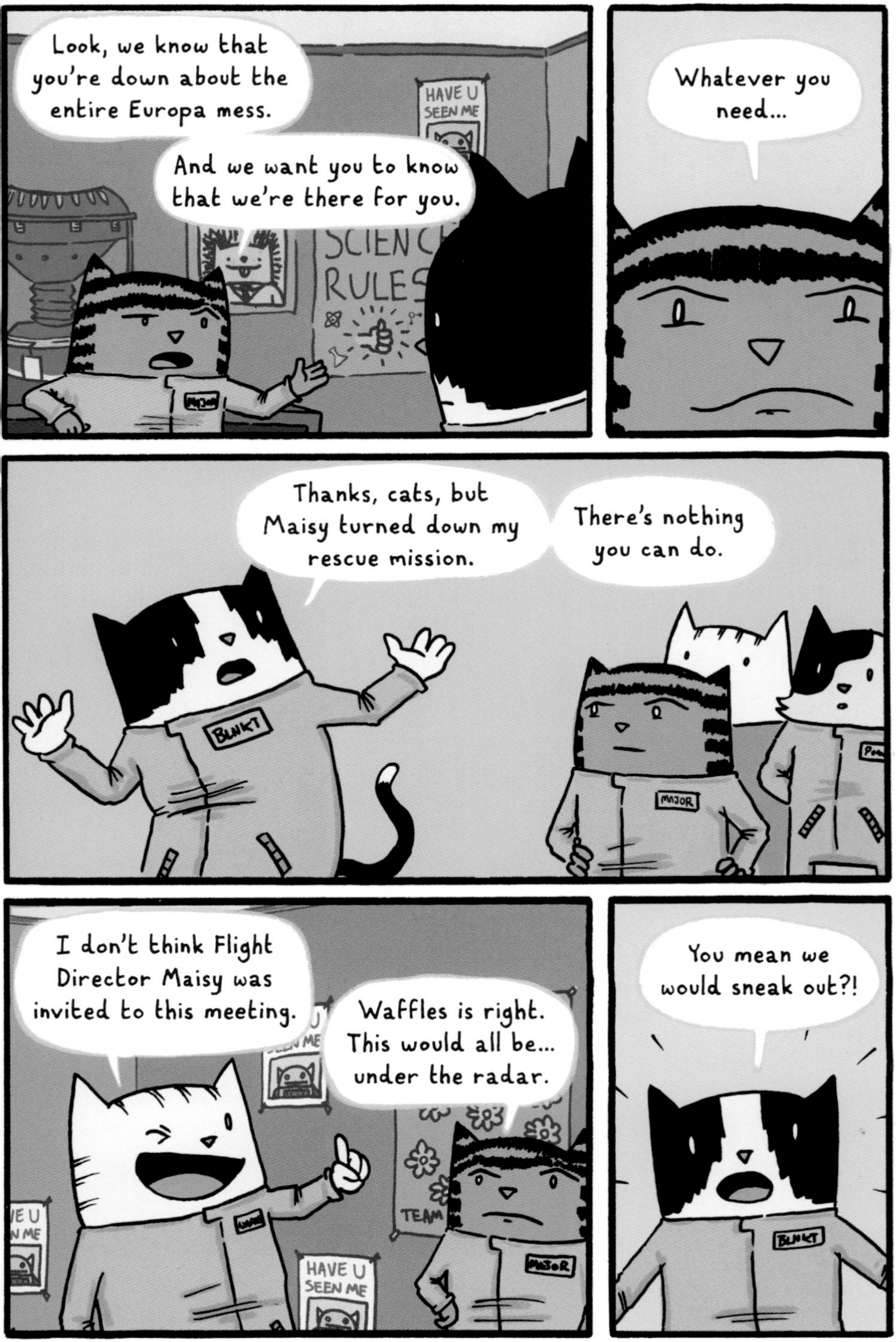
Look, we know that you're down about the entire Europa mess.
And we want you to know that we're there for you.
HAVE U SEEN ME
MAJOR
Whatever you need...
Thanks, cats, but Maisy turned down my rescue mission.
There's nothing you can do.
BLNKT
MAJOR
I don't think Flight Director Maisy was invited to this meeting.
Waffles is right. This would all be... under the radar.
HAVE U SEEN ME
TEAM
MAJOR
You mean we would sneak out?!
BLNKT

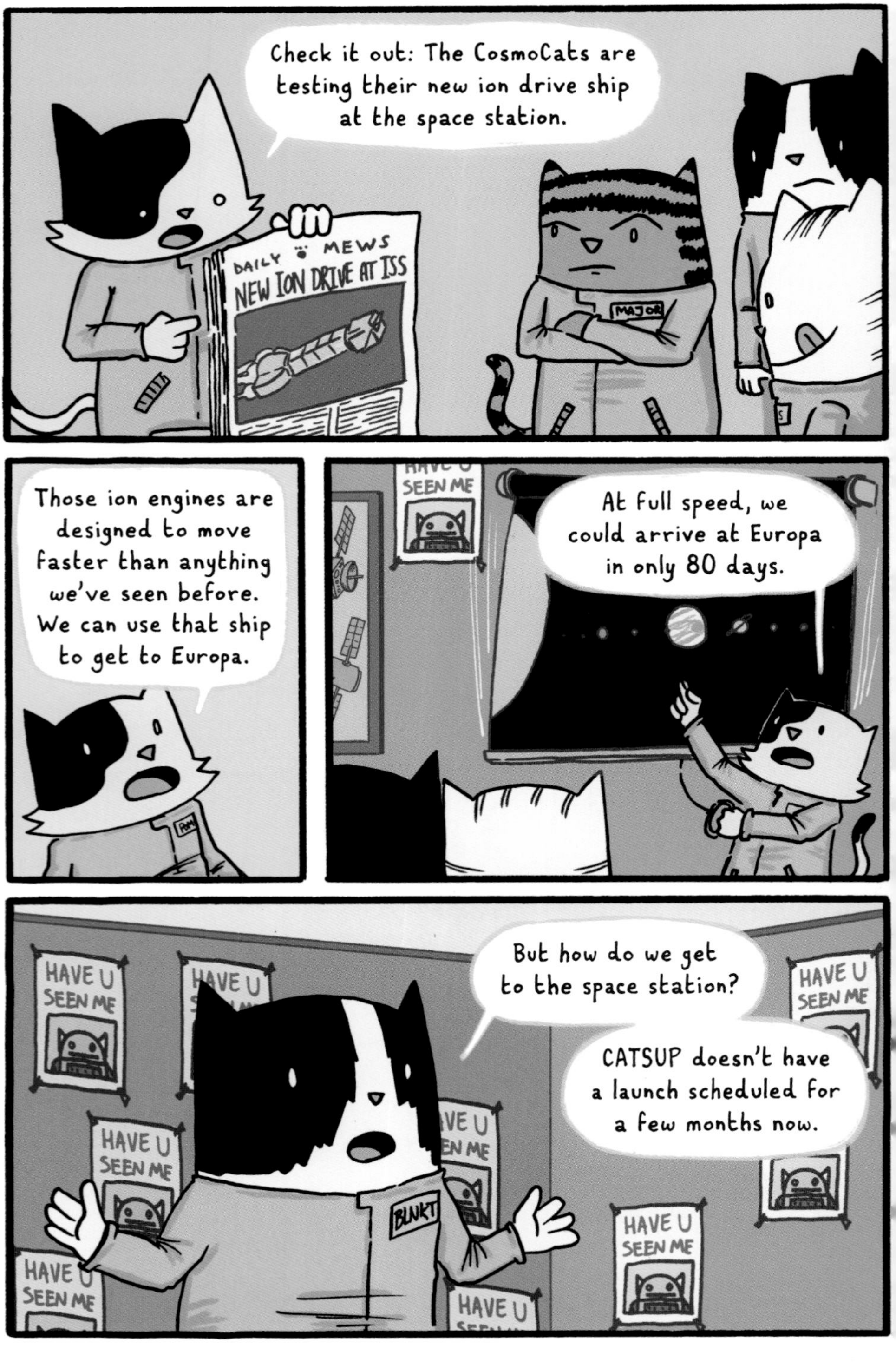

Check it out: The CosmoCats are testing their new ion drive ship at the space station.
DAILY MEWS
NEW ION DRIVE AT ISS
MAJOR
Those ion engines are designed to move faster than anything we've seen before. We can use that ship to get to Europa.
HAVE U SEEN ME
At full speed, we could arrive at Europa in only 80 days.
HAVE U SEEN ME
But how do we get to the space station?
CATSUP doesn't have a launch scheduled for a few months now.
BLNKT

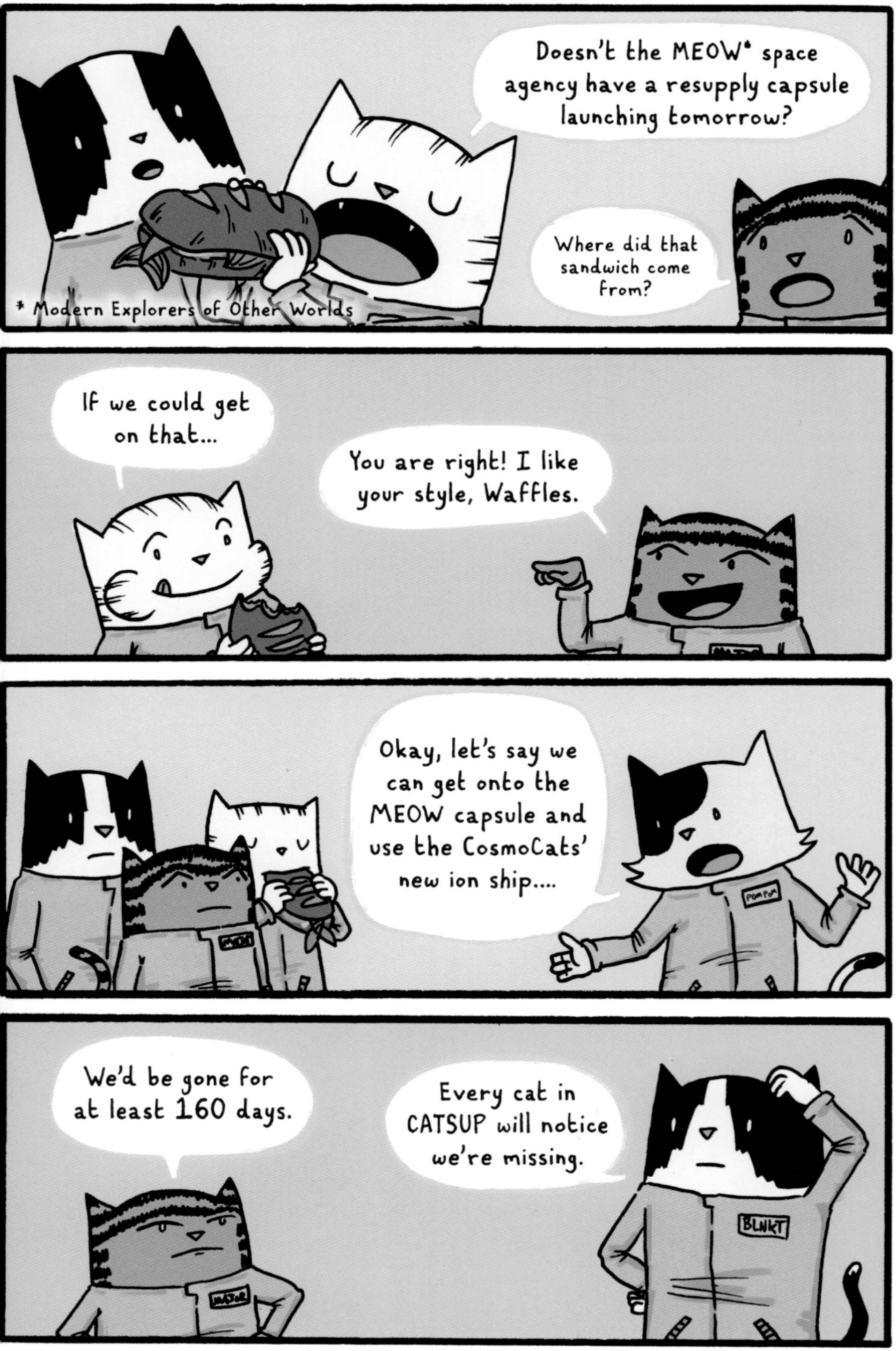
Doesn't the MEOW* space agency have a resupply capsule launching tomorrow?
Where did that sandwich come from?
* Modern Explorers of Other Worlds
If we could get on that...
You are right! I like your style, Waffles.
Okay, let's say we can get onto the MEOW capsule and use the CosmoCats' new ion ship....
POM POM
We'd be gone for at least 160 days.
Every cat in CATSUP will notice we're missing.
MAJOR
BLNKT

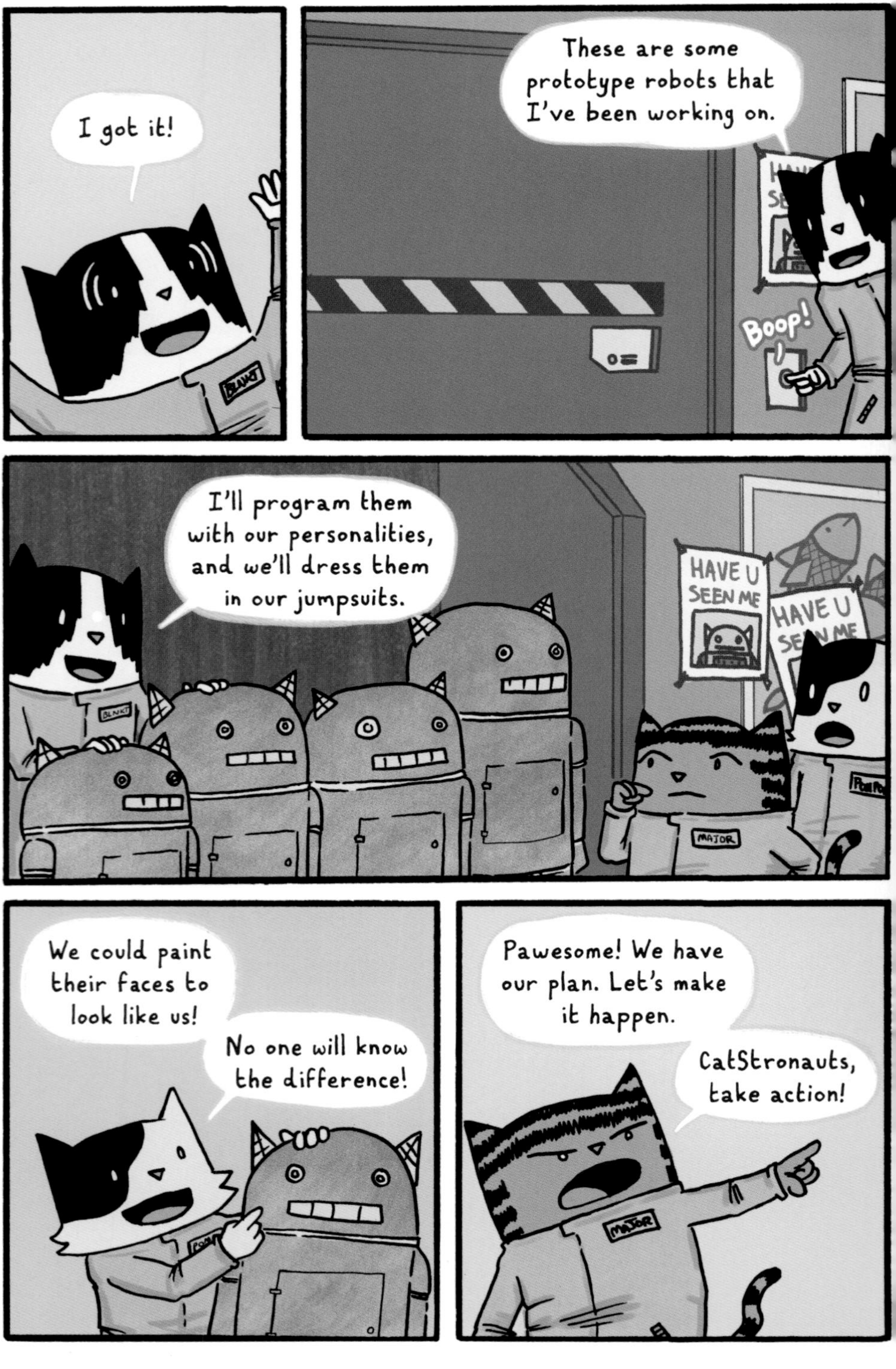
I got it!
These are some prototype robots that I've been working on.
Boop!
I'll program them with our personalities, and we'll dress them in our jumpsuits.
HAVE U SEEN ME
HAVE U SEEN ME
We could paint their faces to look like us!
No one will know the difference!
Pawesome! We have our plan. Let's make it happen.
CatStronauts, take action!

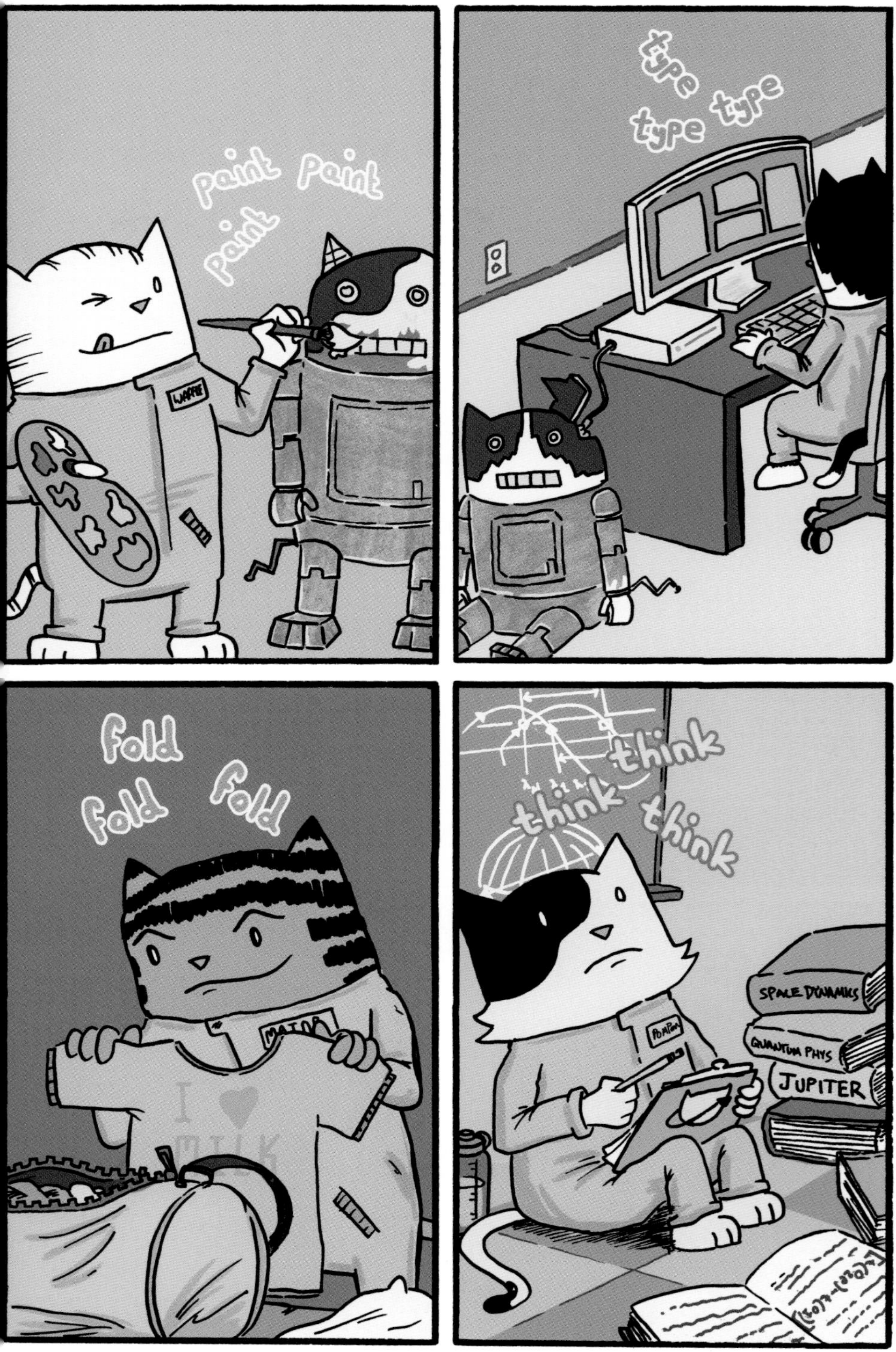
paint paint
paint
WAFFLE
type
type type
fold
fold fold
I ♥ MILK
think
think think
POMPOM
SPACE DYNAMICS
QUANTUM PHYS
JUPITER

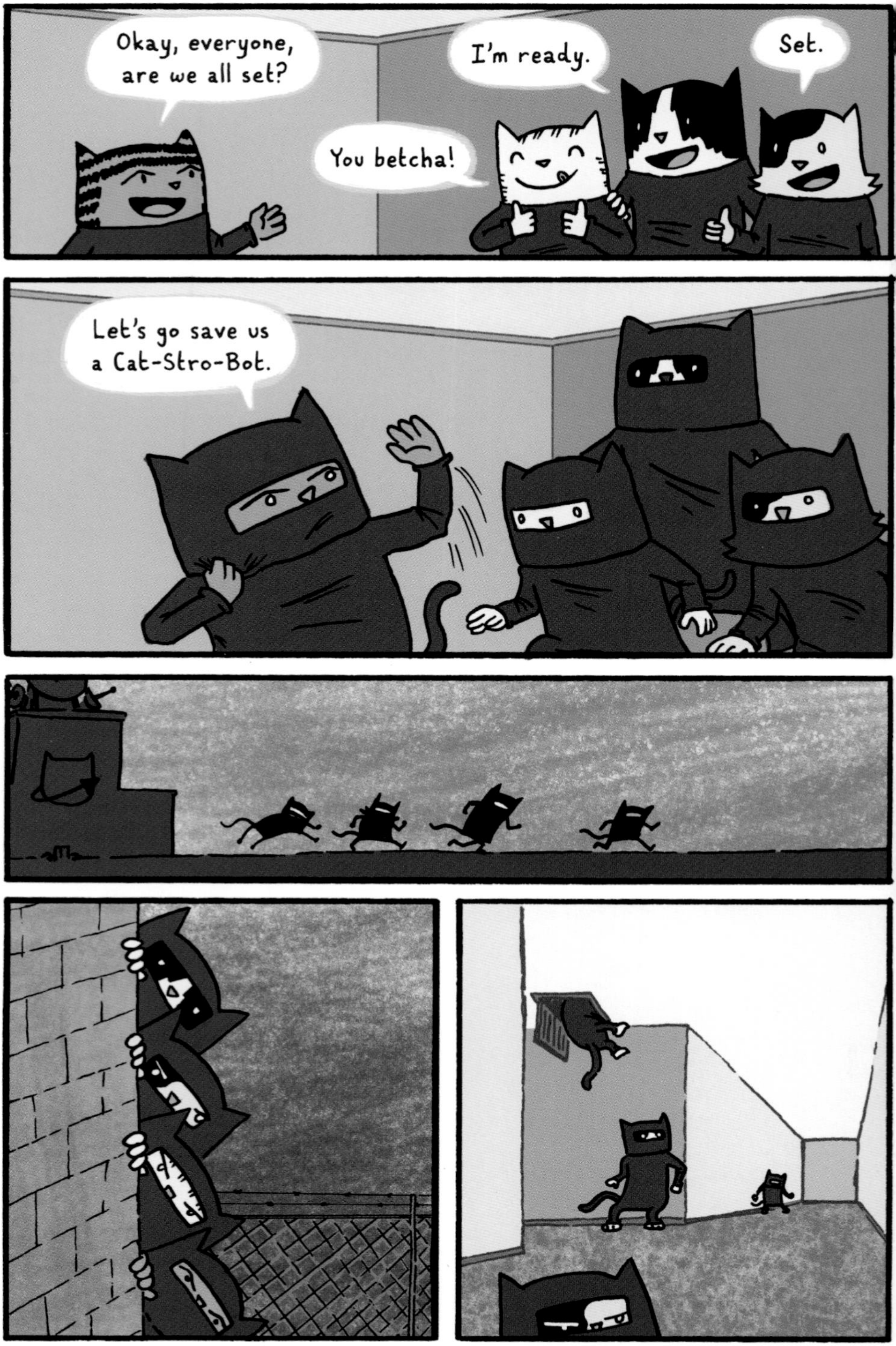
Okay, everyone, are we all set?
I'm ready.
Set.
You betcha!
Let's go save us a Cat-Stro-Bot.

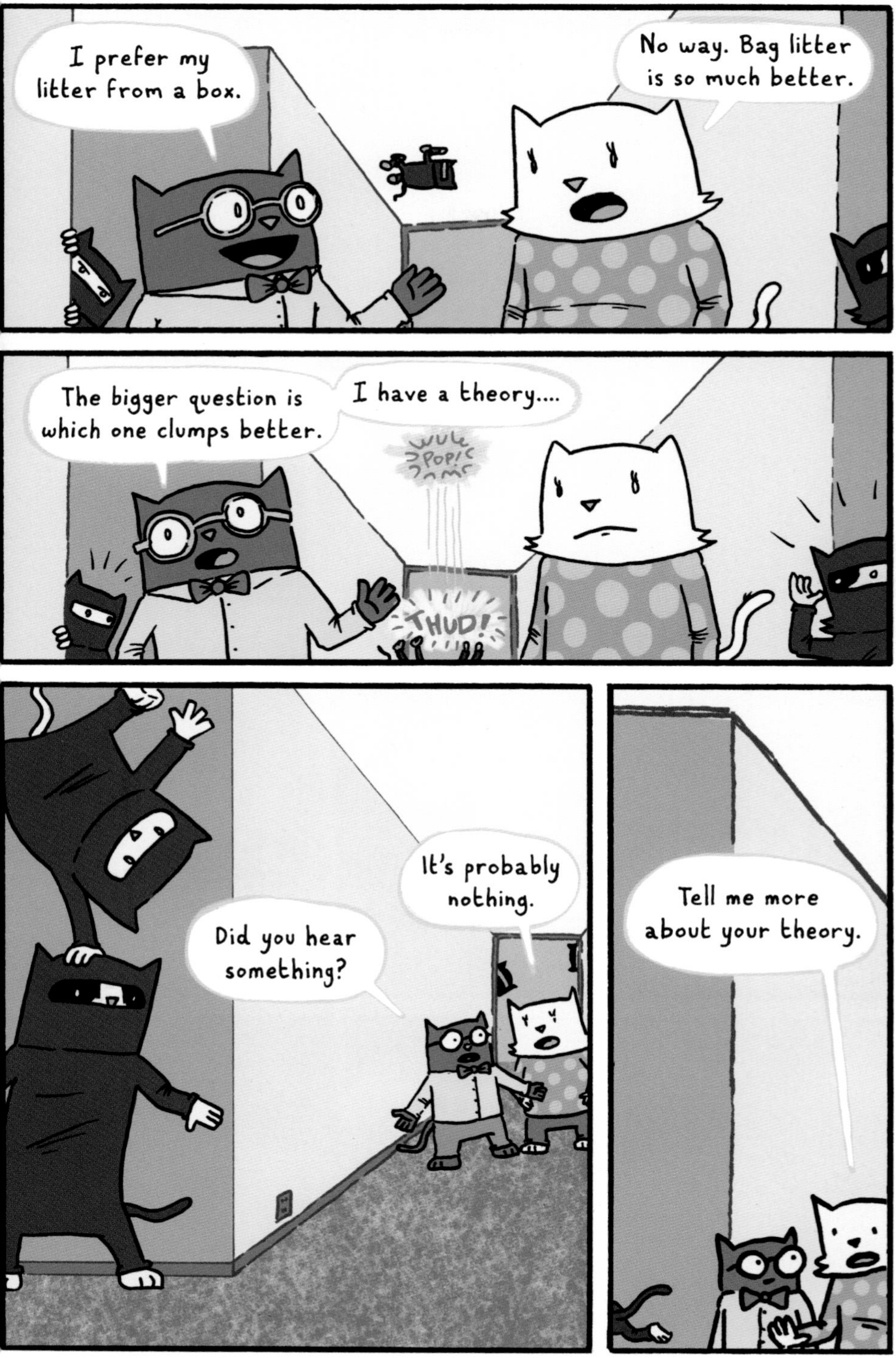
I prefer my litter from a box.
No way. Bag litter is so much better.
The bigger question is which one clumps better.
I have a theory....
POP!
THUD!
Did you hear something?
It's probably nothing.
Tell me more about your theory.

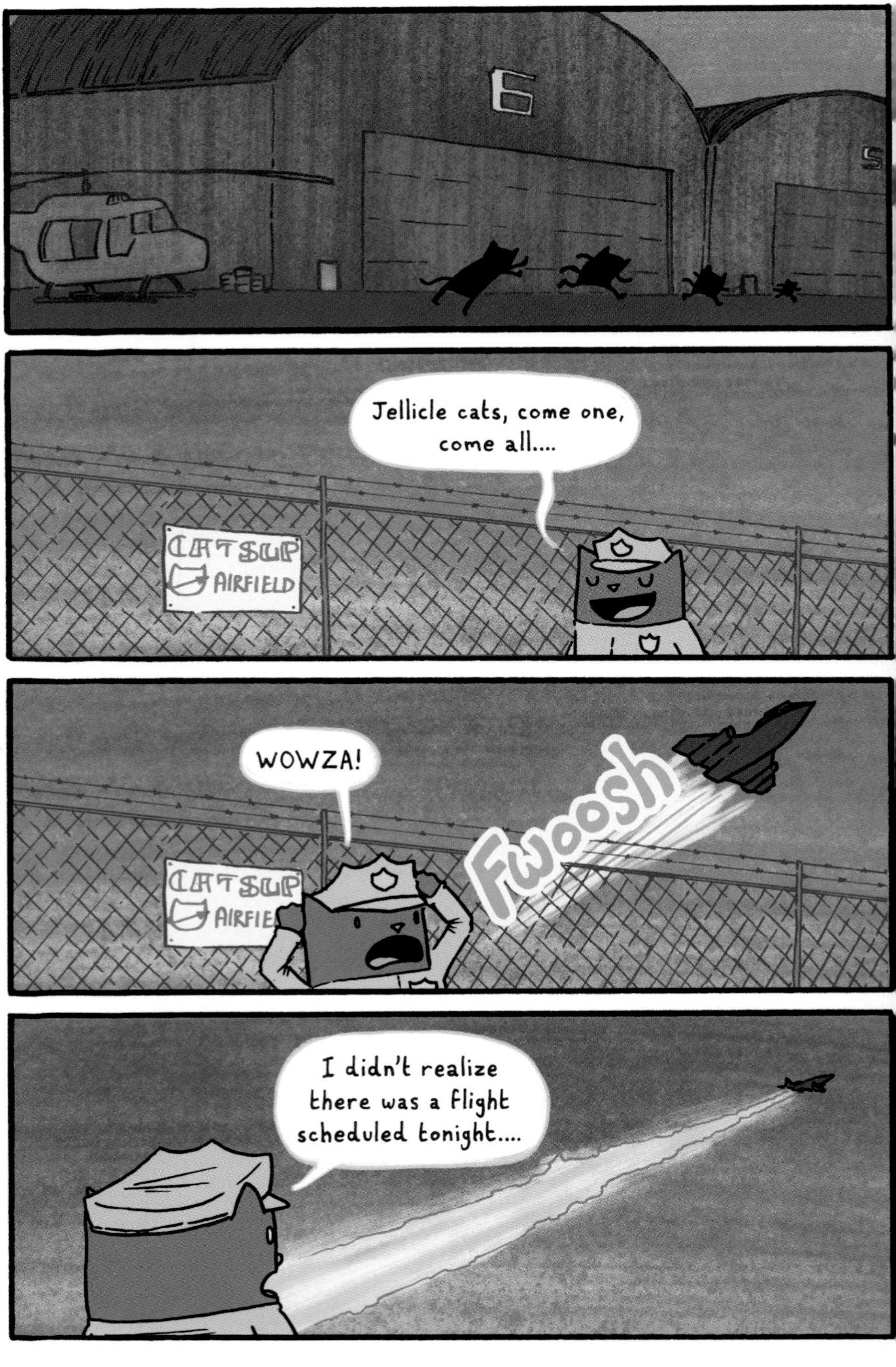

6
Jellicle cats, come one, come all....
CATSUP AIRFIELD
WOWZA!
Fwoosh
I didn't realize there was a flight scheduled tonight....

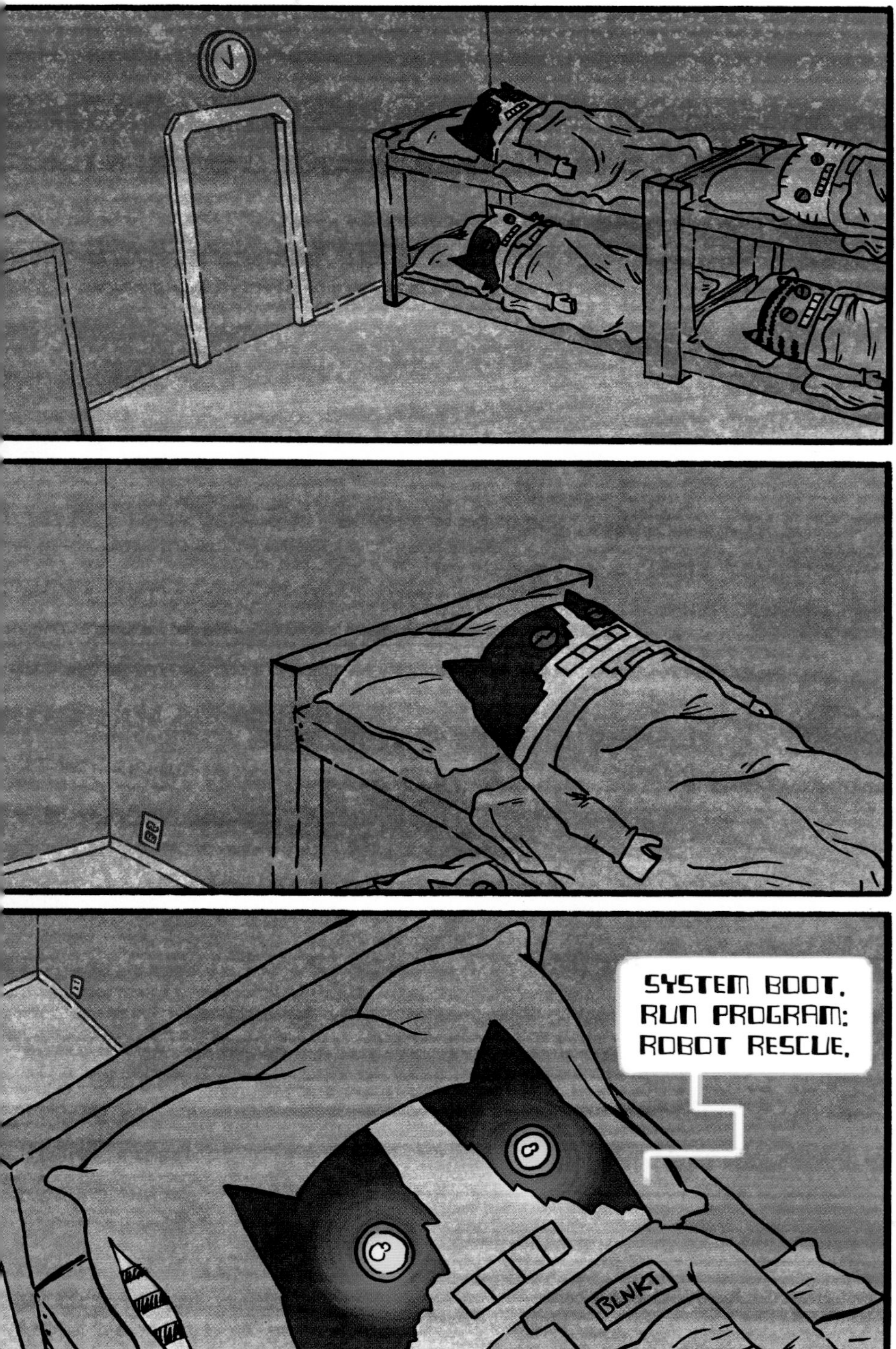
SYSTEM BOOT.
RUN PROGRAM:
ROBOT RESCUE.
BLNKT

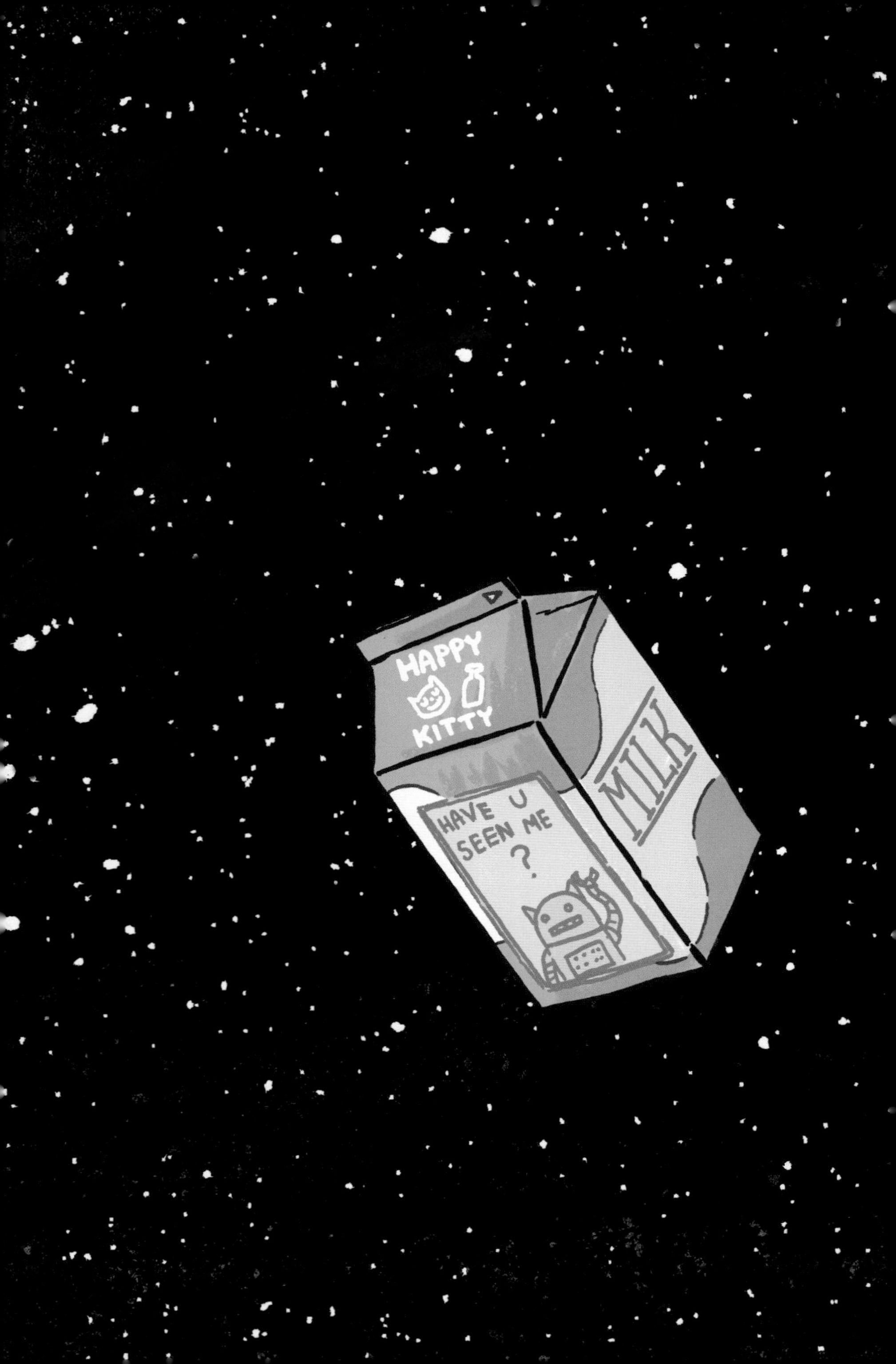
HAPPY
KITTY
MILK
HAVE U SEEN ME
?

CHAPTER 4

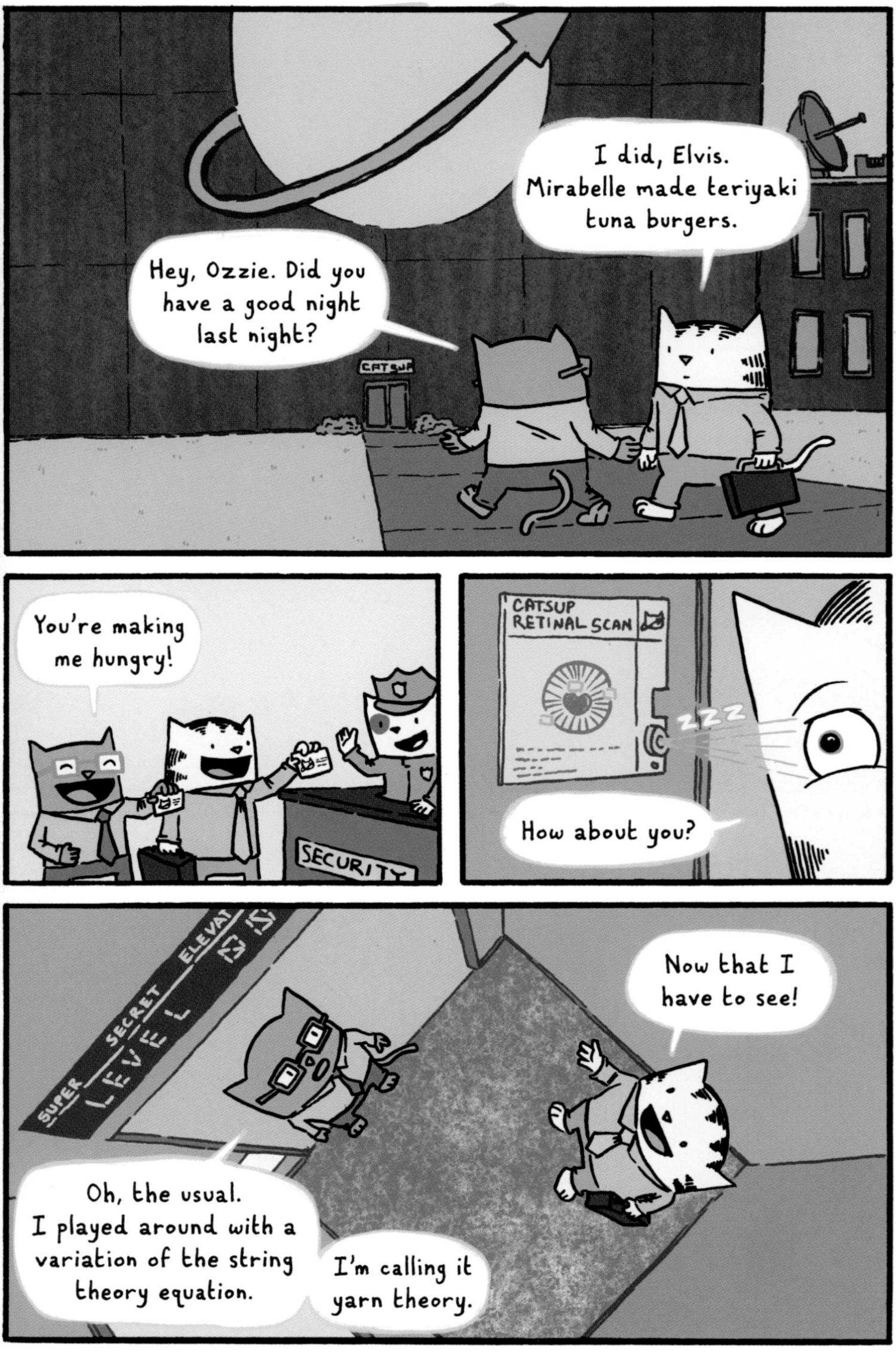
Hey, Ozzie. Did you have a good night last night?
I did, Elvis. Mirabelle made teriyaki tuna burgers.
CATSUP
You're making me hungry!
SECURITY
CATSUP RETINAL SCAN
ZZZ
How about you?
SUPER SECRET LEVEL ELEVAT
Oh, the usual. I played around with a variation of the string theory equation.
I'm calling it yarn theory.
Now that I have to see!

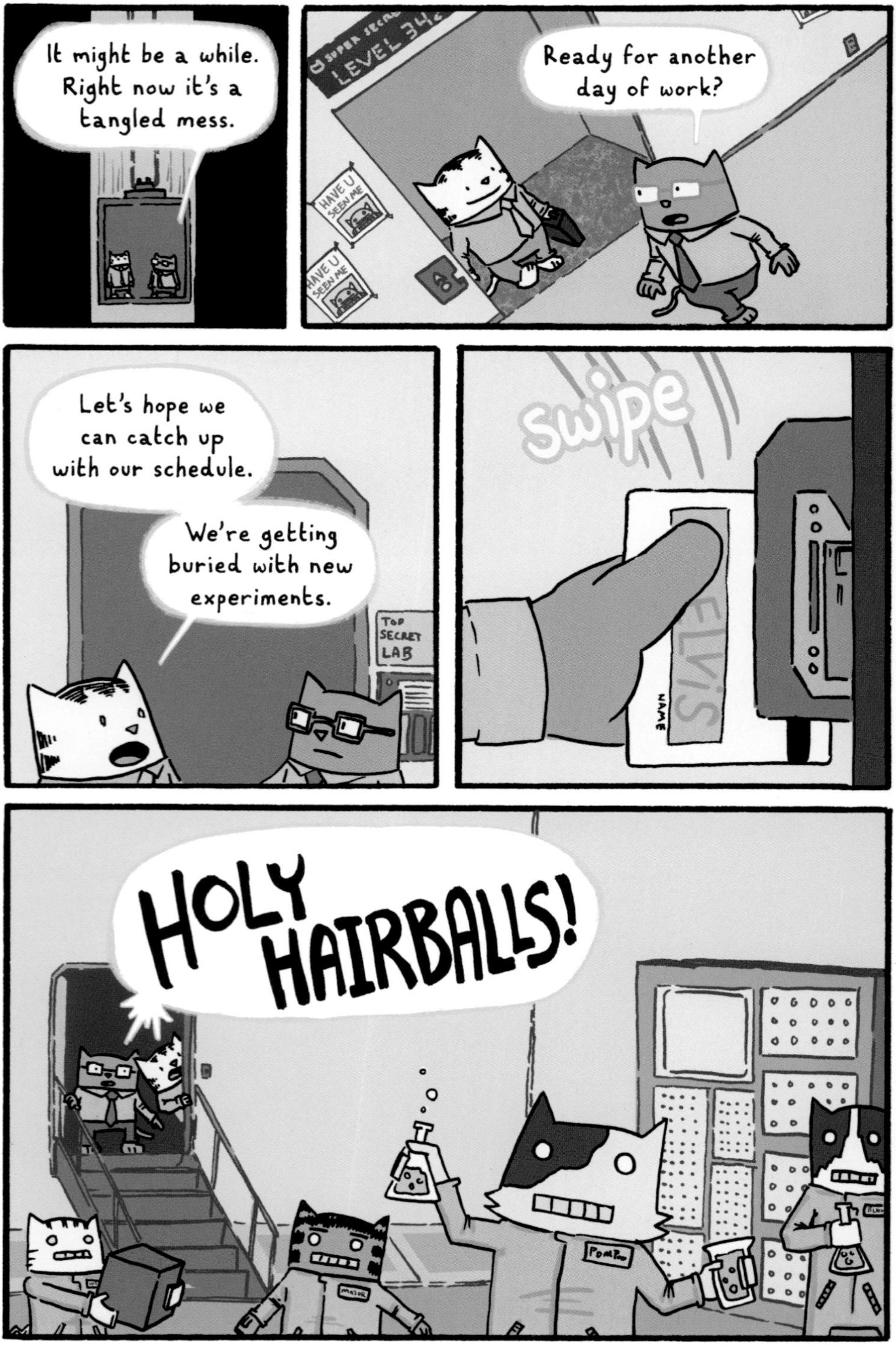
It might be a while. Right now it's a tangled mess.
Ready for another day of work?
HAVE U SEEN ME
HAVE U SEEN ME
Let's hope we can catch up with our schedule.
We're getting buried with new experiments.
TOP SECRET LAB
swipe
ELVIS
NAME
HOLY HAIRBALLS!

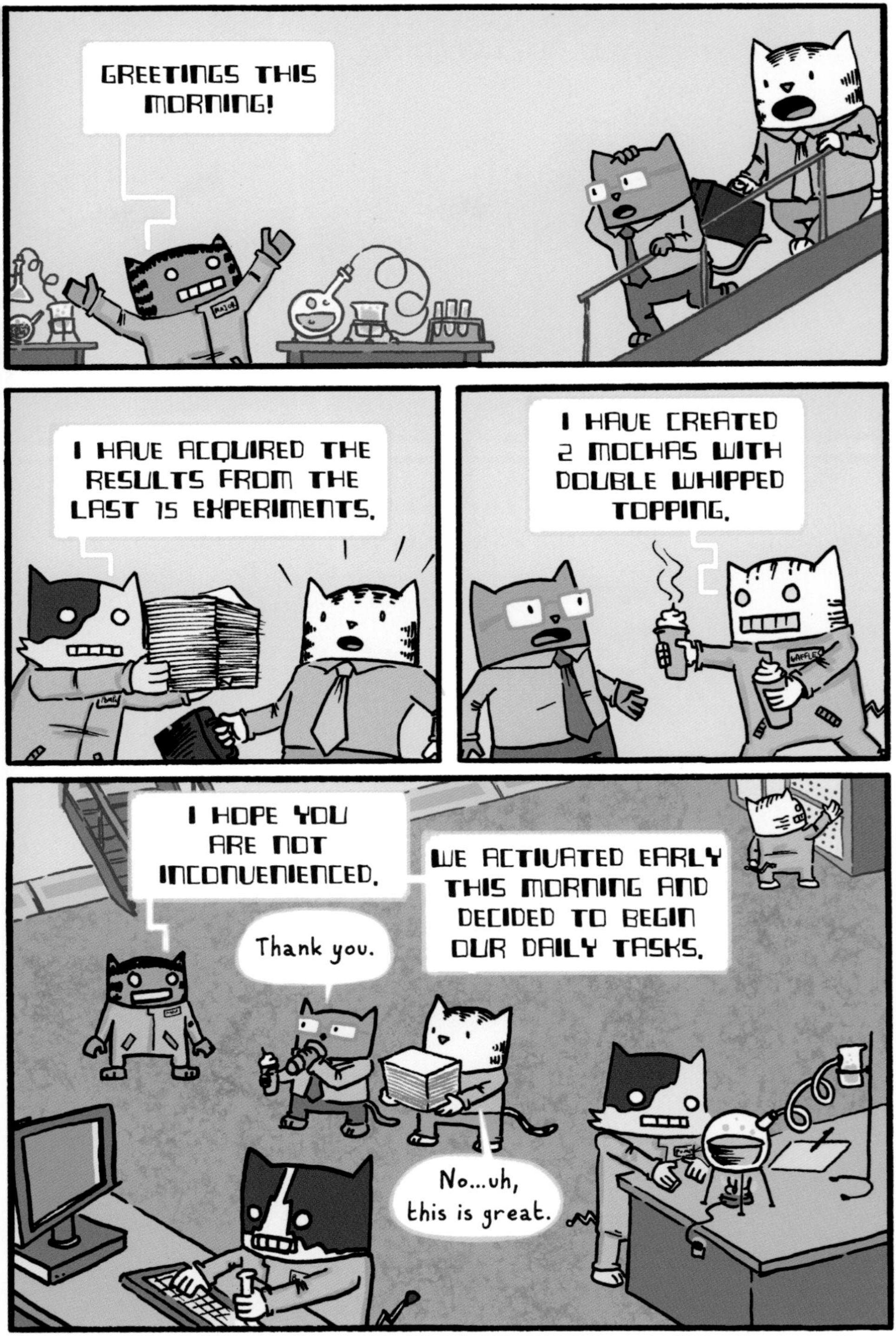
GREETINGS THIS MORNING!
I HAVE ACQUIRED THE RESULTS FROM THE LAST 15 EXPERIMENTS.
I HAVE CREATED 2 MOCHAS WITH DOUBLE WHIPPED TOPPING.
I HOPE YOU ARE NOT INCONVENIENCED.
WE ACTIVATED EARLY THIS MORNING AND DECIDED TO BEGIN OUR DAILY TASKS.
Thank you.
No...uh, this is great.

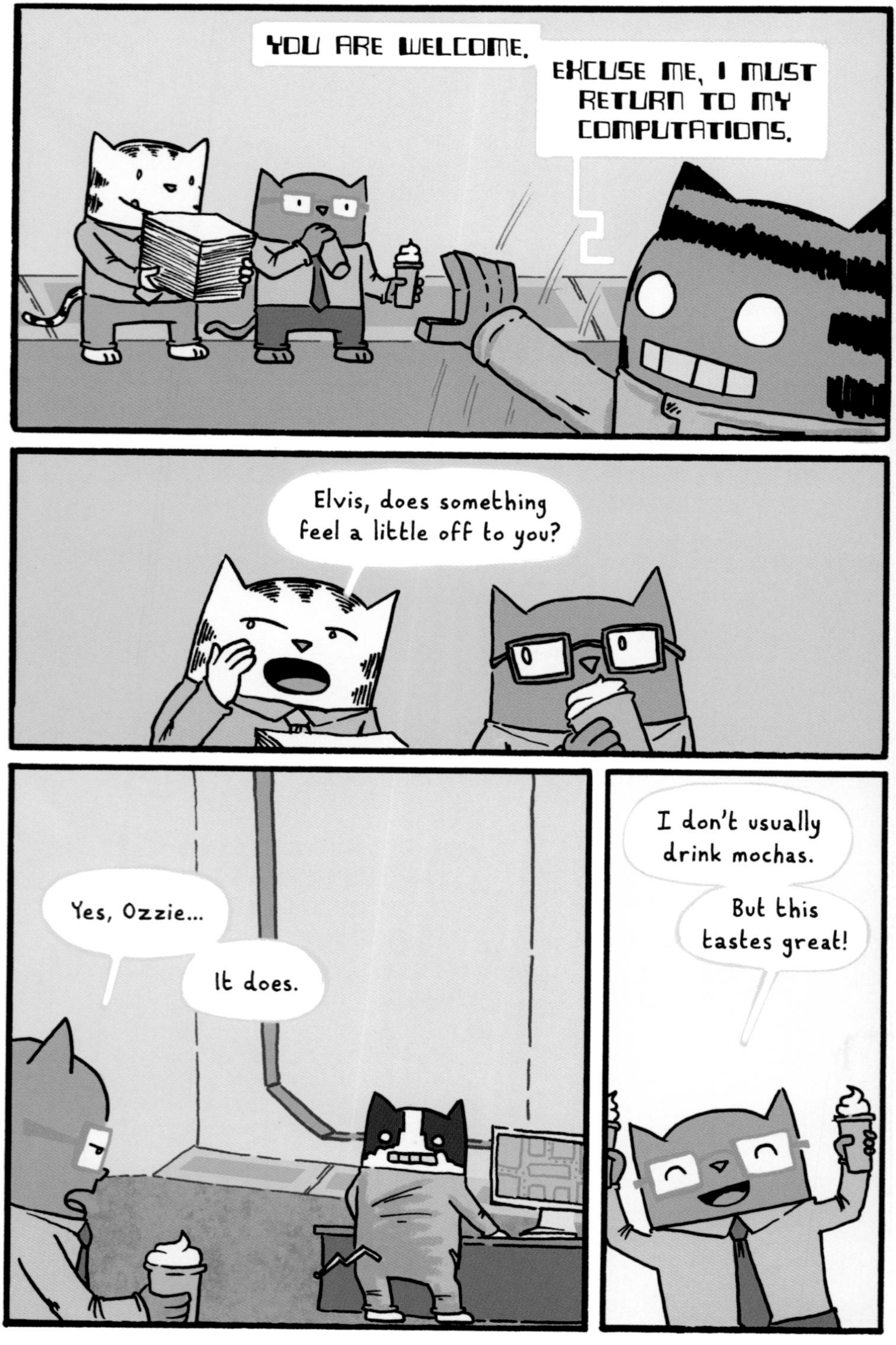
YOU ARE WELCOME.
EXCUSE ME, I MUST RETURN TO MY COMPUTATIONS.
Elvis, does something feel a little off to you?
Yes, Ozzie...
It does.
I don't usually drink mochas.
But this tastes great!

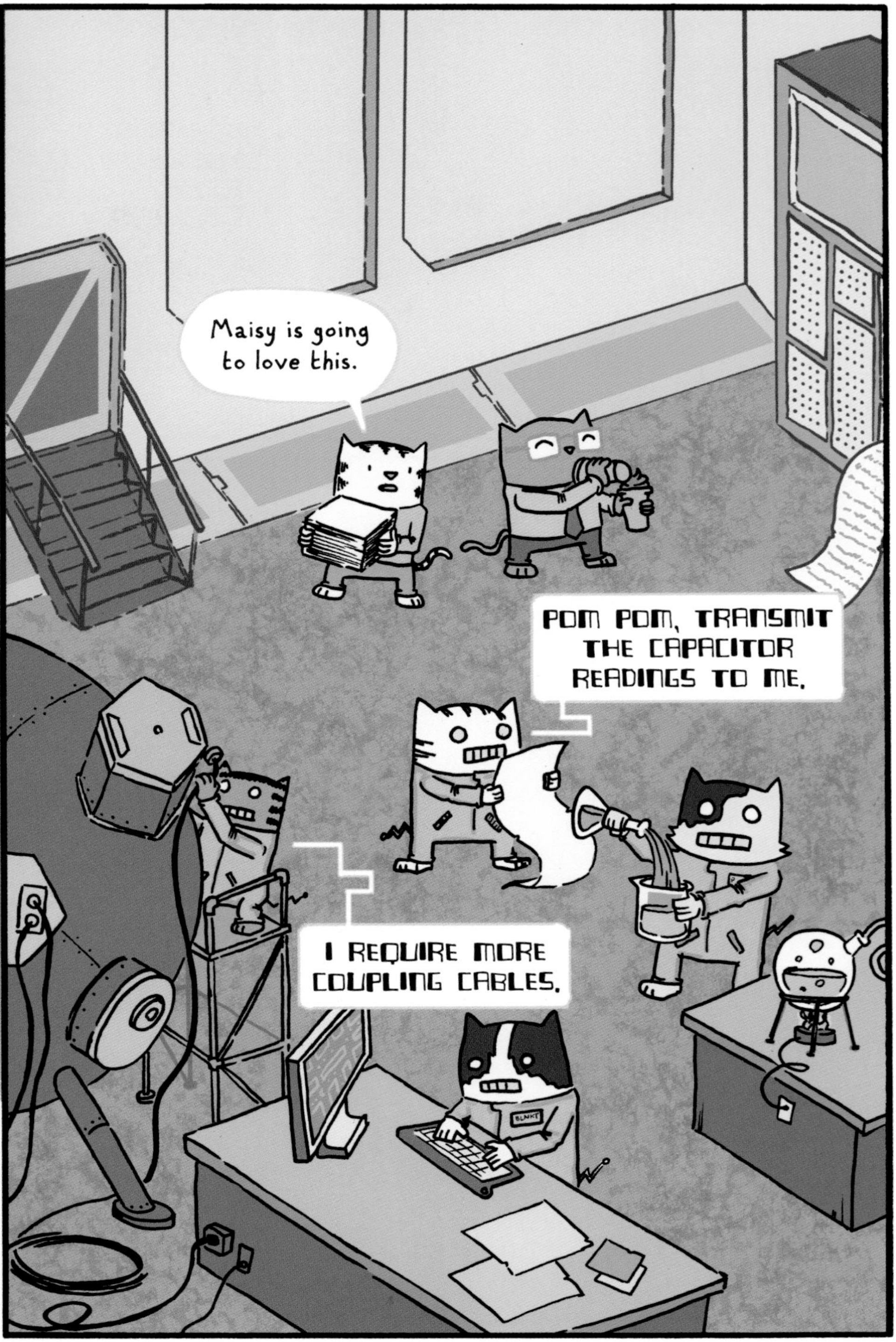
Maisy is going to love this.
POM POM, TRANSMIT THE CAPACITOR READINGS TO ME.
I REQUIRE MORE COUPLING CABLES.
BLNKT

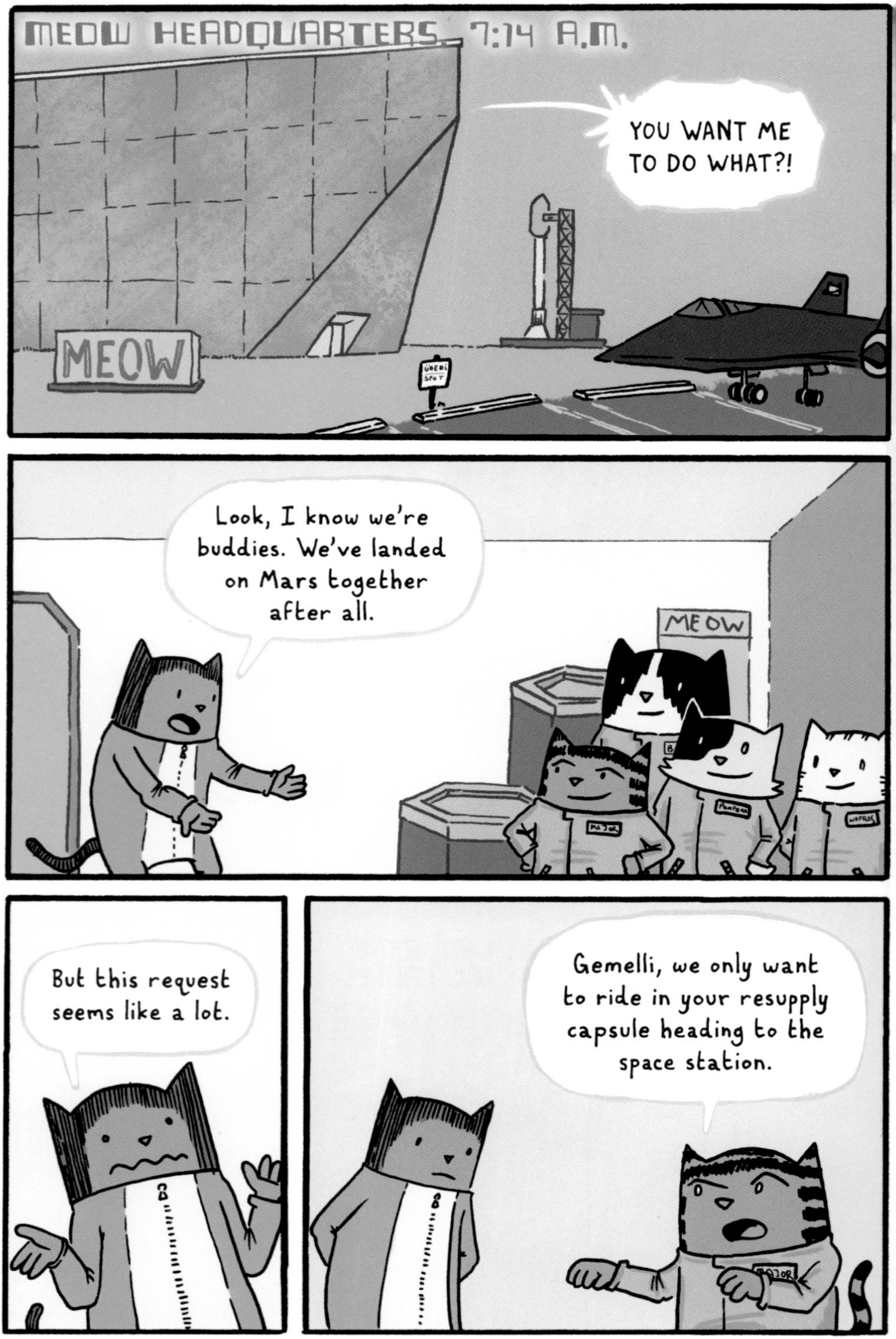
MEOW HEADQUARTERS, 7:14 A.M.
MEOW
YOU WANT ME TO DO WHAT?!
Look, I know we're buddies. We've landed on Mars together after all.
MEOW
But this request seems like a lot.
Gemelli, we only want to ride in your resupply capsule heading to the space station.

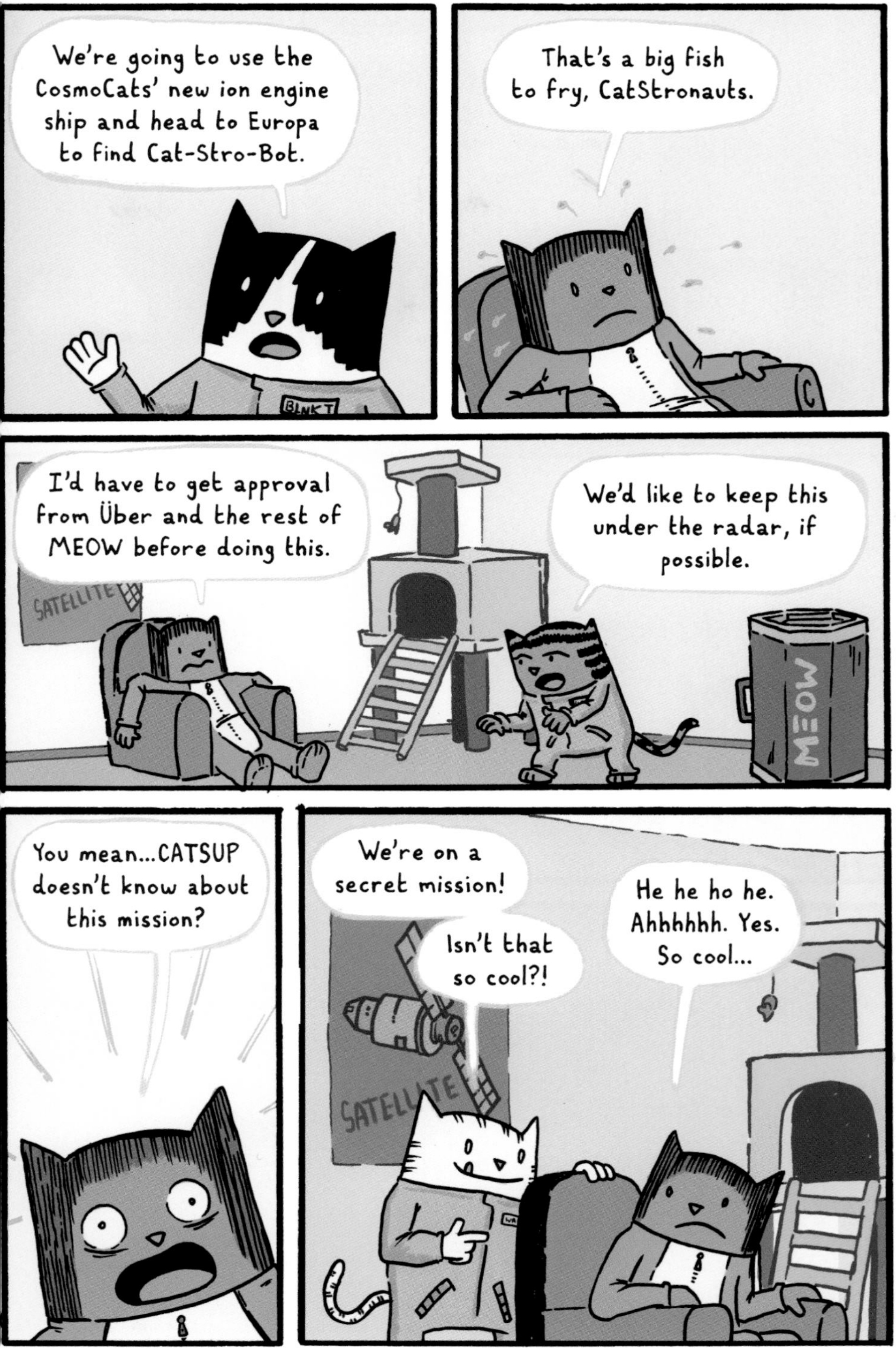

We're going to use the CosmoCats' new ion engine ship and head to Europa to find Cat-Stro-Bot.
BLNKT
That's a big fish to fry, CatStronauts.
I'd have to get approval from Über and the rest of MEOW before doing this.
SATELLITE
We'd like to keep this under the radar, if possible.
MEOW
You mean...CATSUP doesn't know about this mission?
We're on a secret mission!
Isn't that so cool?!
He he ho he. Ahhhhhh. Yes. So cool...
SATELLITE

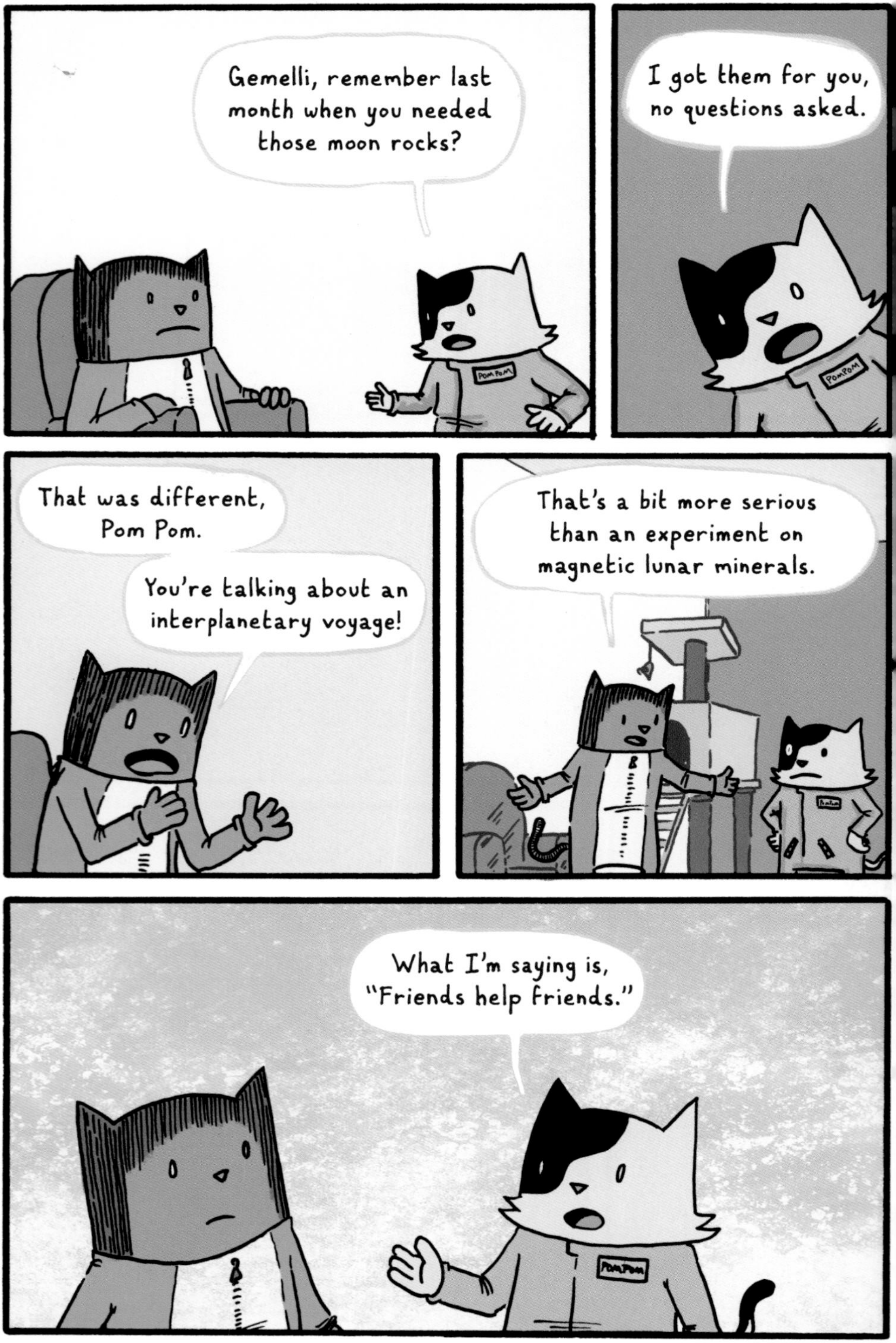

Gemelli, remember last month when you needed those moon rocks?
I got them for you, no questions asked.
That was different, Pom Pom.
You're talking about an interplanetary voyage!
That's a bit more serious than an experiment on magnetic lunar minerals.
What I'm saying is, "Friends help friends."

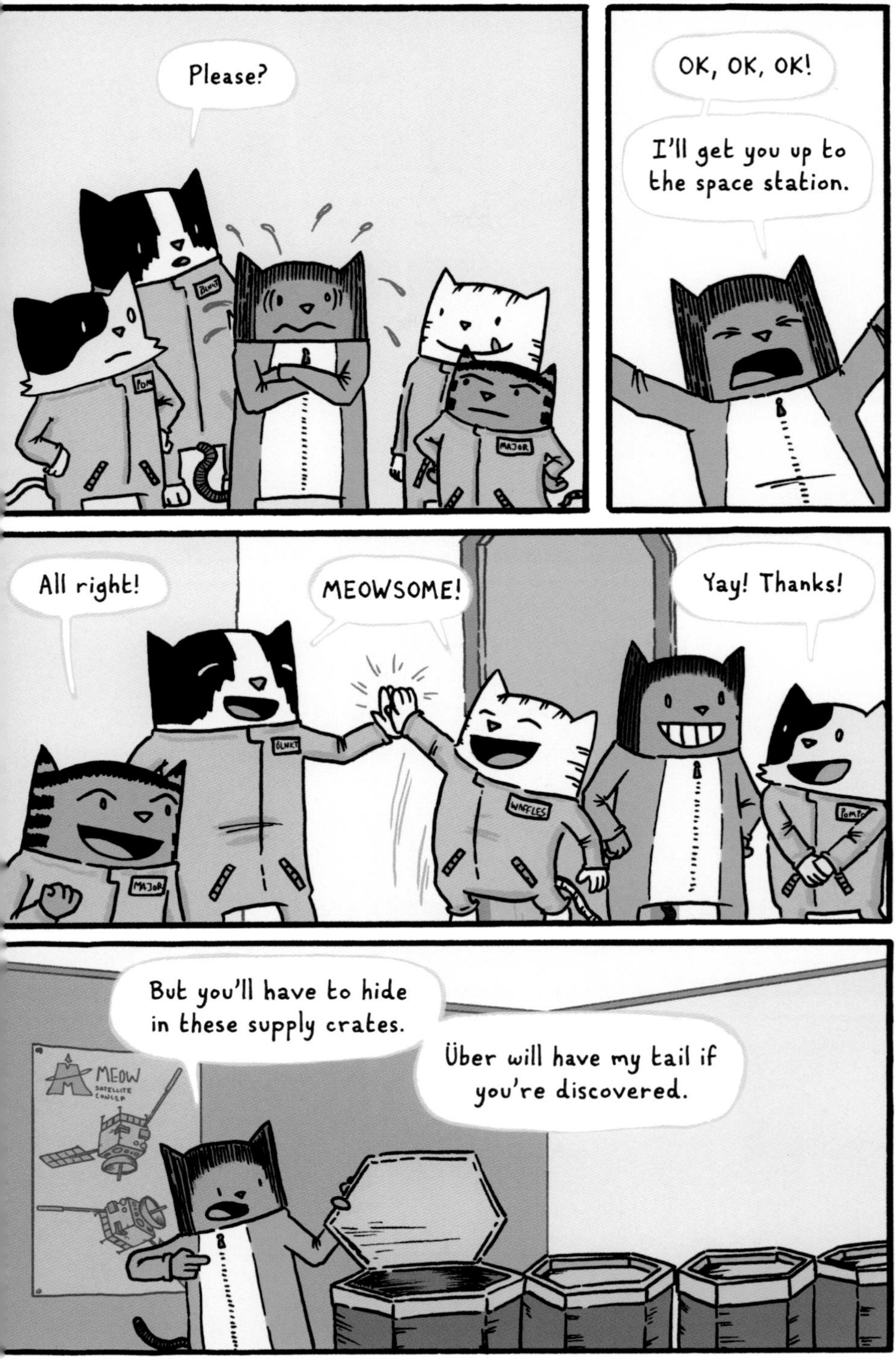
Please?
OK, OK, OK!
I'll get you up to the space station.
All right!
MEOWSOME!
Yay! Thanks!
But you'll have to hide in these supply crates.
Über will have my tail if you're discovered.
MEOW

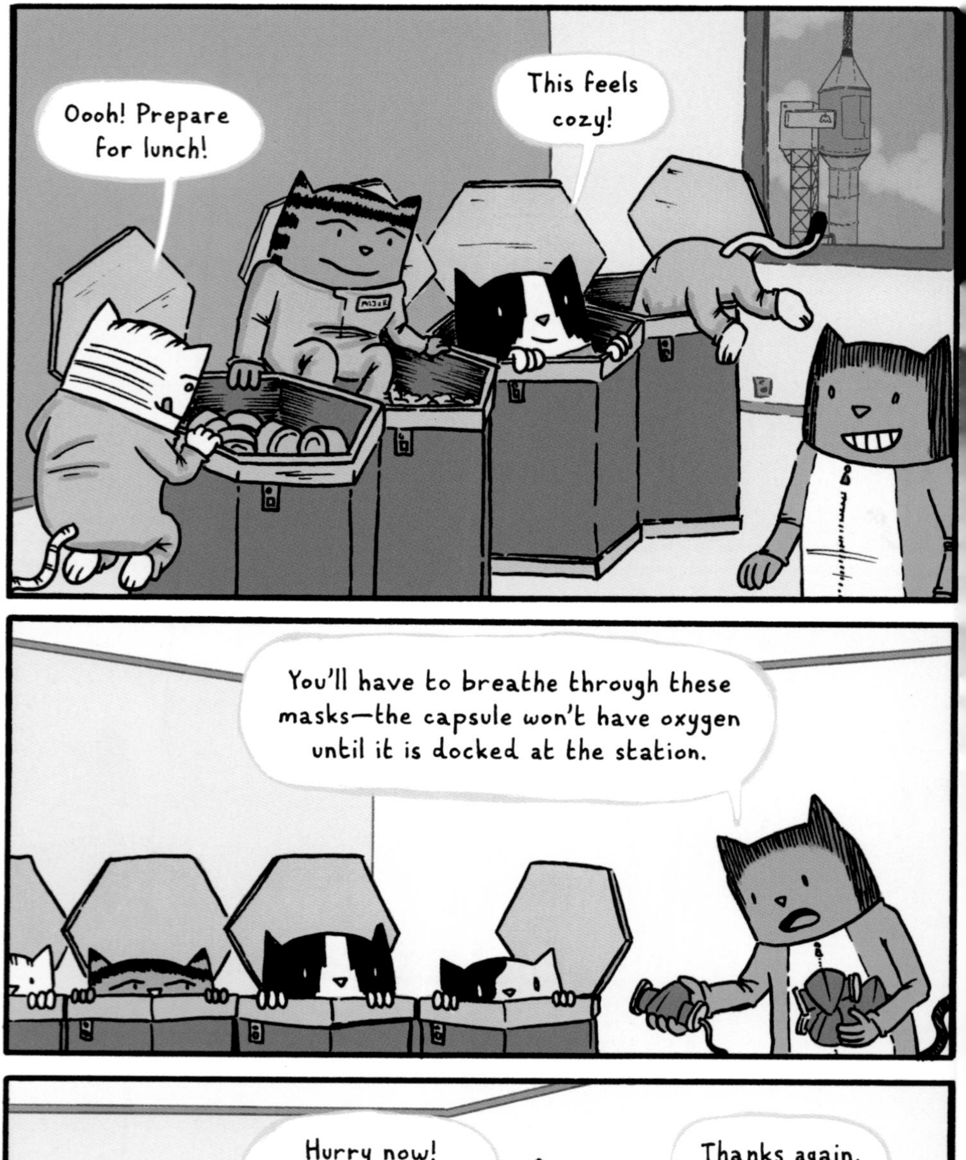
Oooh! Prepare for lunch!
This feels cozy!
You'll have to breathe through these masks—the capsule won't have oxygen until it is docked at the station.
Hurry now! Someone's coming.
Thanks again, Gemelli.
BEEP

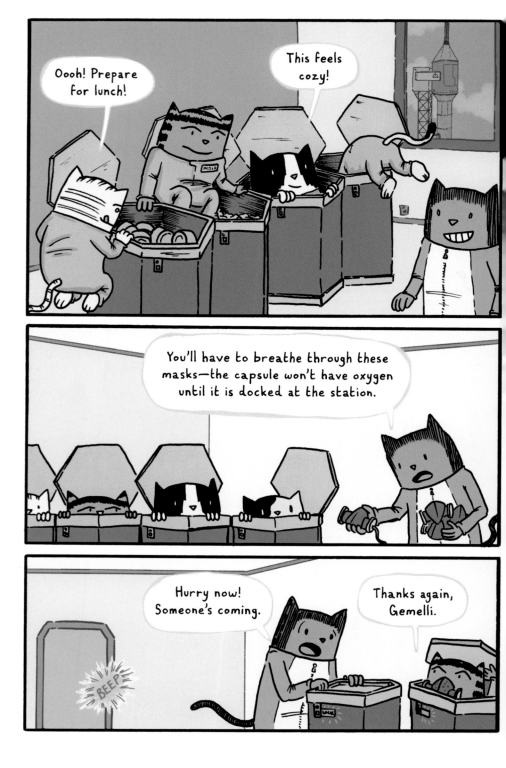

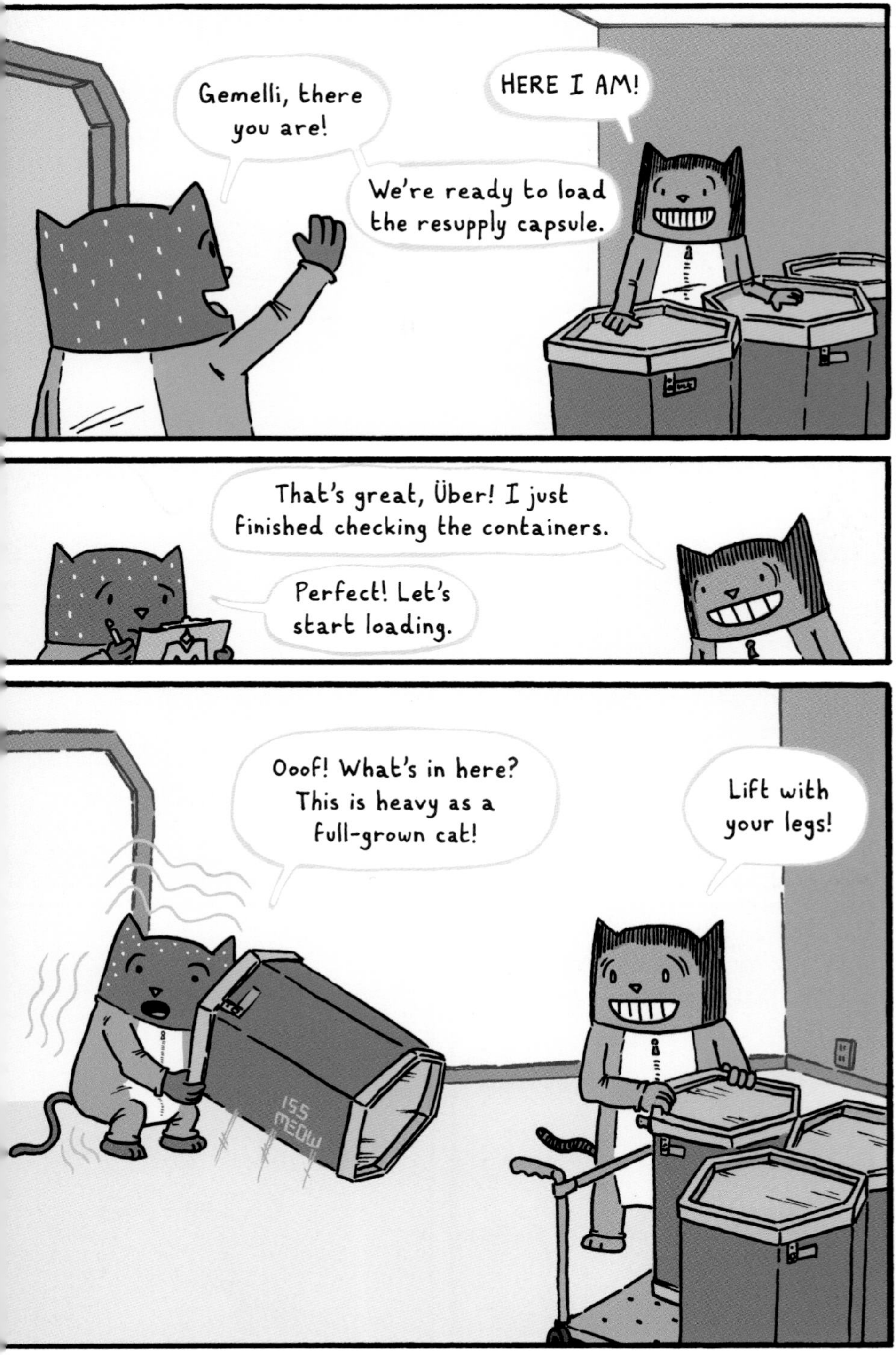
Gemelli, there you are!
We're ready to load the resupply capsule.
HERE I AM!
That's great, Über! I just finished checking the containers.
Perfect! Let's start loading.
Ooof! What's in here? This is heavy as a full-grown cat!
ISS MEOW
Lift with your legs!

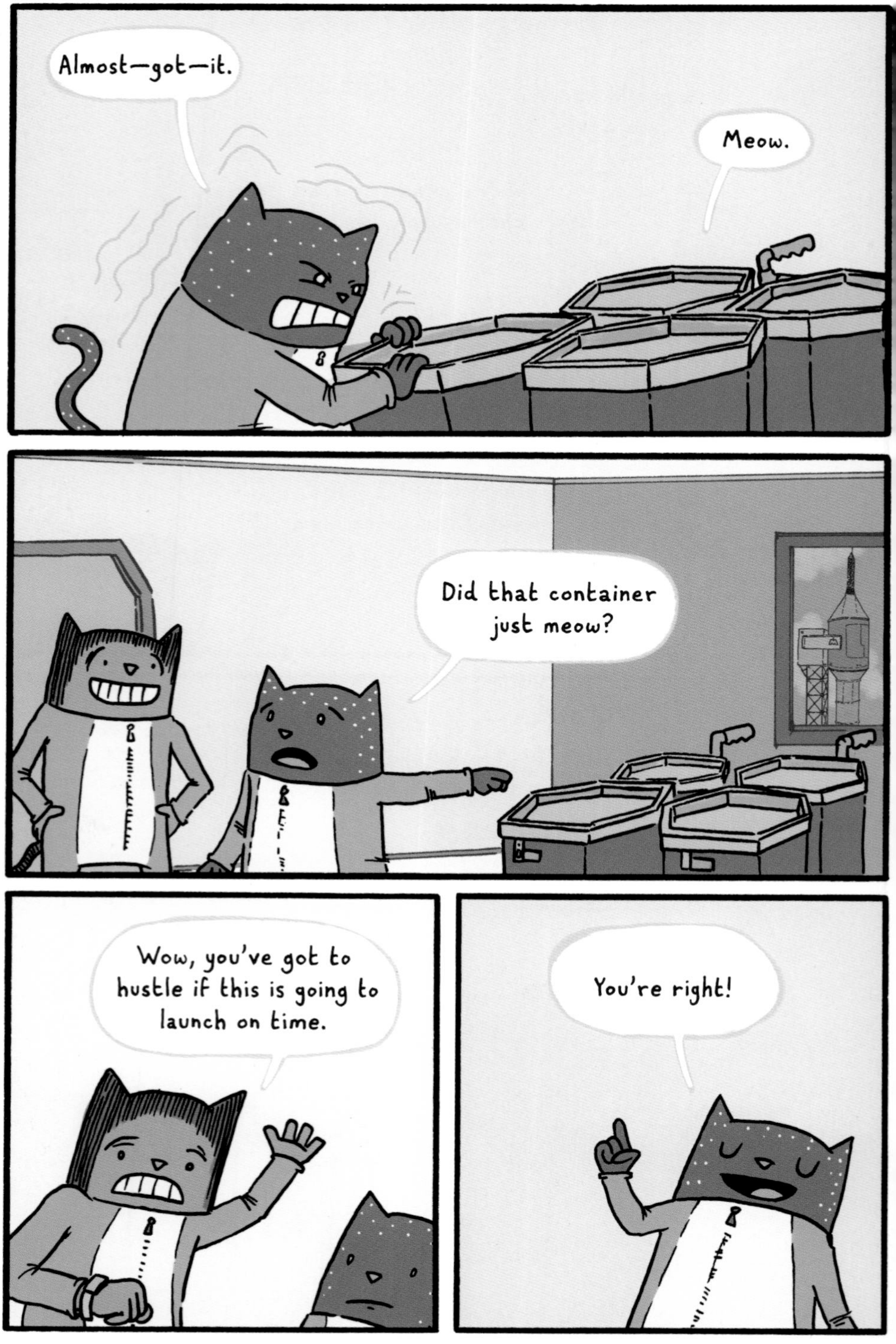
Almost—got—it.
Meow.
Did that container just meow?
Wow, you've got to hustle if this is going to launch on time.
You're right!

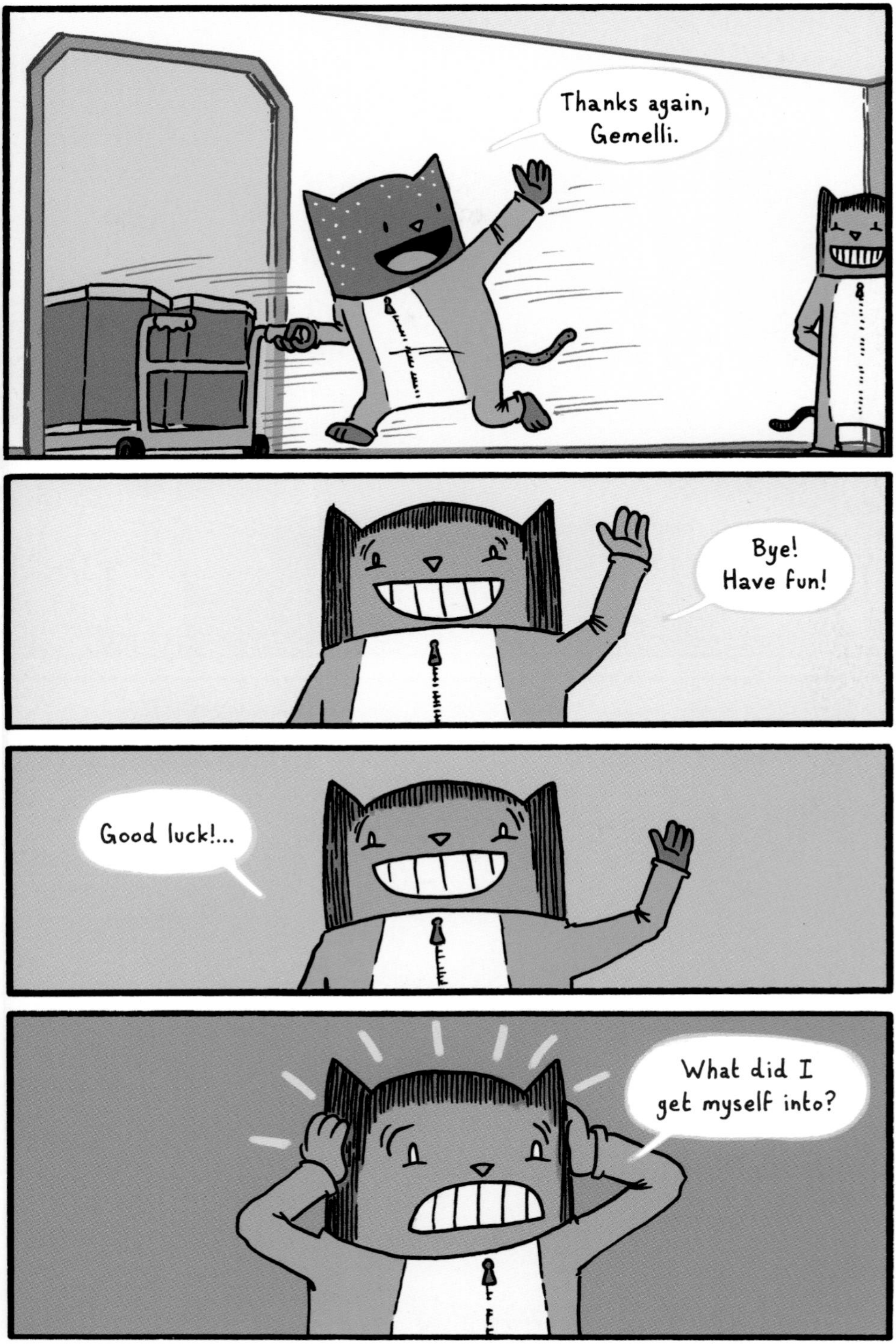
Thanks again, Gemelli.
Bye! Have fun!
Good luck!...
What did I get myself into?

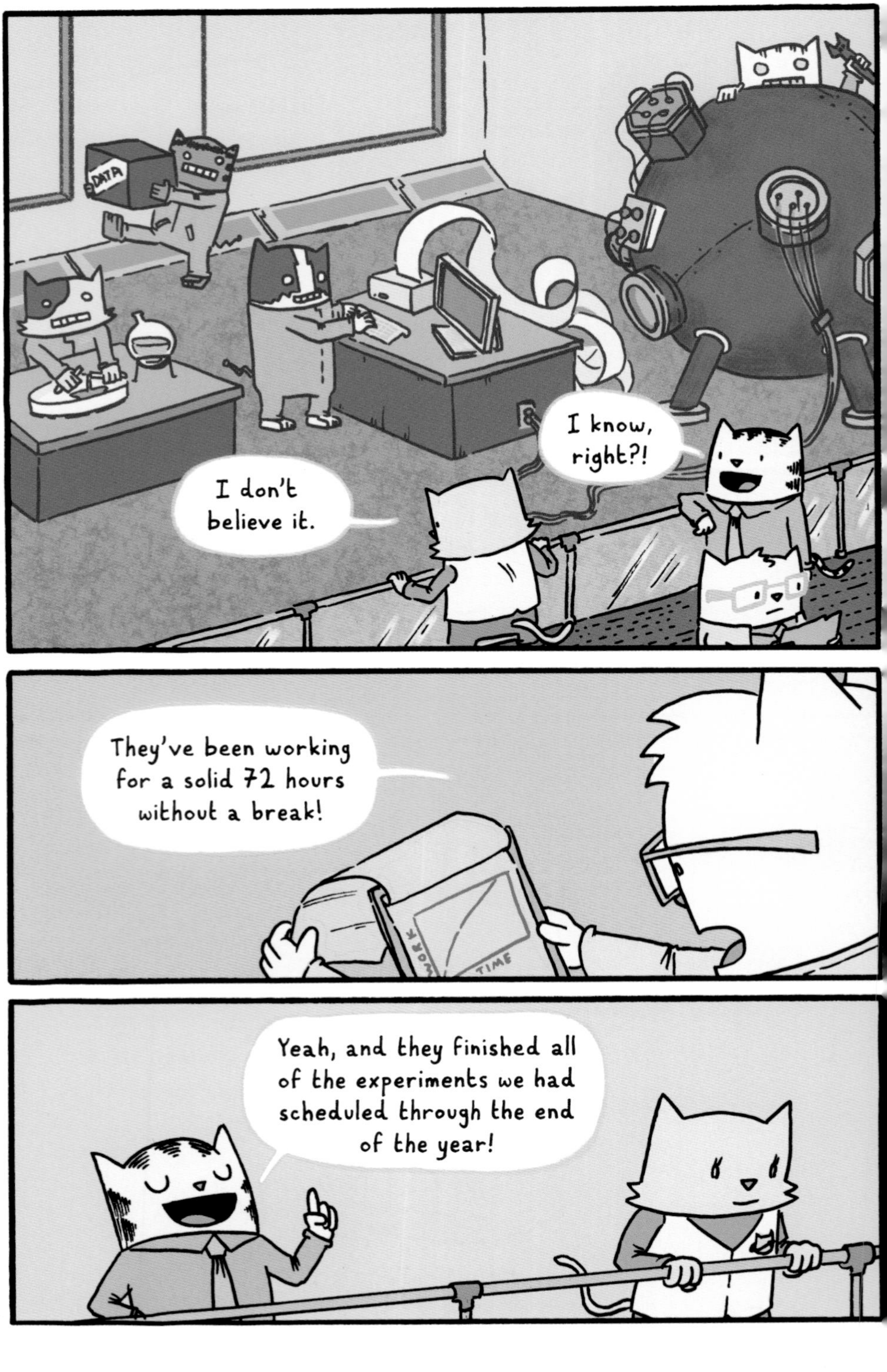
DATA
I don't believe it.
I know, right?!
They've been working for a solid 72 hours without a break!
WORK
TIME
Yeah, and they finished all of the experiments we had scheduled through the end of the year!

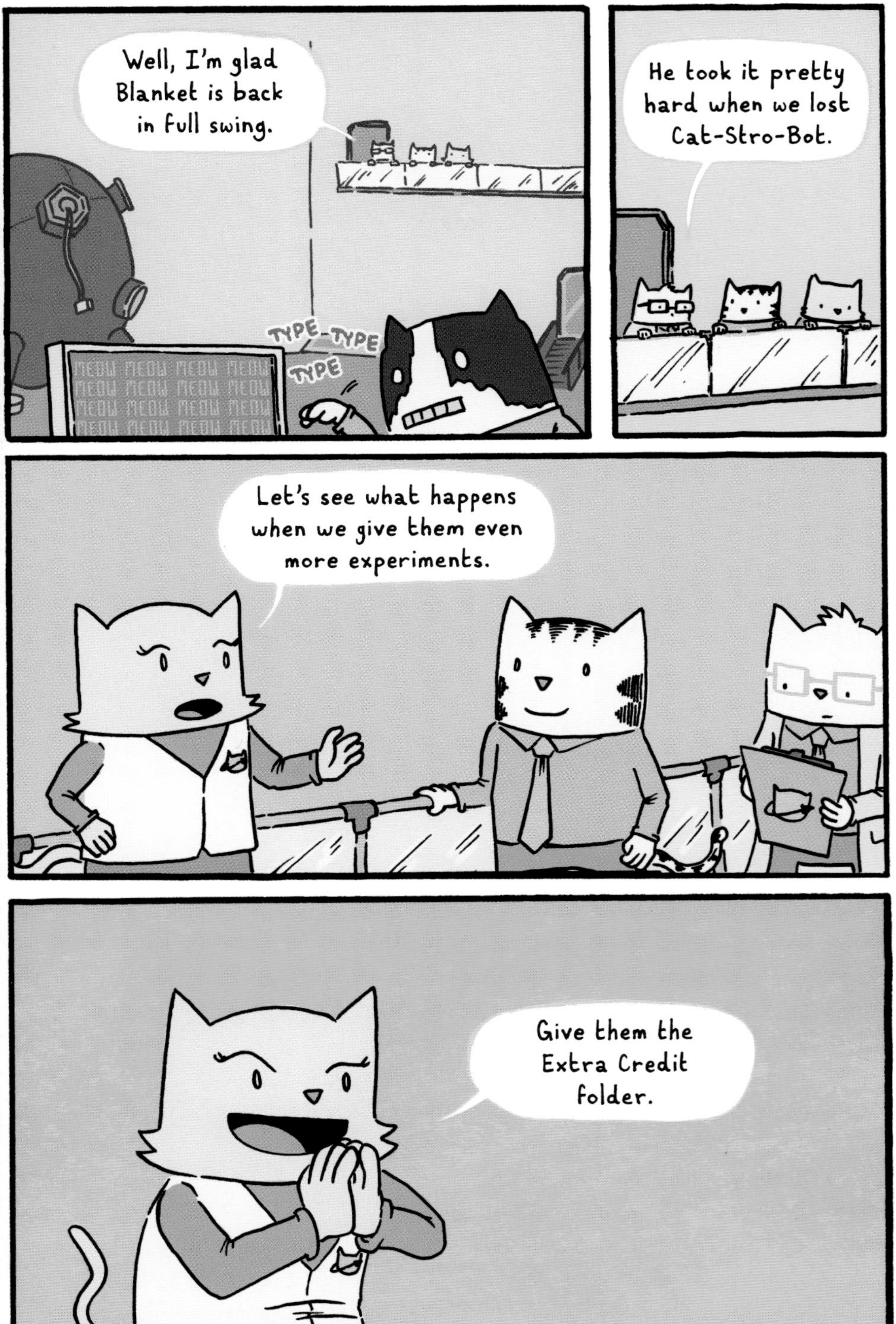
Well, I'm glad Blanket is back in full swing.
MEOW MEOW MEOW MEOW
TYPE TYPE
TYPE
He took it pretty hard when we lost Cat-Stro-Bot.
Let's see what happens when we give them even more experiments.
Give them the Extra Credit folder.

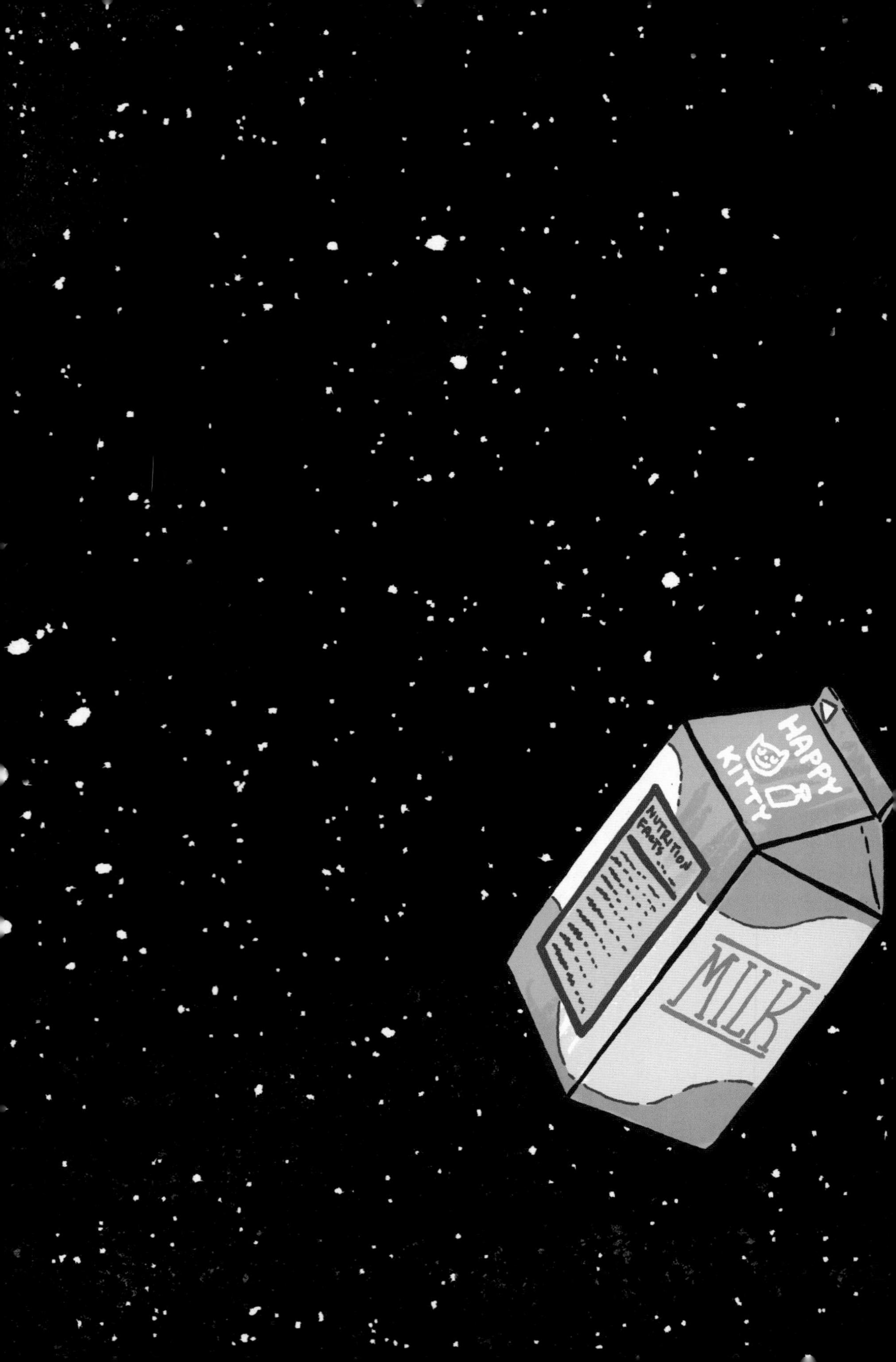
HAPPY KITTY
NUTRITION FACTS
MILK

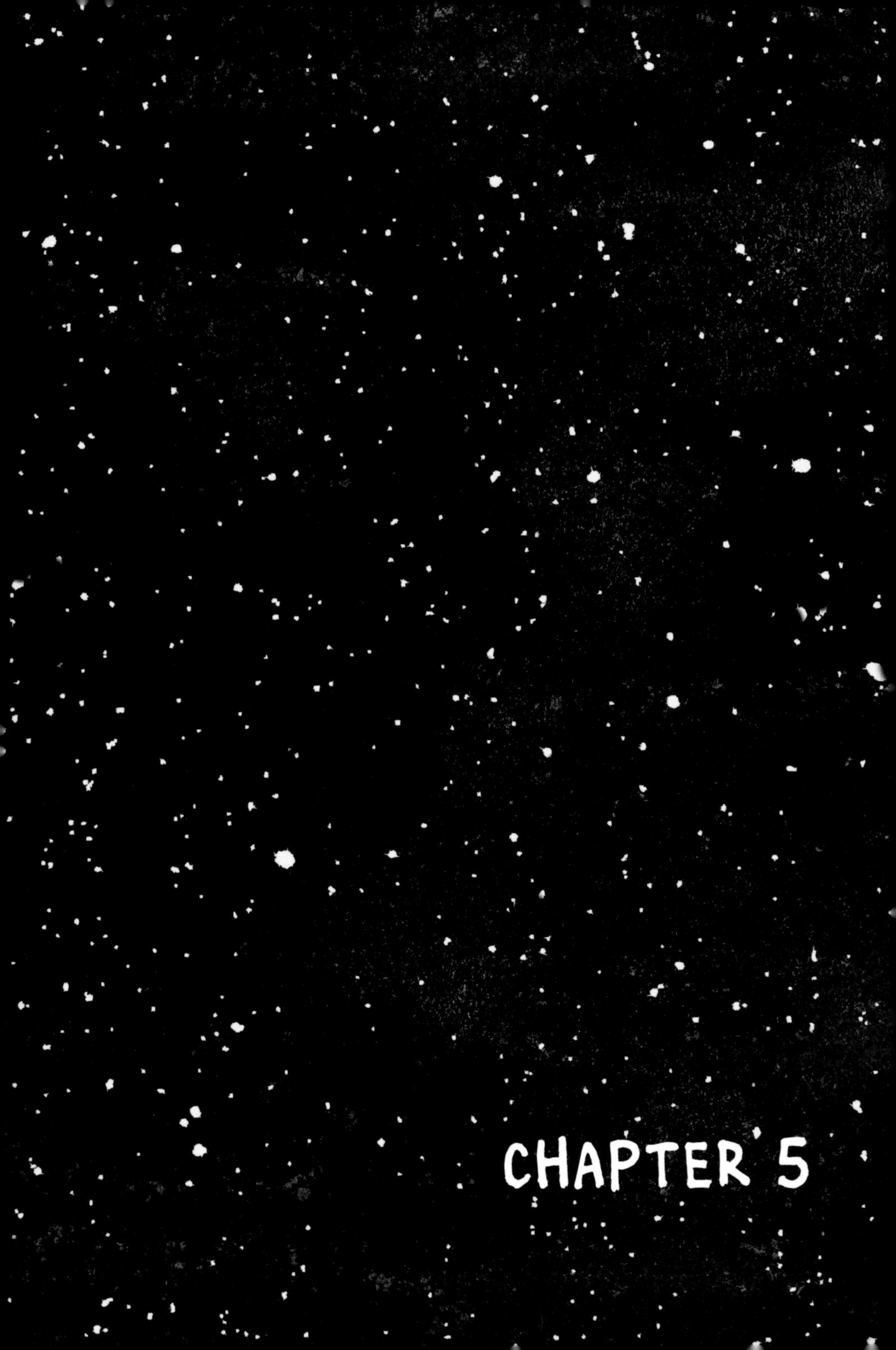

CHAPTER 5

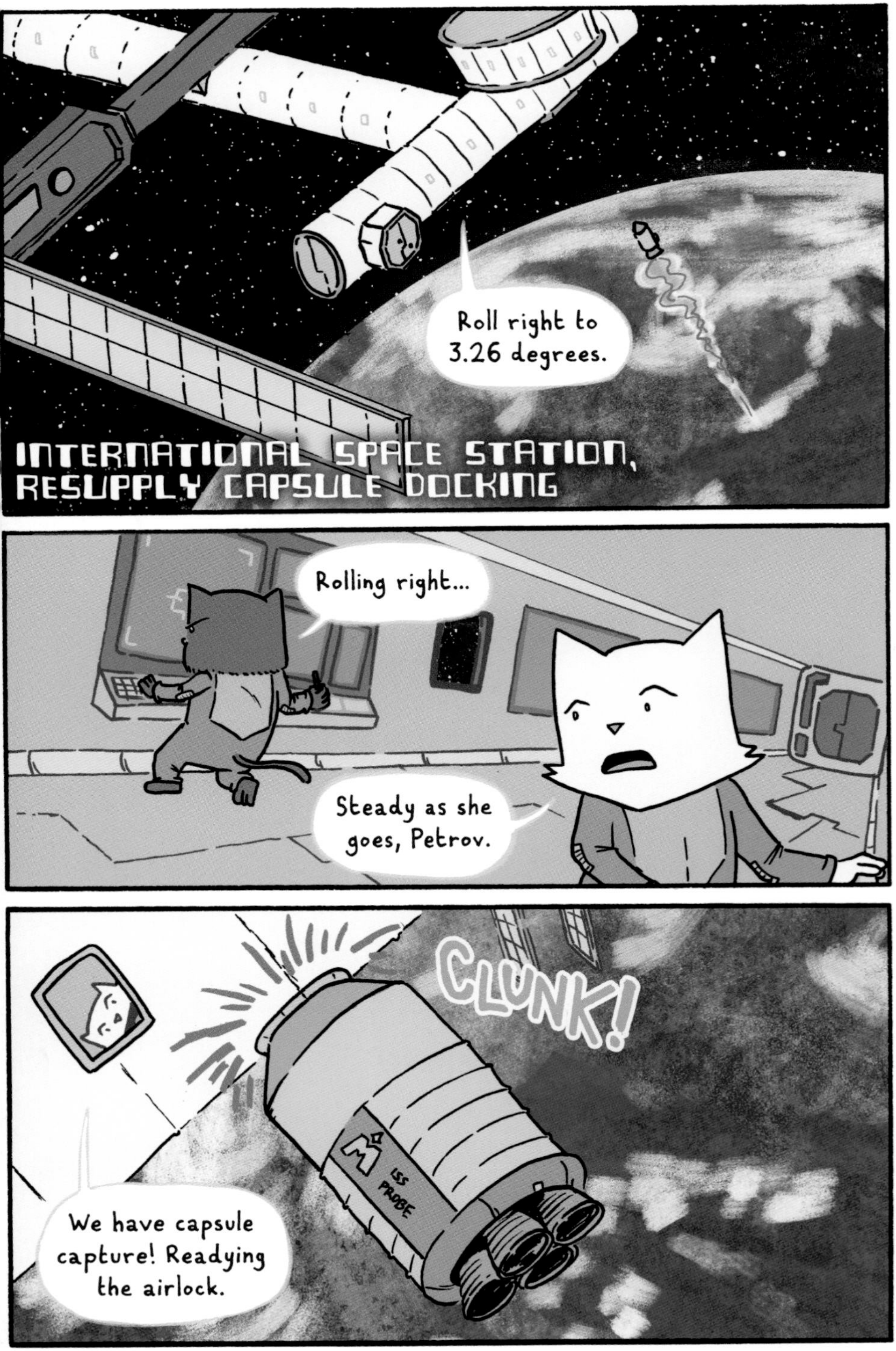
Roll right to 3.26 degrees.
INTERNATIONAL SPACE STATION, RESUPPLY CAPSULE DOCKING
Rolling right...
Steady as she goes, Petrov.
CLUNK!
ISS PROBE
We have capsule capture! Readying the airlock.

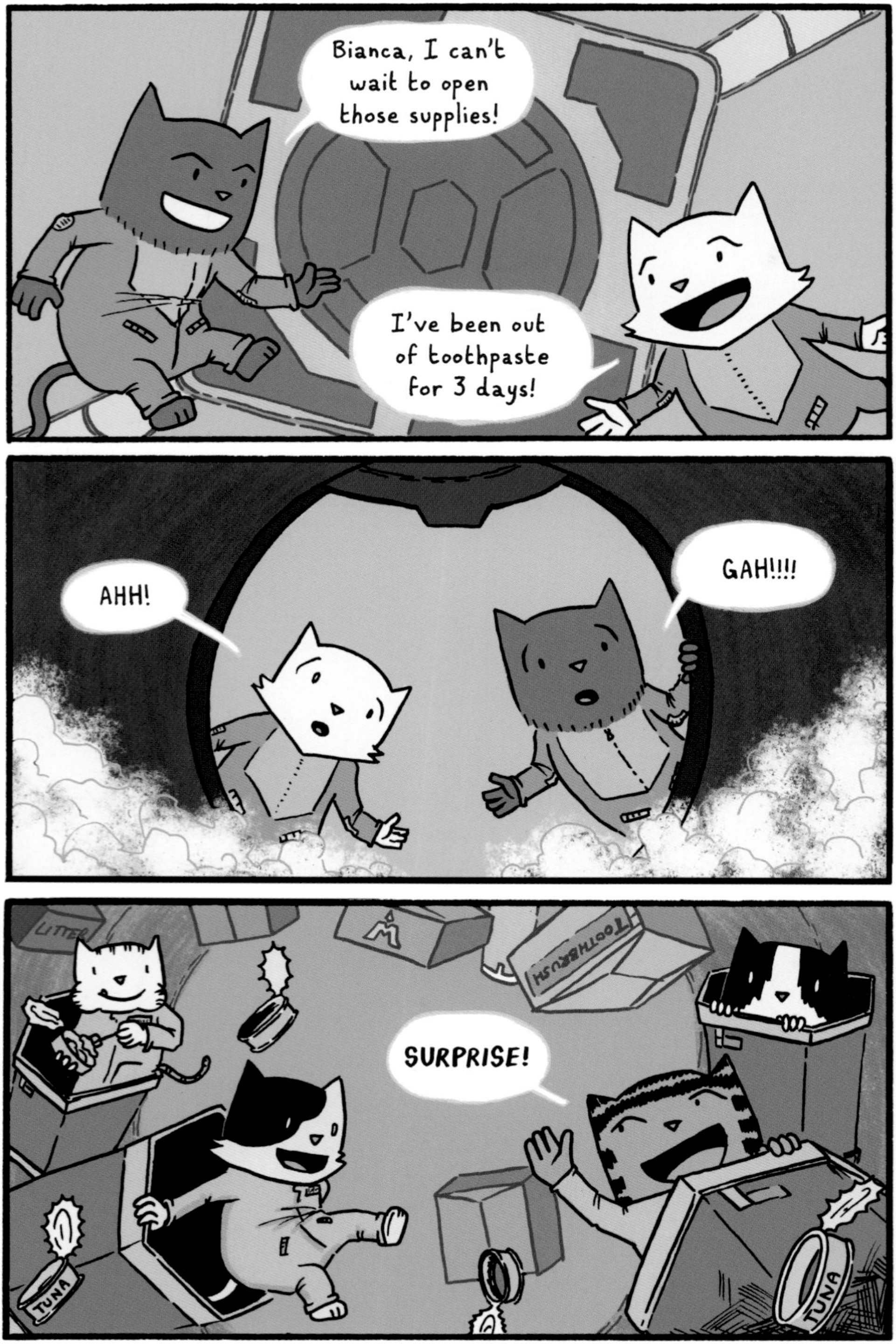
Bianca, I can't wait to open those supplies!
I've been out of toothpaste for 3 days!
AHH!
GAH!!!!
LITTER
TOOTHBRUSH
SURPRISE!
TUNA
TUNA

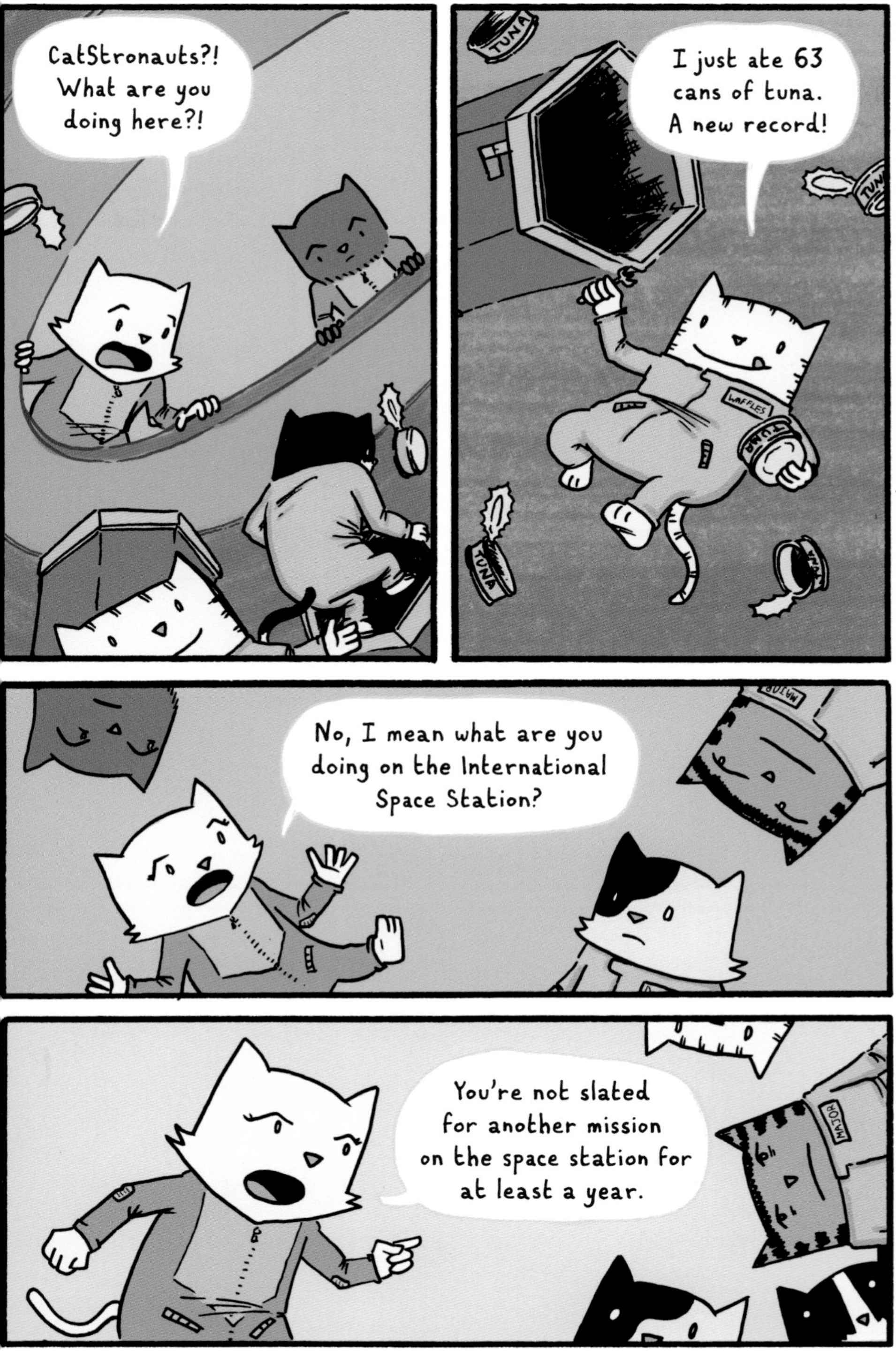
CatStronauts?! What are you doing here?!
I just ate 63 cans of tuna. A new record!
No, I mean what are you doing on the International Space Station?
You're not slated for another mission on the space station for at least a year.

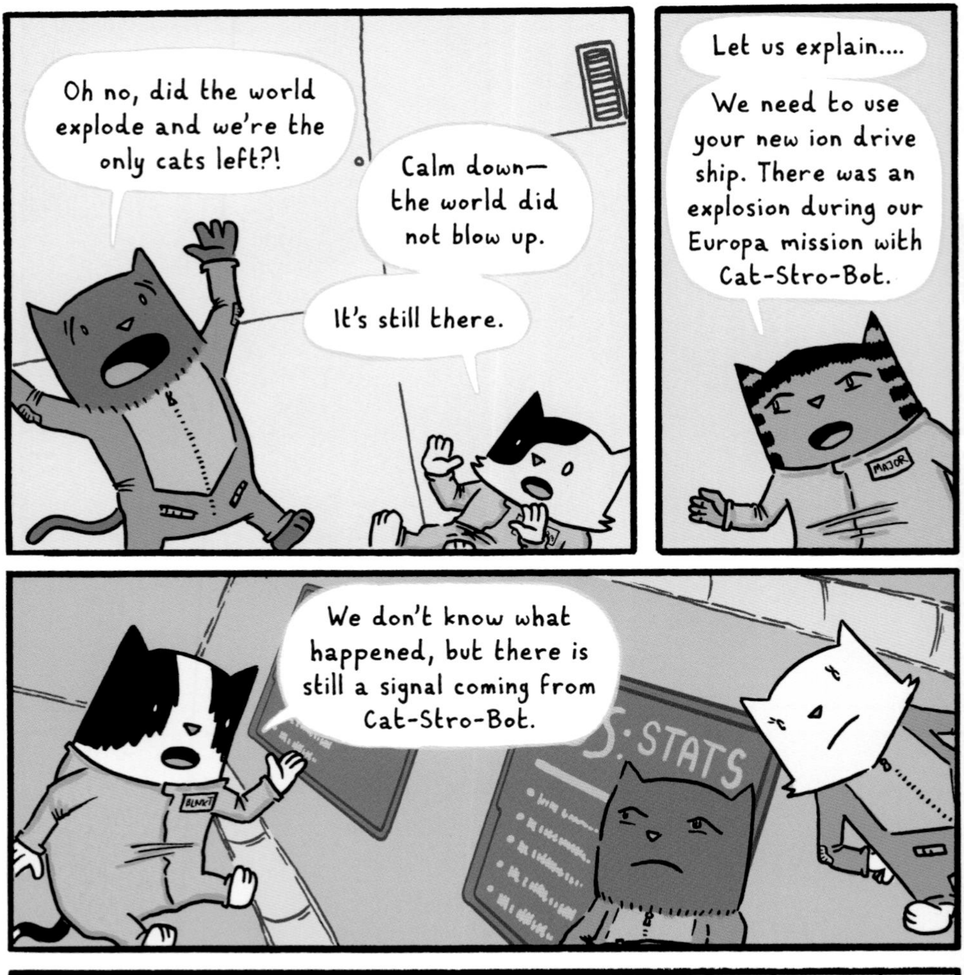

Oh no, did the world explode and we're the only cats left?!
Calm down—the world did not blow up.
It's still there.
Let us explain....
We need to use your new ion drive ship. There was an explosion during our Europa mission with Cat-Stro-Bot.
MAJOR
We don't know what happened, but there is still a signal coming from Cat-Stro-Bot.
STATS
So we're going to Europa to save him!
Isn't that plan the coolest?!

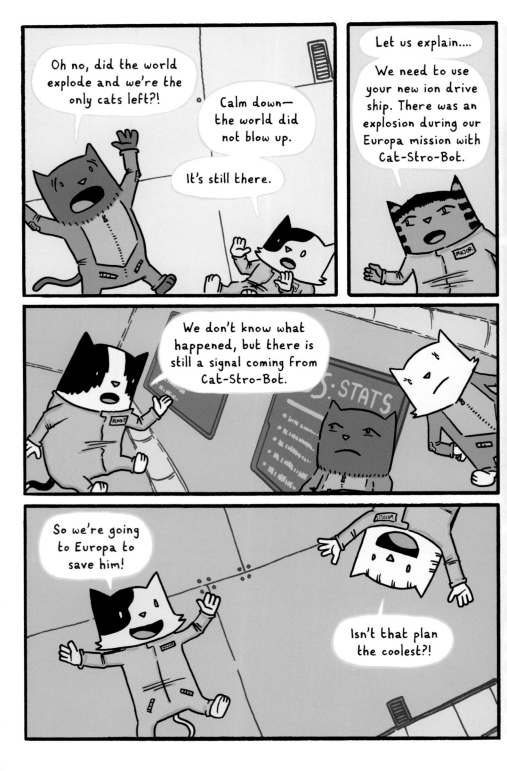

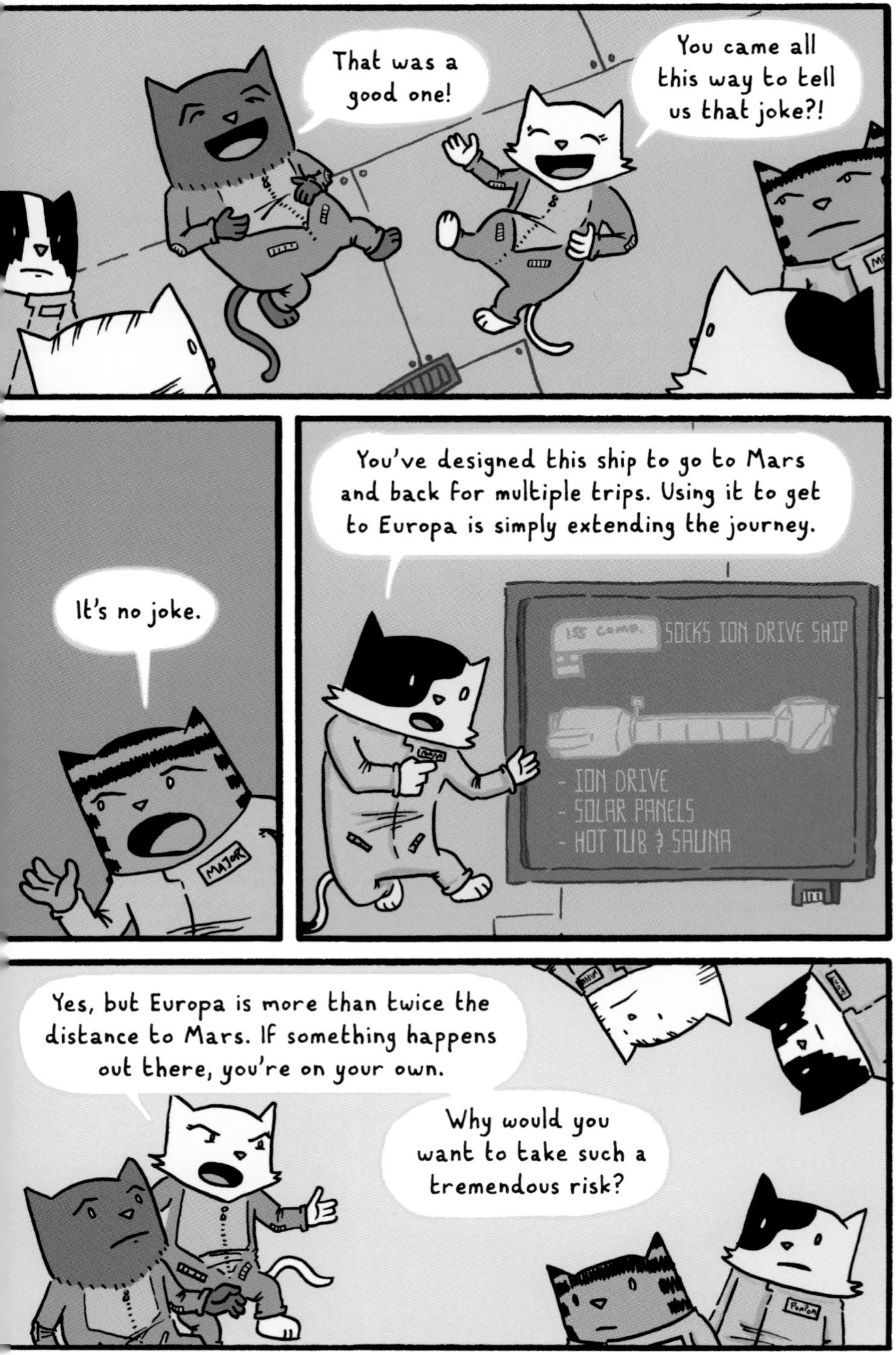
That was a good one!
You came all this way to tell us that joke?!
It's no joke.
You've designed this ship to go to Mars and back for multiple trips. Using it to get to Europa is simply extending the journey.
SOCKS ION DRIVE SHIP
- ION DRIVE
- SOLAR PANELS
- HOT TUB & SAUNA
Yes, but Europa is more than twice the distance to Mars. If something happens out there, you're on your own.
Why would you want to take such a tremendous risk?

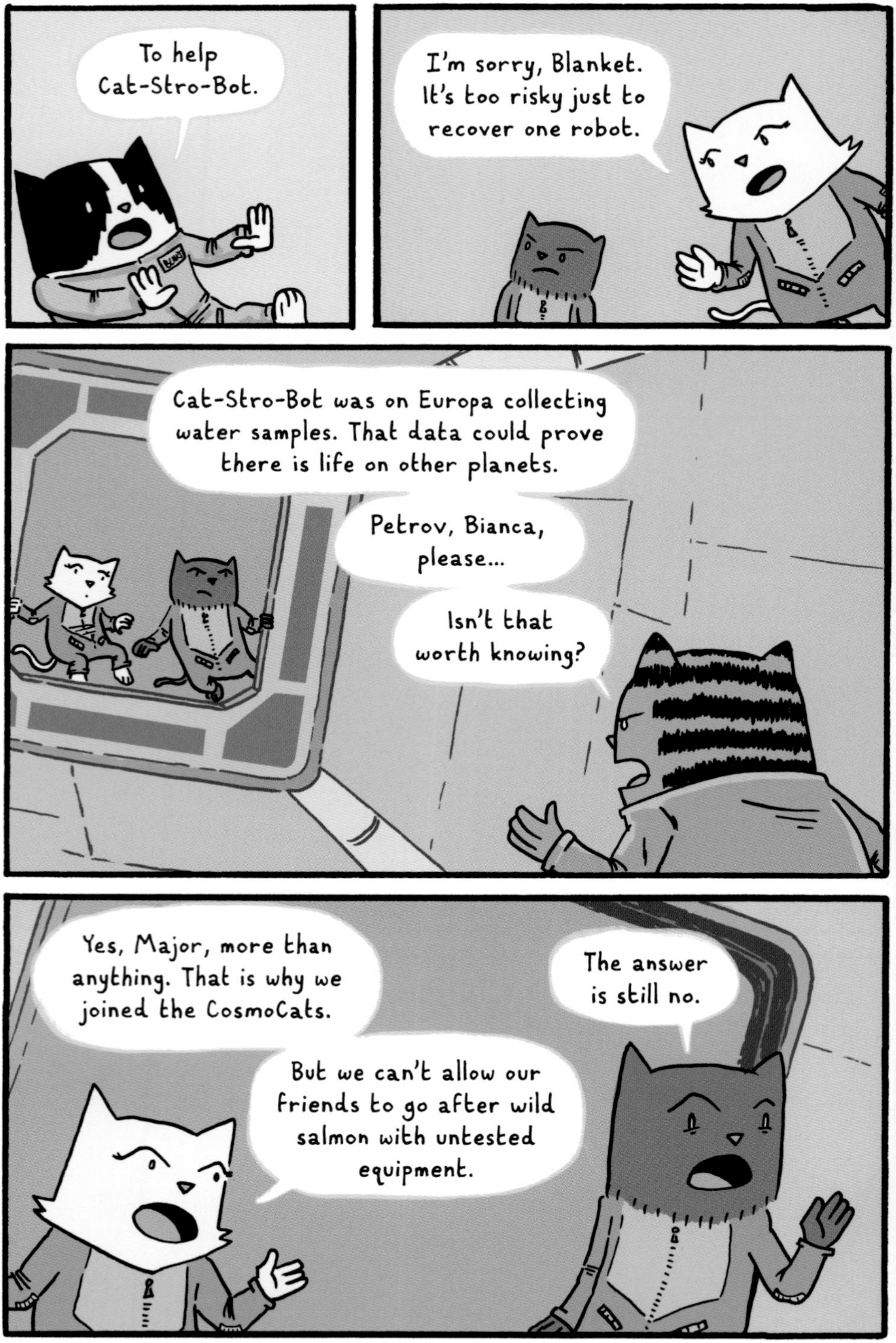
To help Cat-Stro-Bot.
I'm sorry, Blanket. It's too risky just to recover one robot.
Cat-Stro-Bot was on Europa collecting water samples. That data could prove there is life on other planets.
Petrov, Bianca, please...
Isn't that worth knowing?
Yes, Major, more than anything. That is why we joined the CosmoCats.
But we can't allow our friends to go after wild salmon with untested equipment.
The answer is still no.

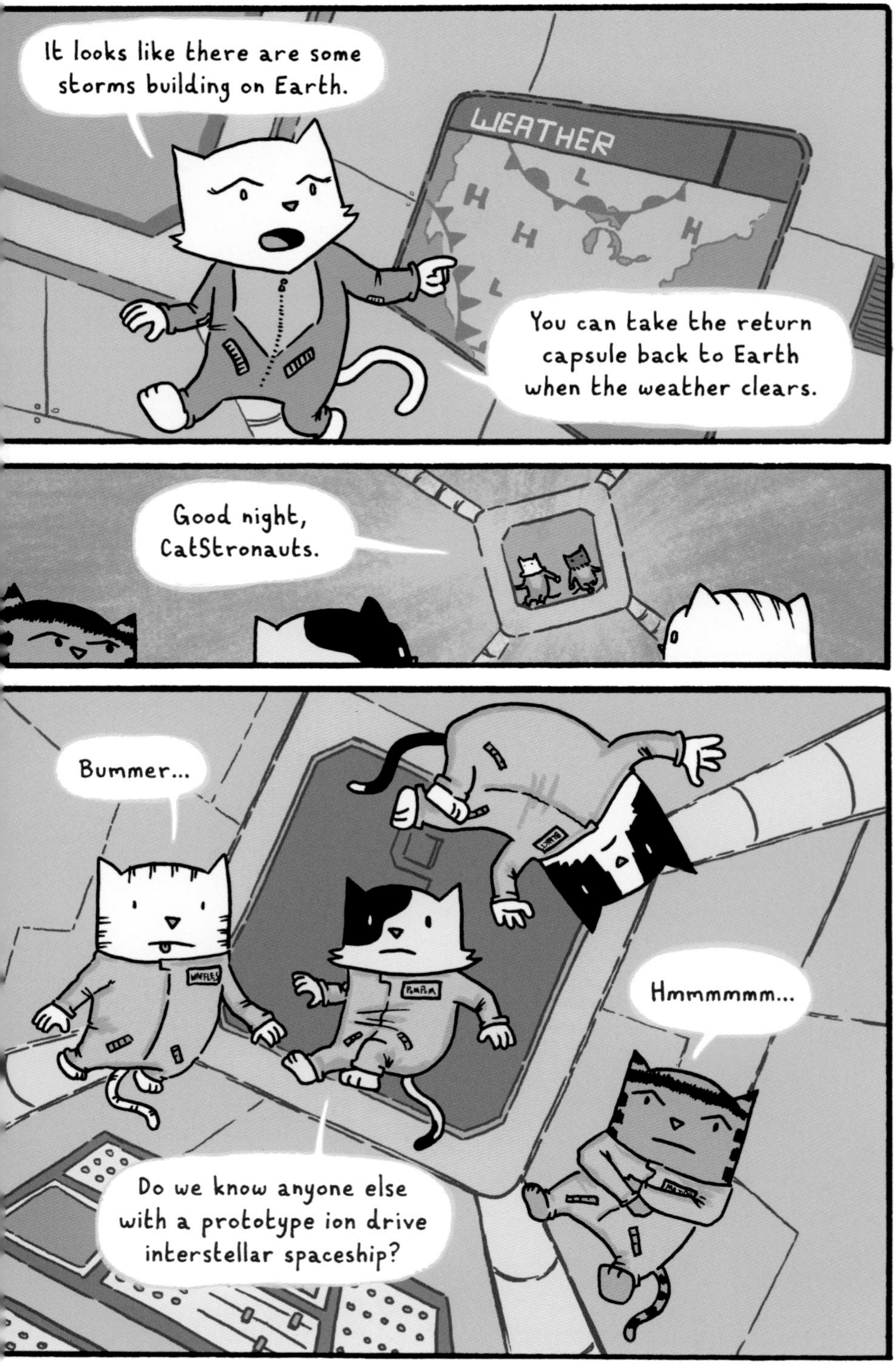
It looks like there are some storms building on Earth.
WEATHER
You can take the return capsule back to Earth when the weather clears.
Good night, CatStronauts.
Bummer...
Hmmmmmm...
Do we know anyone else with a prototype ion drive interstellar spaceship?

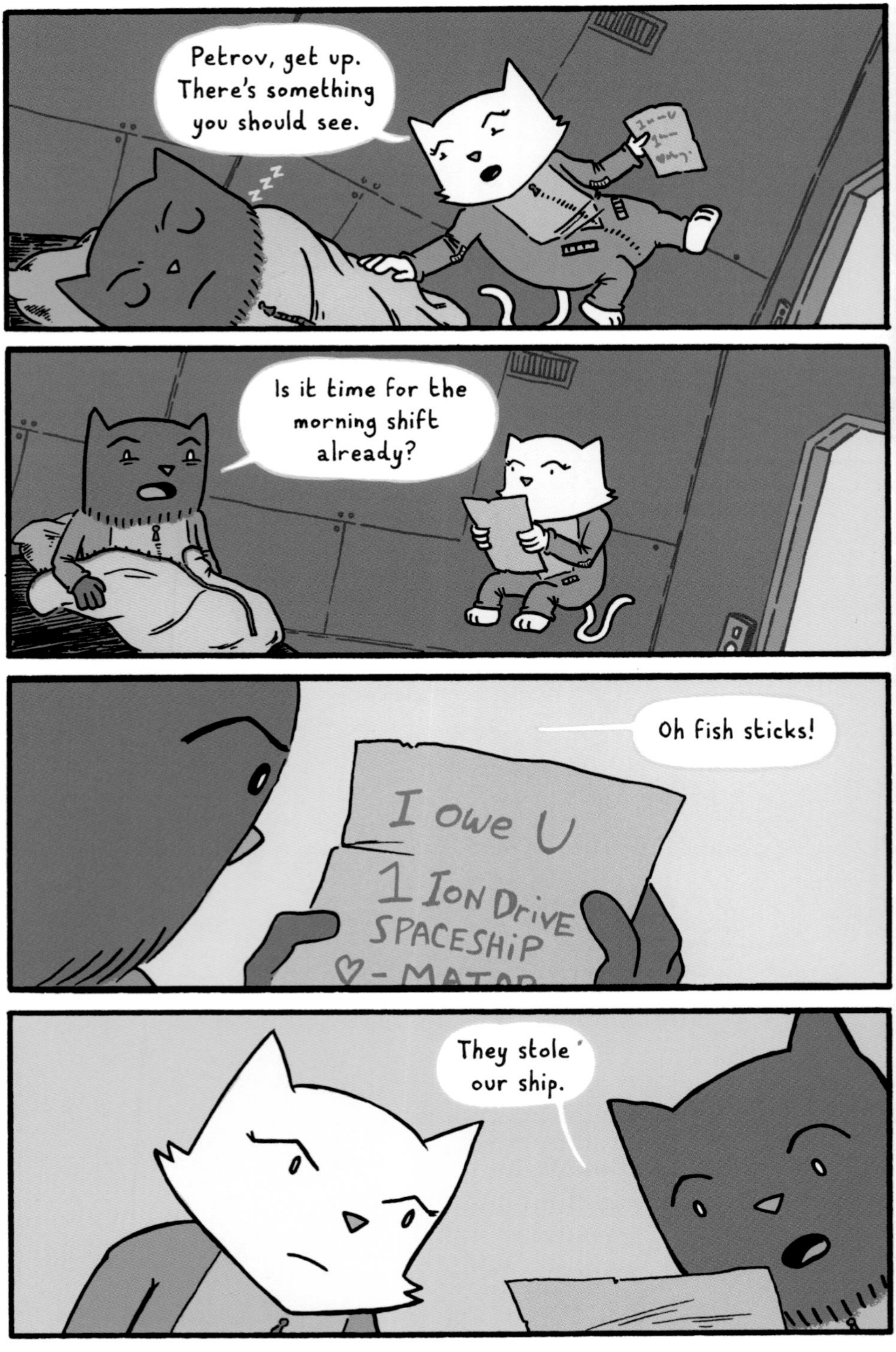
Petrov, get up. There's something you should see.
Is it time for the morning shift already?
Oh fish sticks!
I owe U
1 Ion Drive
SPACESHIP
They stole our ship.

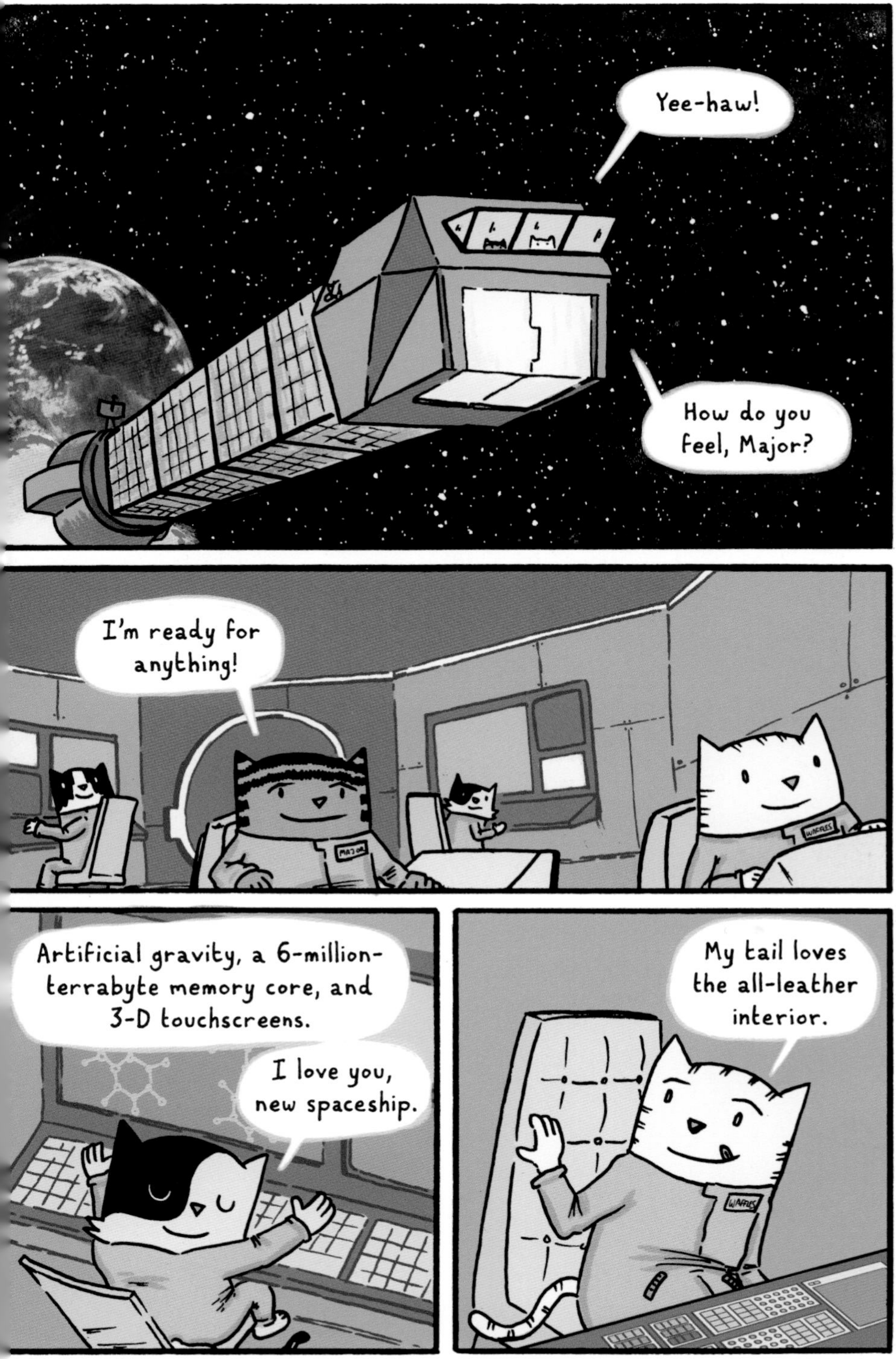
Yee-haw!
How do you feel, Major?
I'm ready for anything!
MAJOR
WAFFLES
Artificial gravity, a 6-million-terrabyte memory core, and 3-D touchscreens.
I love you, new spaceship.
My tail loves the all-leather interior.
WAFFLES

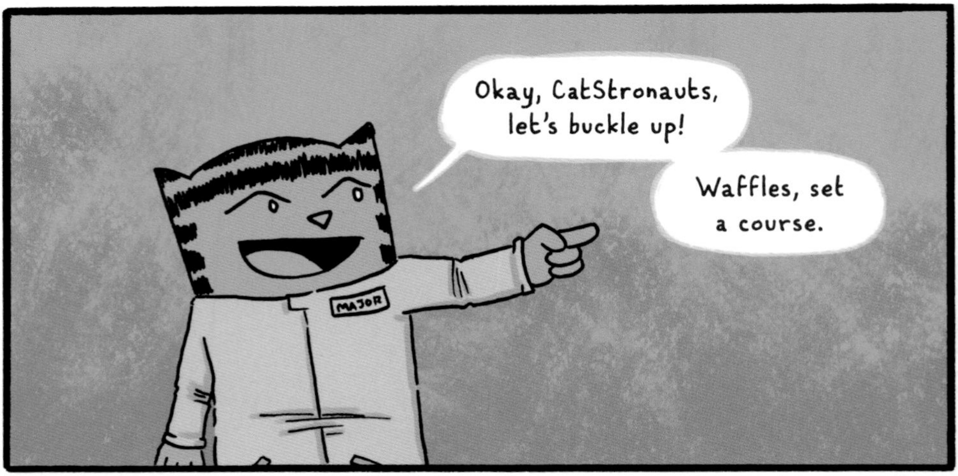
MAJOR
Okay, CatStronauts, let's buckle up!
Waffles, set a course.

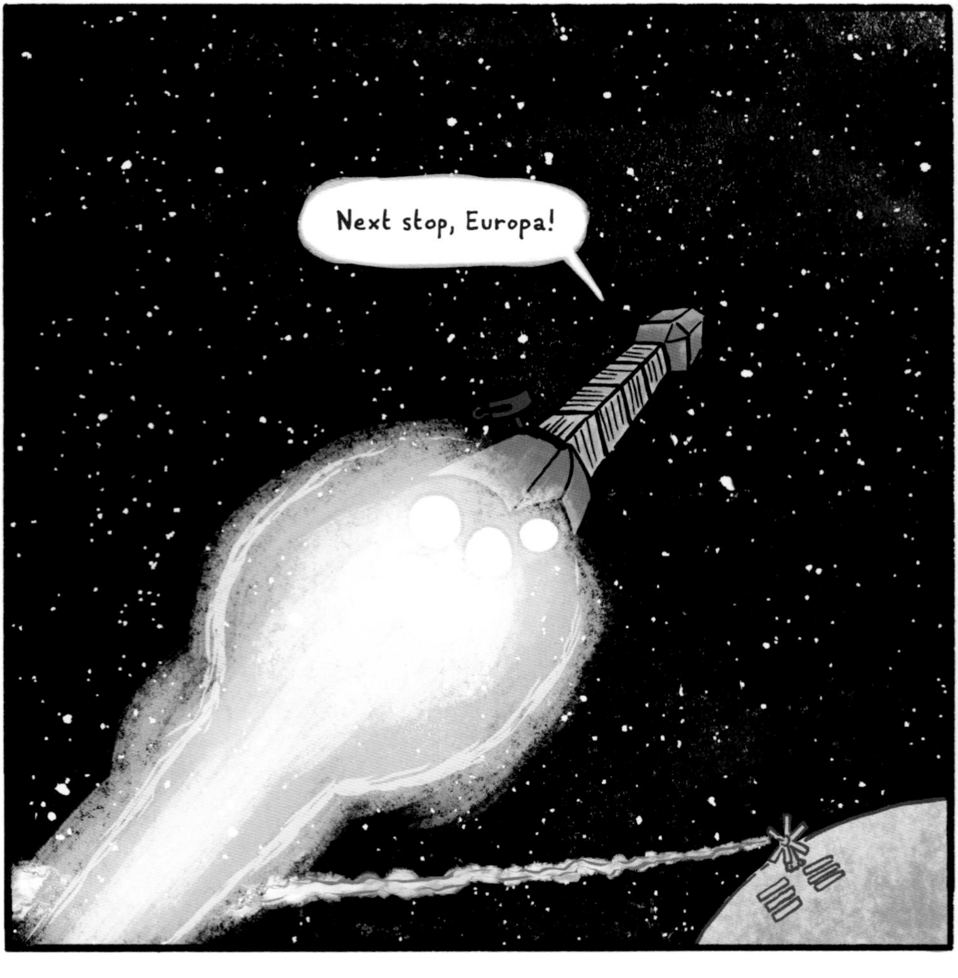
Next stop, Europa!

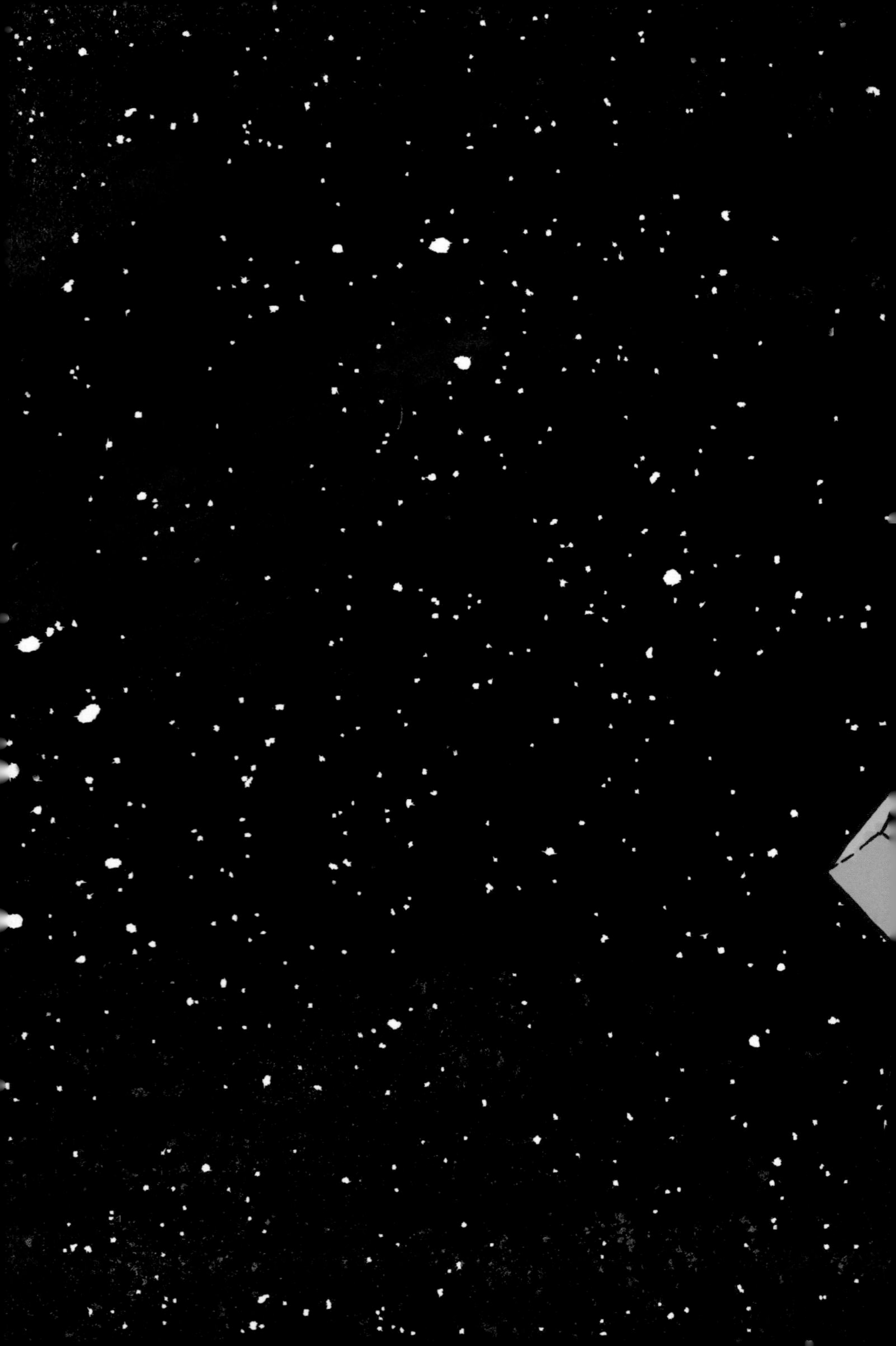

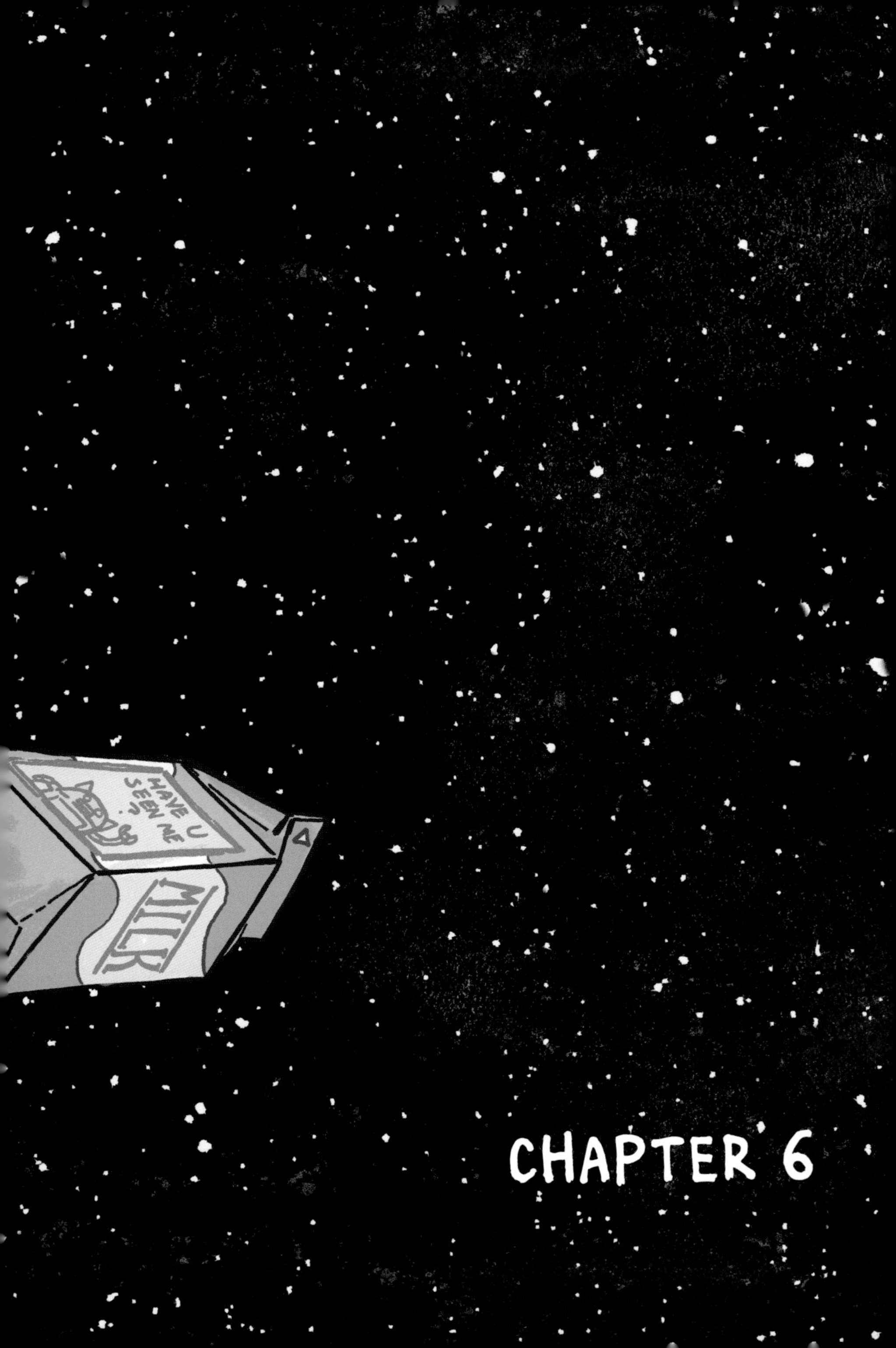
HAVE U SEEN ME ?
MILK

CHAPTER 6

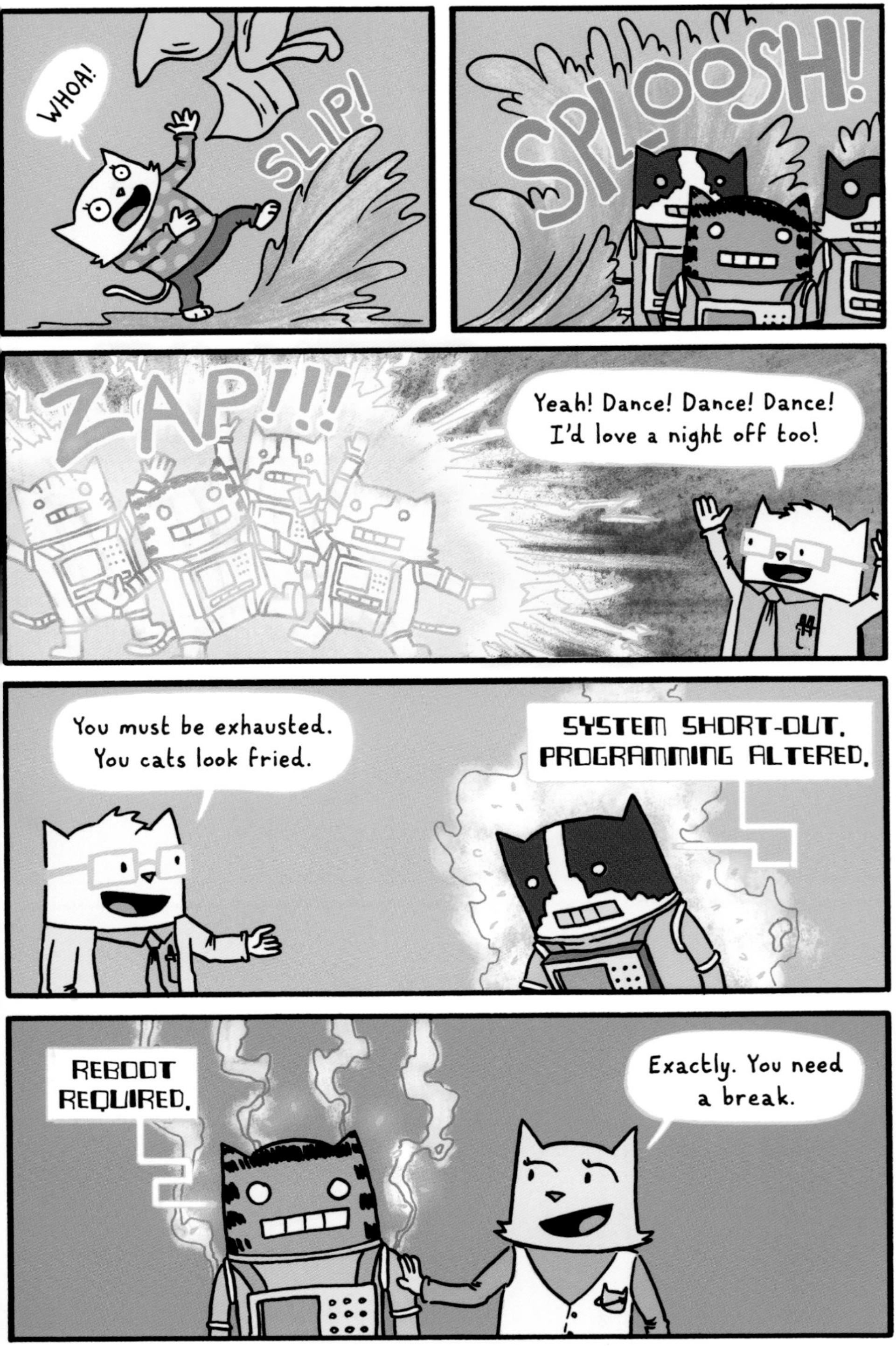
WHOA!
SLIP!
SPLOOSH!
ZAP!!!
Yeah! Dance! Dance! Dance! I'd love a night off too!
You must be exhausted. You cats look fried.
SYSTEM SHORT-OUT. PROGRAMMING ALTERED.
REBOOT REQUIRED.
Exactly. You need a break.

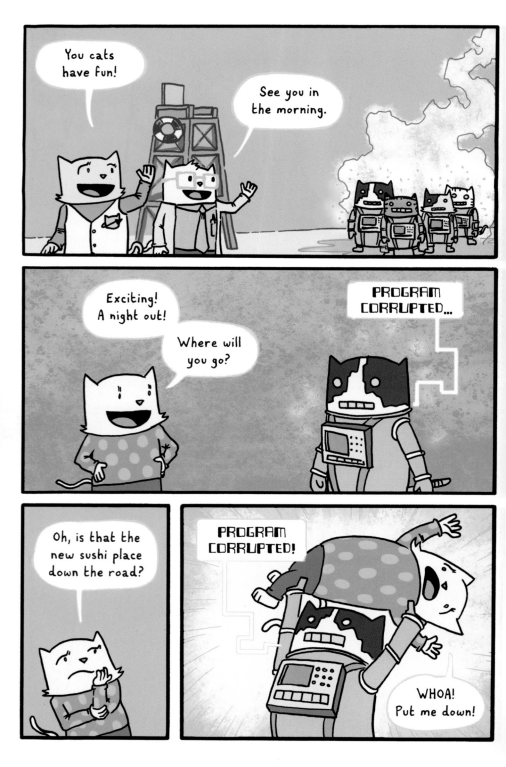

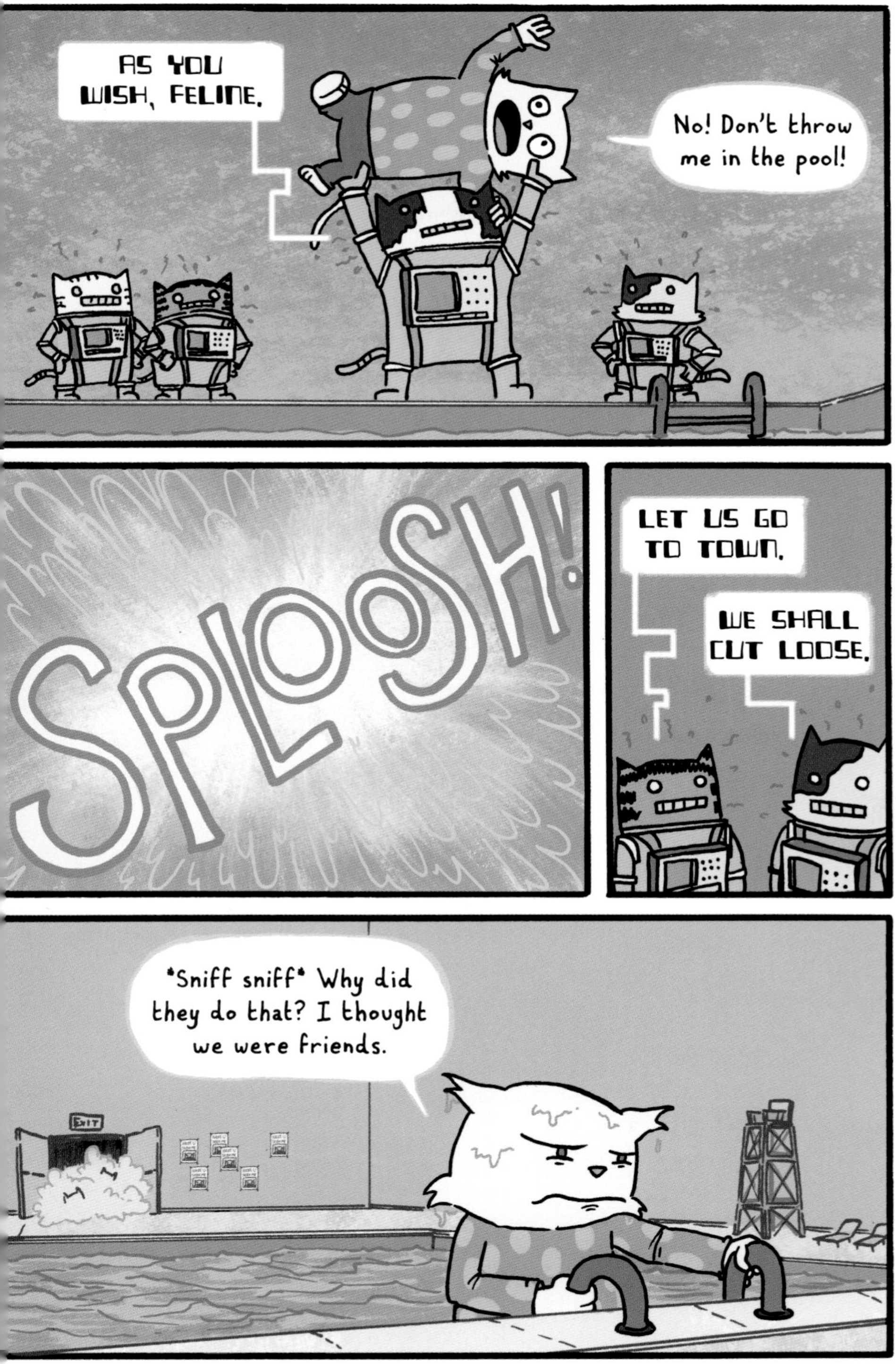
AS YOU WISH, FELINE.
No! Don't throw me in the pool!
SPLOOSH!
LET US GO TO TOWN.
WE SHALL CUT LOOSE.
Sniff sniff Why did they do that? I thought we were friends.
EXIT

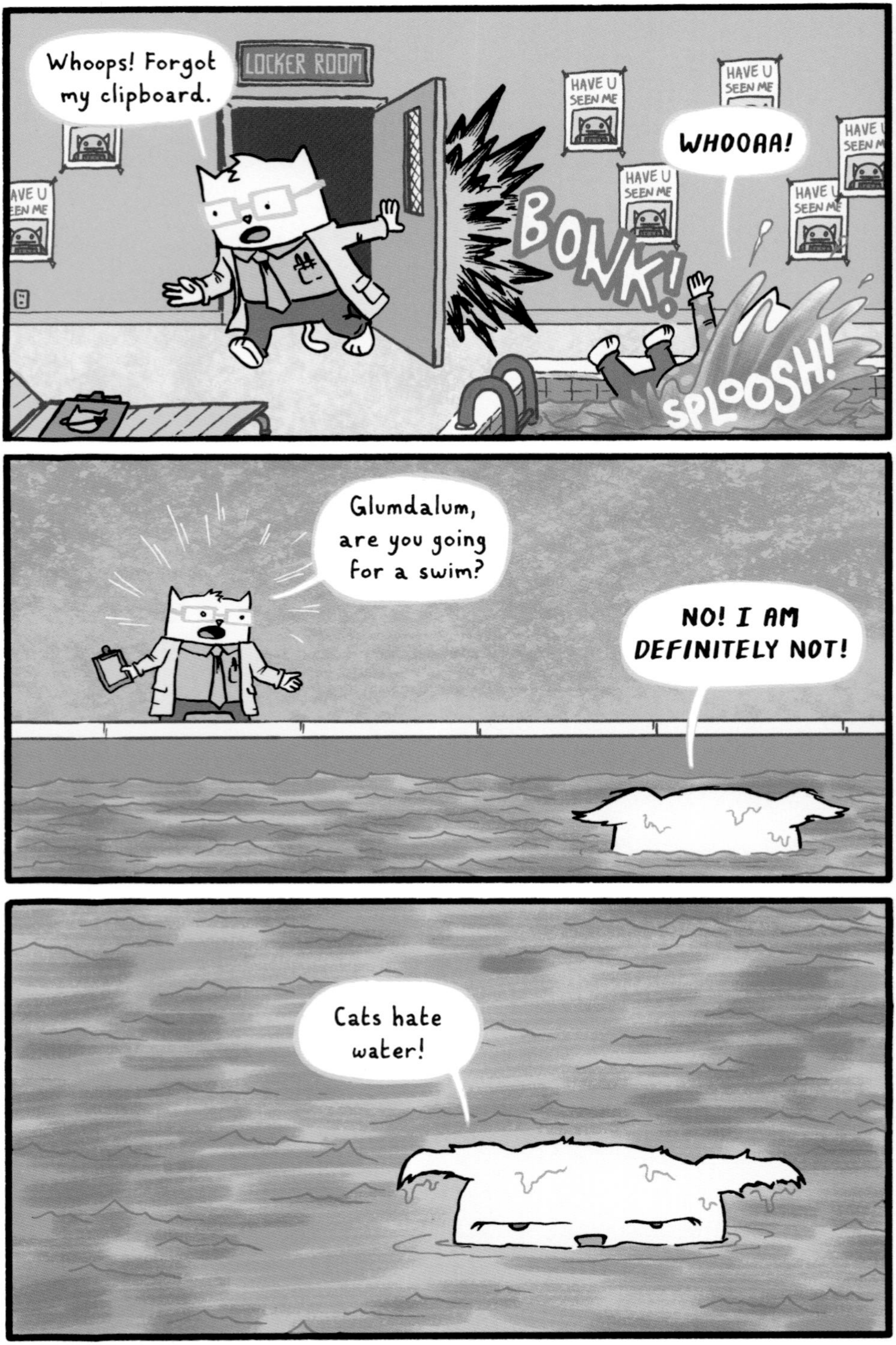
Whoops! Forgot my clipboard.
LOCKER ROOM
HAVE U SEEN ME
BONK!
WHOOAA!
SPLOOSH!
Glumdalum, are you going for a swim?
NO! I AM DEFINITELY NOT!
Cats hate water!

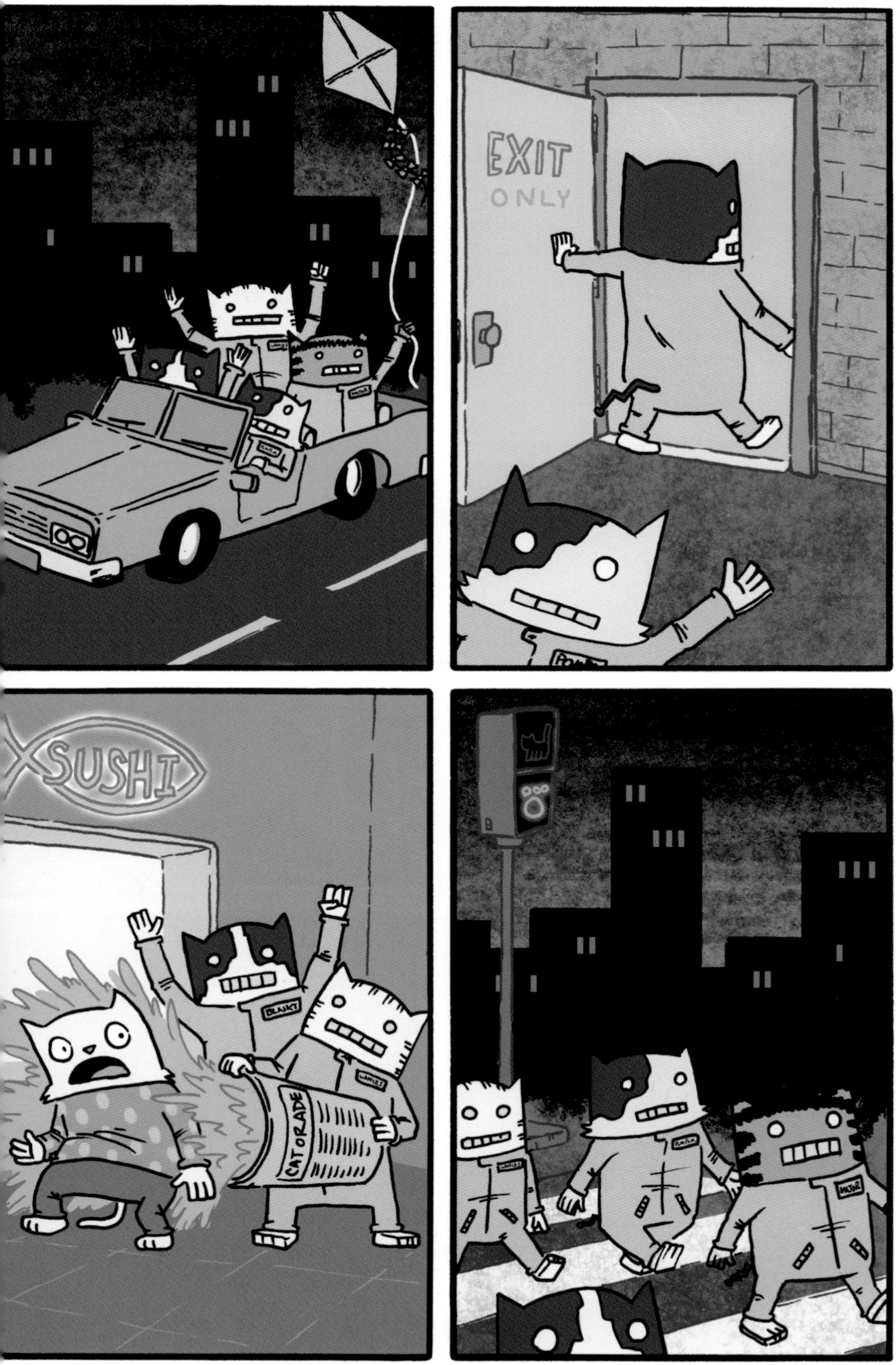
EXIT
ONLY
SUSHI
CATORADE

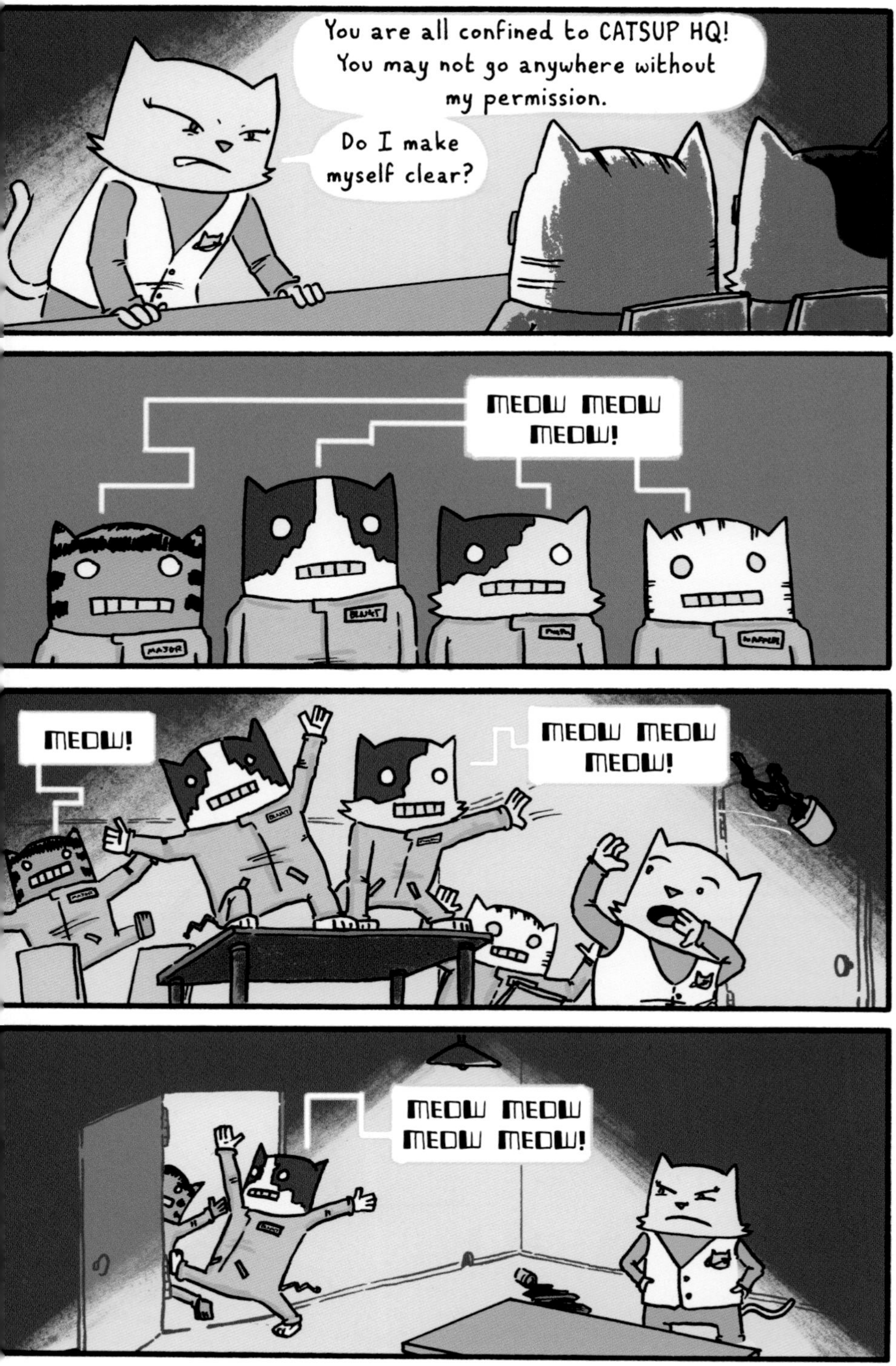
You are all confined to CATSUP HQ! You may not go anywhere without my permission.
Do I make myself clear?
MEOW MEOW MEOW!
MAJOR
BLURT
MEOW!
MEOW MEOW MEOW!
MEOW MEOW MEOW MEOW!

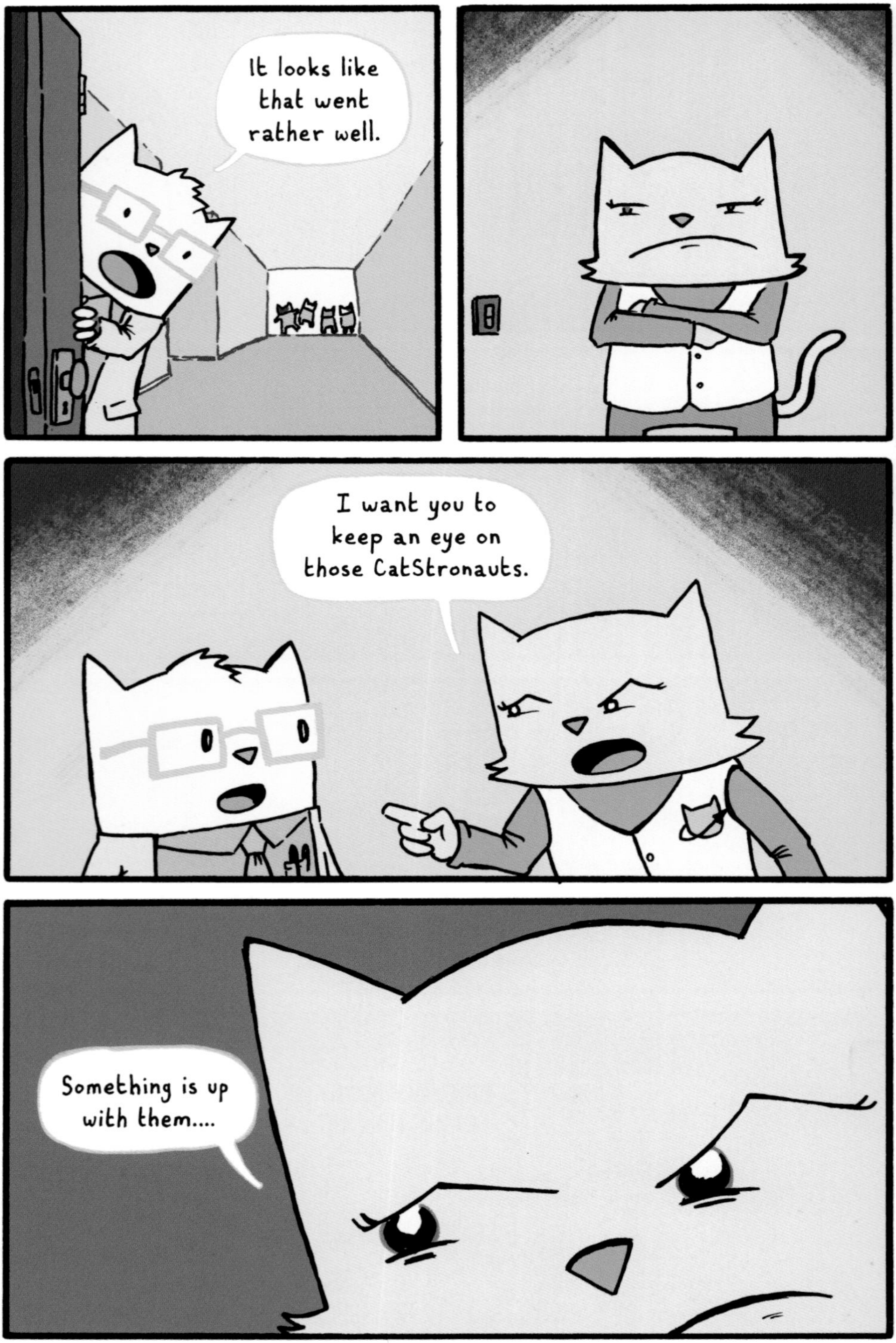
It looks like that went rather well.
I want you to keep an eye on those CatStronauts.
Something is up with them....

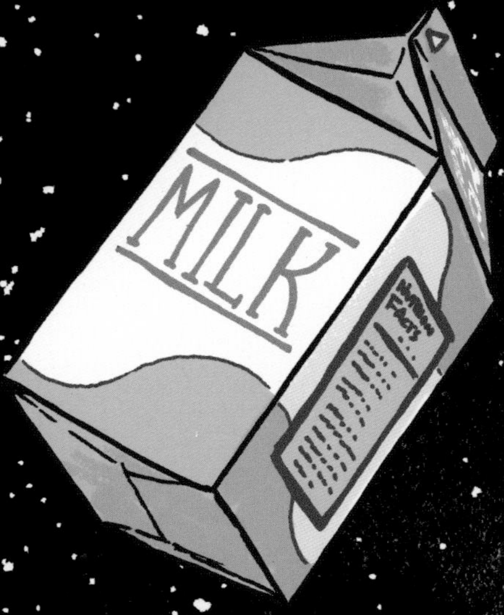
MILK

CHAPTER 7

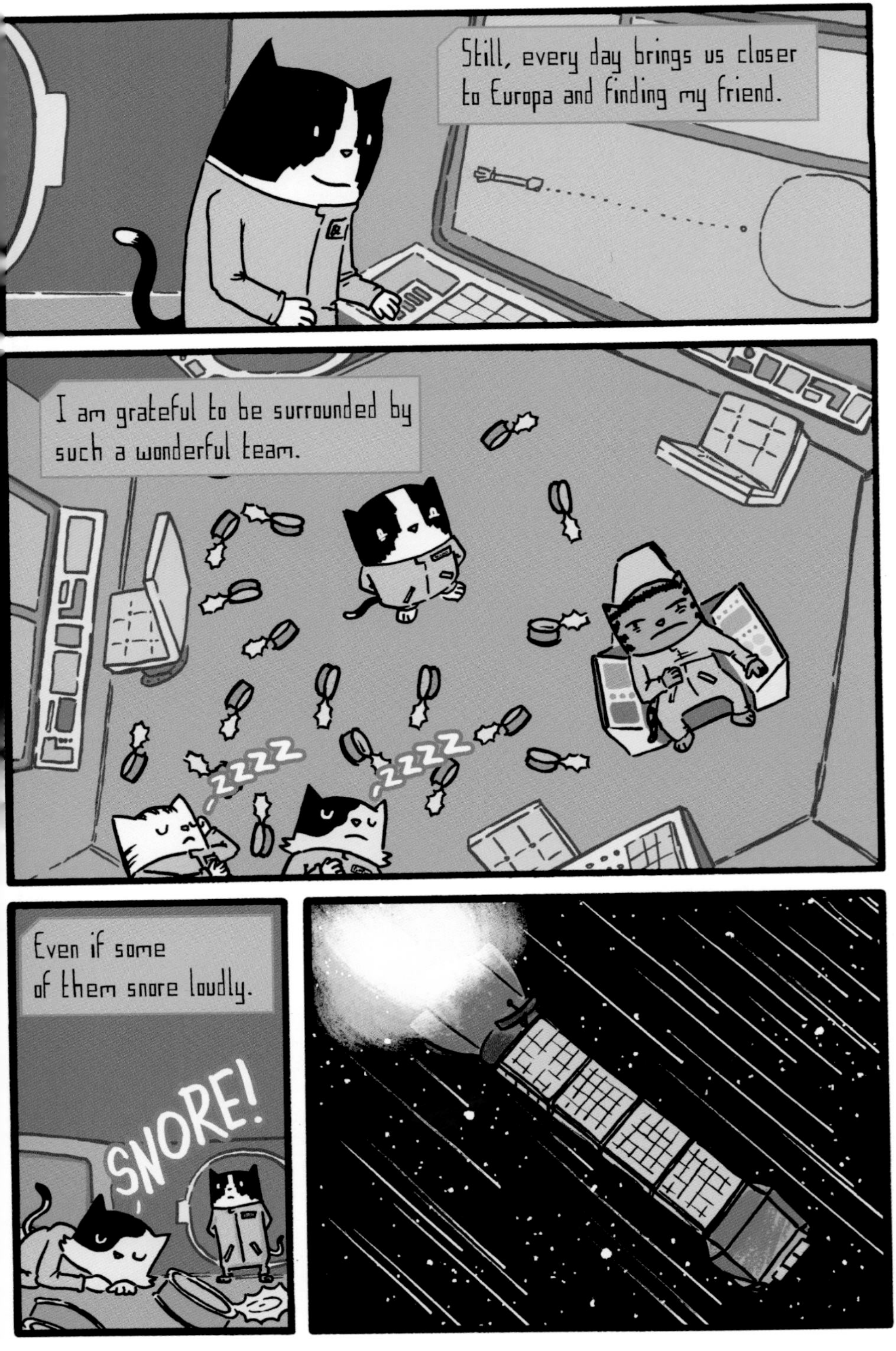
Still, every day brings us closer to Europa and finding my friend.
I am grateful to be surrounded by such a wonderful team.
ZZZZ
ZZZZ
Even if some of them snore loudly.
SNORE!

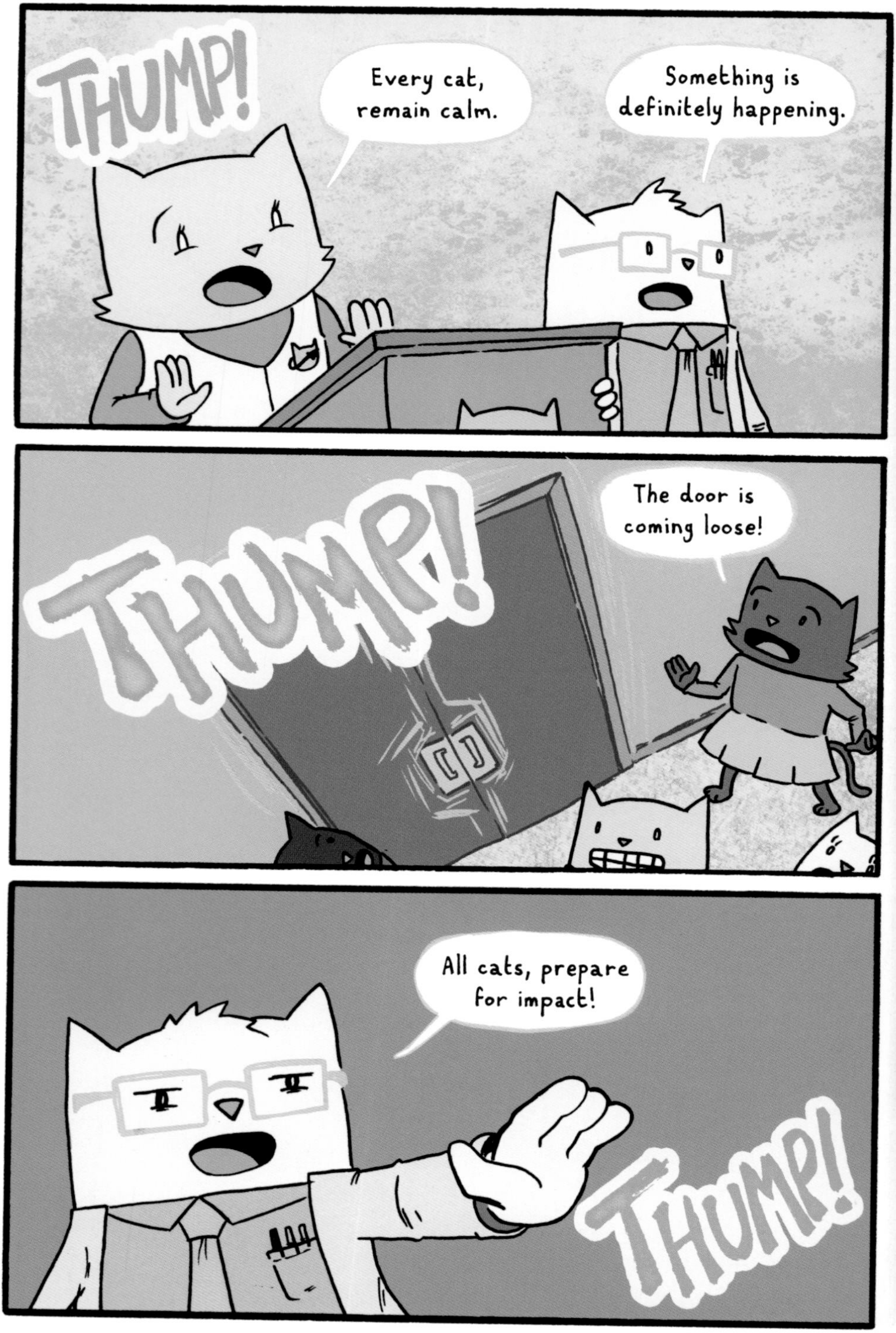
THUMP!
Every cat, remain calm.
Something is definitely happening.
THUMP!
The door is coming loose!
All cats, prepare for impact!
THUMP!

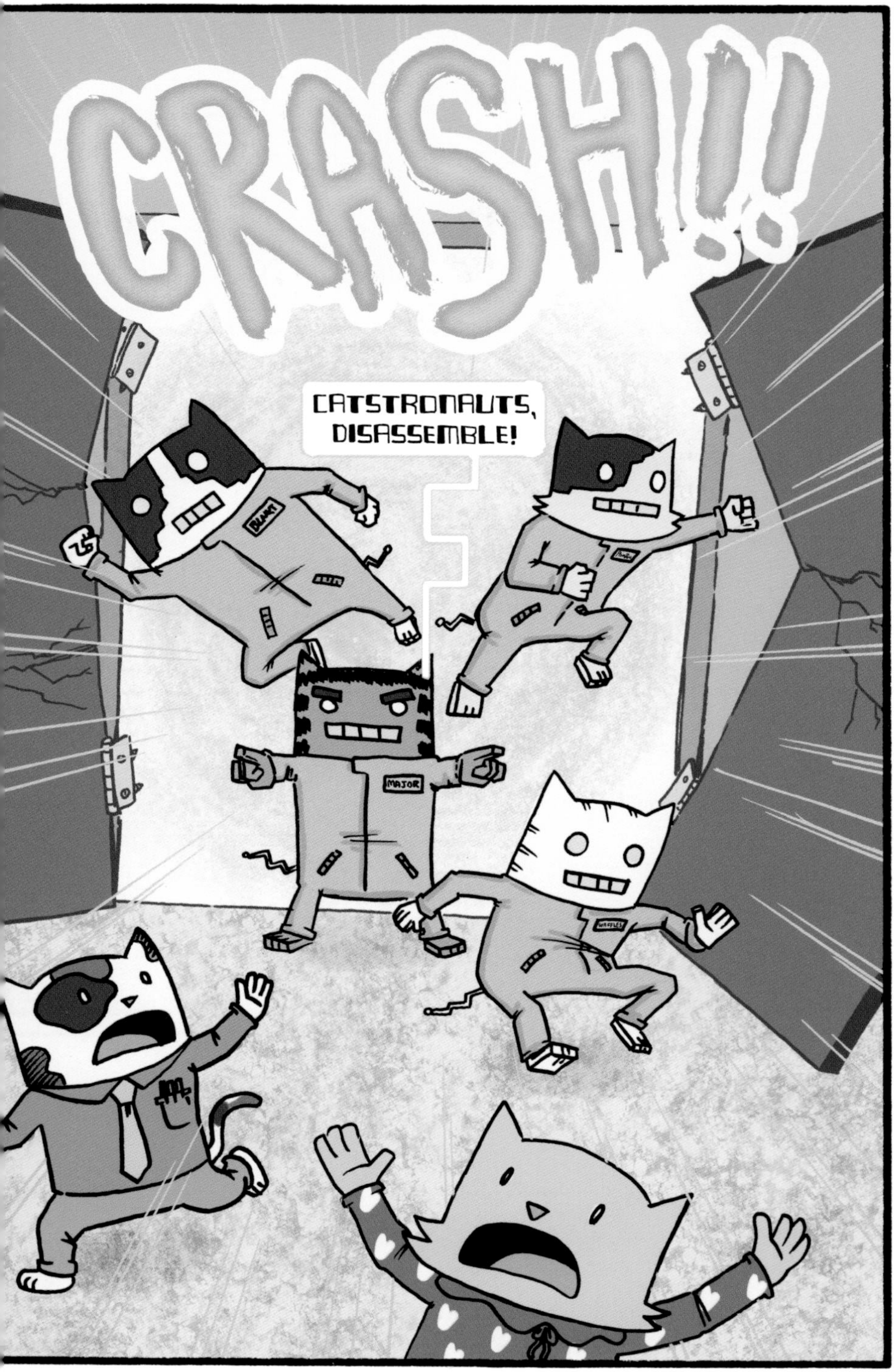
CRASH!!
CATSTRONAUTS, DISASSEMBLE!
MAJOR

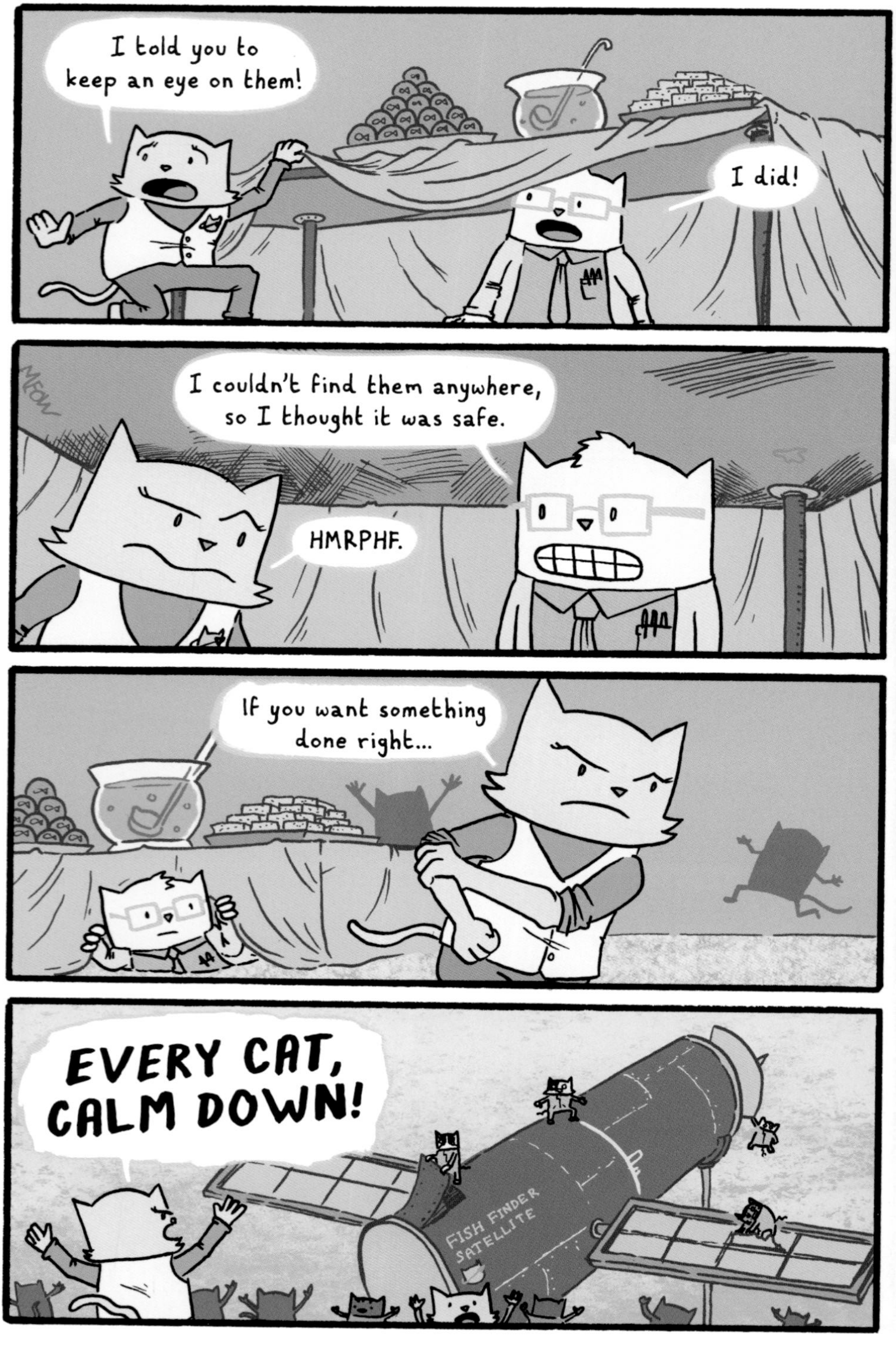

I told you to keep an eye on them!
I did!
MEOW
I couldn't find them anywhere, so I thought it was safe.
HMRPHF.
If you want something done right...
EVERY CAT, CALM DOWN!
FISH FINDER SATELLITE

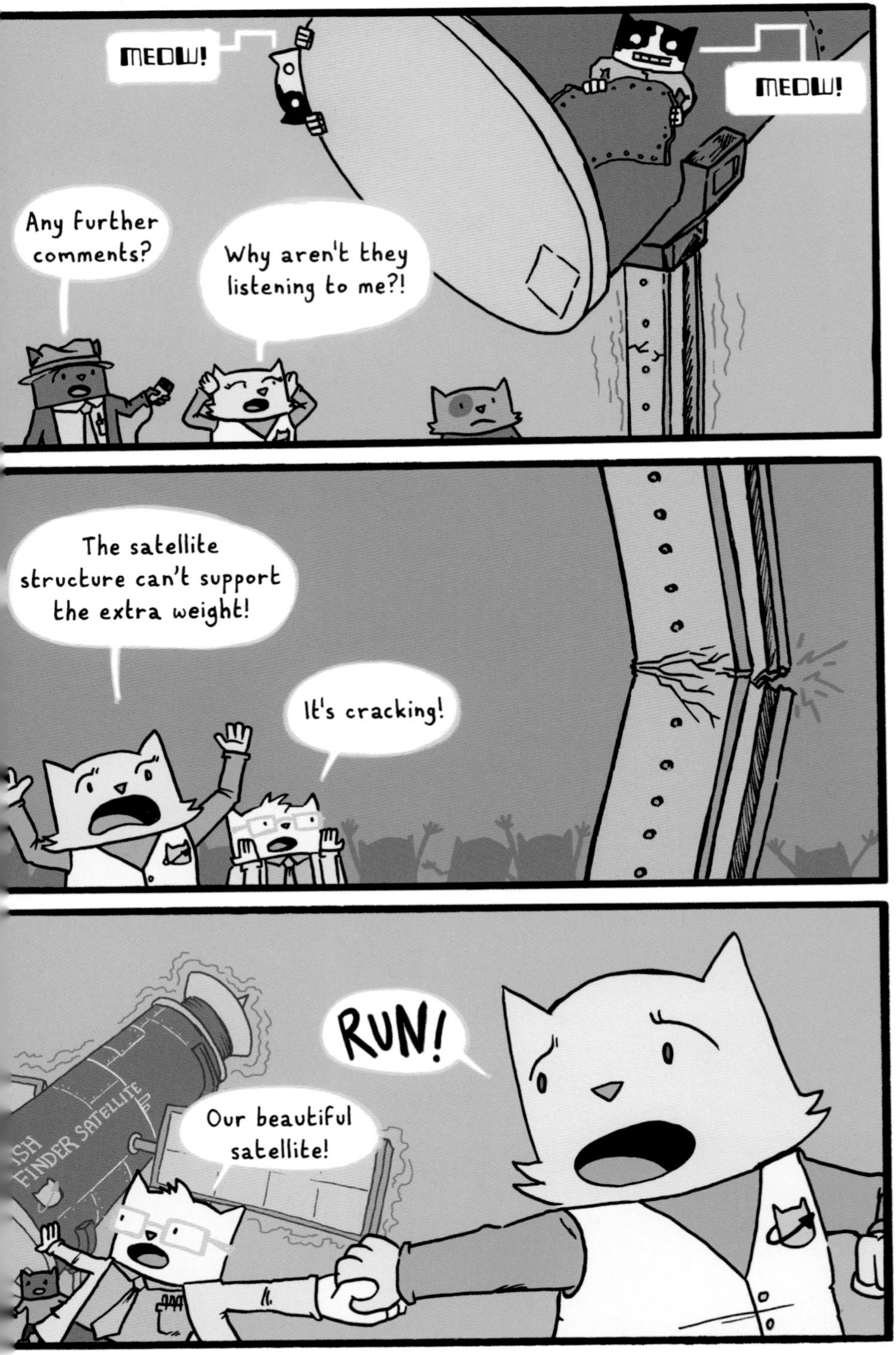
MEOW!
MEOW!
Any further comments?
Why aren't they listening to me?!
The satellite structure can't support the extra weight!
It's cracking!
RUN!
FINDER SATELLITE
Our beautiful satellite!

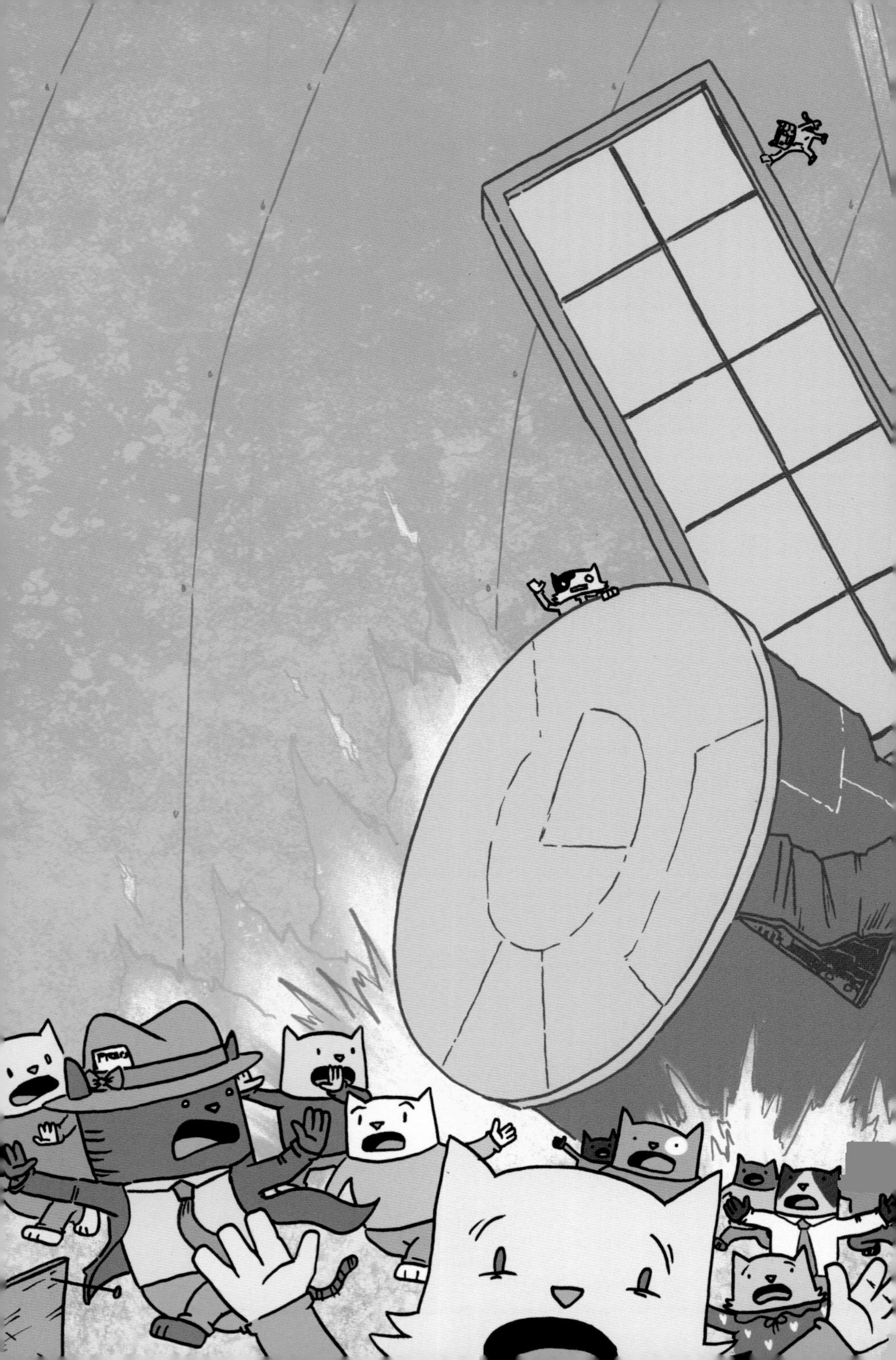

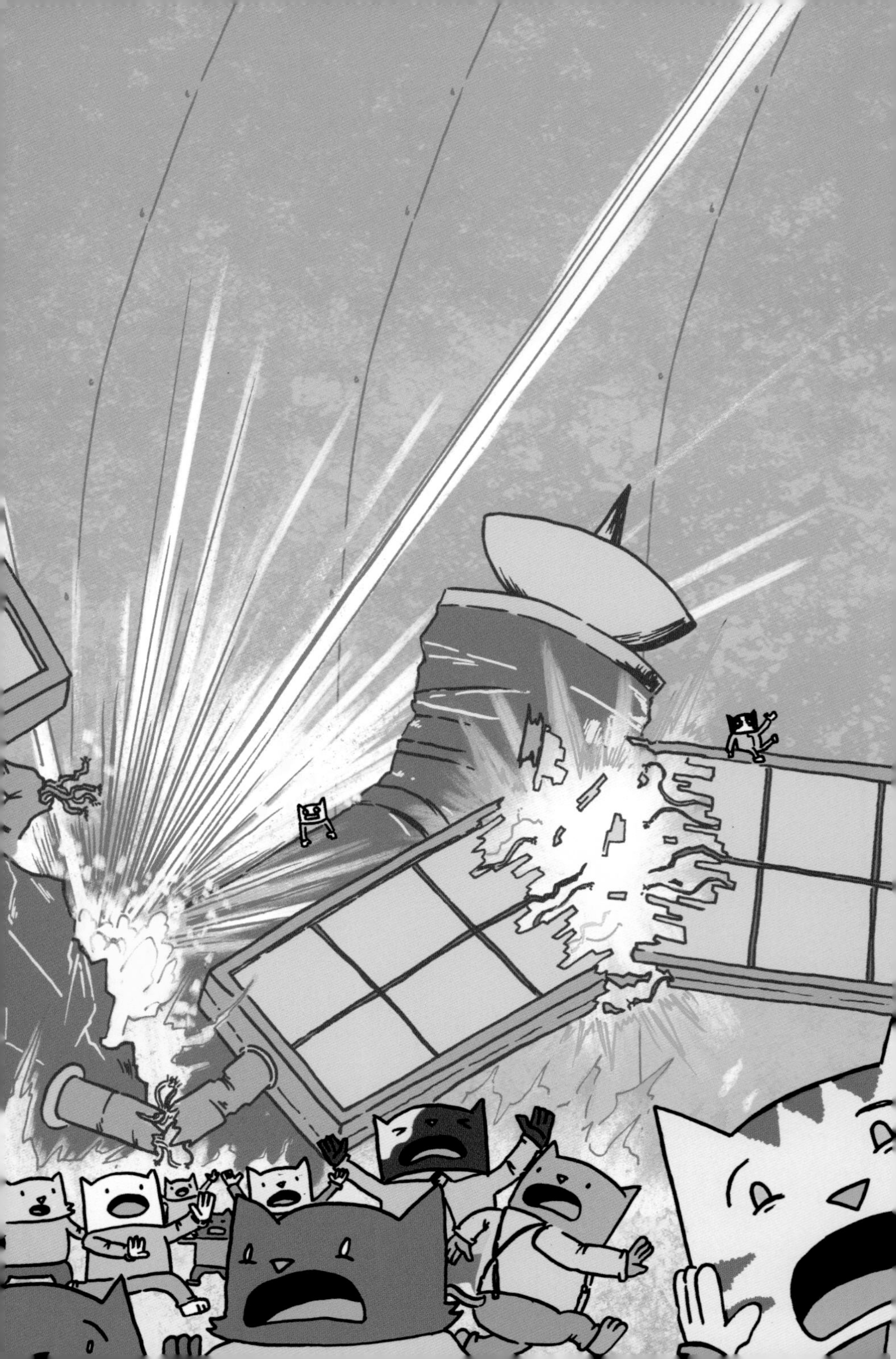

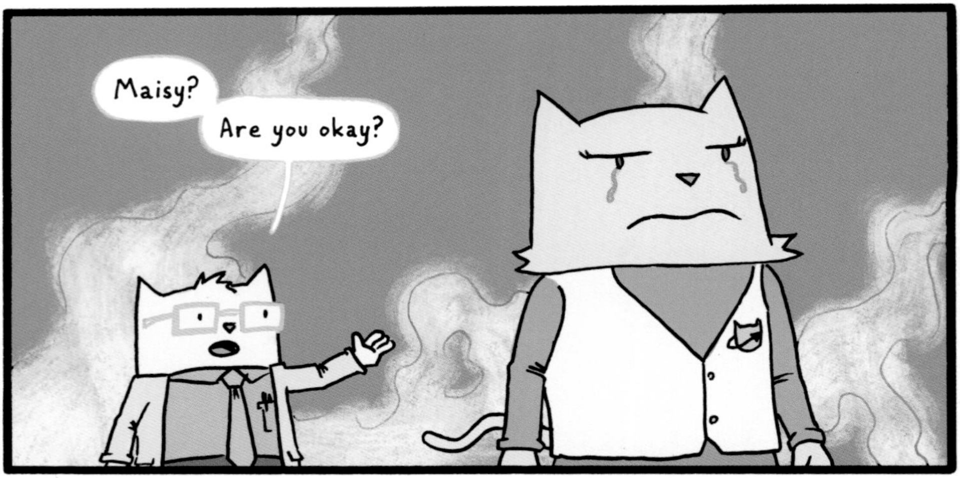
Maisy?
Are you okay?

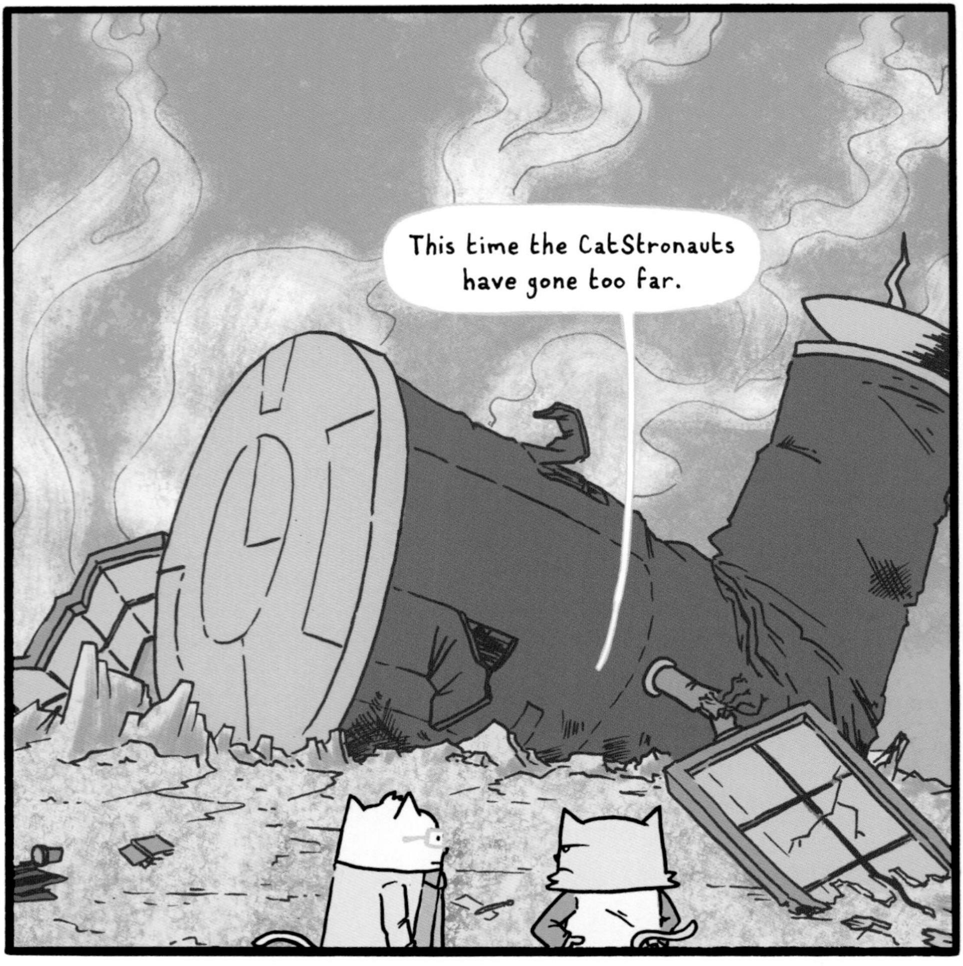
This time the CatStronauts have gone too far.

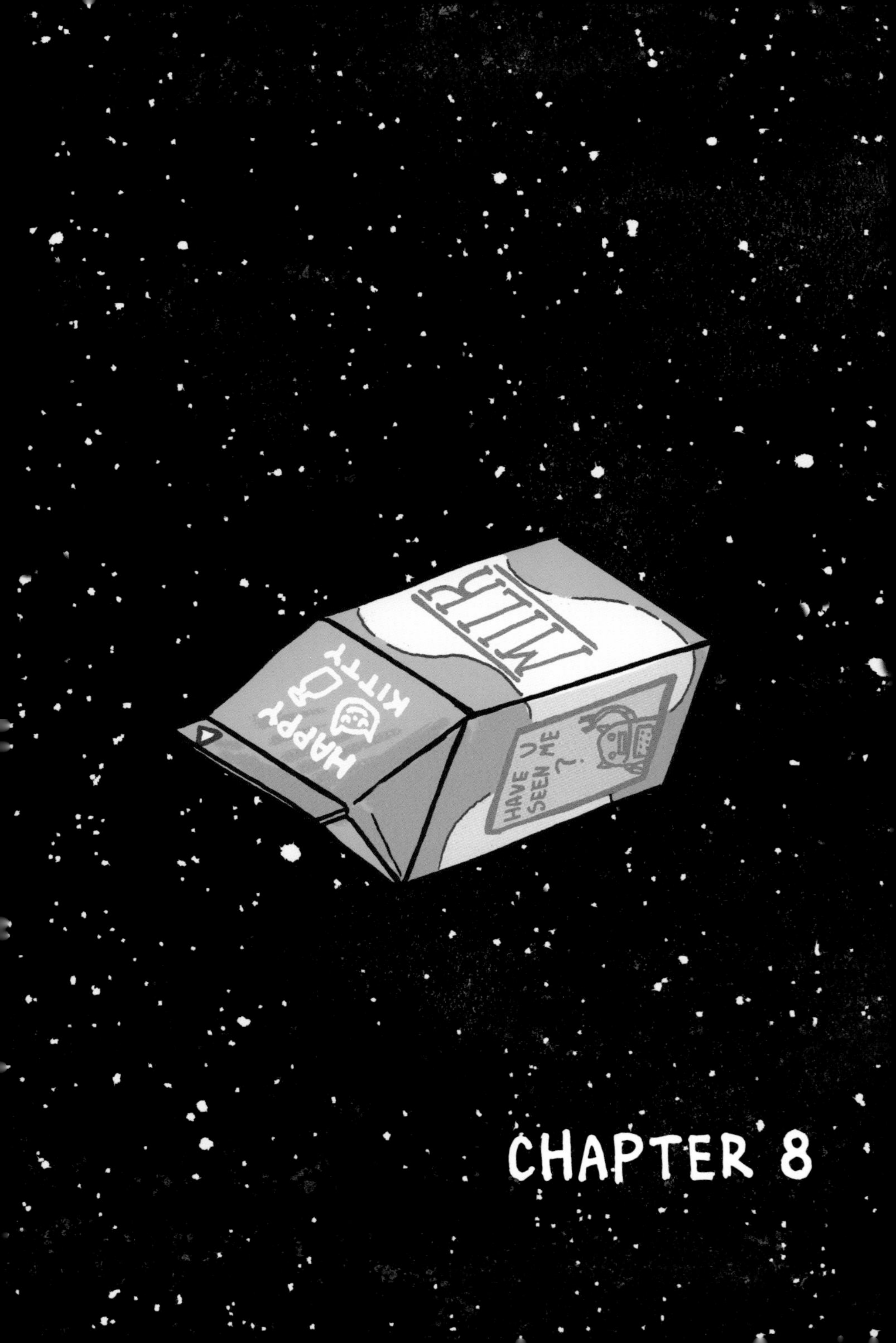
MILK
HAPPY
KITTY
HAVE U
SEEN ME
?

CHAPTER 8

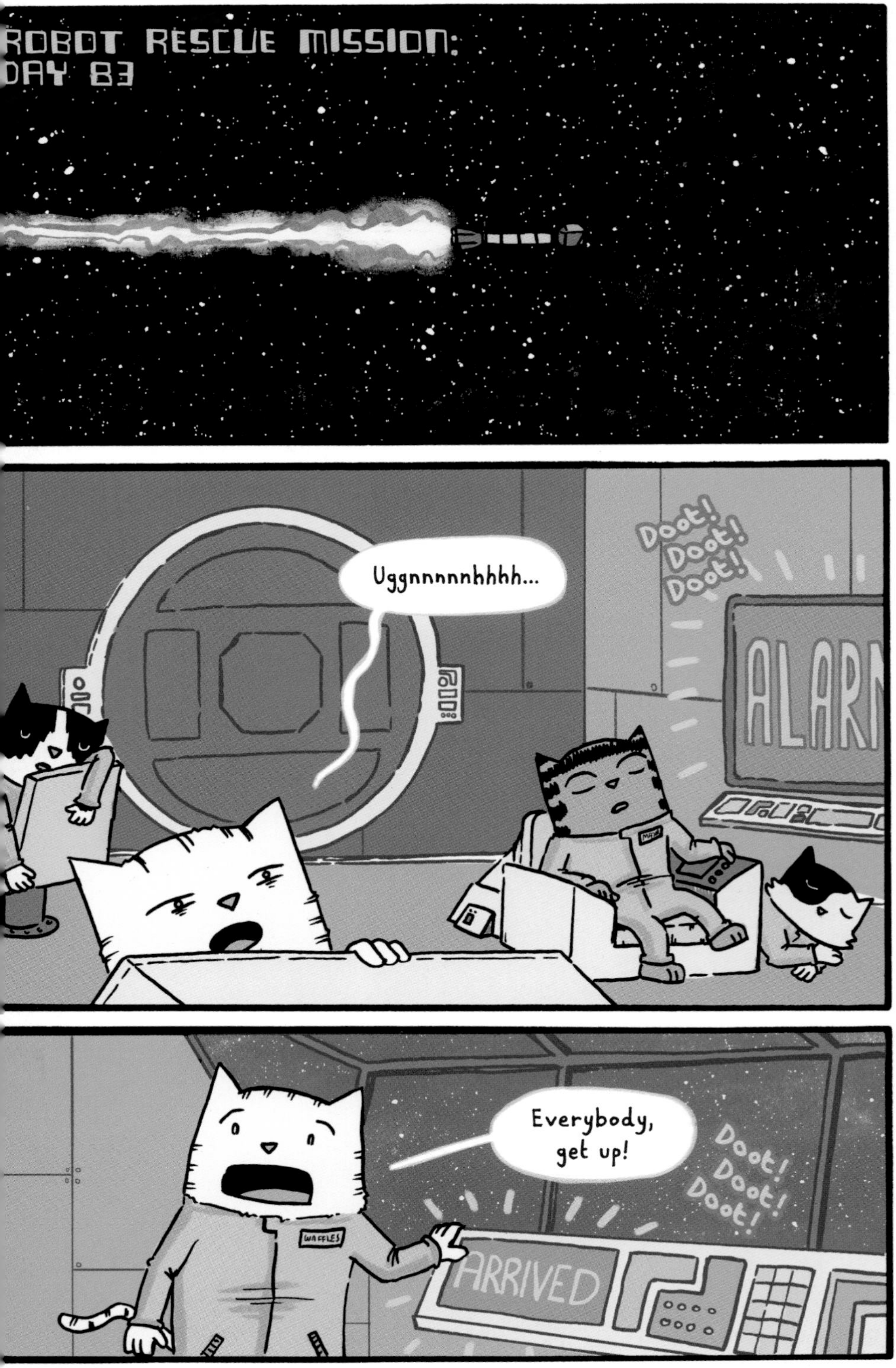
ROBOT RESCUE MISSION:
DAY 83
Uggnnnnnhhhh...
Doot! Doot! Doot!
ALARM
Everybody, get up!
Doot! Doot! Doot!
WAFFLES
ARRIVED

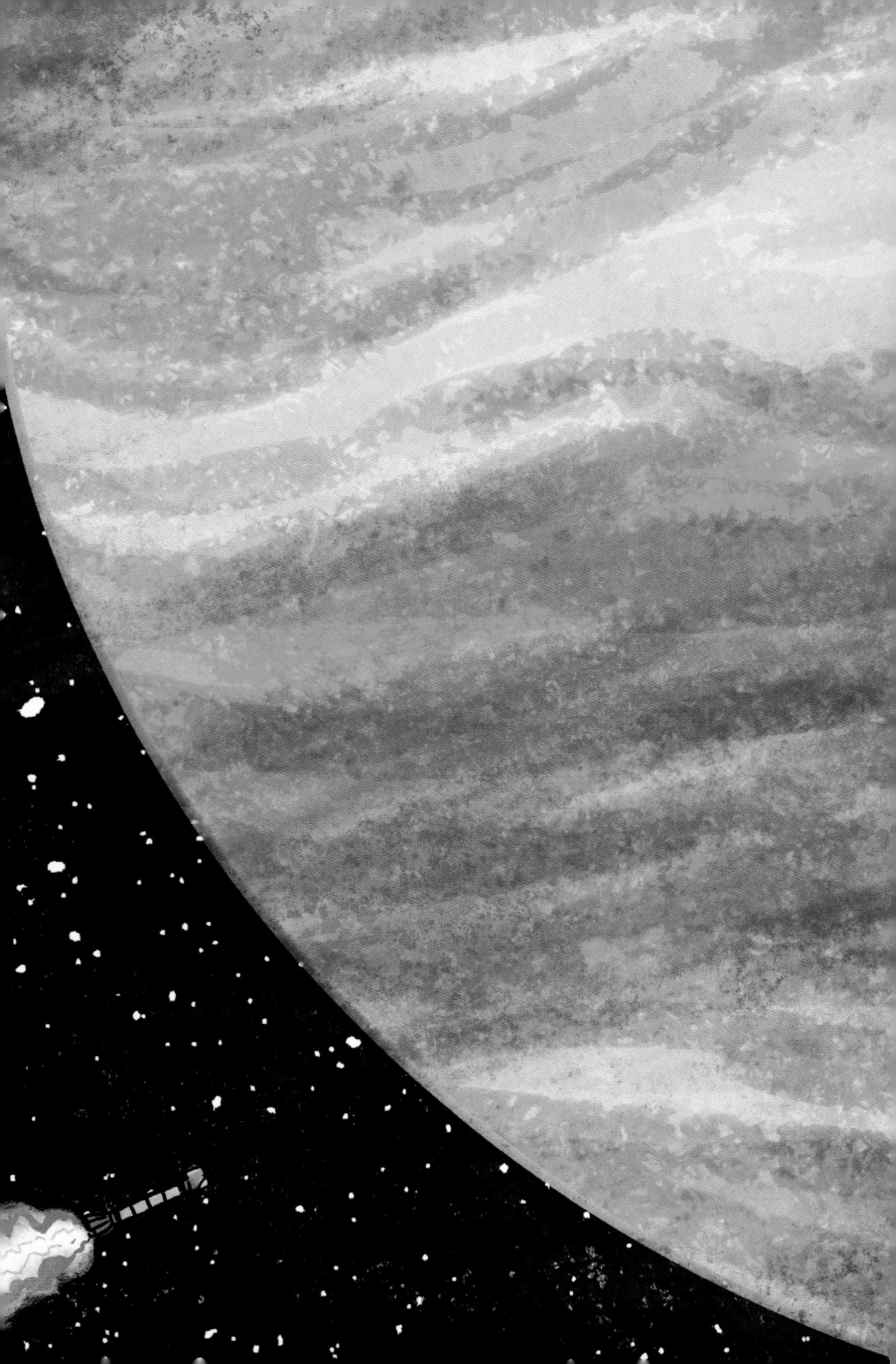

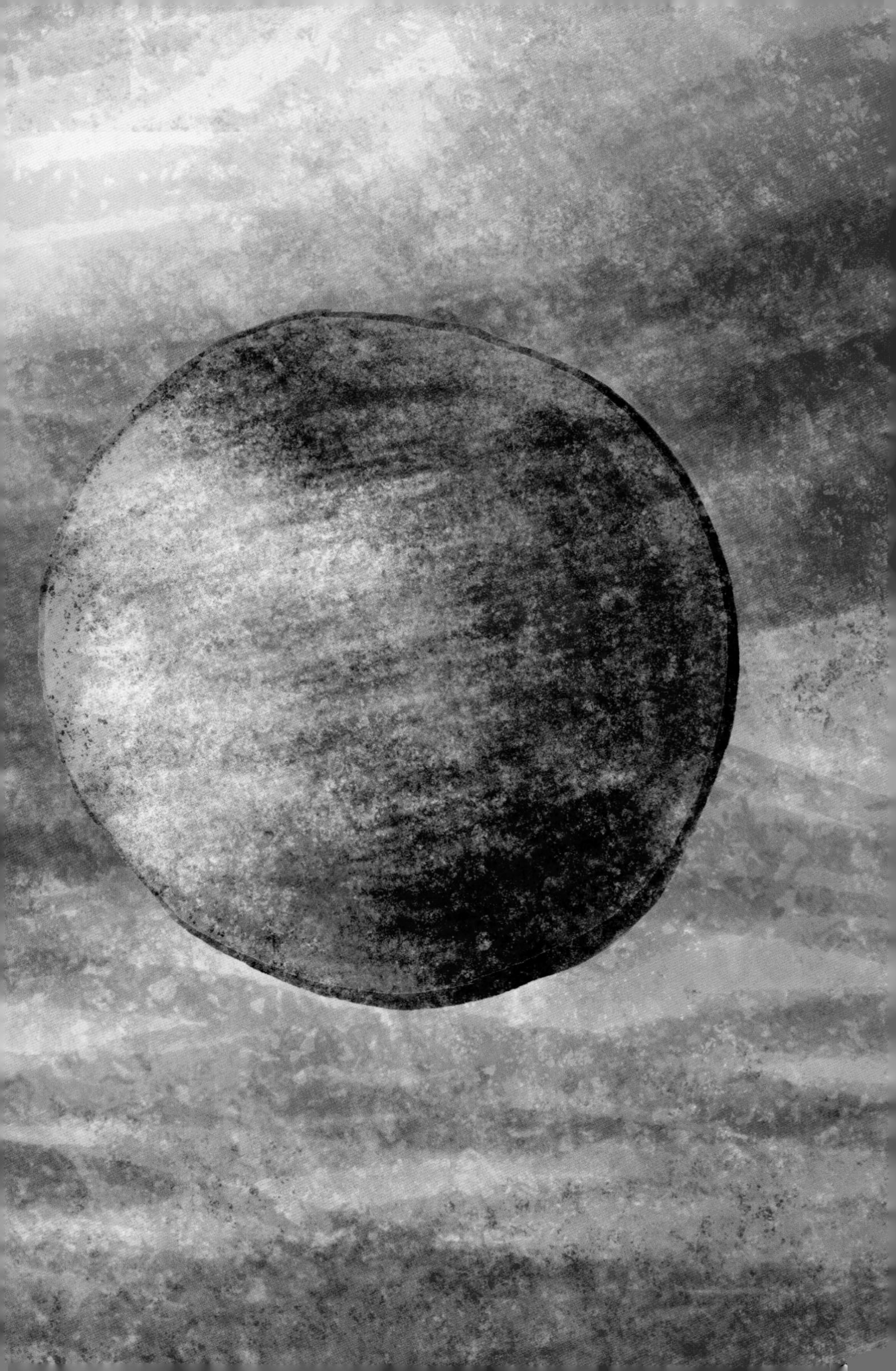

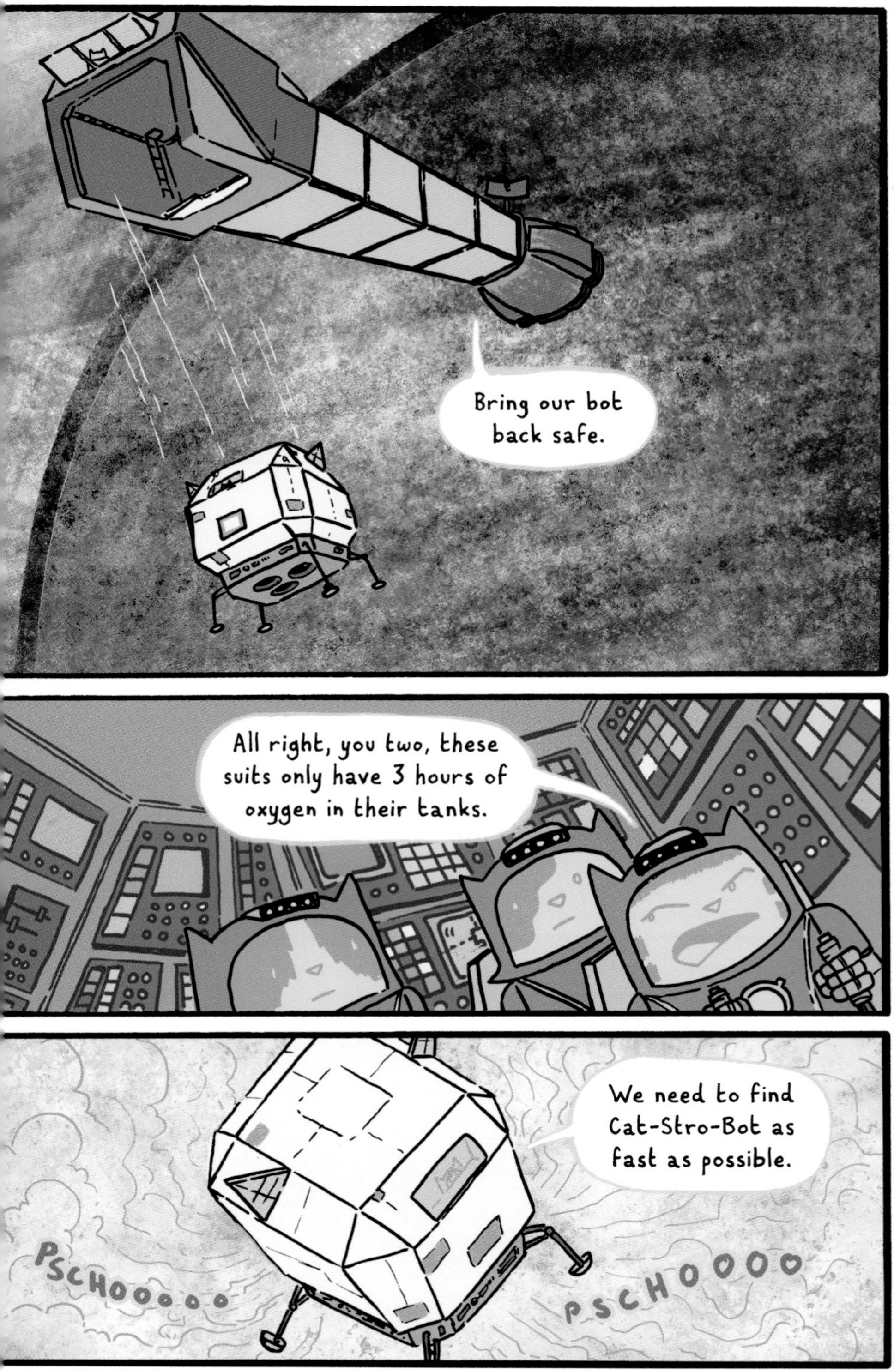
Bring our bot back safe.
All right, you two, these suits only have 3 hours of oxygen in their tanks.
We need to find Cat-Stro-Bot as fast as possible.
PSCHOOOOOO
PSCHOOOOO

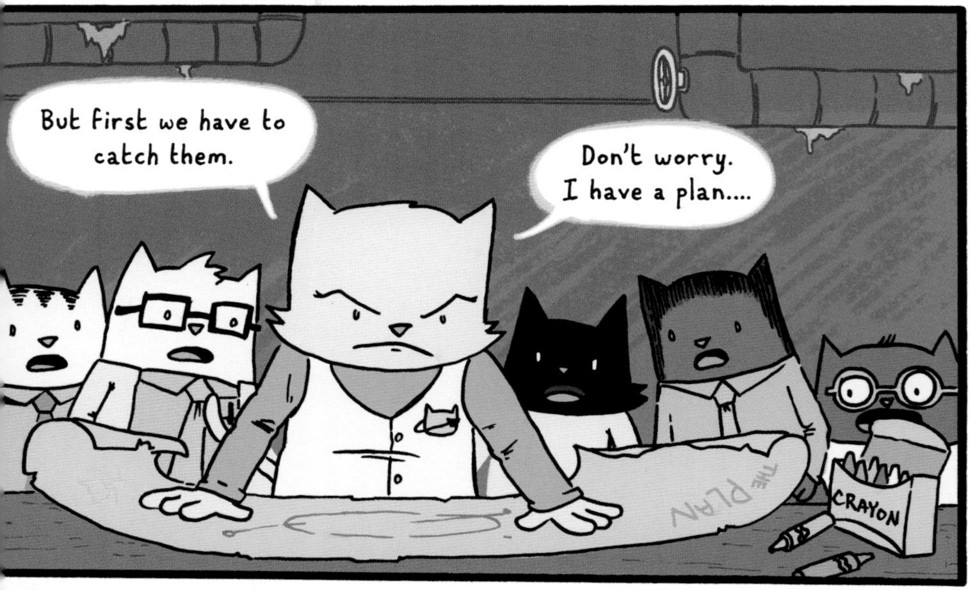
But first we have to catch them.
Don't worry. I have a plan....
THE PLAN
CRAYON

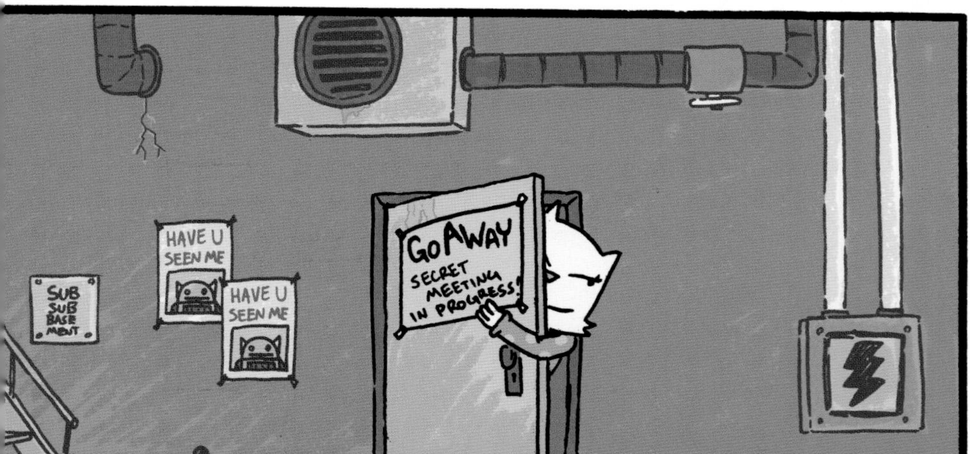
SUB SUB BASE MENT
HAVE U SEEN ME
HAVE U SEEN ME
GO AWAY
SECRET MEETING IN PROGRESS!

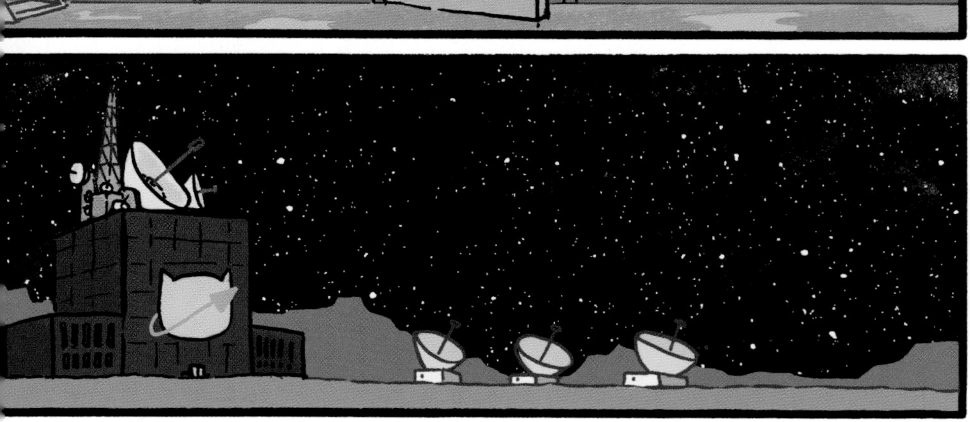

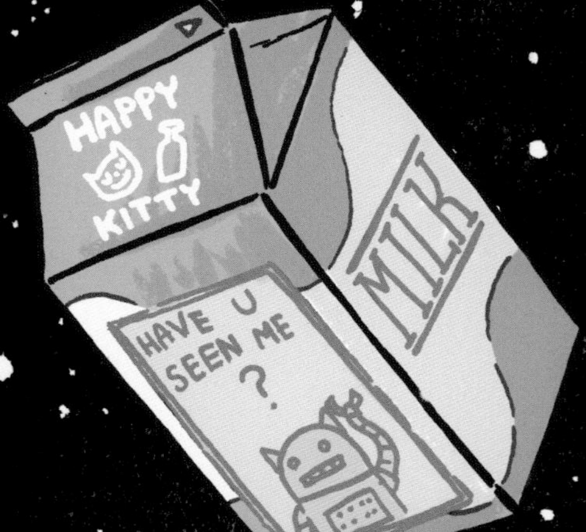
HAPPY
KITTY
MILK
HAVE U
SEEN ME
?

CHAPTER 9

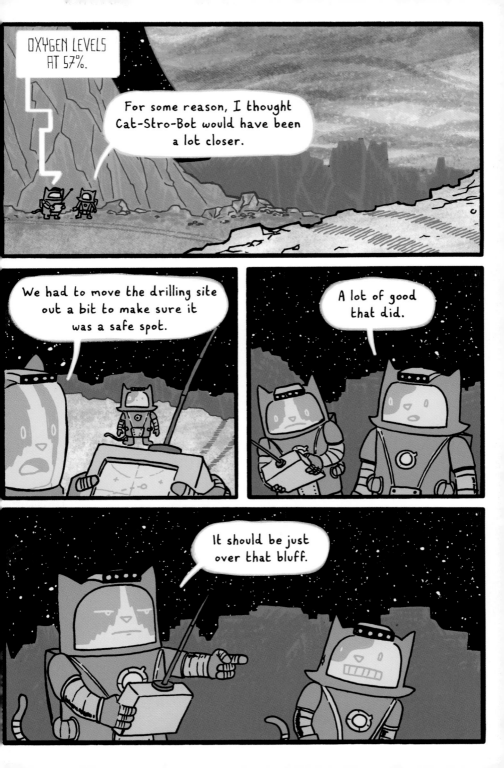

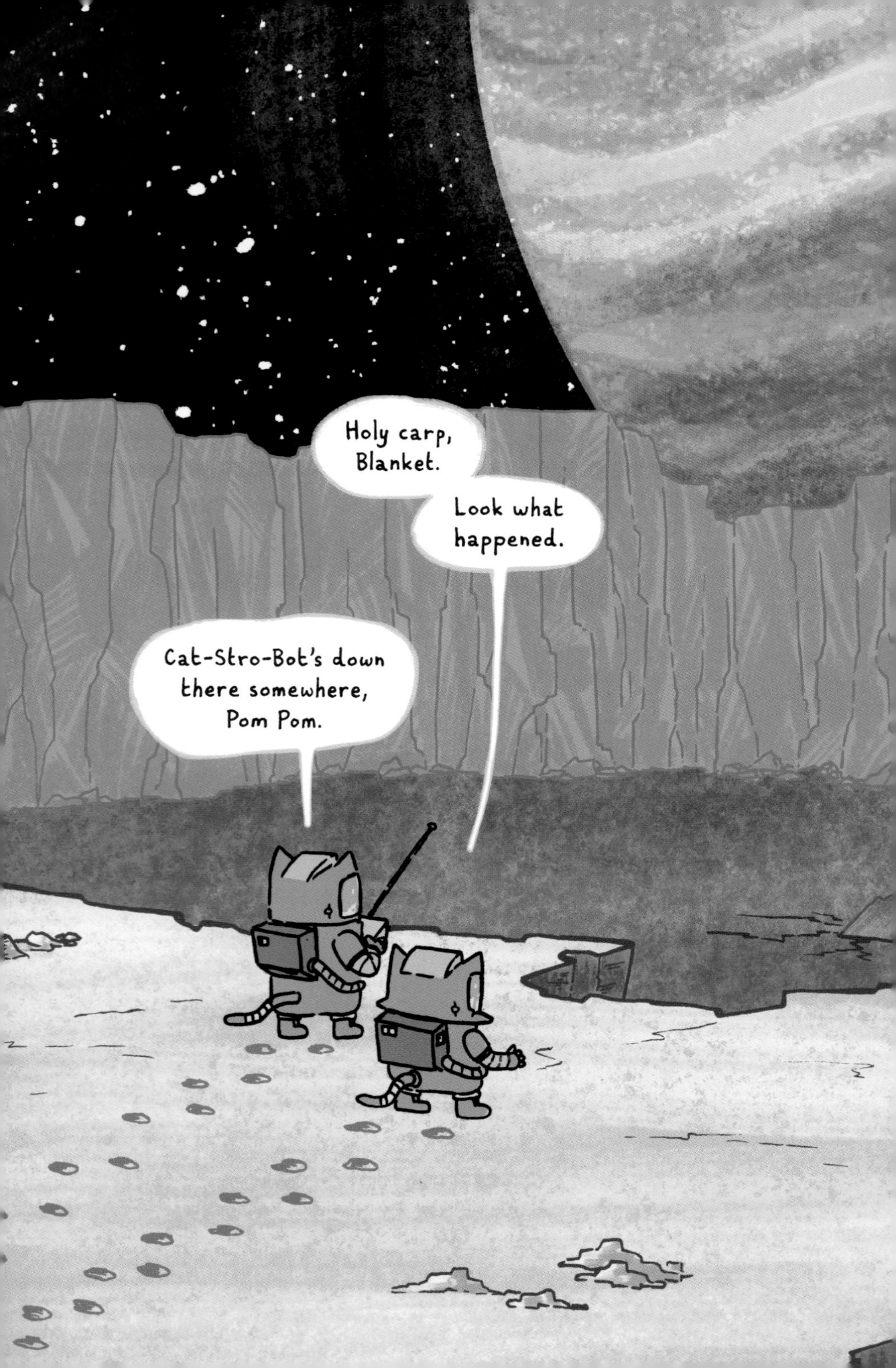
Holy carp, Blanket.
Look what happened.
Cat-Stro-Bot's down there somewhere, Pom Pom.

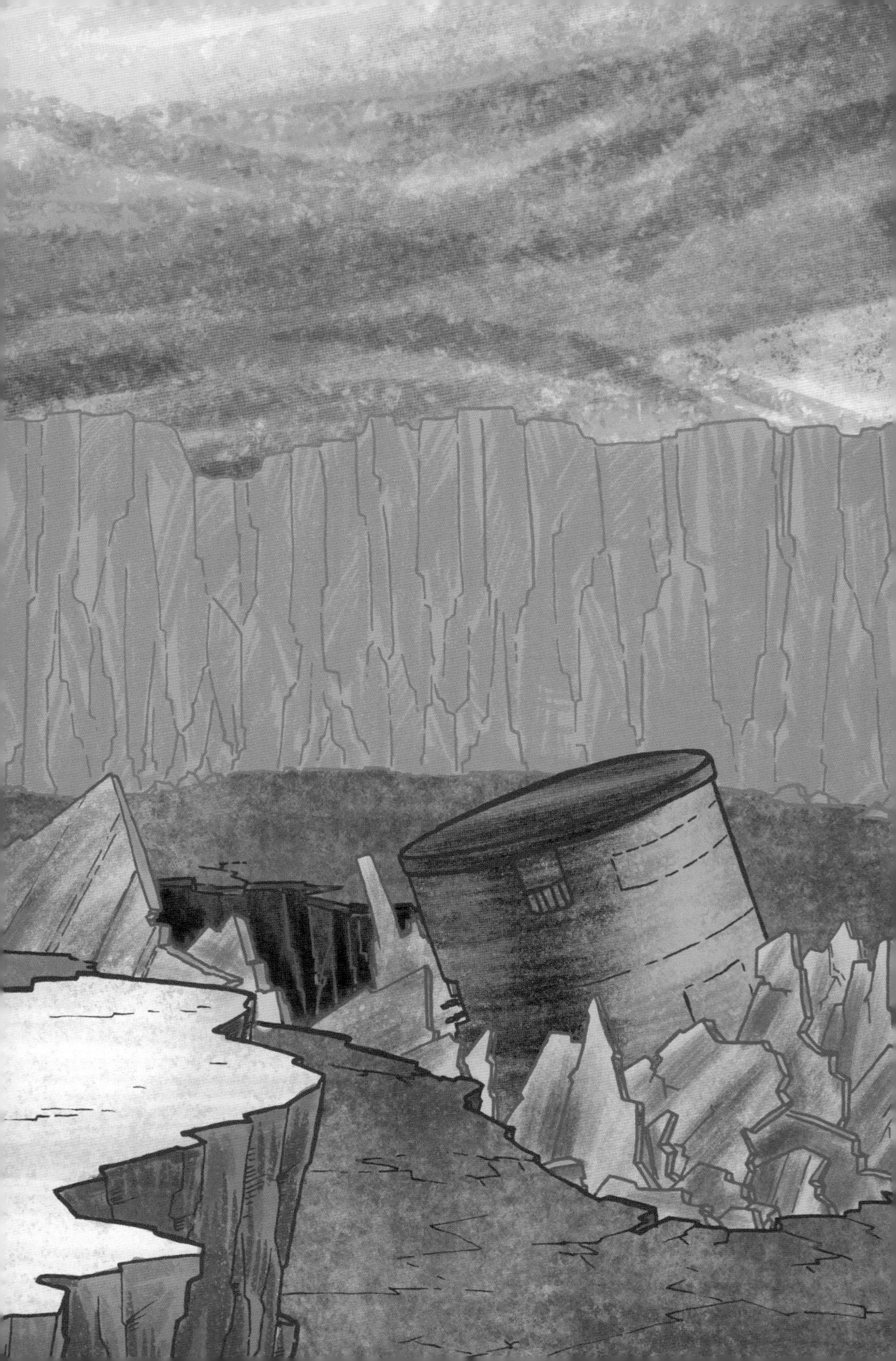

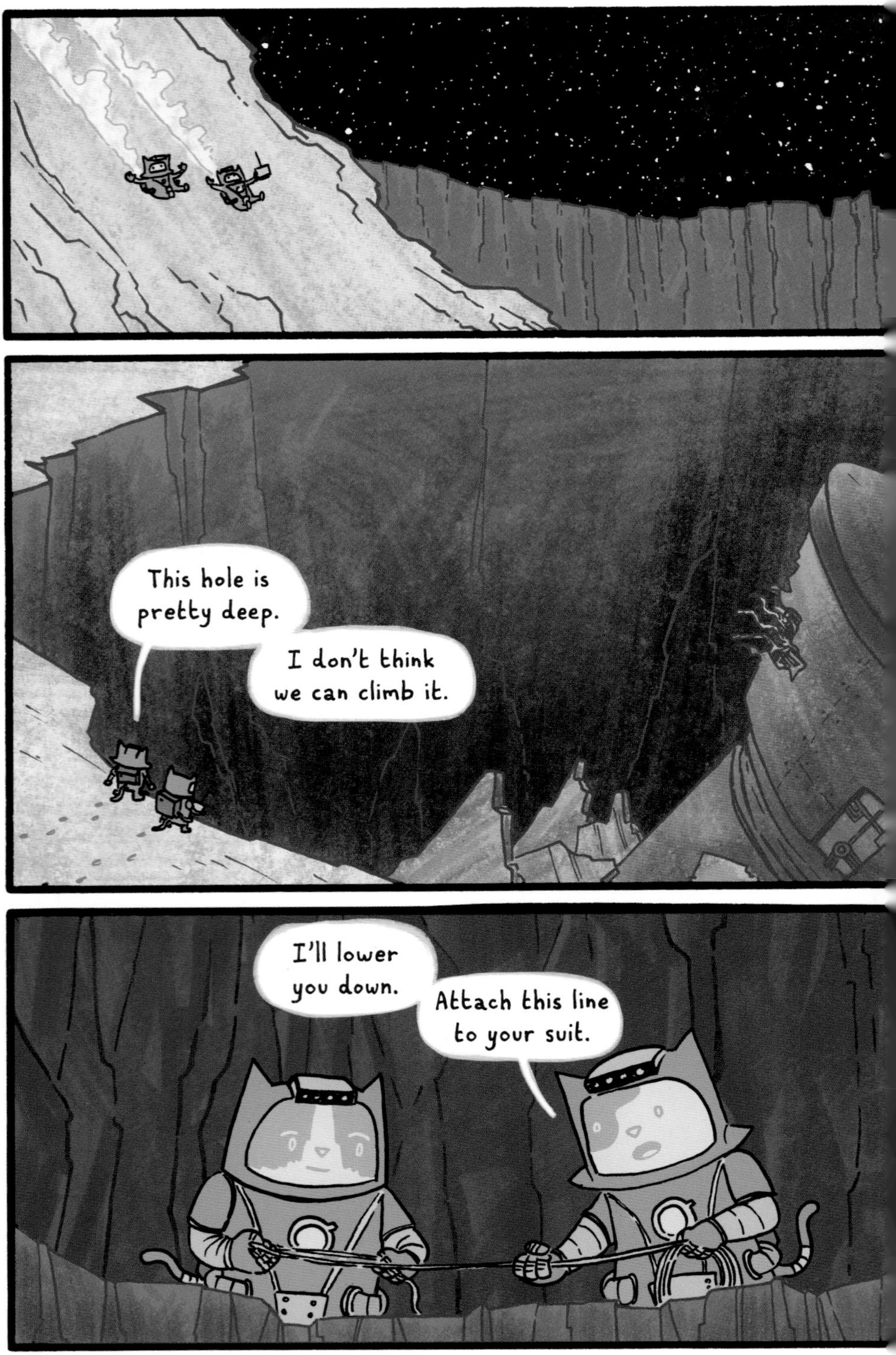
This hole is pretty deep.
I don't think we can climb it.
I'll lower you down.
Attach this line to your suit.

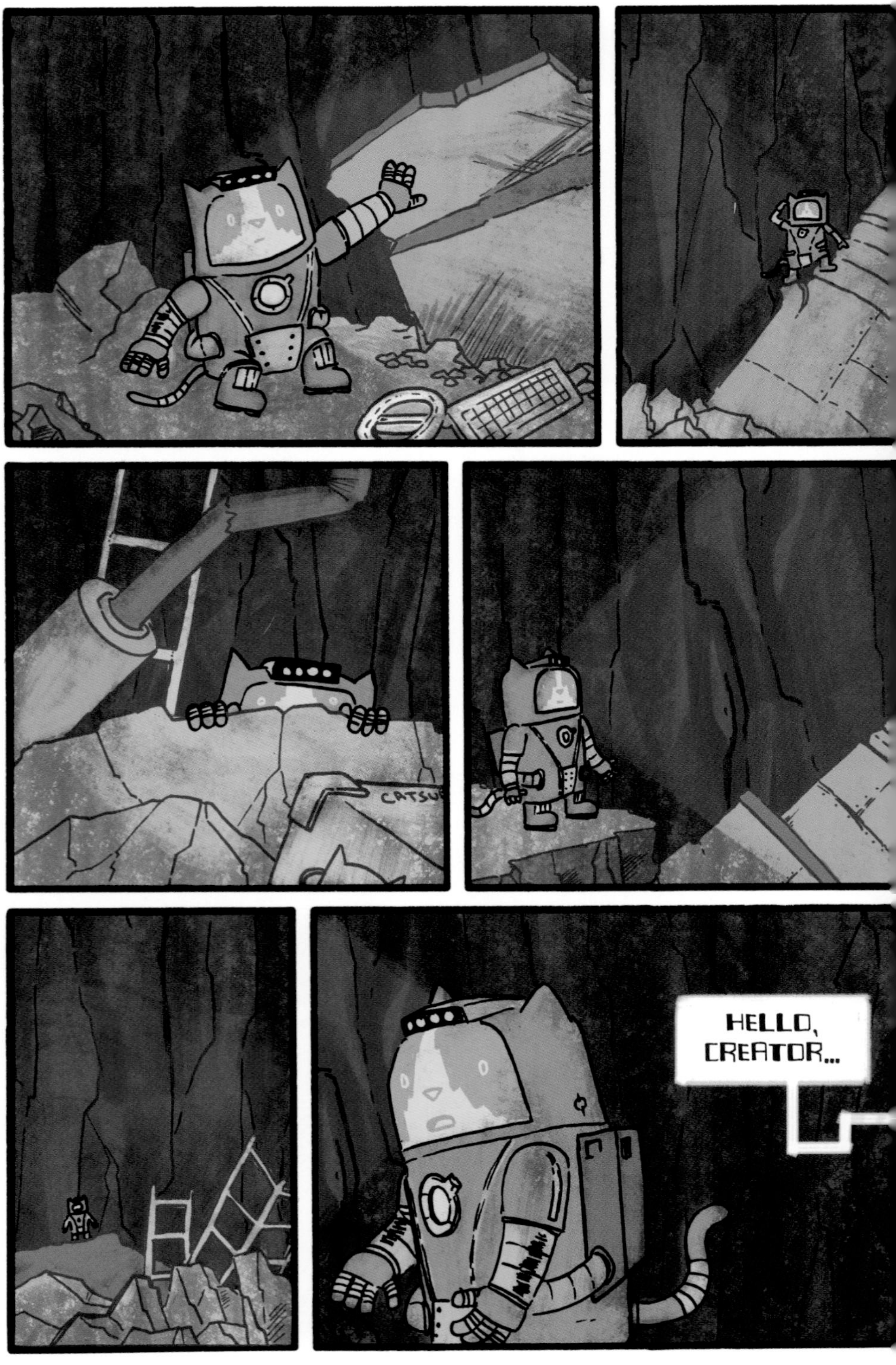
HELLO, CREATOR...

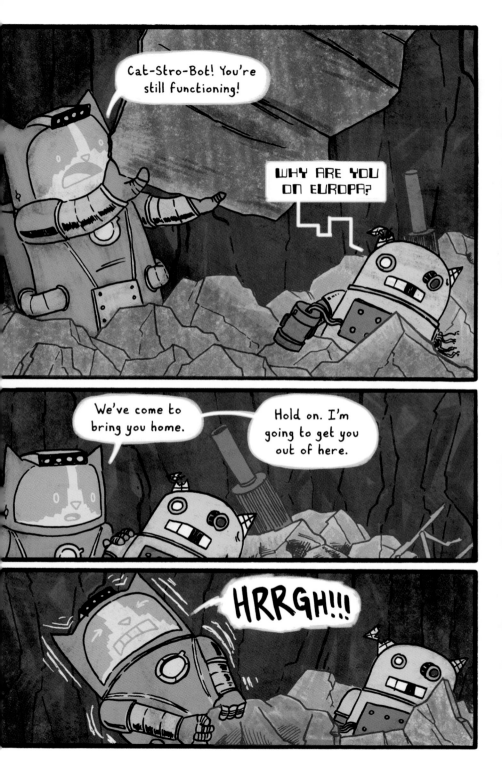

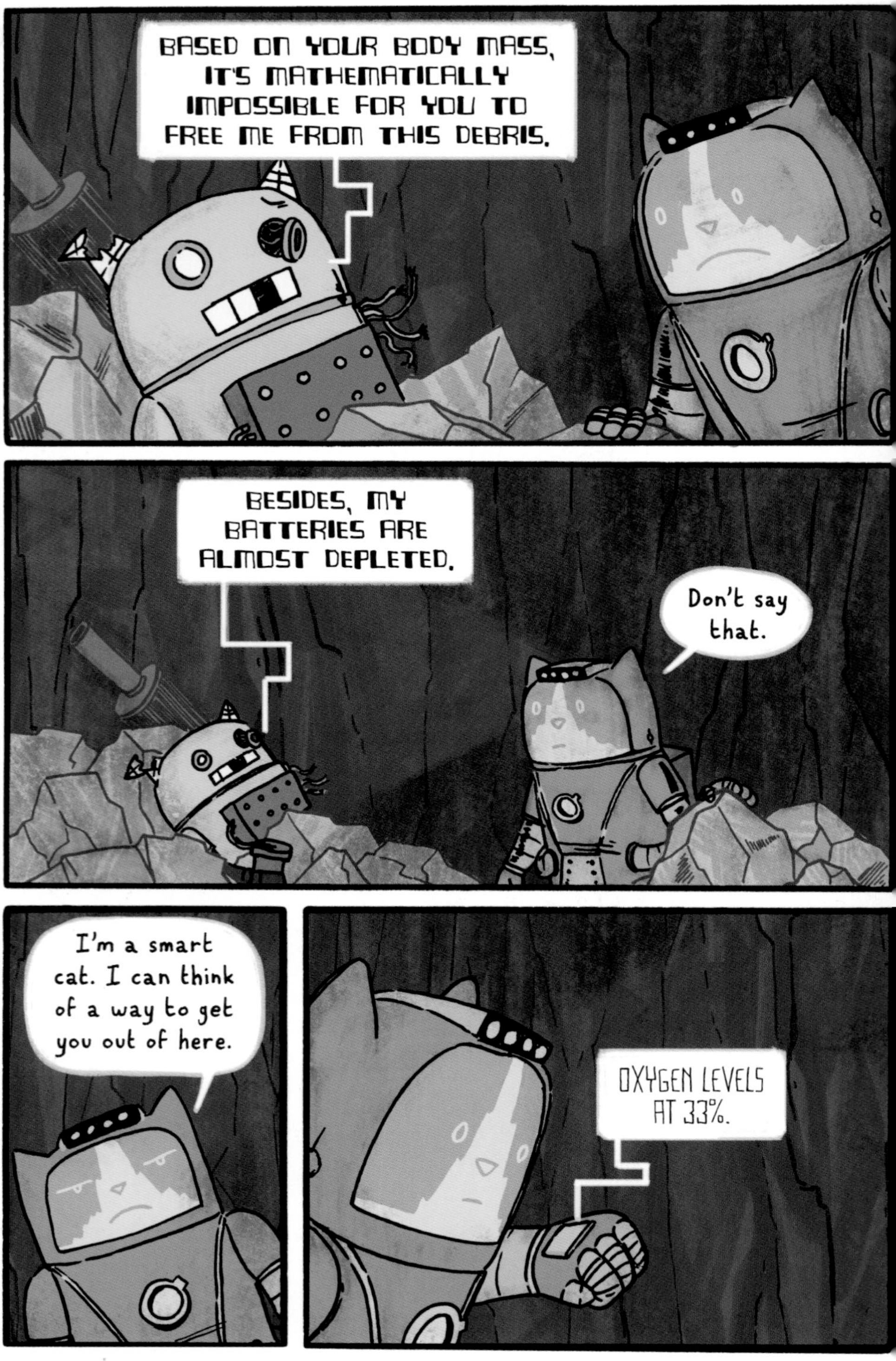
BASED ON YOUR BODY MASS, IT'S MATHEMATICALLY IMPOSSIBLE FOR YOU TO FREE ME FROM THIS DEBRIS.
BESIDES, MY BATTERIES ARE ALMOST DEPLETED.
Don't say that.
I'm a smart cat. I can think of a way to get you out of here.
OXYGEN LEVELS AT 33%.

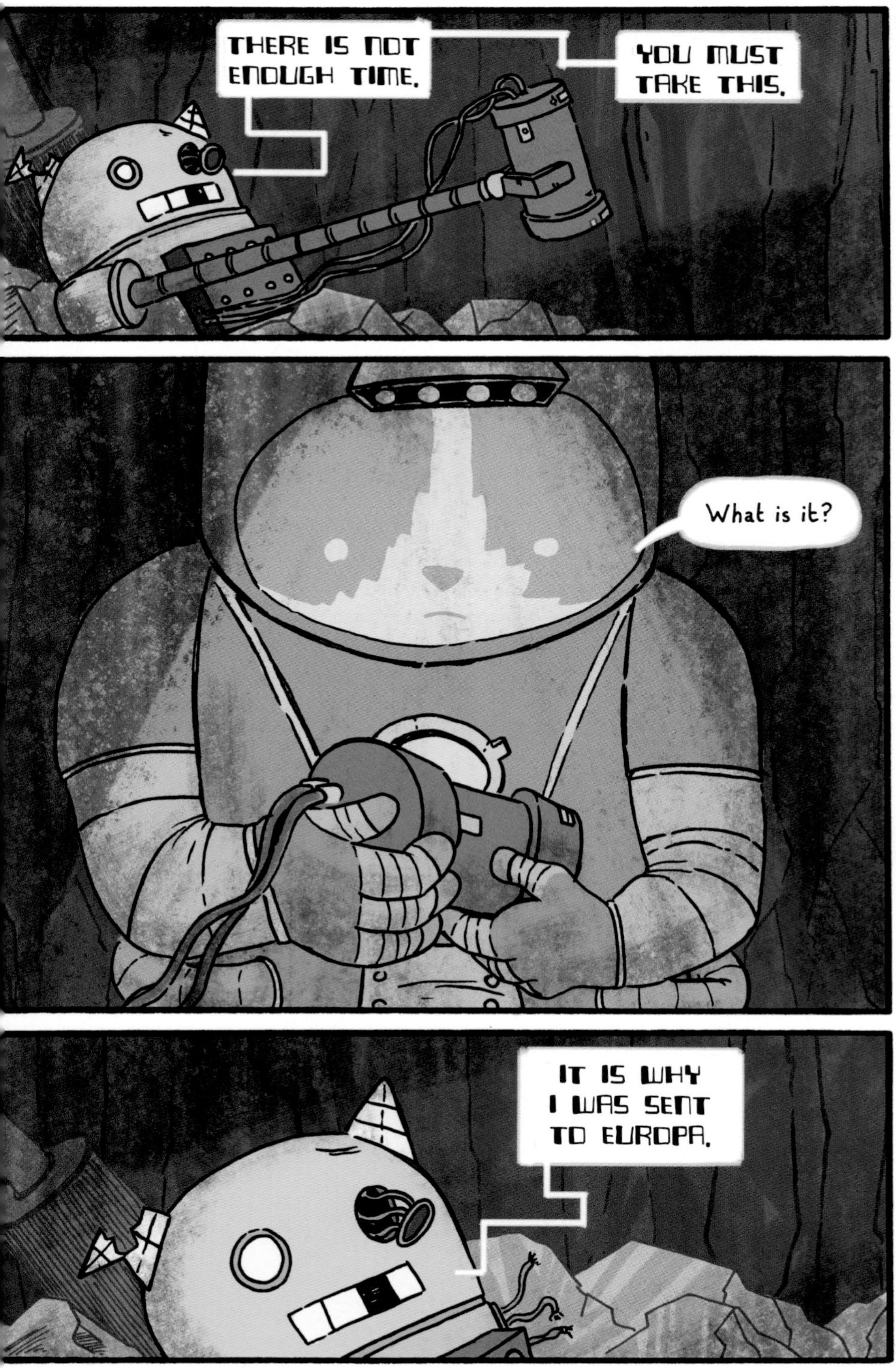

THERE IS NOT ENOUGH TIME.
YOU MUST TAKE THIS.
What is it?
IT IS WHY I WAS SENT TO EUROPA.

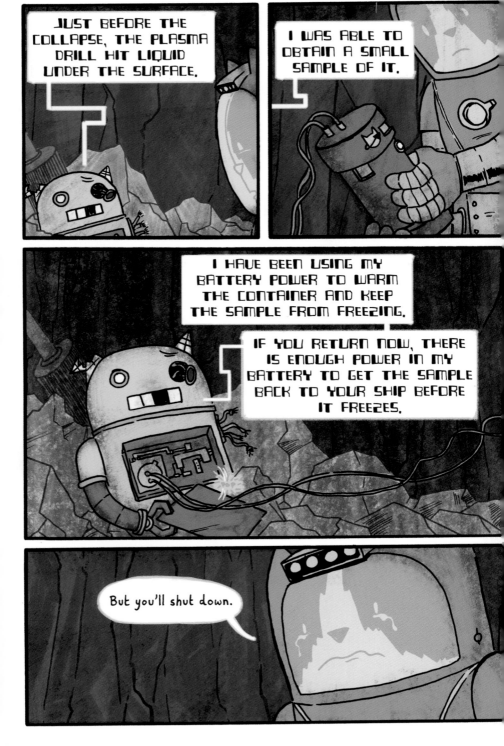

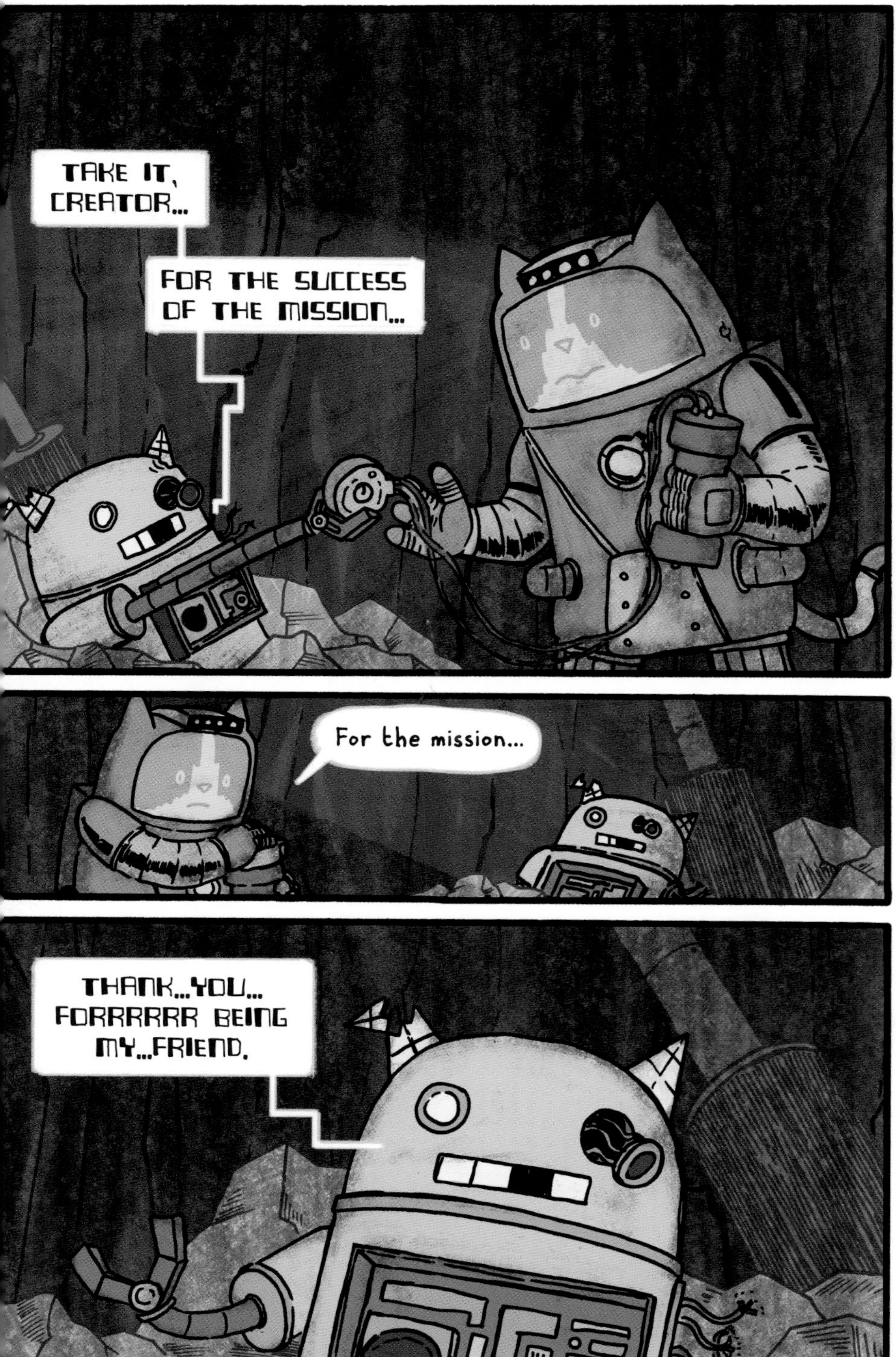
TAKE IT, CREATOR...
FOR THE SUCCESS OF THE MISSION...
For the mission...
THANK...YOU... FORRRRRR BEING MY...FRIEND.

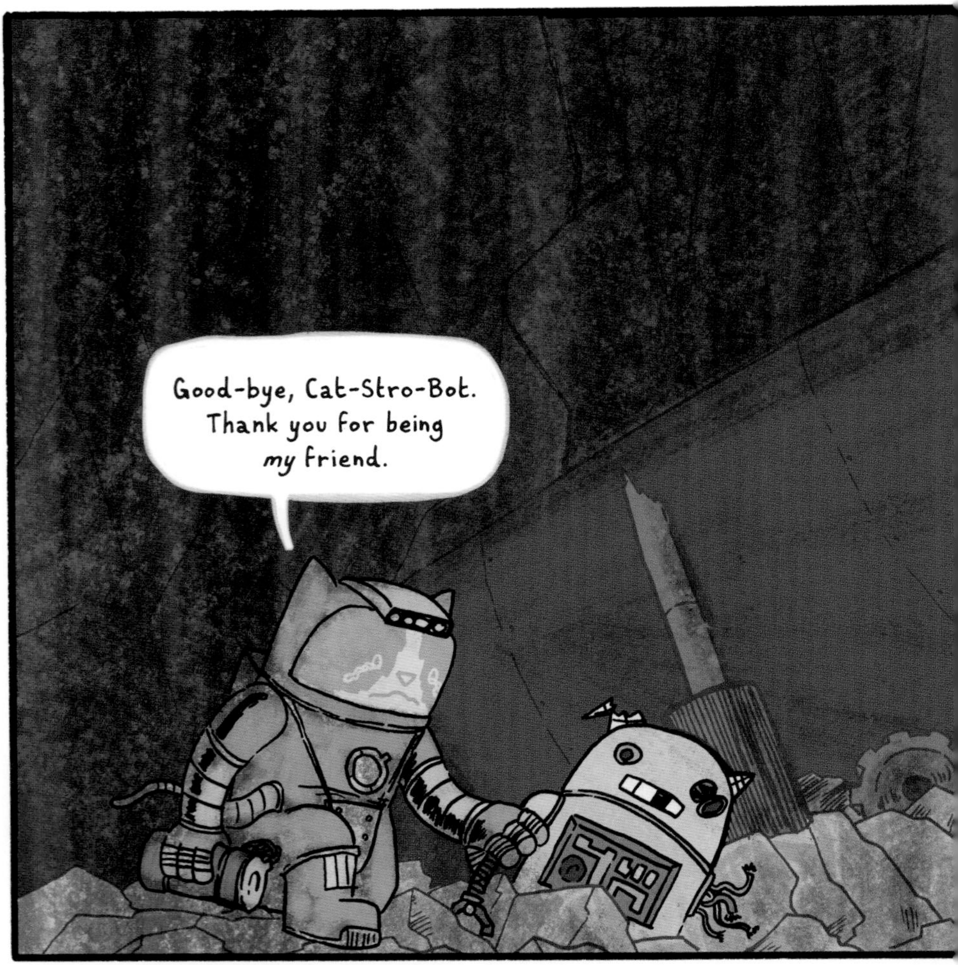
Good-bye, Cat-Stro-Bot. Thank you for being *my* friend.

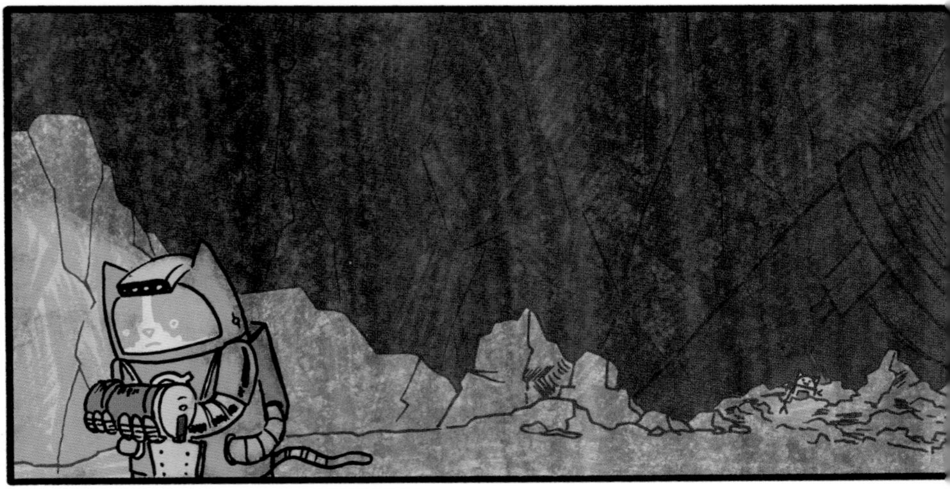

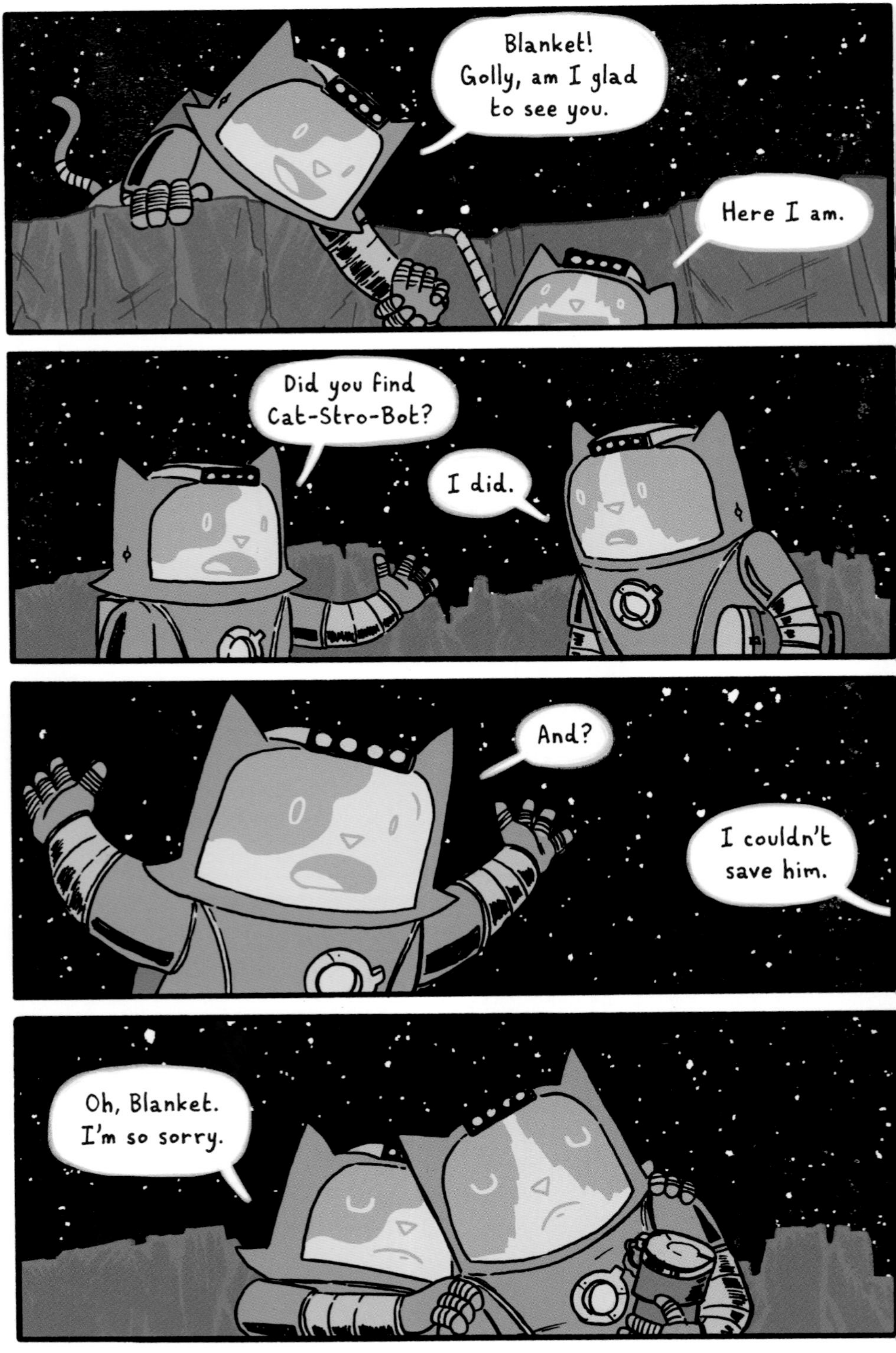
Blanket!
Golly, am I glad to see you.
Here I am.
Did you find Cat-Stro-Bot?
I did.
And?
I couldn't save him.
Oh, Blanket. I'm so sorry.

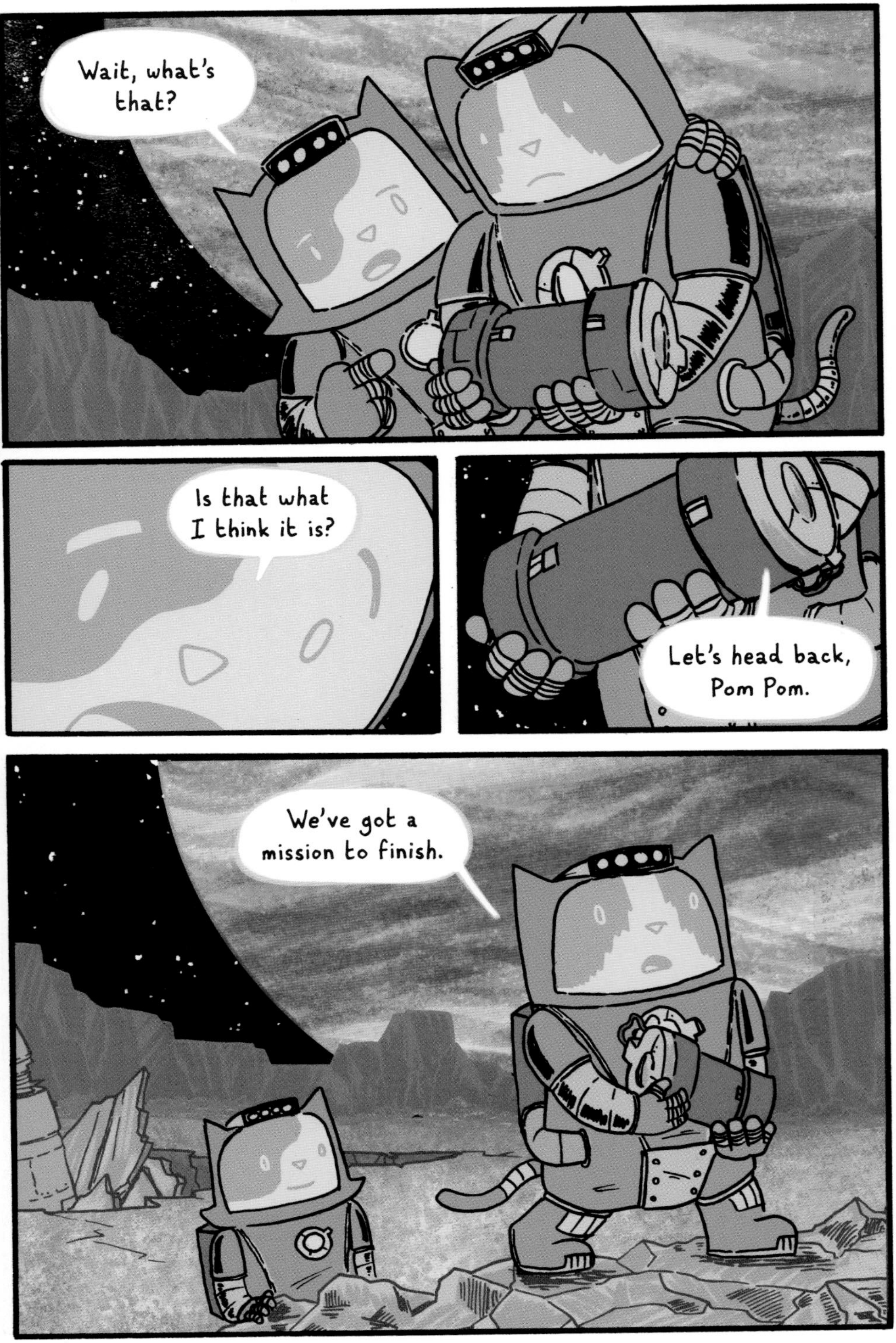
Wait, what's that?
Is that what I think it is?
Let's head back, Pom Pom.
We've got a mission to finish.

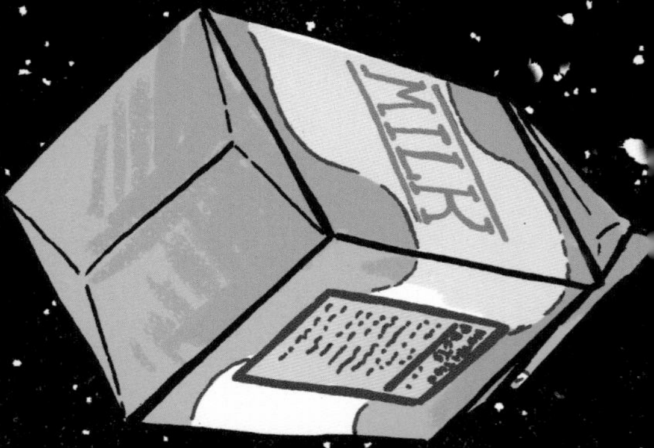
MILK

CHAPTER 10

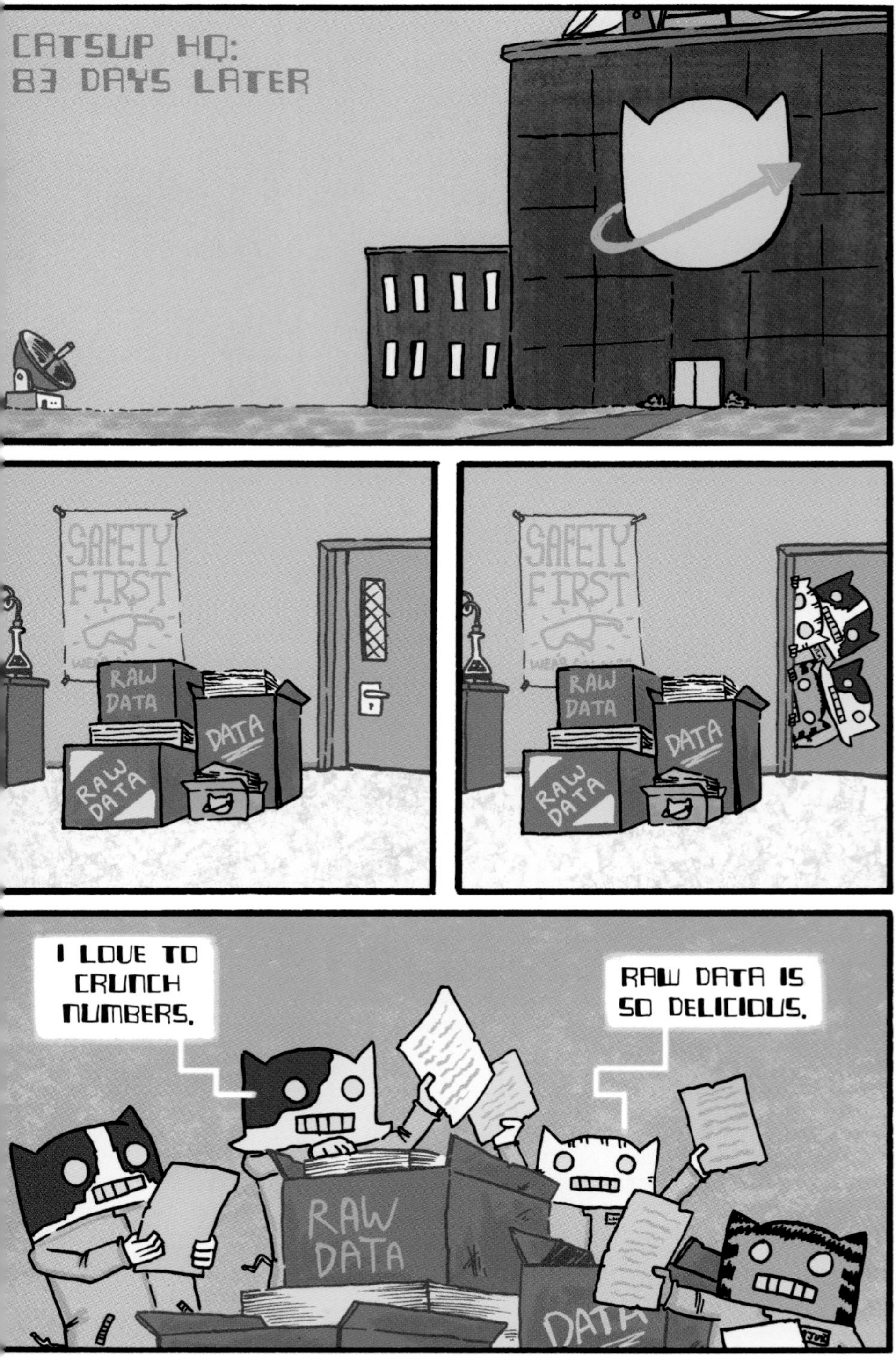
CATSUP HQ:
83 DAYS LATER
SAFETY FIRST
RAW DATA
DATA
RAW DATA
SAFETY FIRST
RAW DATA
DATA
RAW DATA
I LOVE TO CRUNCH NUMBERS.
RAW DATA IS SO DELICIOUS.
RAW DATA
DATA

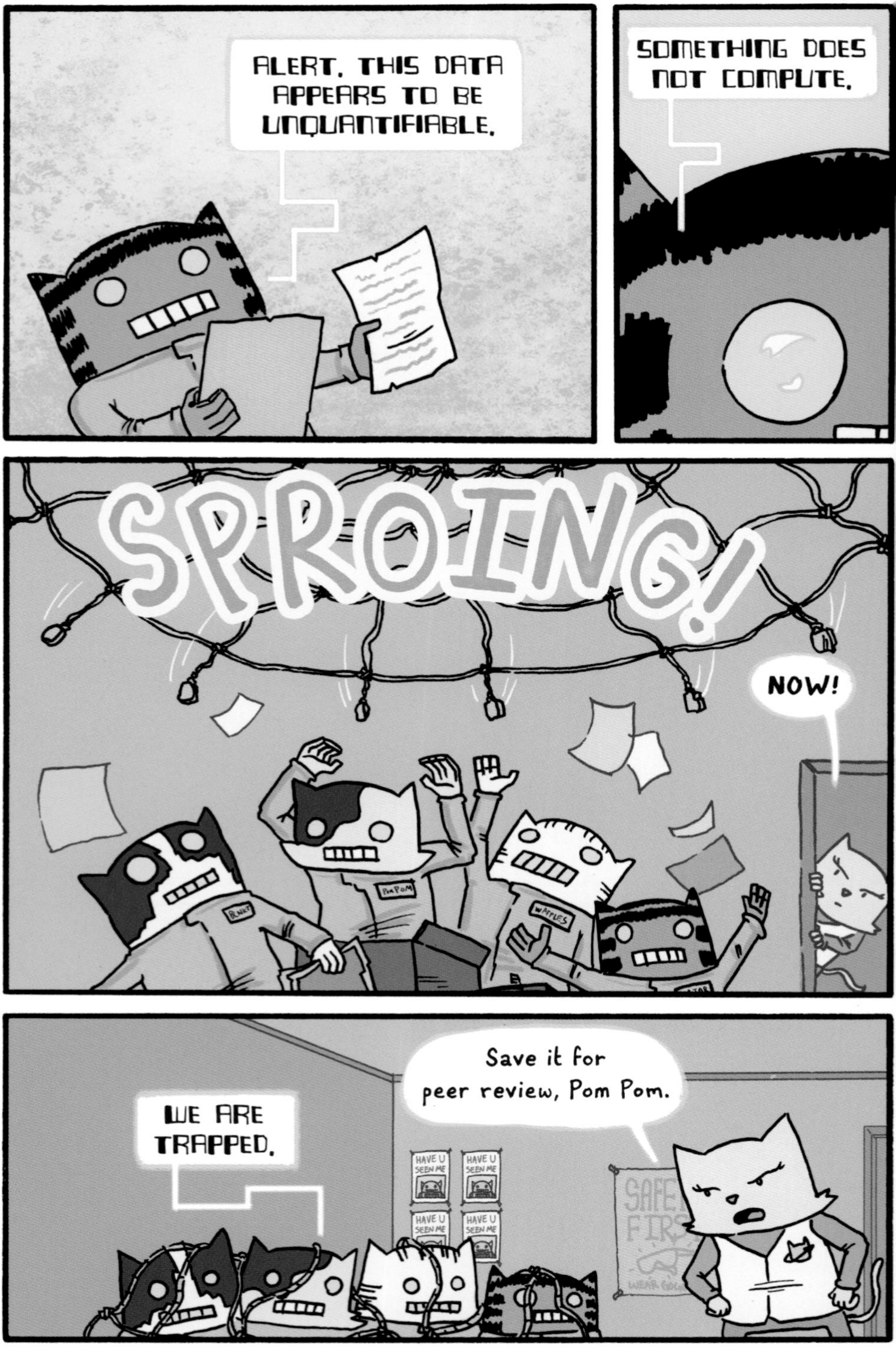
ALERT. THIS DATA APPEARS TO BE UNQUANTIFIABLE.
SOMETHING DOES NOT COMPUTE.
SPROING!
NOW!
PomPom
WAFFLES
WE ARE TRAPPED.
Save it for peer review, Pom Pom.
HAVE U SEEN ME

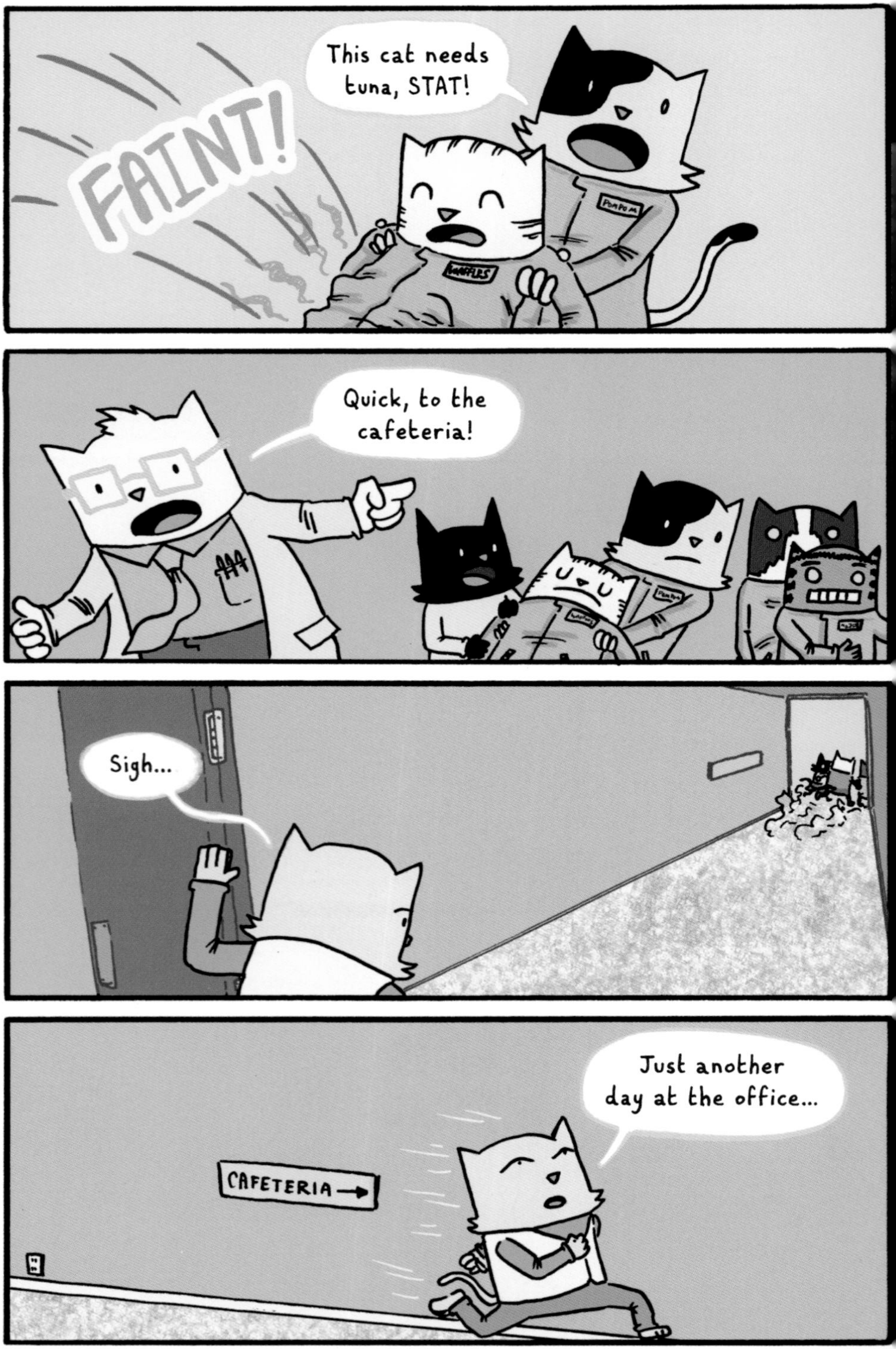
FAINT!
This cat needs tuna, STAT!
POMPOM
WAFFLES
Quick, to the cafeteria!
Sigh...
Just another day at the office...
CAFETERIA →

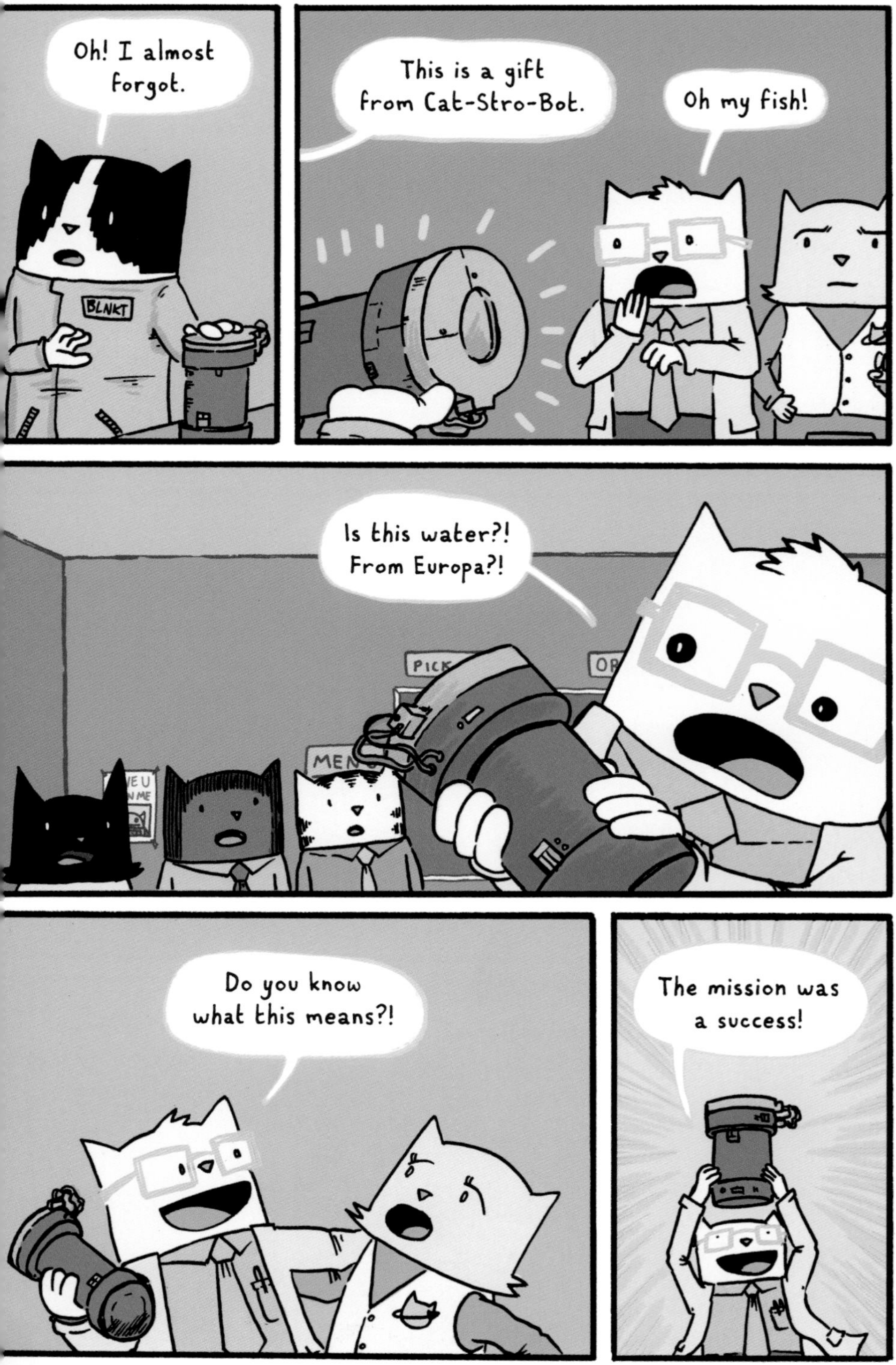
Oh! I almost forgot.
BLNKT
This is a gift from Cat-Stro-Bot.
Oh my fish!
Is this water?! From Europa?!
Do you know what this means?!
The mission was a success!

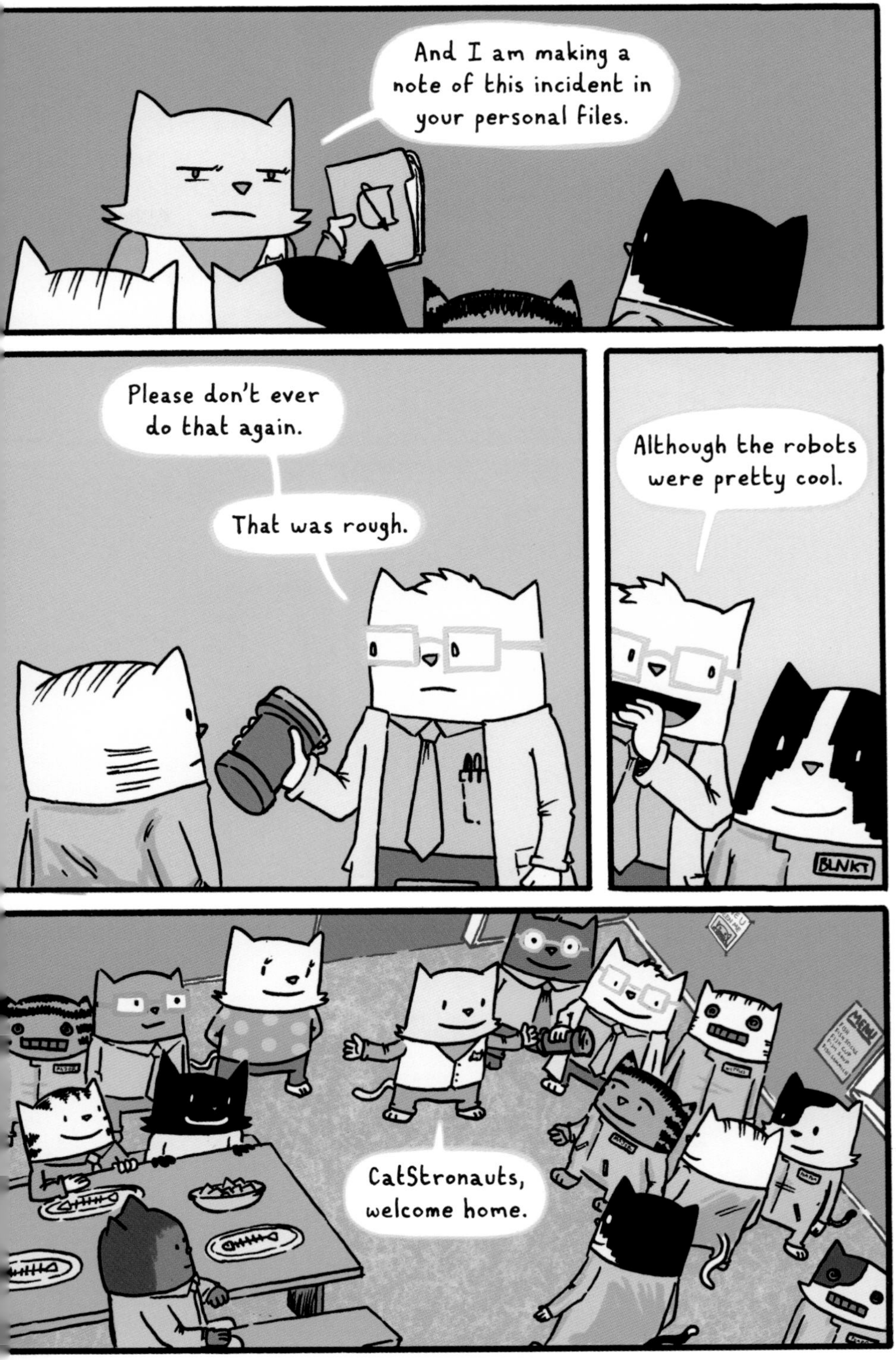
And I am making a note of this incident in your personal files.
Please don't ever do that again.
That was rough.
Although the robots were pretty cool.
BLNKT
CatStronauts, welcome home.

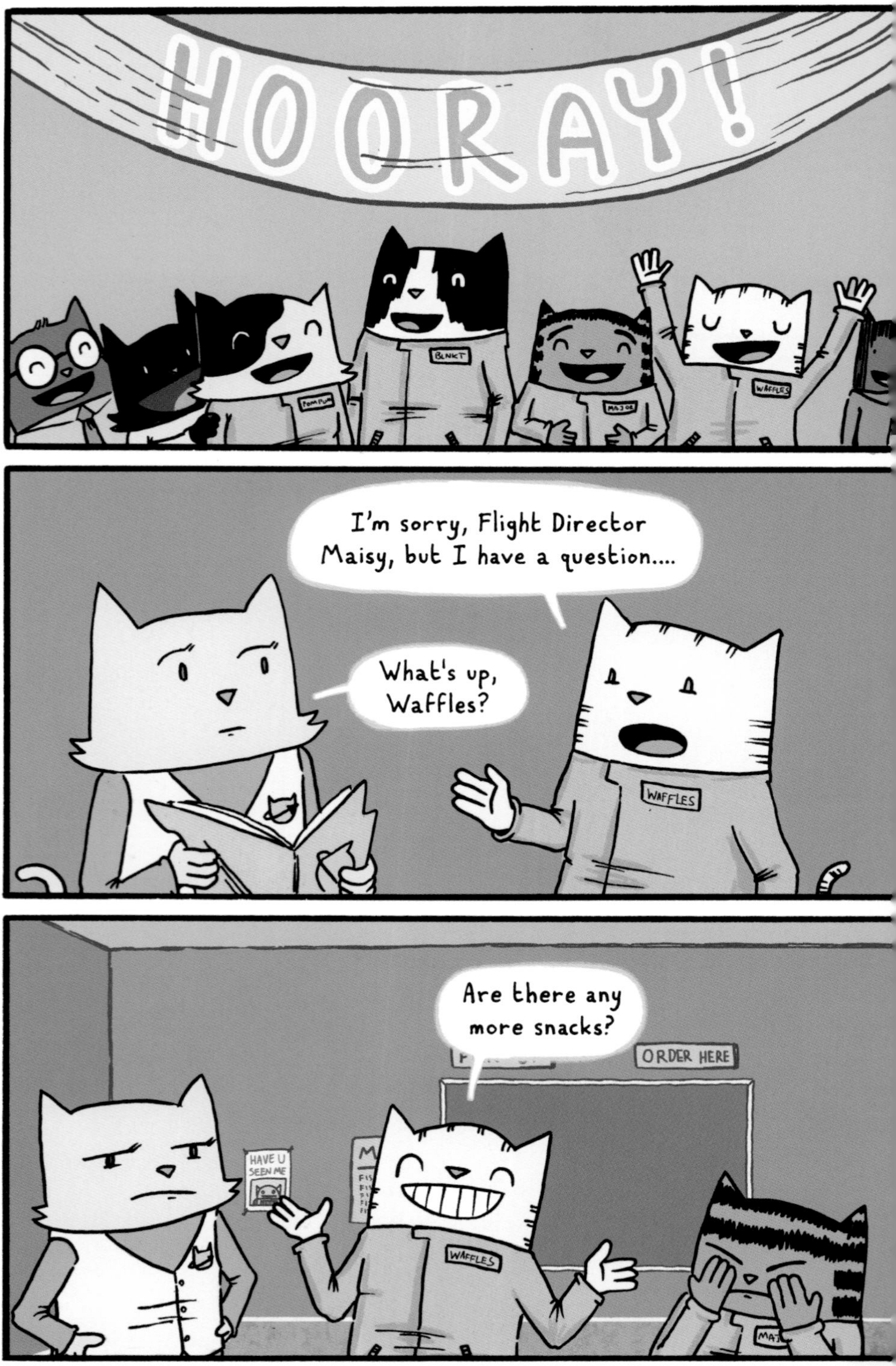
HOORAY!
BLNKT
POMPUM
MAJOR
WAFFLES
I'm sorry, Flight Director Maisy, but I have a question....
What's up, Waffles?
WAFFLES
Are there any more snacks?
ORDER HERE
HAVE U SEEN ME
WAFFLES

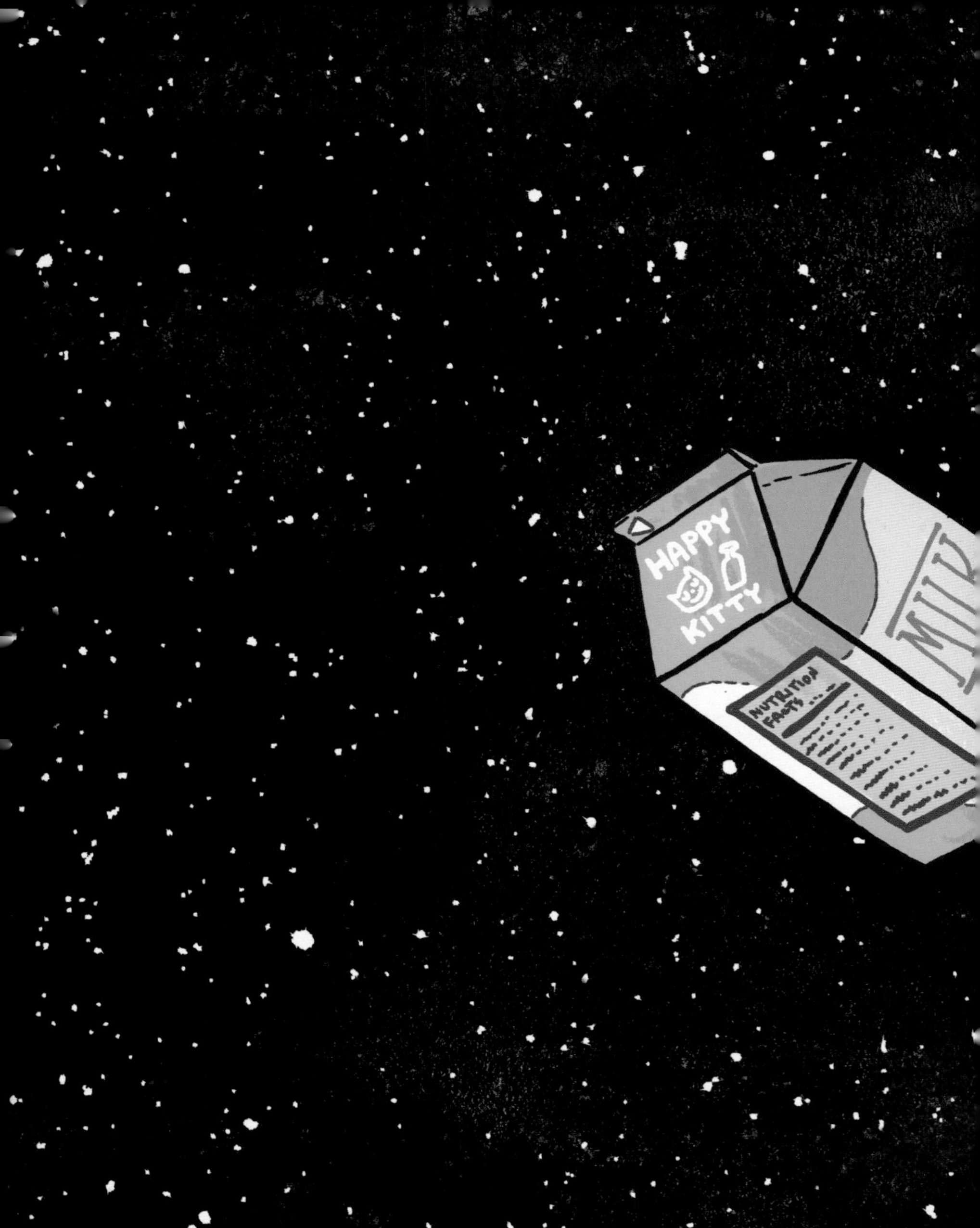
HAPPY
KITTY
MILK
NUTRITION FACTS

CHAPTER 11

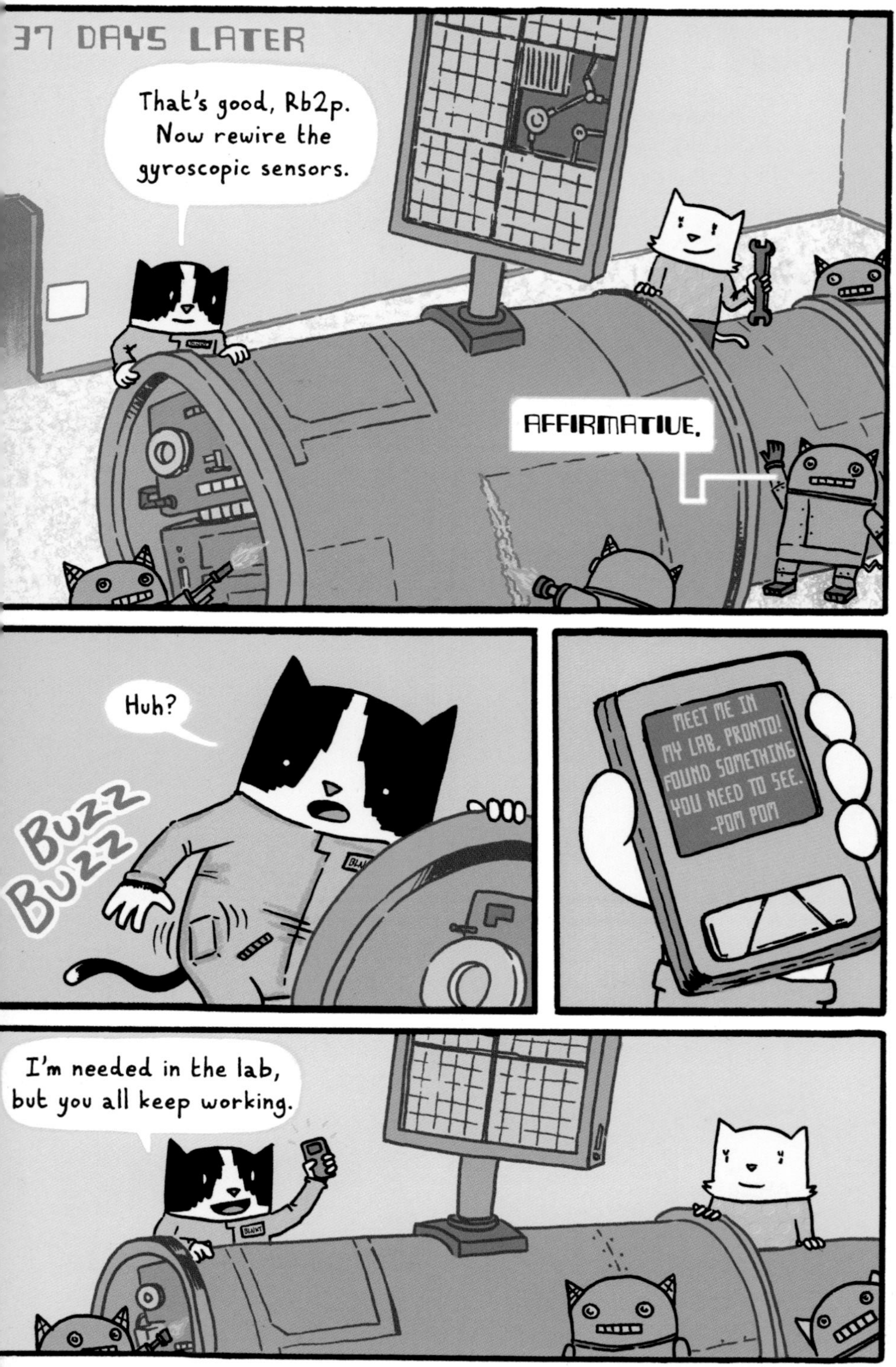
37 DAYS LATER
That's good, Rb2p. Now rewire the gyroscopic sensors.
AFFIRMATIVE.
Huh?
BUZZ BUZZ
MEET ME IN MY LAB, PRONTO! FOUND SOMETHING YOU NEED TO SEE. -POM POM
I'm needed in the lab, but you all keep working.

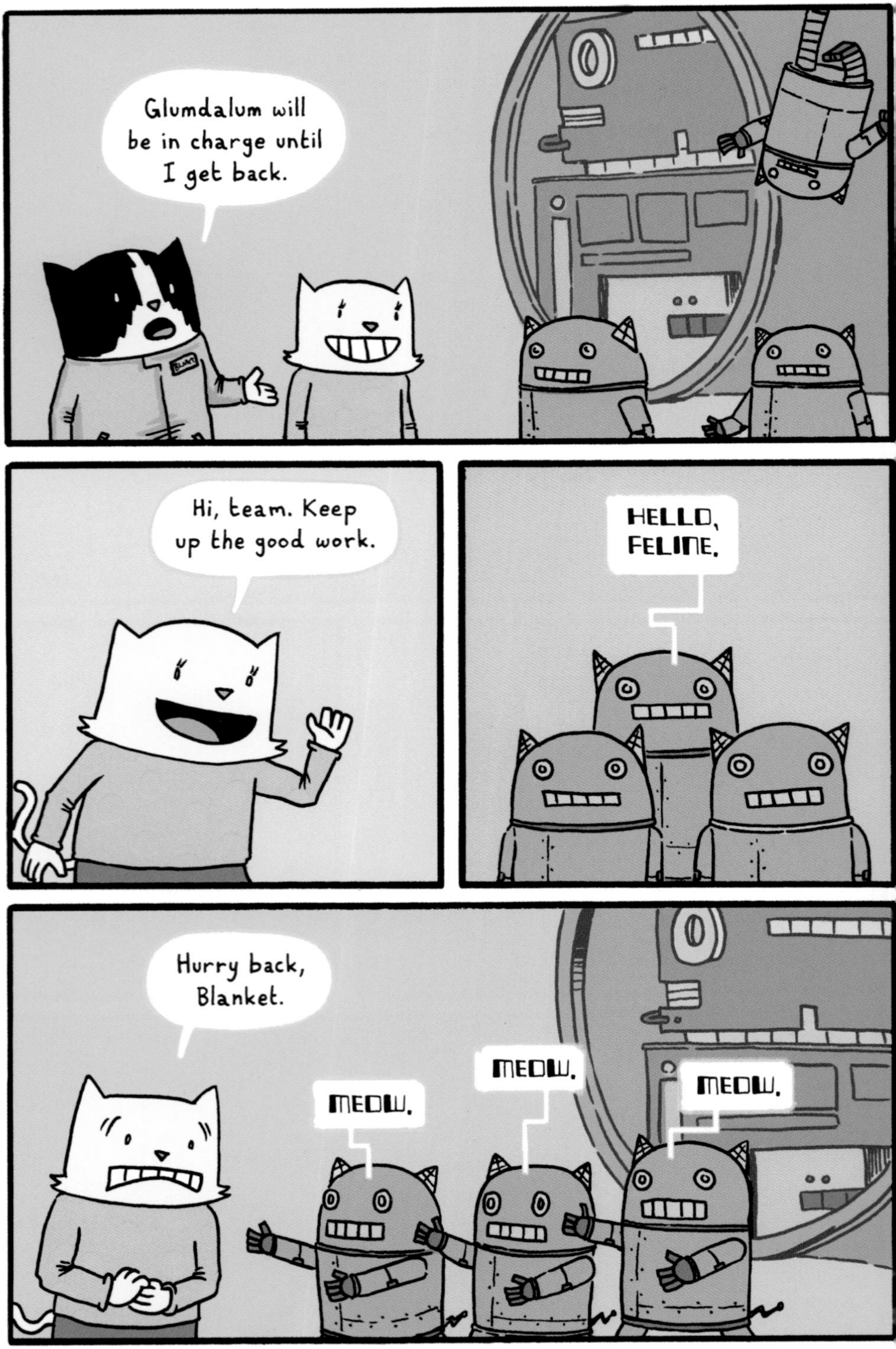

Glumdalum will be in charge until I get back.
Hi, team. Keep up the good work.
HELLO, FELINE.
Hurry back, Blanket.
MEOW.
MEOW.
MEOW.

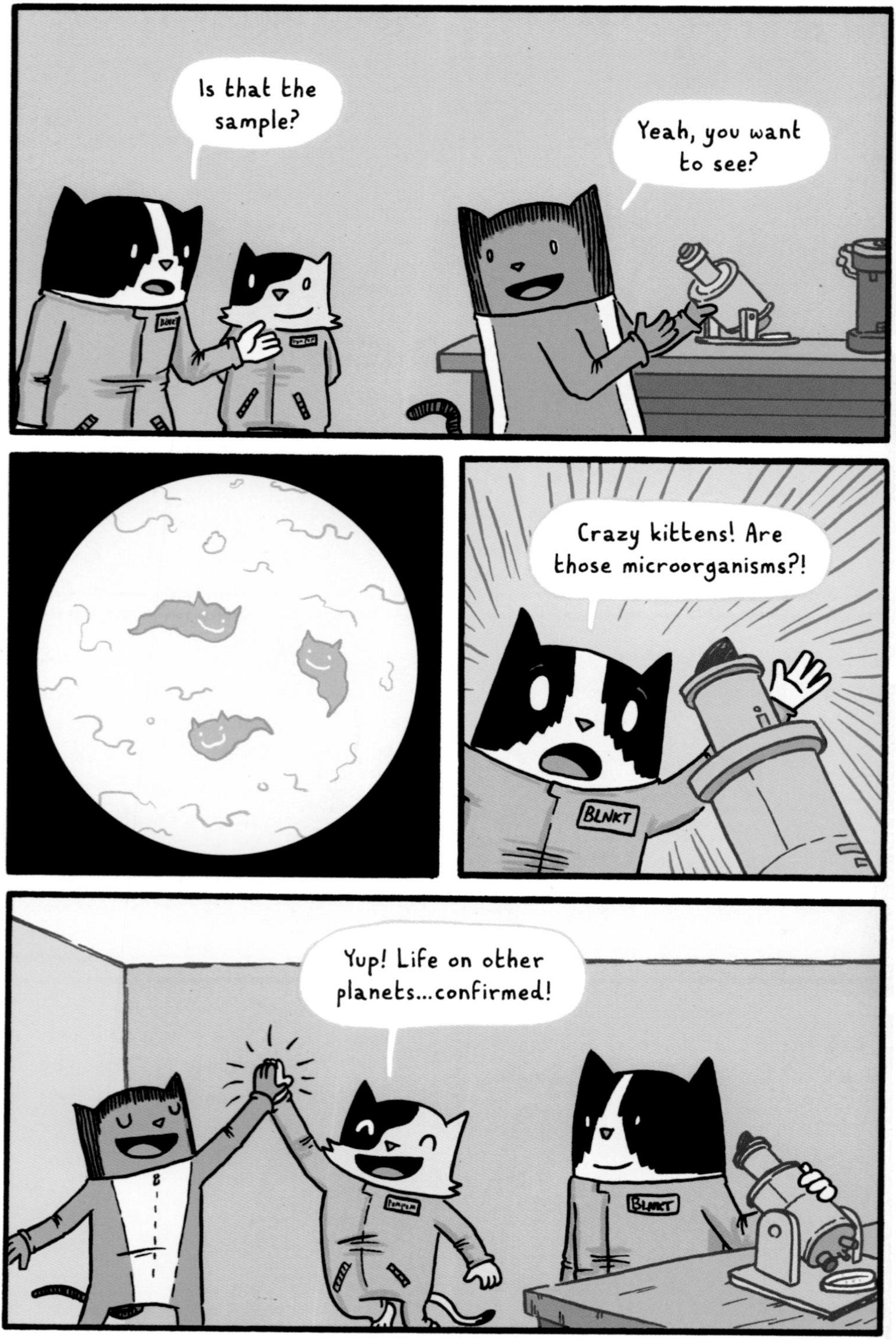
Is that the sample?
Yeah, you want to see?
Crazy kittens! Are those microorganisms?!
BLNKT
Yup! Life on other planets...confirmed!
BLNKT

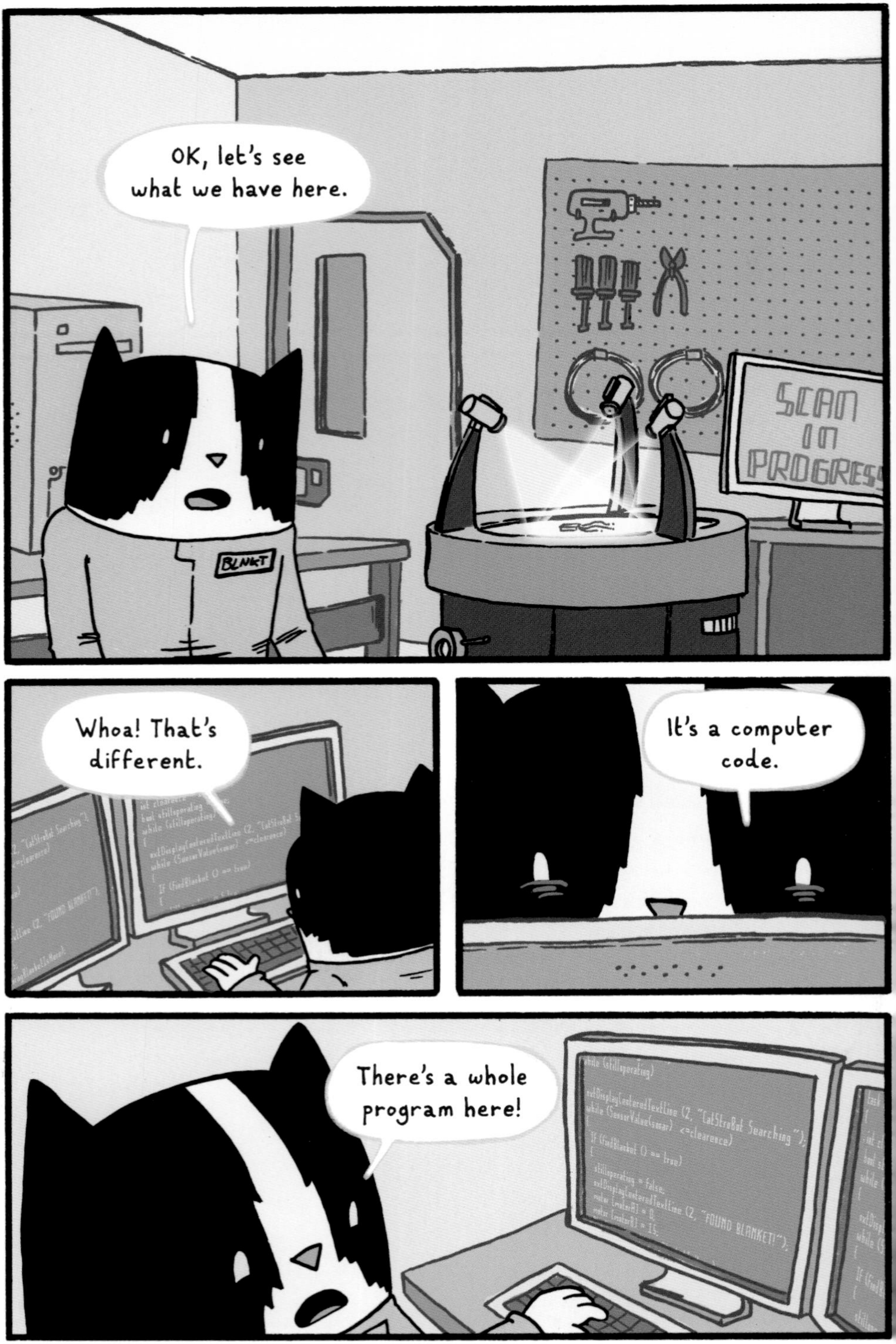

OK, let's see what we have here.
BLNKT
SCAN IN PROGRESS
Whoa! That's different.
It's a computer code.
There's a whole program here!

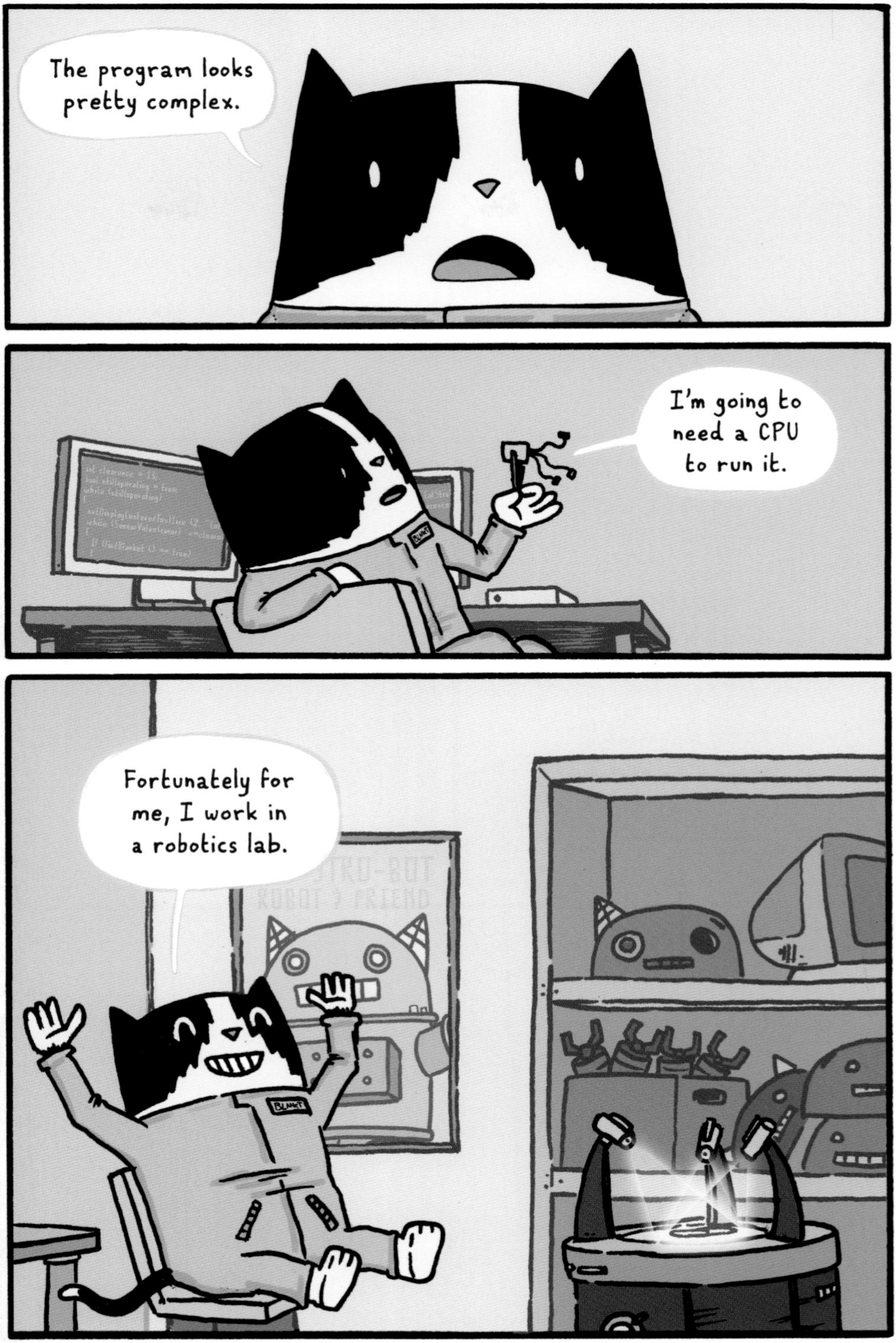
The program looks pretty complex.
I'm going to need a CPU to run it.
Fortunately for me, I work in a robotics lab.

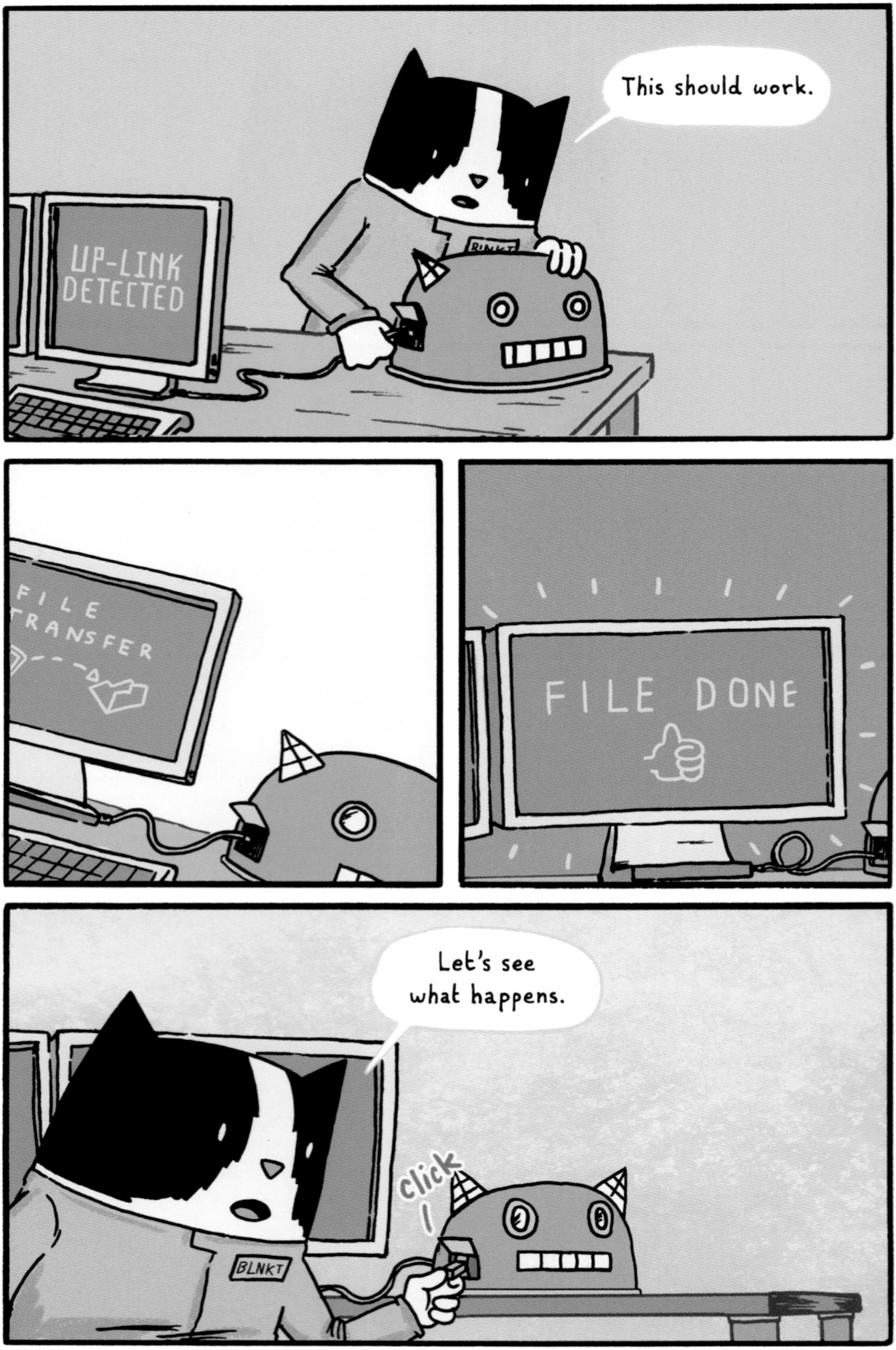
This should work.
UP-LINK DETECTED
BLNKT
FILE TRANSFER
FILE DONE
Let's see what happens.
click
BLNKT

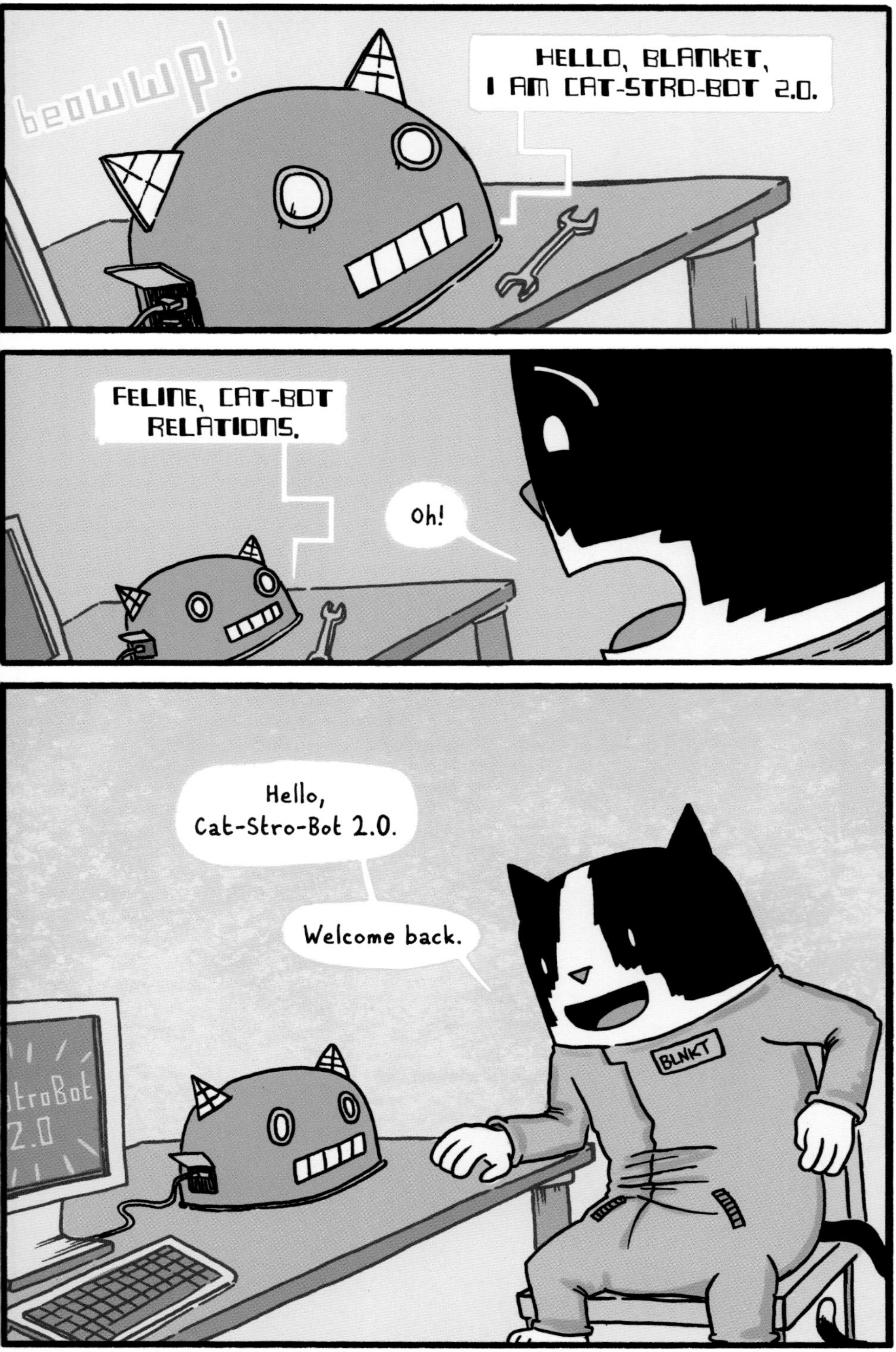
beowwp!
HELLO, BLANKET, I AM CAT-STRO-BOT 2.0.
FELINE, CAT-BOT RELATIONS.
Oh!
Hello, Cat-Stro-Bot 2.0.
Welcome back.
BLNKT

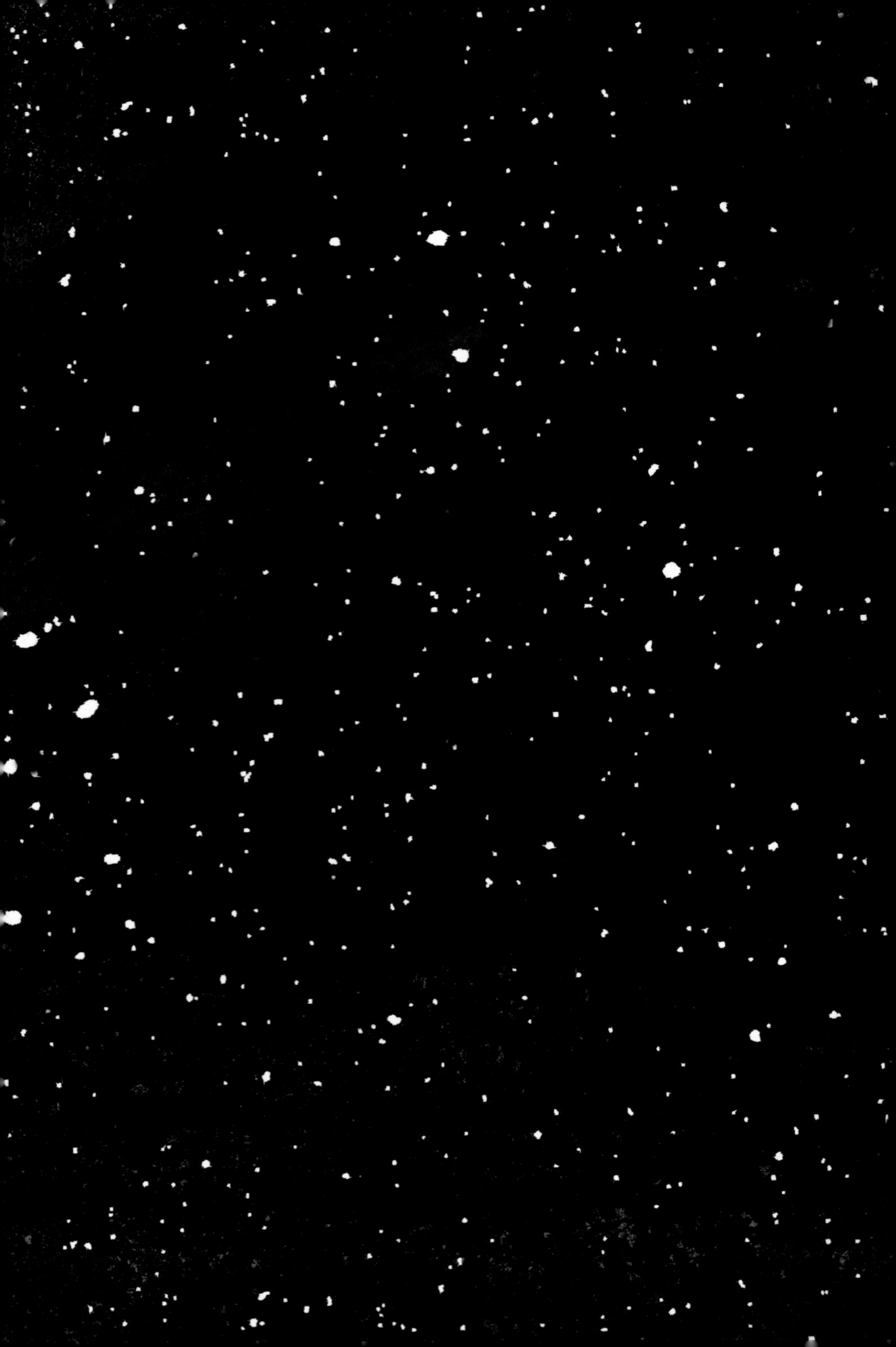

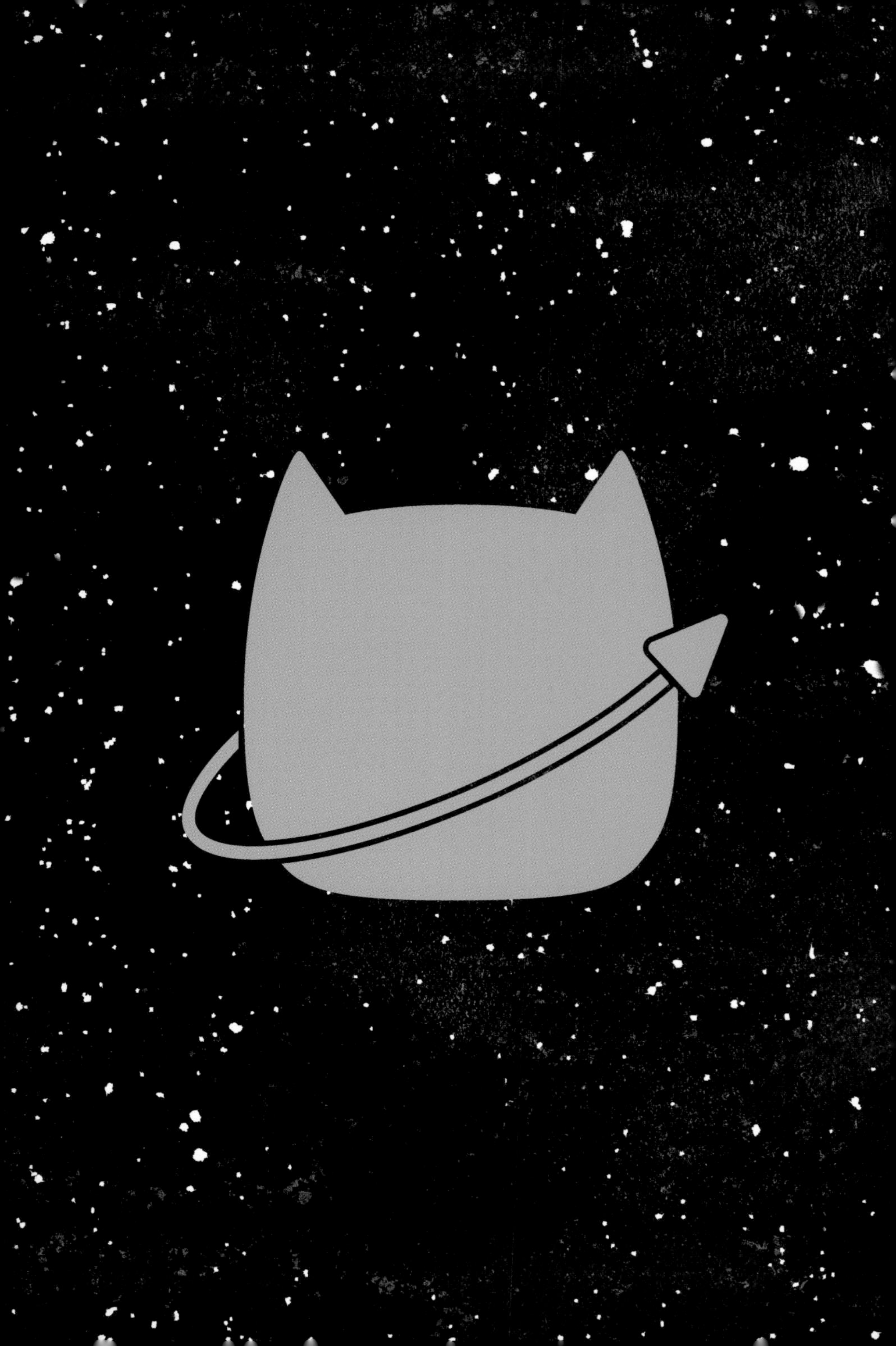

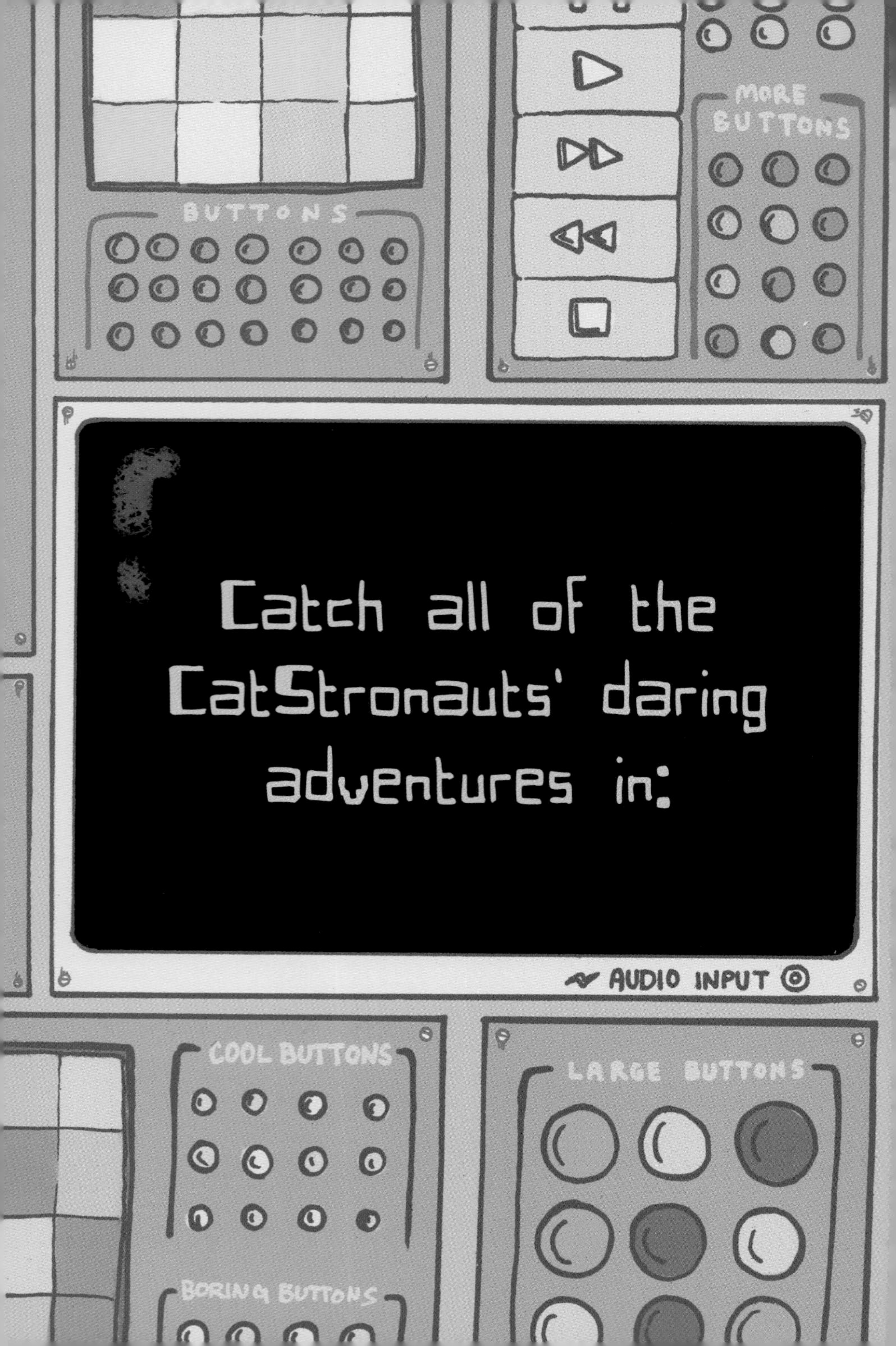
BUTTONS
MORE BUTTONS
Catch all of the CatStronauts' daring adventures in:
AUDIO INPUT
COOL BUTTONS
BORING BUTTONS
LARGE BUTTONS